THE STORY OF A BEAUTIFUL MURDER

REVOLV3R

Go Cougs!

DK

REVOLV3R:

The Story of a Beautiful Murder

Dustin L. King

Copyright © 2019 by Upstate Creative Group LLC

For more information, email:
UpstateCreative3@gmail.com

First paperback edition November 11, 2019

Book design by C.M. King
ISBN 978-1-6958-4562-6 (paperback)

DEDICATION

This book is dedicated to The Hilinski Family in memory of Tyler Scott Haun Hilinski, Washington State University Quarterback #3. May 26, 1996 to January 16, 2018.

The Hilinski's Hope Foundation (www.hilinskishope.org) was formed to help save lives by eliminating the stigma for student athletes. It is never too late to get involved to help others.

ACKNOWLEDGMENTS

This book would never have been completed without the continual support and motivation from Andrea Nagel, Alli Beck Design, Eileen Loughney, Anthony King, my amazing family, friends, and work-family. I can never repay them for the time they invested in this project. I hope seeing the words in print is equally as rewarding for them as it is for myself.

Special thank you to my wife, who I married on a beach in Depot Bay, Oregon many moons ago. We were blessed with a perfect sunset ceremony, surrounded by our irreplaceable friends and family. It was a serendipitous day that I wish we could recreate with each anniversary. There were several times when I wanted to scrap this project and move on with our lives. She encouraged me to see this book through to completion. I love her for believing in me more than I believe in myself and for continually pushing me to become a better version of myself.

1
EXTRA EXTRA, READ ALL ABOUT IT

A single bullet sent a chilling pulse of emotions across the nation. The devastating tragedy was plastered across every media outlet on a crisp October morning. Before acknowledging any human life form, individuals instinctively gave up their sovereignty to their mobile devices and began checking their feeds. Communities did not know what to do with actual news, instead of filler-pieces, sending speculation running rampant.

Stories began materializing from coast to coast on social networks, suppressing the impulsive appetites of even those who were unfamiliar with the couple. Reporters and influencers jumped at the opportunity to be the first to break the sensational story on the national stage. Most major news networks were pulling material from social media, scouring for reasons to dramatize the event.

USA Today published a shocking revelation on the front page of their newspaper and website with the headline reading "Multi-millionaire named 'triggerman' in a classic murder-suicide." Mr. and Mrs. Skilli remained as majority-shareholders in an extensive portfolio of companies, all of which originated in their Colorado living room. Heart-wrenching testimonies from friends and family made it even more difficult to process the events that had transpired.

The captivated audience was troubled not knowing how a beautiful marriage could end so violently. They were once crazy kids in love, who traveled the world in search of meeting wonderful new friends. Every relationship has its highs and lows, but they continually exhibited that they were an inseparable team no matter what challenges life threw on their path.

As a result of the negative press and conspiracy theories surrounding the murder-suicide, the company stock began to plummet on the New York Stock Exchange. Those who were close friends of Mr. Skilli could not comprehend his actions and refused to believe the fabricated stories they were hearing.

"What could drive a successful man, who had endless luxury at his fingertips, to such madness?" the news reporters continued to question.

One would think that after fifty years of being with the same person, any marital issues would have been ironed out. Besides, Mrs. Skilli was an absolute angel. She was one of those special people in the world that everyone naturally wants to please and be friends with. There was no logical explanation for her life to be taken. Especially by the hands of Mr. Skilli, the man who felt bad hurting a fly.

Typically, the actions of an old man, in his early eighties, would not have any correlation to the going concern of a well-established business, but that was not the case in this matter. As it turns out, Mr. and Mrs. Skilli provided the heartbeat of their company. Even though they were no longer active in day-to-day operations, their leadership skills were unrivaled. Mr. Skilli made a lasting impression on everyone he encountered.

Combining his natural ability to motivate, with the positive energy of Mrs. Skilli, created an unstoppable team. Their harmonious connection was the strongest bond two individuals could share. Their greatest joy was to help individuals and families find direction in life. It went beyond that of monetary aid. They lifted spirits and guided lost souls to find strength, courage, and meaning. The success of their business ventures provided them with a healthy revenue stream allowing them to make a positive impact on the world.

Storms of great family controversy swirled around the funeral arrangements. Some argued that Mr. Skilli was a monster for killing his wife and he did not deserve to be anywhere near Mrs. Skilli, dead or alive. While others campaigned that they lived their entire lives together and should be laid to rest side-by-side as they had originally intended.

The opposition from Mrs. Skilli's family stood their ground, resulting in their daughter being placed in the center of the debacle. For her, the decision was simple. She had watched her father love her mother unconditionally all of her life and knew the rumors were untrue. She knew the love her parents had for each other was special, but she made the decision to have the funerals held separately. Their caskets would be laid to rest side-by-side one another in Taft Pioneer Cemetery.

Never wanting to be a burden on their families, Tanner and Annika each had meticulously planned out their funeral arrangements. They did not expect to pass at the same time, but each wanted to surround themselves with the memories they had created and shared over their lifetime. In their typical sentimental fashion, they commissioned to have two caskets hand-carved over the course of several years.

Reclaimed barn wood accented the Florida Cyprus granting depth to the story of their lives. Using only chip and relief carving techniques, the master tradesman retold their love story with exquisite mallet strikes. The centerpiece of Tanner's casket was a tall sailboat in rough waters, reminiscent of *The Old Man and the Sea*. Abraded wood displayed cresting waves beneath the hull of the ship sailing towards the sunset. Running the length of Annika's casket was an African landscape. Three lions were eloquently depicted walking toward a beautiful valley. Precise markings captured the courageous characteristic of a mighty protector, his gentle lioness, and their adored cub.

Independently, the caskets were works of art mapping Tanner and Annika's journey through life. The mesmerizing images were dovetailed with familiar mountain ranges they had climbed, hiked, or skied. Punctilious gouge and chisel marks silently helped evolve their beautiful storylines into one.

Each service was held at their local church where they had been members of the congregation for several years. Mrs. Skilli's funeral was held first, then Mr. Skilli's in the week that followed. Both services filled the pews with people who came from all over to pay tribute to the couple. Mixed-feelings about how it all concluded were an after-thought for those in attendance. Regardless of the rumors, the congregation at Mr. Skilli's service showed admiration and respect for the incredible man that they knew. Not a single bad word was spoken about either party. When the pastor opened the floor to those who wanted to say a few words, the line was endless. Speakers shared their greatest memories of the couple, sniffling their way through stories about how the Skilli's compassion impacted their lives. Despite separate services, the speaker could not distinguish the inseparable couple as individuals.

One of Mr. Skilli's best friends closed the ceremony. With legs shaking so hard the walk to the podium felt as though he was climbing Capitol Peak. He lacked the courage to reach the summit and opted to sit on the top step of the stage. After several attempts to gain his composure, tears began streaming down his cheeks. He knew he would never be able to replace his best friend. After several painfully silent minutes, the pastor gave him a bottle of water and motioned for him to drink. His trembling fingers struggled to grasp, and twist open the white cap, but he finally managed. Tilting the bottle back slightly, he took a small sip, followed by a deep breath and exhale, he began:

"For those I have not yet had the opportunity to meet, my name is Gavin Silva. I was going to say that I was Tanner's best friend. However, as I look around this room, and see tissues being used like they're going out of style, I'm now questioning myself. After hearing the stories of others, it's hard for me to understand how Tanner and Annika found time in their busy schedules to share time on this earth with so many wonderful people.

"Tanner made me feel like I could conquer the world. There was no question in my mind that if I ever needed help, he would be there. Heck, most of the times I didn't even have to ask, he would just call from out of the blue. As I listen to so many similar stories from others, I cannot comprehend how one couple could have such deep relationships with so many individuals. Plainly stated, Tanner and Annika had indescribable faith, they were special.

"If any thoughts are lingering about his alleged actions, I can tell you with complete certainty that he loved his wife more than any human on earth has ever loved someone else. From the very first night he spoke of her, while we were youngsters in Naknek, I knew that Annika had captured his heart.

"Tanner showed me that I can achieve anything in life, with hard work and honesty. If I wanted to give up on a relationship or project, Skilli refused to let me quit. There were countless times that I wanted to cash in my chips or throw in the towel, but he would never allow it. He pushed me towards reaching a level of potential I doubted, and for that, I will be forever thankful.

"Not only did I respect the man and trust him with my life, but I also tried to emulate his ways. His moral compass was always calibrated toward honesty and he made a point to keep every relationship-bridge intact.

"Most people only think of bridges as a means to get over a ravine or water. Tanner also saw them as a shield from the sun or shelter from the rain. The bridges provide brief relief when driving through a torrential downpour. Even with the windshield wipers working overtime on high, but still unable to keep up with the intensity of the downfall. Tanner loved traveling under bridges during storms. He would drive with the radio turned off and water droplets pummeling his windshield. The momentaneous pause under the bridge was a refreshing method to refocus his mind.

"One night, during our summer in Naknek, we drank beers on a bluff overlooking Bristol Bay. Tanner gave me the best wisdom a human can hear. 'We only get one shot at this life and with that, a single opportunity for trust. Think of trust as the most stunning building in the world. People can build the foundation from the ground up, but once compromised, the building will never be the same during their lifetime. Repairs can be made over time, but the structural integrity will always be questionable,' Tanner said while we watched the evening tide retreat into the Pacific Ocean.

"Tanner always explained to me that we are in a sea of life. Much like the ebb and flow of the tide, there will always be highs and lows, but that's what makes it an exciting journey. Most people desire smooth water at the forgettable cost of not having wind, thus their sails are slack leaving them immobile. In order for them to propel forward in life, wind and rough waters are essential. I will leave you with his favorite quote, 'You can't run from the wind. You trim your sails, face the music, and keep going.' "

2
PARTY OF THREE

Their story began when Tanner was just a twinkle in his father's eye. Tanner Skilli's parents attended a Young Life camp their junior summer of high school. His father, Tripp, was a jock back then and held a handful of track and field records in the high jump and triple jump. Tanner's mother, Judy, was the quiet, nerdy type and kept to her studies. She had little interest in sports and spent her spare time reading and volunteering around the community. Being the only daughter of a mechanic, she developed an infatuation for beautiful vehicles. Judy's parents lived a simple and loving life with a single goal, they wanted to raise an exceptional human.

Tripp and Judy's journey to camp began on a train carrying twenty-five campers from their school. Prior to the trip, his parents had never spoken a single word to one another. When Judy took her seat across the aisle, Tripp quickly assessed his options. He figured she was cute enough to pass the time. Tripp struck up a conversation with the bashful young lady as the train cars rumbled down the tracks, never expecting it to reshape the rest of his life.

Camp was amazing. Waves of kids from around the country arrived for a week of adventure. After a few days of going their separate ways, Judy and Tripp's paths crossed once again. Day three on their itinerary was a ropes course out in the woods. When they arrived, they were instructed to pair up before the activity began. Judy was the only familiar face in the group and Tripp bashfully asked her if she would navigate him through the forest. Neglecting the fact that there was an even number of campers, Judy secretly feared she would get left out. Her timid discomfort was relieved and she happily obliged.

Placing the blindfold over his eyes, Judy helped tie it in the back. She felt comfortable with him and could not help but take advantage of his vulnerable state and tickled his side. The gesture was well received and ignited their friendship. Out of sixteen teams, Judy flawlessly guided Tripp through the course three minutes ahead of the competition. When they reached the finish line, they enjoyed a marathon celebration from the instructors. From that point forward they were referenced as the *Dream Team* for the duration of camp. They formed a great friendship that moved a little too fast and went a little too far.

Flames soared into the night sky, lighting up the forest trees for their final night at camp. Counselors strummed their acoustic guitars to classic country songs and the campers happily joined. Tripp spotted Judy across the way and slowly maneuvered his way toward her throughout the night. The setting was perfect and he wanted to feel the embrace of another against his own. When Tripp finally reached Judy, the desire was mutual. Judy wrapped his arm around her shoulder and leaned back into his chest. The two swayed from side to side and sang their hearts out to "Sweet Home Alabama."

Sitting around the bonfire was magical and filled Tripp's soul watching the flames dance to the music.

Judy looked up at the star-filled sky directly above and softly whisper, "Wow! Did you see that?"

Tripp tilted his head back in time to catch the tail-end of a shooting star lighting up the night's canvas. As he squeezed Judy gently, he felt a finger poking him in the back. Wondering how she grew an extra arm, he released her and stepped back. Judy was enjoying the warmth of his body and turned to see why Tripp broke away. Both were confused until they realized the pokes were coming from fellow campers inviting them to sneak back to the bunks. A small group of defiants were cutting out for a spicy round of spin the bottle. They looked at each other, shrugged, and slowly disappeared from the crowd.

Two months following camp, Tripp received an unexpected

call.

"We need to talk. Can you come over?" she whispered into the phone.

Allowing his arrogance to misguide him, Tripp thought she was preparing to confess her love. Summer harvest had been keeping him busy and the thought of a possible make out session was appealing. Then the guilt of preying on an innocent teenager began to set on his conscience. Only a year separated them by age, but he knew that she was too pure in heart. Using her to pass the summer days at camp was unfair. As much as Tripp enjoyed their time together, he was acting selfishly to make camp interesting. In his mind, life beyond camp did not have Judy in the picture.

Moments of painful silence passed before Tripp heard a sniffle on the other end of the line. Not wanting to kindle unintended emotional ties, Tripp was hesitant to drag her along any further. He knew he had to face the music and agreed to visit Judy. He slammed the door to his old Ford, after leaping into the standard-cab and firing up the V8 engine. Driving across town, Chris LeDoux played on the radio as Tripp rehearsed his speech to sever ties. Hearing her cry was a clear indicator that there would be no kissing involved. They had not kept in touch since the end of camp, making the urgency for the meeting peculiar. Tripp could sense she had something weighing on her heart and was bracing for impact after letting her down gently.

The tires came to a slow stop in the gravel driveway. Tripp took his focus off the top of his steering wheel to see Judy sitting on the front porch with her arms wrapped around her legs. Her swollen eyes were hard to disguise. It was obvious that mixed-emotional tears had been falling all morning and she was hurting.

"Judy, what happened? Are you okay?" he asked with concern.

Tripp wrapped his warm arm around her and felt convulsions rippling through her body. A few words were muffled into his shirt and all she could do was squeeze him tighter against her body.

Following a heavy sigh, she was able to whisper, "We messed up big time. You are going to be a dad."

Stepping back, Tripp began pacing while staring blankly at the ground. A warm sensation worked its way up from his toes. Once the warmth reached his head, both of his legs gave out.

The misty wind wrestling in the wheat fields damped the mood further. Feeling the weight of the world resting on his unsteady frame Tripp was forced to take a seat on the step beside her. Placing his face in the palm of his hands, he leaned forward to rest his head against his knees.

"I've taken the test three times and you are the only person I have ever done anything like that with," Judy said with devastation.

Tripp sat up and without thinking blurted out, "It was only for a couple of seconds and was far from going all the way. I wasn't planning for this and I'm sure as hell not ready to be a dad."

She looked up with tears streaming down her face.

"How do you think I feel? How do you propose we explain to our kid that I got pregnant from a stupid camp dare?" she countered.

His reaction to the news made Judy feel tarnished and alone. They both sat in silence as salty-emotions began trickling down their faces. Tripp, fearful for his life, as well as the wrath of his parents, made him oblivious to his lack of compassion for his future son's mother.

The magnitude of the news was too much to process in a single day. The two agreed that they would keep thinking about it and pray until they figured something out. Tripp got back in his truck and drove frantically down the backcountry roads.

Staring off into the open horizon, his mind declared war upon itself. Closing out all external stimulations, he was forced to combat dismal fears of being a bad father. When Tripp arrived home, his mother had prepared his favorite lasagna dinner. Surprising his mother, Tripp politely declined the offer and went directly to his room. His appetite was of little concern, with his inner turmoil winding tighter and tighter in the pit of his stomach.

After shutting the door, he clasped his fingers together and clenched them behind his head.

His upper body collapsed into his lap, as he quietly cried out, "What have you gotten yourself into this time?"

Hatred for himself filled his veins with anger. Tripp clenched his fists tightly, attempting to find a release for his frustrations. He was not yet mentally prepared to deal with adult situations that have life-shaping implications.

Unfolding his body, he leaned up and gasped for clean air. A small gleam of light, from the closet, captured Tripp's attention. Turning his head to find the source, he found that it was coming from the side of his father's revolver.

Earlier in the day, Tripp's father had taken the revolver out to shoot gophers. Those varmints had been digging holes in their field and getting on his last nerve. His father had instructed him that the peacemaker was due for a cleaning. Tripp pulled the Bulldog .44 Special out of its holster and checked to see if it was loaded. One round remained in the chamber.

Staring blankly at the developed camp photos stacked on his nightstand, he felt lost in the world.

"I'm not ready for this. I'm not ready to be a dad at seventeen," he murmured to himself while shifting his focus down the barrel of the revolver.

He was empty as a young man and fearful of the wrath that would eventuate for the remainder of his time on earth. Distorted judgment misguided Tripp's mindset, leaving him lost in his crisis. The road he had traveled was a dead end. At that point in his life, dealing with struggles and adversity was uncharted waters. His parents had taught Tripp many things, but they never educated him on the true value of life and how precious a gift he had been given.

"I'll leave this one up to fate," Tripp said as he sat back down on the side of the bed in solitude.

With the gun pointed at the floor, Tripp squeezed the grip with his dank right hand. His lips pressed tightly as he inhaled through his nose. Questioning himself he searched for answers in the air that filled his lungs but exhaled with disappointment. To pour gasoline on the fire, his left hand slipped as he first attempted to spin the chamber downward. The mishap perpetuated his determination further. Tripp secured his grip on the handle and then correctly spun the chamber before placing the barrel in his mouth. Wrapping his thumb across the front of the hammer, he delicately pulled back on the cold stainless steel until it was cocked.

Feeling warm beads of sweat roll down the side of his cheek, he winced his eyes and slowly squeezed the trigger. The sound of the cylinder rotating sent a surge of adrenaline through his veins. His heart began pounding frantically, as though it were trying to escape from his chest in search of a soul who could feel compassion. The trigger clicked and the hammer fell with deliberate life-determining violence. Tripp's neck gave way and his head snapped back before dropping to the mattress. His limbs went numb, causing his arms to crumble to his sides. It was over. From his lifeless grip, the revolver fell out of his hand onto the pillow beside him.

The white noise inundated his room for several confusing minutes and eliminated all thoughts from his mind. Suspended in the darkness of an unmapped space, his closed eyes impulsively began shedding tears. Tripp was on the verge of hyperventilation and attempted to move his right arm. His skepticism, of no longer having a physical presence in the world, slowly diminished. First placing his hand on his chest, to verify the rapid beating of his heart was not illusory. Then reaching over with his left arm and squeezing his thigh, he briefly shamed himself for gambling on his life in such a careless manner.

Sobbing uncontrollably as he slowly started to open his eyes, Tripp continued to explore his body with his hands. Pinching his limbs several times before attempting to open his eyes completely, he took a deep breath and forcefully exhaled. As he slowly peered back into the world he was nearly blinded by the light of the moon.

That same moon had hung in the sky every night of his existence, but the beauty of its presence held a deeper significance that night. He was captivated by the way the moon was slowly rising over the mountains. First presenting itself with mighty reign and power, then slowly looming across the night sky as a silent protector. The old wisdom from Tripp's father resurfaced.

Growing up, Tripp's father would constantly try to educate him on perspective. He had a gift that he wanted to bestow upon his son, the ability to see situations from various approaches and to remain open-minded. His father believed that everything in life hinged on perspective and resistance to greed. Rather than focusing on material goods, he recognized the amazing gifts of human life that surrounded him.

For Tripp's father, the moon was a reminder to be thankful for the ultimate gift of life. Most people take the moon for granted, both in its massive size and its dependability. Only when the moon slowly rises behind mountain ranges do we fully appreciate its intrinsic grace. Without comparative contrast, everyone's perspective is misled. They think it is just a fun little light that sometimes looks like God's fingernail suspended in the night sky, but its sheer mass and reliability is deserving of higher admiration.

Tripp sat up and gazed at the spectacle of one of life's certainties. After nearly exiting the world with five pounds of pressure from his finger, he saw the world with new eyes. Beauty and light replaced the pain and darkness drowning his soul.

Emotions of fear, anger, guilt, and disappointment were banished out of him. Fate had given him a second chance.

Never had Tripp backed down from a challenge and he could not explain why he was so afraid to bring life into the world. Procreation was how mankind evolved, yet he feared the burden of commitment and the chance that he might be a poor father. Nearing death compelled him to accept his challenge of being fully responsible for the life of another human.

Tripp was not certain how he would make it work. However, he did know that no matter what happened in his life, the sun would always rise in the east and set in the west. The moon would be a constant reminder that the sun is still present in the universe, even when it cannot be directly seen.

In a rush, Tripp grabbed the camp directory off his dresser and raced out of his room. He bolted down the hall toward the rotary phone, frantically flipping through the crumpled directory looking for Judy's number. Bingo, there it was. Tripp picked up the phone to dial. Judy's mother answered.

"Hello ma'am, is Judy home?" he asked, voice shaking.

"She's not available right now. Can I take a message?" she asked with an unconvincing tone.

"Ma'am, it is imperative that I speak with her. It's urgent!"

After thirty seconds of negotiation, Judy picked up the phone.

"Judy, it's me, Tripp. I'm sorry for the way I reacted. When I pictured receiving the news of my first child, I never expected to feel an overwhelming sense of guilt. I'm so sorry for not taking your feelings into consideration. Your mind is probably racing more than mine right now," he said with deep conviction.

Judy sniffled, "Thank you, Tripp. I appreciate you saying that. Don't worry, this won't affect your future. I talked with my family tonight and they are going to help me raise the baby."

Taking a moment to decide his next move, Tripp lost all sense of diplomacy and begged, "Can I come back over?"

Judy sighed, gathering her thoughts.

"I think I'm just emotionally exhausted and I have reached my crying threshold for the day. Let's meet up in the morning," she said, voice somber, exhausted.

Tripp agreed to meet Judy in the morning. He walked downstairs to meet his family sitting around the dinner table. With his most crowd-pleasing ear-to-ear grin, he announced he was going to be a father. The news was received better than anticipated. Tripp's mother quickly interjected with the interrogation questions, an attempt to diffuse the situation and lighten the mood. His father wanted to be angry but could see the look in his eyes. Oddly enough, he was proud of his son. They had spent years teaching Tripp that admitting guilt and accepting responsibility was a requirement of being a man. His parents respected his honesty and offered their support.

At daybreak, Tripp drove over to Judy's house with a fresh bouquet of white daisies, handpicked from his mother's garden. He boldly walked up to the front porch and knocked on the door. Greeted by her father's double-barrel shotgun, Tripp leaped back from the door.

"You've got a lot of nerve coming around here, boy. There are only two reasons I live my life. One of them is my wife and the other is my only daughter."

Bending slowly, Tripp placed the bouquet on the wood porch, raising his hands up to shoulder height in truce.

"Sir, I know I messed up. This was my mistake," Tripp said with a shaky voice.

Judy's trigger-happy father cut him off, "My daughter is no mistake! You got that, boy?"

Judy peered around the corner of the door frame and gestured to her father to put the gun down.

Speaking softly, Judy told her father, "I got this daddy. Can I talk to Tripp without the fear of God running through his veins?"

She stepped out onto the front porch and placed her hand across her father's chest. Judy delicately positioned herself between them and her father backed through the doorway. After the door closed, Tripp took a seat on the old wooden steps and tried to catch his breath.

As Judy delicately seated herself on the steps beside Tripp, he reached across and grabbed her hand.

"Again, I apologize profusely for my reaction yesterday. I thought good and hard about all this last night. Judy, I want to make an honest woman out of you. I know, I know, this sounds absolutely crazy, but we can make this work," Tripp assured.

Lowering her head, Judy took a deep breath.

"I don't know, Tripp. We barely know each other, and we are in high school for heaven's sake," Judy said with disbelief.

She shook her head slowly and looked up at him. Meeting his eyes, she said, "That better not be your way of proposing."

Smirking, Judy leaned over and rested her head on Tripp's chest. Wrapping his arms around her, he kissed her on the forehead.

He held her in his arms and said softly to her, "We can do this Judy. We're going to be the best damn parents a kid could ever ask for."

3

TRAILER TRASH

By the time Tanner Skilli reached twelve years old, his family lived in a cozy, double-wide trailer. There was a whole lot of nothing for a poor boy to do in the outskirts of Casper. His 822-square-foot home forced him to stay outside unless hail and lightning filled the Wyoming sky. There was one other kid in the rundown Golden Sunset Community, but Tanner was strictly forbidden to be friends with him.

A deep history of living on the wrong side of the tracks plagued Brode's family. Their trailer was four apart from the Skilli's and he hated Tanner's guts. They were once friends and palled around the Golden Sunset trailer park. As youngsters, they shared adventures and played in the field. The boys would spend afternoons digging holes, which always sent Judy into a fearful panic. Tripp encouraged the boy's bravery, believing that a man must learn the skills of venturing into nature. He would always caution Tanner to be on the lookout for the poisonous prairie rattlesnakes and bobcats. Feeling the trust of his father, infused courage within Tanner and reinforced his desire to please Tripp.

Shamefully, Tanner and Brode's friendship was lost in the collateral damage from their father's childish ways. Brode's dad, Lefty, started hitting the sauce a bit too early on Sunday afternoon. Over a meaningless preseason game, he began terrorizing the complex and making a fool of himself. The Cardinals had just lost to the Seahawks. Not only did Lefty's team lose, but he also lost the $200 he wagered. Questioning who bets on a preseason game, Tripp took matters into his own hands. He felt he must defend his beloved Seahawks against Lefty's hatred forecast for their season.

Fists started flying after a colorful shouting match. Tripp ended up landing a quick jab, while casually sidestepping the drunken haymakers. Watching Lefty drop to the gravel sparked rage within Brode. Ashamed of his father's actions and poor fighting skills, Brode instantly despised the Skilli's. He developed a self-appointed mission to seek revenge for his family's disgraced name.

Following school, The Natrona County school bus would drop Tanner off down the road from their trailer. Most days, he would quickly exit the bus before Brode and briskly walk two blocks to an old, desolate park. Barely meeting the requirements to be classified as a recreation area, being called a park was the best compliment it ever received. The park had an old basketball hoop with a chain net and a tennis court that looked like it was the first one ever constructed. The playground, if they could even call it that, had faded plastic side panels and a rusted slide. The whole place looked like ground zero from a small war. It was no surprise the community had petitioned to demolish the whole thing before someone got seriously hurt, but Town Hall said they needed it to meet quota.

Occasionally, there were some other kids around, but it was infrequent. They would try to throw together a pick-up game on the only hoop still functional, but most fizzled out after a couple of points. For the most part, the playground was desolate and Tanner was the king of the court. An older gentleman, Pete, would stop by from time to time and tell anybody with a ball about his glory days. Tanner always worried the gentleman's knees were going to give out, but he still enjoyed the friendly banter.

Although Pete had trouble getting around, he could dribble the ball like it was magnetized to his hand. Over many decades of practice, he had truly perfected his craft. His between-the-legs, behind-the-back, and ankle-breaking crossover were awe-inspiring. But the true beauty of his game was his ability to pass. It did not matter if it was behind the back, between the legs, or a simple bounce pass. Pete had an ability to deliver the ball to the perfect place, with the precise velocity for the receiver to handle the pass.

Pete always made sure to give Tanner a few drills to develop his ball-handling and passing skills. Tanner was not mature enough at the time to accurately express his appreciation for the advice, but he logged every word to memory like it was scripture from God himself. Whenever Tanner found himself alone on the court, which was more common than not, he worked tirelessly on the drills. Accepting the wise words of the old man, a true talent began to emerge from within. Success surfaced as Tanner's self-guided motivator. Basketball was a perfect outlet to free him from being a silent juror of the trailer domestic disputes. Whenever Tripp came home from a rough day, which had become more often than not, Tanner's signal to head over to the courts was when his father reached for the fifth of Wild Turkey.

By the end of his sixth grade school year, things got tough for Tanner. He felt trapped in a Bermuda Triangle between home, school, and internal struggles. Tanner started to gain weight, as his body began to transform. His face erupted with acne and his reflection was no longer familiar. The kids in class were more than willing to poke fun at every given opportunity. Brode's vendetta intensified when Tanner received praise from his teacher for his academic excellence in the classroom.

On the playground, Brode and his friends would perpetually torment Tanner. All they needed was an opportunity to get him alone. Once the playground supervisor was out of sight, they would corner Tanner and threaten to pummel him. At first, it was just words and shoving. However, it started to slowly escalate as the days went on. Tanner told his dad about the bullying, but his father just brushed it off, telling him it was simply a part of growing up and that he had bigger issues to deal with like paying the rent.

Tanner had no one to turn to, no one in his corner. Embarrassed to tell his mother, he kept his emotions and difficulties bottled up inside. She had enough on her plate to deal with, so he refrained from further contributing issues. One day, he put on his worn-out jeans that barely fit him anymore, already dreading the day ahead.

Walking into the classroom, Tanner noticed Ms. McCutcheon had not yet arrived to begin class.

Brode seized the opportunity and yelled out in front of everyone, "Tanya, are you waiting for a flood?"

The whole class started to laugh at him. As he sat down, the girl next to him asked if he had taken a shower that week.

"You smell like a dumpster," she said with disgust.

A trailer trash comment from the critics trailed off as the teacher entered the classroom.

The day progressively got worse. When the bell rang for recess, Tanner continued to sit at his desk and do his earlier assigned math homework. Most kids enjoyed the freedom of not having to sit in a classroom, but Tanner feared any moments that went unsupervised.

"Tanner, what are you still doing in here?" the teacher asked. "Go outside and enjoy some fresh air."

Tanner reluctantly put his schoolwork away and walked outside. Brode and his minions were already on high alert. He tried to avoid making eye contact, but they were missile-locked on his every move. They followed him around the corner and when they saw their opportunity, pounced.

Brode and his army circled around Tanner and started shoving him back and forth. His passive demeanor absorbed each blow until he reached his breaking point. Just as the teacher rounded the corner, Tanner clenched his fist and landed a solid right-hand jab on Brode's chin, dropping him to the ground. He was then knocked to the ground by a punch to the back of his head. The boys took turns kicking and spitting on him as he curled up in the fetal position, clenching his hands behind his head in an attempt to absorb the blows.

Ms. McCutcheon ran over to Tanner's rescue, or so he thought. Grabbing him by the arm, she lifted him to his feet and marched him directly to the principal's office.

Looking down at him, Principal Martinez spouted, "Well Tanner, what do you have to say for yourself?"

"They started it," he uttered as tears started to pool in his eyes.

"Ms. McCutcheon said she saw you throw the first punch. Is that not the case? This is very unexpected from you," the principal replied.

Tanner took a deep breath. "Yes, but they forced me to do it."

"We are going to have to call your father to come pick you up," Principal Martinez said as he prompted his secretary to get him on the phone.

"My mother is at home. Can you please call her instead?" Tanner pleaded.

The principal shook his head, "I'm afraid not. Fighting falls under your father's jurisdiction."

After Tripp received the call at work, he sped over to the school. Crossing his arms across his chest, he listened to Mr. Martinez and Ms. McCutcheon recount the fight. Tripp looked at his son is disgust and pulled him by the arm to leave. An eerie silence filled the truck cab as they pulled out of the school parking lot in their old Ford. Once they were out of earshot from others, the remainder of the ride was a non-stop verbal beating. Tanner was instructed to go to his room the minute he walked through the door. According to Tripp, a letter of apology was in order for wasting the time of Principal Martinez.

Putting pencil to paper, his inner rage intensified. *What the hell am I supposed to be sorry for? I didn't do a damn thing wrong. I hate this place. I hate school. I hate all the kids. I hate this crappy life,* he thought to himself before getting up and storming out of his room.

Tripp had gone outside to chop wood for the fireplace, otherwise, Tanner would never have dared to release such emotional frustration. As he walked past his parents' room, he saw his father's gun sitting in the holster. After surveying his surroundings, he slowly walked into the decrepit master bedroom. Tanner pulled the Bulldog .44 Special out of the holster and devised his exit strategy.

Forget this place. No one would even realize I was gone. Their lives would be better without me anyways. Gripping the handle, he intrinsically looked down the barrel and saw the solution to fix all of his problems.

Startled by the old door screeching, Tanner quickly placed the gun back into its holster. After covering his tracks, he exited the room and inconspicuously walked down the hallway.

Judy yelled across the trailer, "Come on over here Tanner. We need to talk."

When he rounded the corner and made his way down the hall, he saw his mother sitting at the kitchen table with a stack of mail next to her. She was holding a letter in her trembling hands and asked Tanner to have a seat. He had never seen his mom in such an emotional state. Her typical demeanor was absent. There was an uncertainty if she was sad, angry, or overjoyed.

"What is it, Mom? What's with the letter?" he asked curiously.

Replying in her soft, motherly voice, she said, "Your ever-so-sweet Uncle Perry has blessed us. He never had any kids of his own and told me that he would always love me like a daughter. Would you please go get your father?"

Tanner jumped up from the chair and pried open the squeaky door.

"Pops! Pops! You gotta come in the house," Tanner yelled over to the shed.

"I thought I told you to go up to your room and write an apology," his dad shouted back.

"Of course. I'm working on it, but mom wants to tell us something really important. She got a letter. I think something might be wrong. She's shaking," he yelled back.

Tanner stood by the door as Tripp put the ax away and loaded up his arms with firewood. Stepping back, Tanner ushered his father through the door. Tripp and a buddy had spent the previous weekend cutting a hole in the side of the trailer, constructing a makeshift fireplace. Tripp was more than pleased with the outcome and utilized it every night since. Tripp, lacking a sense of urgency, stacked the wood next to the fireplace and then took his seat at the table.

"Well, as you know, my uncle Perry passed away not too long ago. I received a note from him today," Judy tried to calmly explain.

"What does it say?" they asked in unison.

Judy took a deep breath and began reading the letter aloud.

My Dearest Judy,

All my life I was searching to find something. I did not know exactly what that something was, so I focused my energy on accumulating things. As you know, we were not very well off when I was growing up. When I was old enough to work, I took a job at the local auto dealership washing cars. By the time I graduated high school, I had moved up the rungs at the dealership and decided to forgo getting a college education. Do I regret it? Well, yes and no. I had a great life, there is no question about that. Never would I ever have imagined that washing cars one summer would lead to owning a string of dealerships throughout California.

Nothing came easy on my drive to success; it was a constant grind to get where I am today. Like a dynasty, I have more money than I can spend in three lifetimes. College would have certainly made my journey in the business world a lot smoother, but I never went. Each year I would tell myself that I would go back one day and get my degree. When the time came to enroll, there would always be a dozen reasons that prevented me from going to class. You could say I preferred the path less worn. I would like to think of it as a more scenic journey on life's trails.

Money was always my key motivation. Fixating on the next car, boat, or toy I was going to buy. The hope was that material possessions would bring me joy. Sure, they did for a short while, but the novelty always wore off. To tell you the truth, I found some kind of sick pleasure in having others admire what I could afford. Overhearing them make comments about how they wished they were me, gave me satisfaction. The harsh reality I learned too late in life, is that things do not make anyone happy.

Being in the car business, I was successful because I knew how to sell the illusion of true happiness. I would paint a breath-taking pictures of living in the lap of luxury. I conveniently left out the part about the added pressure they were going to have each month. That new monthly payment was just an afterthought to their next material fulfillment. Even if the vehicle was more than a year's salary, the pursuit of happiness came at a price.

I'm sure you're wondering why I'm telling you all this. You have always been the most caring and genuine person in my life. You loved me for me and never once asked for anything. I know things have not been easy for you and Tripp, but you two have always done the right thing when it comes to being a family.

My cancer has started to take over my brain and my days on earth are numbered. I have made arrangements for you and your family to move to California, so you can have the lives you always dreamed. You will be contacted in the next few days with all the details. My wish is that you go to college like you originally set out to do. I have sold off all the dealerships and have given the contractors the directive to renovate my home as you wish. It has never had a woman's touch and I doubt you want to live in an oversized bachelor pad.

I am forever indebted to your parents for allowing me to be a part of your life. Being able to watch you grow into the amazing woman you are, has brought me the greatest joy. I could not be more proud of you. I leave you with all my material possessions because I trust that you know what is meaningful in this world. If there is anything you do not like, donate them to the individuals that touch your heart the most. Please live out the life that I wish I would have had with family and friends. Make sure to tell them that you love them each and every day.

You will always be my little angel,

- *Uncle Perry*

Judy set the note on the table and sat back in her chair. The room fell silent, that was until the neighbor fired up his ol' jacked-up suburban and started revving the engine like he was Richard Petty.

"Mom, tell me this means we get to get out of this town and live in a real house," Tanner said with a grin from ear to ear.

"I can't say I'm going to miss the sound of that redneck race car," Judy replied with a wink.

With only a few weeks left in the school year, Tripp and Judy decided that it was best for Tanner to finish out the year at his current school. They wanted him to start with a blank slate going into Junior High. Tripp Skilli quit his job at the War Surplus Store, Judy gave her notice at The Golden Corral, and they started packing their belongings. A new life was waiting for them in the quaint town in the northeastern corner of California. Wellington would soon be called home.

Judy's co-workers were heartbroken over her departure and threw the Skilli family a makeshift going away party. The good folks of Casper had treated them well and they were sad to see the faces of old acquaintances. Party planning was limited with such a small window, but the Skillis appreciated the send-off in the back room of The Golden Corral. Although excited about the move, Tripp and Judy had settled into a routine over the years. Such a drastic change and uncertainty of the future frightened Tripp. Judy was less anxious and ready for a change in scenery. Tanner could not get out of Dodge fast enough, he wanted to distance himself as far from Brode as possible.

As Tanner grabbed the last duffel bag off his bedroom floor, he said his final goodbyes. Emotions began to take over as he retraced his steps from the weeks before. It took him back to when he felt helpless and lost in the world. Then, in a blink of an eye, a single letter changed his direction in life. There was a light at the end of the tunnel and hope for his future.

4

WELLINGTON

The Skillis walked out of their rusted old trailer with the last items to load in the U-Haul. Tripp pulled Judy and Tanner in by his side.

Turning them to face their old home, like Clark Griswold presenting the first burst of electricity to breathe life into a Christmas illumination masterpiece, he said, "Family, this is it. Our next venture in life is down that road. This goes to show you that being a good person, doing the right things, and working hard will eventually pay dividends. Let's get this show on the road!"

They headed down Interstate 25 towards Cheyenne and then jumped on to Interstate 80 westbound, leaving Casper in the rearview mirror.

Tripp decided it was best if he drove the U-Haul for the first leg of the trip, which allowed Tanner and Judy the opportunity to enjoy quality conversation.

"Well, are you excited, Son? I spoke to the construction crew last week, and they said the finishing touches are going on a special gift your Uncle Perry left just for you," Judy said as she briefly took her eyes off the road and glanced over with a smile.

Tanner could tell that his mother was overjoyed to get out of Casper. It had been a long time since he had seen her with such a genuine smile.

"Mom, what are you looking forward to the most when we get

23

there?" Tanner asked.

"I don't know where to begin," she said. "I've always been told that anyone can be poor, but it takes a lot of discipline to be wealthy. We have been so blessed. To tell you the truth, it's not even about the money. Although, I'm looking forward to going to the store and not having to worry if there is enough money in the bank account to cover the cost of a gallon of milk. I am more excited for you to have a real home and not some dinky little trailer. I've thought about going back to get my college degree as I had originally planned."

As Judy continued, it finally hit Tanner like a ton of bricks. He was the reason she had not been able to fulfill her dreams. She had sacrificed so much for him and he rarely showed her any sign of appreciation.

She was mid-sentence about how she was going to plant a garden when he interrupted, "Mom, I am sorry. I love you so much. I've never pieced it together, until just now, how much of your life you have given up for me. I love you."

Gazing upon the western horizon she replied, "Son, you are more than worth it."

Both, with tear-filled eyes, continued talking about anything and everything. It was the most time Tanner had ever spent with his mother one on one. He had no idea about all her life's aspiration that she was never given the opportunity to pursue. The Beach Boys "California Girls" was playing on the radio, as he looked out the window at the barren land. An internal struggle with guilt began consuming his every thought. It made so much sense now; he was a mistake, a mistake that led his own mother to sideline her dreams. Judy hoped Tanner would one day be able to see his dreams all the way through to a fulfilled life. Before bringing her son into the world, she committed to herself that she would always put his needs before her own.

Pulling into the Candlewood Suites in Winnemucca, Nevada for the night, the two felt a bond like they had never experienced before. They had not even reached California yet, and already the next chapter in their story was looking brighter. He had always loved his mother dearly for the way she treated others, but a much deeper appreciation and respect for her was now anchored in Tanner's heart.

The next morning they got back on the road. Much to their

surprise, the trip flew by faster than anticipated. They pulled out their trusty guide, Mister Rand McNally, and navigated their way through Wellington. Two wrong turns later, they located a long private driveway that took them back up into the tree-covered hills. Not a single word was spoken as they passed by the gorgeous scenery on the way to their new home. When they reached the circular driveway at the top, they were greeted by a well-dressed man leaning up against his white Audi R8. He introduced himself as Jordan Rockwell, as he was handing them the keys to their new home.

"Mr. and Mrs. Skilli, she is all ready for you," Jordan said as he gestured them to follow him in the front doors. "Mr. Perry spared no expense when designing this shack."

As they were making their way towards the large entrance doors, Tanner commented about Jordan's fancy Audi.

"It fails in comparison to some of the rides your family has in the shop," he said while glancing back.

They scattered like cockroaches throughout the house, as each began their self-guided tour. No more than a few seconds would go by, and there would be shouting from the other end of the house, "You gotta see this," or "This place is incredible." Once the exploration had concluded, they reconvened in the great room.

With a big smile on his face, Jordan looked at Tanner and said, "Are you ready for your special gift?"

They walked to the back sliding door and made their way to the edge of the deck. Tanner glanced over the edge and looked out at the backyard.

"Is that a Helipad basketball court?" he said as excitement and shock emanated from him.

He ran down the stairs and opened the powder-coated black chain-link gate. The surface provided a regulation full-size court, with NBA hoops at each end. Jordan and the Skilli parents made their way down to join Tanner.

Judy wrapped her arm around her son.

"Uncle Perry figured we wouldn't be taking the helicopter to work as he did. You won't believe how badly I wanted to tell you. Ever since I heard he had made arrangements to convert this into a basketball court, it has been so difficult restraining myself from telling you."

Jordan chimed in, "There is one minor catch. This basketball court comes at a cost. Mr. Perry was very adamant that we have you sign this contract."

With a baffled look, Tanner repeated, "Contract? What exactly do you mean by contract?"

Jordan opened his briefcase and pulled out a legal document with "BINDING CONTRACT" bolded across the top and three stipulations written below.

One - I promise to get good grades in school and go to a four-year college.

Two - I promise to shoot 100 free throws every day of the year, even when there are traces of snow or graupel on the ground.

Three - I promise that when I play basketball at a professional level, I will put half of my salary, signing bonus, and advertising endorsement money into a savings account that is to remain untouched while still in the league.

Jordan reached into his pocket, pulled out a fancy pen, and handed it over to Tanner.

"I understand that this is a big commitment, but I'm going to need you to sign and date the document at the bottom," Jordan said in absolute seriousness.

Looking over at his parents, Tanner nodded in agreement. He put ink to paper, and his first contract was in effect before stepping foot in a seventh-grade classroom.

5
LINCOLN

L incoln Middle School, which the town simply called "Lincoln," hosted grades seven and eight. It was a big deal for the recent sixth-grade graduates to make the jump to seventh grade, because the two elementary schools got combined. The town of Wellington was small enough that everyone knew the gossip about most families, but having new classmates added to the excitement. No one would know Tanner as the new kid at school since half the faces were going to be unfamiliar.

The night before the first day at Lincoln, Tanner began to panic. He was more than thankful to have made it out of Casper, but he was not fully prepared for a new school or making friends. Different scenarios and approaches played out in his mind. Tanner was unsure of himself and tried to devise his strategy for the next year.

He impulsively questioned if he should try to keep his head down and lay low, or if he should try to make as many new friends as possible. One thing was for certain, he did not want to be known as the rich kid. No one would understand that he grew up poor and was far from an entitled silver spoon kid. Trying to explain that he grew up in extreme poverty would likely fall on deaf ears.

In an attempt to calm his nerves, Tanner jumped into the shower to rinse off before heading to bed. The warm water, delivered at the optimum fifty-one psi, was as a subtle reminder of how his luck had shifted. Their old shower, in the trailer, was barely large enough for a grown adult to turn around in, forcing them to lean against the wall. If showers failed to properly maneuver, water would spray out the side and flood the bathroom. It had happened countless times over the years. Forgetting to lean was a surefire way to enrage Tripp Skilli. At their new home, having his very own bathroom was a true luxury. The dueling rain showerheads accompanied by body sprayers was a lavish upgrade the Skillis could appreciate.

Feeling fresh as a flower, Tanner crawled into his plush bed. Two hours tickled by as he tossed and turned like a rotisserie. The air conditioning had dropped to sixty-six degrees at night, but it felt as though he had fire burning through his veins. He tossed his covers to the side when he was roasting, only to scour for them minutes later when he became cold.

The clock, projecting the time on the ceiling, read 12:03 AM. With the fear of never being able to fall asleep again, he wandered down the hall into the bathroom and pulled out the medicine box. Grabbing the bottle of Benadryl, he pressed in on the cap and twisted it open. Three pink pills fell into his hand. He paused for a moment and shook the bottle once more. A dozen more pills piled on the others. Looking up to the mirror, he stared deeply at his reflection with a piercing glare.

"Get it together you pansy," he said under his breath.

With a slight shake of his head, he shifted his focus back to his hand and scooped up all but two of the pills. Drinking like a cat from the faucet, he placed his head in the sink to wet his whistle. It took less than twenty minutes for the diphenhydramine to kick in. Nightmares about showing up to school not wearing pants and being singled out in a choir class began to haunt him. Through the night he wrestled with a conglomeration of fears that junior high beholds.

Like clockwork, his alarm began playing the local country radio station at 6:00 a.m. Tanner woke up in a Benadryl-haze that made him question if he were still alive or in the form of a ghost. He hit the snooze button and laid back down with his back on the bed. His heart began racing. There was no chance of enjoying the extra ten minutes of sleep that was sure to make him well-rested. Shock was starting to set in. He had convinced himself something would ultimately prevent him from having his first day at the new school. Realizing his arms were crossed over his chest as if he were in a coffin, he came to terms with the fact that he was not going to die that morning. It was time to face the music and get ready.

Judy was adamant about snapping a few photos of Tanner on the front porch, before granting access into the vehicle. It was an embarrassing ritual that Judy took great pride in continuing. The routine grew old after third grade, but Tanner knew how much it meant to his mother. He would play into the theatrics and show resistance, fully accepting the inevitable future. As they approached the school, he could feel his blood pressure rising and instructed his mother to pull over a block before the drop off zone.

"I can walk from here, Mom. Thank you for the ride," he said as he reached for the door handle.

"Have a great first day, Sweetie. Your mommy will be here after school to pick you up. Be nice to your teachers," she said while using her best parade wave.

Before Tanner closed the Range Rover door, he looked at his mother and said, "If I don't make it out of this alive, know that I love you. Tell Dad goodbye for me."

With an unencouraging smile, he shut the door and began the walk of doom.

Computer Education was Tanner's first class. Lincoln was one of the thirty-three middle schools selected to receive a substantial donation from a small software company out of Washington. The company provided a classroom full of personal computers with CRT monitors. Tanner had never actually got to use a computer. When he signed up for the class, he thought they were only going to learn about them. He was stoked to learn how to operate the data machines.

The teacher spent most of the first class introducing himself and welcoming the students to the new school. His name was Mr. William Baugh, but he preferred "Coach." He was the eighth-grade baseball coach, known for his competitive brilliance and love for the game. Tanner's excitement about the class was knocked down a notch once he realized that the coach was going to use the same direct approach in the classroom as he used on the diamond. The coach scanned the room as if he were scouting new talent and then instructed them all to press the power switch on their computers. A giant image of fluffy clouds, on a light-blue backdrop, filled the screen. It was as if Tanner was entering another dimension, the experience was mesmerizing. Life as a seventh grader was shaping up to be a joyous adventure.

Coach instructed them to have their feet flat, back straight, and to begin with their fingers on the home row. The students all looked around in confusion, wondering where the home row was located. Their uncertainty led to various configurations of their hands on the keyboard. Tanner pressed his eight fingers together and positioned them on the spacebar. His stoicism led others to follow his lead. Coach Baugh enjoyed watching them squirm for a few seconds before providing further instruction. He then informed them that the home row is when you have your pointer fingers on the F and J. *That explains the little bumps on the keys*, Tanner thought to himself. With his fingers securely on the home row, the feeling of being in control warmed his body. The most advanced piece of technology was literally at his fingertips.

Following lunch, things took an abrupt turn for the worse. The science building was located on the portion of Tanner's school map that was earlier used as a coaster. His fourth hour biology classroom had been masked by an orange juice stain. Wandering aimlessly down the halls, he finally swallowed his male pride and asked for directions. A kind student-teacher pointed to the other end of school, sending him off in a mad dash.

He slid in the doorway, like Indiana Jones, just as the bell was sounding. Tanner quickly surveyed the room in search of an open chair. The only empty seat was located on the other side of the largest man-child Tanner had ever seen. No one was sure of his real name, but he went by Bubba. A full head of red hair was sculpted into the finest mullet in all of the land, not to be overshadowed by the lightning bolt shaved into the left side above his ears. He wore a sleeveless shirt beneath his faded pair of coveralls. One strap over his shoulder allowed the other strap to hang to the side like a rope swing. Tanner's summer growth spurt became apparent to him when he towered over everyone in that hall that morning. However, sitting next to Bubba made him feel like a dwarf.

After handing out the syllabus, Mr. Frazier began a discussion about electricity. He drew pictures on the chalkboard and then wheeled in a new state-of-the-art Panasonic television for the pinnacle of his lecture. After ejecting the VHS from the fancy built-in player, Mr. Frazier noticed he had roughly ten minutes to spare. Following the video on wind energy, he posed a question to the class about whether or not dams were good for their planet. When Mr. Frazier asked if anyone knew about how hydroelectricity worked, and how dams create energy, Bubba threw up his hand with confidence. Once called on, he articulated that water passes through the big wheels and the dams suck out all the electricity in the water.

"That's why the water on the lower part of the dam is white. Water that is blue has electricity, you know? When it passes through the dam and stuff, it has all the electricity pulled out," Bubba elaborated.

Not sure how to respond to Bubba, Mr. Frazier shifted his eyes to Tanner, "How about you, what's your name?"

Stunned from being singled out, Tanner could barely mutter an introduction, "Tanner, Tanner's my name," he said.

"Well Tanner, can you tell us how water creates electricity," Mr. Frazier asked.

Vaguely could Tanner recall the earful Tripp had given him about dams at last week's supper. As his father continued on about how fascinating the concept was, Tanner neglected to fully appreciate the lesson at the time. Shocking both himself and the class, Tanner was able to regurgitate just about every word his father had told him.

Impressed by the eloquent response, Mr. Frazier paused, "Hmm, that's incredibly accurate. Thank you, Tanner."

In hindsight, Tanner should have just kept his mouth shut and said that he did not know. The bell rang, dismissing class. Tanner grabbed his backpack and mapped out his path around the angry ogre. As he walked behind Bubba, a sharp elbow jabbed into his walking path. He stepped around the elbow and a haunting feeling crawled up the back of his neck. Without wavering he continued walking towards the door, feeling daggers being hurled at the back of his head. Bubba sat silent and squinted his hateful eyes while trying to think of something to say, but his anger scrambled his thoughts.

Tanner burst out of biology class like he had just robbed a bank and was trying to locate his getaway car. Zigging and zagging through hallway traffic, he frantically looked back to see if he had a tail. Once he reached his locker he felt a strange sense of comfort.

It was as though the locker was a safe haven with protective powers. His sweaty palms smeared the locker combination he had written on his hands.

"0-40-30. Nailed it on the first try," he mumbled to himself in victory.

Tossing his biology book into the locker, he noticed a six-pack of Mountain Dew had appeared since last period. He leaned down with his right hand and pulled a can from the pack. As he postured back up, a large hand grabbed the side of his locker.

"Hey Dipshit, thanks for trying to make me look like an idiot in front of the whole class. I knew all that crap that you said, I just didn't want to say it," Bubba said as he backed Tanner up against the neighboring locker.

"I didn't have to try to make you look like an idiot at all, you took that liberty on your own," Tanner said with unfamiliar confidence.

Seeing himself in a new light, he refused to tolerate being bullied and fought through the urge to run and hide. He wanted to be seen, and this new sense of self was boiling to the surface with every second that passed. Tanner was no longer going to tolerate being pushed around and knew he must approach the confrontation with an entirely different perspective.

Tanner's passive demeanor had suppressed his willingness to stand his ground too long. The old Tanner was left back in Casper. Still holding the soda in his hand, he tried to shove Bubba backward. It was a failed attempt. There is no way that gangling little boy was going to move that behemoth of a young man, especially since he could not gain any leverage. Even if Tanner climbed up the side of the lockers, and tried to leg-press him out of the way, it would have ended in embarrassment.

"I'm not afraid of you," Tanner said while looking up and staring Bubba directly in the eye.

That is when Dermot Sinclair was introduced into Tanner's life.

"Hey, don't even think about wasting that Mountain Dew by smashing it over his head. That's the nectar of the gods, you know," Dermot said while gesturing for Bubba to step away from his locker-mate.

Dermot was the youngest of six boys in his house and showed zero hesitation standing up to boys bigger than him. Bubba saw the ferocity in his eyes and decided to back down. Bubba gave Tanner a quick shove in the arm and instructed him to not make the same mistake again.

"What the heck was that all about?" Dermot asked. "Looks like you're making new friends already. How about another? I'm Dermot, looks like we are sharing a locker this year."

Tanner handed him the can of Mountain Dew, "Well then, this must be yours. I was picking it up when Big Red launched his surprise attack on me. The name is Skilli, Tanner Skilli."

Just like that, a lifelong friendship was born. For the first time in his life, Tanner felt courageous. He was not sure what compelled him to stand up to Bubba, but those few moments were pivotal in Tanner's life.

Courage is a strange thing. The way one gains courage and the way one loses it are not always the same for everyone. The most difficult aspect of courage is it has to first be revealed before one could strengthen it. Before that first day of middle school, Tanner's courage and self-worth had slowly been declining. After feeling the euphoria of standing up to a bully, he was able to transform all his anxiety about being the new kid in school. A newfound confidence replaced all of his doubts about not being good enough. The infusion of self-worth ignited a transformation.

Tanner began to develop a newfound sense of self in the weeks that followed. The change was seen in the classroom, on the court, and in his overall demeanor. He walked the halls with his head held high and shot the ball like he knew it was going to hit nothing but the bottom of the net.

As it is with everyone, junior high was far from perfect. Filled with a plethora of highs and lows, Tanner experienced all the unavoidable rites of passage that early teenhood provides. The braces phase and having his voice crack while asking the teacher a question was embarrassing. The discomforting trauma of dressing down in the locker room, with a bunch of boys going through puberty, began to subside as the year progressed.

Tanner became the standout basketball player, while Dermot earned the title of the school's top wrestler. They received plenty of attention from the young women in the school, but Tanner never reciprocated the interest. Mostly in part to him not picking up on any of the obvious hints that were getting hurled his way. Dermot on the other hand, took full advantage of the situation and had a new girl hanging by their locker every week. By association, Tanner got to know most of the girls but never found one that he wanted to pursue. He was hesitant to date any of the girls, for fear of ruining his chance with a better-suited match down the road.

Tanner figured, a broken-hearted girl can do a tremendous amount of damage to one's reputation. Plus, they were all girls that his best friend had already dated. It was a calculated risk that Tanner was not willing to take. If he chose incorrectly, just one time, his character could get tarnished from untrue rumors she could spread. A life free of drama was his desired route, so he remained a young bachelor.

When he was not on the court, or in the classroom, Tanner took refuge in the computer lab. The lab became his safe haven from the drama-filled junior high life. Coach Baugh was usually situated in front of his computer checking the market and enjoyed the intellectual company. Tanner found it easier to relate to Coach's personality and age than that of his confused and socially awkward peers, making it mutually beneficial.

Through various discussions, Coach Baugh gave Tanner a gift that he was unable to appreciate at the time. The two had developed an odd friendship. Although the coach would occasionally drop a subtle hint about Tanner turning out for the baseball team in the spring, he also found Tanner to be fascinating and enjoyed their conversations. After throttling back his aggressive coaching persona, the two would talk about economics and the future of technology. It was not the normal coach-to-player, or even teacher-to-student relationship, they were just comrades.

During study hall, Coach Baugh let Tanner into the computer lab so he could learn how to write computer programming codes on projects outside of the normal curriculum. Coach would sit at his desk and monitor the stock market. When he spotted his next potential investment, he would ask Tanner what he thought. The two would weigh the pros and cons of the potential purchase. Tanner would then ask if the Coach had any ideas of the direction he should go on a program. They enjoyed the insight from each other and would then carry on with their separate business.

Junior high went by in a flash. Tanner was successful on the court both years and was able to maintain a 3.90 GPA in the classroom. As a reward for his good grades, his parents let him pick out a computer of his choice. Every night when Tanner arrived home, he would update Tripp and Judy on the program he was working on at school. Technology was a foreign dimension to both of the Skilli parents. They would nod along as though they understood the dialect he was speaking, but they were clueless. Having a computer at the house would allow them an opportunity to see the mastermind Tanner had become in the computer world.

That summer, Tanner spent most of his time on the basketball court with Dermot. Abiding by his contract with his Uncle Perry, he faithfully continued to shoot 100 free throws each and every day. If he knew he wasn't going to be home one day, he would shoot 200 and bank them towards days he would miss. Shooting that many times consecutively, from the same spot, became mind-numbing. Tanner grew hesitant to ever travel to areas that would not have a court. Free throws became an addiction once he witnessed his work was paying off. After having the highest free-throw percentage in the league, he could not wait for the next season.

6

SUMMER ON THE WATER

Only one month remained until Tanner's sophomore year of high school was recorded on the books. Not wanting Tanner to be lazy around the house all summer, Tripp Skilli reached out to a buddy who worked at the Tall Oak Mill. Luckily the mill was looking for a few cheap labor summer hires. Judy sat Tanner down and made him fill out his first application for employment. The inside connection helped get his application to the top of the pile. Tanner reluctantly went through the formality of the interview process. It was a fixed gig, but Tanner still impressed the young Human Resource manager. They offered him the job at a pay rate of seven dollars an hour, making him officially part of the working labor force.

The thought of spending his summer indoors was punishment enough. Having to wear thick jeans, long-sleeves, steel-toed boots, and a hard-hat only added insult to injury. Tanner had no idea of what to expect, but quickly perked up when he was told to get a pair of steel-toed boots. The HR manager said, "With a steel-toed boot, heavy lumber will just cut 'em all off. If you smash your toes in those other boots, there is no chance of gluing them back on."

The starting whistle blew at 5:15 a.m. without fail. Tanner wasn't well known for being a morning person. His quarrel with the evil snooze button only grew stronger as the summer progressed. Never learning from the past, he brainlessly expected the extra ten minutes to fulfill his rest. Each day he would wait until the very last moment before finally getting up. It was a miracle in itself that he always managed to punch the time card before the first whistle blew.

Aside from being called "Newb" or "Grunt," the days at the yard were honest and rewarding. Most mornings were spent with the simple task of slinging sawdust with a barn shovel. It was mindless work, but "slinging saw" offered a great way to get the blood flowing first thing. Initially, the days were rough on his upper body, but he refused to show any sign of weakness. As his muscles strengthened, he began to develop an appreciation for hard-work and a glimpse of where other mill workers spend their entire lives. Knowing that it was only for a summer, and he had greater aspirations, was the only encouragement that made it bearable. Tanner would constantly have to reassure himself that he was college-bound and would do anything to not live the life of a mill worker.

July Fourth was a day Tanner Skilli would never forget. He got lucky and only had to work a half-shift to celebrate America's Independence Day. He was already three hours into his shift before any of his friends had even hit their first snooze button. The mill workers took their morning break at 8:15. Tanner grew restless, bird-dogging the clock. He was ready to cut loose and enjoy the summer as every teenager should. Once he was off at 10 a.m., the plan was to head to the river for the day and hit up the town festivities with Kurt, Anders, and their good buddy Dermot.

The boys pulled into the loading docks just after 11 a.m. The town's favorite pastime was already well underway. The origin was unknown, but it had been a long-standing tradition. In Wellington, they had what was known as "The Buoys." These were the town's people who loved to drink beer but couldn't afford a boat. They had developed their own modified boat experience during major holiday weekends, to capitalize on the fun that should be had when living near the water.

The Super Bowl equivalent for The Buoys was the 4th of July. They'd set up camp next to the two boat ramps as if they were at a college tailgater. Special lawn chairs, pop-up tents, coolers, and barbeques were reserved for the sacred event. The boat ramps were the only public ramps within 74 miles, which ultimately created a bottleneck of trucks and trailers. During holidays, it seemed like everyone suddenly had a boat. The race to launch the boats under such scrutiny was the toll that all captains had to pay, which made for an exciting spectacle in itself.

To *assist* in expediting the process, The Buoys judged each driver on their skills by holding up scoring cards ranging from double-zero to ten. A driver's ability to stay focused, and ignore the heckling, was a crafted skill that boosted scores up above a six. If a driver found themselves in a position that they had to pull forward to straighten out, they braced for the backlash. Obstructing the flow of the boat launch parade was the ultimate faux pas.

Anders' engine sputtered as he reached the front of the line. Regripping the steering wheel he noticed his clammy palms, anticipating the scrutinized launch. As a Chevy Silverado slowly drove passed with an empty trailer, Anders knew it was go-time. He pressed in on the clutch and rattled the stick before throwing it into first gear. The Buoys could smell his fear like a cackle of savage hyenas. Side conversations took a brief intermission as they shifted their heartfelt words of *encouragement* toward Anders.

Everything was going to plan.

Tanner was guiding the boat down the ramp at a steady pace, when a member of the peanut gallery yelled out to Anders, "Lucky you have your girlfriend back there to show you where to stick it."

Tanner looked over and flashed them a quick middle-finger trying to defend his fellow mate. It was a grave mistake and an instant regret. The Buoys suddenly rose up from their cushioned chairs with cold Keystones in their hands. The heckling was throttled into full pursuit. Anders looked over at his passenger-side rearview mirror and saw that he was headed straight for the piling. He paused for a second as the roar intensified.

Tanner yelled up to the truck, "Anders, sorry brother, you've gotta do it."

With great remorse, Anders pressed his lips together in disappointment and slammed his hand on the steering wheel. With no other options, he reluctantly pushed down on the clutch and grabbed the gear shift.

Adding insult to injury, as he moved the stick from reverse to first gear, a screeching sound shrieked out.

"If you can't find it, grind it!" shouted a member of the mob.

"You gotta treat her like a woman," an old drunk lady cackled.

The Buoys lost their minds. Cowbells started going off, only to be muffled by the foghorns. Anders questioned himself, *How imperative is it to be on the water today? Is this even worth it?*

Dermot shouted from the dock, "Pull out your string man. Let's get this thing in the water."

Finally, the boat and trailer gently splash into the water. Kurt guided her into deeper water with the bow-line securely in hand.

Embarrassed, Anders popped the clutch too fast and killed the truck. There was nothing he could do but smile and wave. He fired up the engine and sped up the ramp, pulling into the first parking spot he could find.

After parking his father's truck, Anders hurried across the parking lot and down to the dock. His only saving grace was the circus show that strolled in behind them to launch their dingy. The Buoys immediately shifted their attention to the fresh bait and the boys were off the hook.

"One of y'all is gonna have to back it in when we take this thing out. I've done my part for the day. That was the most nerve-racking experience of my life," Anders said as he kicked off his flip flops and jumped in the boat.

Kurt looked over at Anders in his disheveled state, grinning, "No need to tell us, my friend. I don't think we saw a score above a three."

Although the river was relatively small, it was long enough that it rarely got too crowded. They motored away from the flotillas and found their favorite spot. Dermot strapped on the wakeboard while the others lathered up with sunscreen.

Looking disapprovingly at their safety measures, Kurt pulled a different bottle from his pack.

"I need to get bronzed up for my trip to Acapulco next month."

He squirted a large dollop of baby oil on his palm and lathered up.

They took turns getting towed up and down the river that afternoon, weaving around the other boats. Naturally, each of them had to try and outmaneuver the others. Their skills had progressed throughout the summer, raising the bar to new heights each outing - literally.

Tanner had been on a solid ride when his fatigued hands started to cramp. He took one last carve outside the wake, making him almost parallel to the boat. With a white-knuckle grip on the handle, he leaned back and started his cut back. The boys all postured up, waiting to witness a spectacle. From out of nowhere, a dumb jet skier came flying in from the other side to jump their wake. Tanner released the rope and threw his hands up in the air, gesturing toward the jet skier.

Kurt was up next and helped Tanner back onto the swim deck.

Kurt jumped in the water and Dermot tossed him the rope. All the while, Anders held the flag from the back corner of the boat, still suffering from post-traumatic stress from The Buoys. Tanner commandeered the captain's chair and slowly began idling in gear until the slack was removed from the line.

"Hit it," Kurt shouted from the water.

After a solid five-minute performance on the board, Kurt's heart was still beating rapidly from Tanner's epic jump to nowhere. He gave out a cab-whistle and motioned to Tanner to double-up.

Grinning, Tanner looked back at his rider and his captive audience.

"Here we go boys. We are way overdue."

Tanner took a slow wide right turn, in preparation of the launchpad.

Conveniently, they had forgotten all of their previous experiences and dismal failures. Reasonable logic apparently goes out the window when teenage boys reach that level of testosterone-fueled competition. Tanner, Dermot, and Kurt had tried the double-up countless times, yet their timing continued to be pitiful. Anders felt he appreciated life too much to attempt such an outlandish feat and shook his head in objection for the stunt.

To execute a proper double-up, the wakeboarder has to hit two wakes as they converge. The captain circles the boat so the two wakes morph into a super-wake for a brief second. Hitting the super-wake is guaranteed to launch the boarder to heights upwards of twenty feet.

Dialing in his speed on the pre-turn, Tanner looked to the side of the boat and saw Kurt searching for the most comforting grip on the handle.

Dermot promotingly shouted to Tanner, "Kurt is locked and loaded, start making your turn. The perfect T'd Double Up is next on the stage."

Tanner received the head nod of acceptance from Kurt and nodded back.

The waves were just moments away from colliding. Kurt leaned back with all of his might and began his cut. As he made his approach, the formation of the super-wake developed. His mind went blank with surmounting fear, as he hit the massive liquid launchpad with impeccable timing. The trajectory shot him into the sky like a mortar being fired.

Seeing him perfectly execute the jump was uncharted territory for them. No one had ever hit the double-up, before that moment. The magic unfolded before their very eyes and then things went sideways in a hurry. Kurt's arms began flailing as he soared parallel through the air. After what seemed like an eternity of hang time, the next thing heard was the loud clapping of his belly-flop echoing across the water. The wakeboard had come up and hit him in the back of the head as he face-planted, forcing him to drink the river. Kurt's world went black upon impact.

Tanner throttled forward, as far as he could, and spun the boat around. Without giving it a second thought, Anders jumped off the bow with textbook rescue dive precision that The Hoff himself would be proud to witness. All of those years watching Baywatch, because *he truly enjoyed the storyline*, had finally paid off. With Dermot's assistance, Anders pulled Kurt to the swim deck and began a sad attempt of CPR. After just a few moments of weak compressions and lackluster mouth-to-mouth, Kurt began coughing up water and gasping for air. Fortunately for Kurt, Anders did not have to resort to drastic measures like using a pen for a tracheotomy as he saw on television.

With labored breathing and river-soaked lungs, Kurt slowly started coming to. Unfamiliar faces hovered around him, leaving him dumbfounded as to how he got in a boat.

"What the hell just happened? That was the most intense three minutes of my life. I don't smoke, but I sure could use a cigarette right now," Dermot inappropriately blurted out from the corner as a true spectator.

Faint applause broke out from the shoreline. The boys looked over and saw an entire beach of people standing at the water's edge, with their eyes glued to their boat. The cat-calls started, followed by an eruption of cheers. It was at that moment that Anders felt redemption for the day.

Kurt's brief brush with death was a sign to call it a day. As the sun began to set, they motored over to their dock. Well, it wasn't *technically* their dock, but it was the closest one they had access to. The dock was top-notch and belonged to a wealthy computer programmer who uses the 4,000 square-foot home as his third vacation destination. In the nine years he had owned the house, no one saw him there. He had a few huge parties, which were broken up by the police. For the most part, the house was deserted and remained dark and mysterious. The boys had gotten so accustomed to using it as their personal dock that they had forgotten that it wasn't even their own.

After mooring the boat in the slip, they grabbed their backpacks began a short walk to downtown. Their destination was easy to find. All they had to do was follow the bright lights and music, as the party was already underway. Tanner looked over towards Kurt, who had his arm thrown over Tanner's shoulder.

"Hey man, we should probably take you to the hospital to get checked out," Tanner said in nonchalant, but very concerned tone.

"Nah man, I'm good. We can go after we watch the parade," Kurt paused. "And why the hell do I feel like I'm on fire?"

Kurt massaged his shoulder once it began to pulsate with a heartbeat of lava.

"Dude, the parade was this morning. You feel like you are on fire because you doused yourself with that baby oil. You wanted to get bronzed before Acapulco," Tanner tried to remind him.

Kurt snapped his head around, so they were nearly giving each other Eskimo kisses.

"I'm going to Acapulco? Hell yeah, man! That's awesome, I can't wait," he said with the excitement of a kid going to Disneyland.

Dermot spotted a group of girls huddled up next to one of the local vendors' booths.

"I think that's Sarah over there. Come on guys," he said strutting toward the ladies.

Anders couldn't help but laugh at the thought that Sarah would ever let Dermot out of the friend zone. She was way out of his league, but Anders was too kind to be completely forthcoming and crush his spirits. Several times during the previous year, Sarah dropped hints about how great of a guy he was and how fortunate she was to have him as a friend. Dermot's ego was too inflated to pick up on the cues and thought that night would be his golden opportunity to capture her heart.

Trying to be cool while walking toward a gaggle of women was one of the more challenging aspects of early courtship. Tanner casually strutted in front of the boys as he locked eyes with the most beautiful girl he had ever seen. His body language made it clear that he had lost interest in watching Dermot fumble his words with his crush.

Dermot attempted to strike up a conversation with Sarah, as they slowly started to infiltrate the circle of friends. With the new girl's shoulder turned away from him, Tanner leaned over introducing himself.

"Hey, I'm Tanner. I don't think we have had the pleasure of meeting before."

As she turned around, he immediately got lost in her soft blue eyes.

"I'm Stefanie, spelled with an *f*."

Tanner glanced down and slowly shook his head in disbelief.

"Wouldn't that be Fefanie?" Tanner questioned with an awkward chuckle.

"Oh, instead of a *p-h*," he said, in an attempt to save face. "That makes a lot more sense. My dad tells me that guys get dumber when they are around attractive women."

As if he had just met his childhood dream woman, he was at a loss for words. He couldn't construct a single coherent sentence. Stefanie with an *f* looked at Kurt, brows furrowed,

"What's with your friend?" she asked.

"Well you see, Kurt here had a regretful burst of courage and got into a fight with a giant wave. Just kidding, sort of — he had a cataclysmic wakeboarding blunder," Tanner said while squeezing his buddy's sunburnt shoulder.

Stefanie burst out with excitement, "Wait. That was you guys out there earlier? We were on the beach and saw the whole thing. Were you the one who jumped in and saved him?"

Tanner sighed, wishing he was the knight in shining armor who saved the day.

"Nope, I was driving the boat," he said sheepishly while looking Anders' direction.

"He is very lucky to have a group of friends who look after him," she said with a bashful smirk.

Dermot called over to his friends, hands signaling toward the beach. The fireworks were about to begin. As the groups dichotomized, Tanner looked back and tried to think of something heroic to say. After a brief moment, he threw up his right hand and waved goodbye instead. Kurt still had his arm around Tanner's neck and decided that he too should wave goodbye. In an attempt to stop Kurt from embarrassing himself any further, Tanner steered him in the other direction. With Kurt's known habit of confessing his love when departing from a particularly beautiful girl, Tanner yanked Kurt to the side, down toward the beach, making a mental note to cover Kurt's mouth during future coed gatherings.

The boys found an old stone wall above the sandy beach and posted up for the firework show.

"Man that was hilarious. You were like Forrest Gump waving to Lt. Dan from the shrimp boat. Who was that girl?" Kurt teased.

Tanner looked distantly out at the fireworks' barge motoring to the middle of the water.

"That was Stefanie, my future wife," he said with conviction.

"That's wonderful!" Kurt exclaimed, then paused. "Am I actually going to Acapulco?"

Only a few fireworks lit the night sky before they realized the firework show would have to play second fiddle to taking their friend to the hospital.

Tanner told the group they should head out because, "Kurt can't remember a damn thing and is becoming a babbling fool."

They turned toward the path to the parking lot, walking nearly single file through the sand. A chill ran through Tanner, igniting goosebumps across his arms. Looking down the beach access stairs, he noticed Stefanie on the corner of a blanket, hands wrapped around her sundress and shoulders, bare skin exposed to the chilly night air.

Reaching into his backpack, Tanner pulled out his letterman's jacket he had been lugging around.

Looking ahead, Tanner called to Dermot, "Would you mind giving me a hand for a minute? There is some unfinished business I need to take care of before we go."

Dermot slowed up and took over the duty of being on Kurt-watch. Tanner galloped down the stairs, casually sauntered up to Stefanie and valiantly placed his jacket around her.

"I don't want you to freeze like Sam McGee before I even get to take you out on a date," he said with a smile. "My mother was gracious enough to put my full name, including middle initial and phone number on the inside jacket tag. I guess she thought our family name in giant letters across the back wouldn't do the trick of identifying the owner. You can give the jacket back to me when I take you out to dinner."

Feeling smug at his recaptured wit, he promptly turned to leave before he could again be thrown off his game.

"Thanks, Taylor," she inaudibly muttered as she watched them carry Kurt away.

They saw the gleam in Tanner's eyes as he hustled back to guys and bumped fists with Anders in celebration.

7

WISHING FOR A RING

Three days went by and there was no word from Stefanie. When Tanner wasn't at work, he was hovering around the home phone, praying she would call. While pacing in the kitchen, something out the window caught his eye. It was Dermot heading up the road.

"Hey, buddy. I was thinking about swinging by to see how Kurt was doing and then heading down to the lanes to throw a little round ball. You in?" he asked.

"Sure," Tanner replied, grabbing his keys, jacket, and glancing wistfully at the phone. "I can use a distraction."

Kurt's concussion coincidentally led them to discover his appendix was about to burst. The doctors said the appendectomy was not a result of the crash. Had they not taken him to the hospital when they did, he could have been in much worse shape. All credit goes to the nurse, who diagnosed him simply because of the grotesque smell of his belch. As soon as she caught a whiff of the putrid odor, she encouraged the doctor to order imaging to confirm her suspicions.

After a few moments of hesitation, entertaining Dermot's proposition to go bowling, Tanner agreed to join his best friend in the nightly festivities. He was twitterpated and battling a ridiculous internal debate that some might argue should have never been an issue in the first place. A potential call from a girl he had spoken to, for a total of one minute and forty seconds, could not be worth more than going bowling with a buddy. As fate would have it, his decision paid off.

The visit to the hospital before hitting the lanes was a bust. Before they could see Kurt's room, the nurse turned them away. Visiting hours had ended more than two hours earlier. Tanner and Dermot tried to crawl past the nurses' station but were caught after Dermot sneezed. After being escorted out by security, the boys jumped back in the truck and headed toward town.

When they arrived at the bowling alley, the joint was hopping. All the usual suspects were in attendance. The mob consisted mostly of town jocks, creating a testosterone-rich environment. Tanner surveyed the crowd like a police officer looking for a runaway. His target was spotted in a split second. Next up on lane three was Stefanie.

She was modeling Tanner's favorite attire on the female body, denim overalls with a long-sleeve blue shirt underneath. Stefanie grabbed her hot-pink seven-pound ball and walked towards her approach. She seemed to be moving in slow motion, Tanner was lost in an alluring spell of lust. With her right toe planted squarely on the bolded middle dot, she stared down the lane. She sent a sharp glare as if the pins had insulted her mother. Like Joan of Arc, she was plotting to teach them a lesson.

Watching her technique was poetry in motion, she delivered a third-consecutive perfect strike. Tanner uncontrollably let out a bantering rooster crow from the viewing deck. The "Cockle-doodle-doo" and lone standing ovation drew the attention of the entire alley. He then looked up at the screen to see the giant symbol of a turkey with three Xs below it.

Dermot hit him on the arm, "Three strikes is called a turkey you idiot, not a rooster. Turkeys don't crow. They say gobble gobble."

Tanner bashfully waved to Stefanie and shrugged his shoulders, displaying his acceptance of the blatantly erroneous birdcall. She jogged over toward him and leaned across the divider between the viewing deck and lanes.

Looking up at Tanner through a mess of chestnut waves and thick, dark eyelashes, she flirtatiously greeted him, "Hey you, I've been meaning to call you so I could give you back your jacket. It's been weeks now and our phone still has not been hooked up at our house. We're still moving in and getting settled. Stick around so we can chat after this round. We only have a few more frames."

Tanner's heart fluttered with an excited sense of relief.

"No rush, I've got all the time in the world," Tanner swooned.

Watching her walk back to her group, he realized he had just told a bold-faced lie. He had to get up early to work at the mill in the morning, but work was the last priority on his mind. Dermot could see Tanner was a lost cause, so he ditched his wing-man and joined their crew on lane 14.

The minutes ticked by as the ball return refused to perform its only task. With each minute that passed, until they reached their final frame, Tanner grew increasingly antsy. *This girl better be worth it,* he thought to himself. Any doubts that he had were quickly swept out the window once Stefanie walked over and gave him a hug before taking the empty seat across from him.

"So the other night," she started, "Who is Sam Wicky? When you gave me your jacket you said something about him."

Tanner promptly shifted his head to the side in confusion. "Oh, Sam McGee! I said I didn't want you to freeze like Sam McGee. Sorry, my family has a deep love for Alaska. In our house, Robert Service, who wrote the iconic Sam McGee poem, is a legendary figure. It's just that any time I get cold he's the first person that I think of."

Her eyes lit up with excitement.

"I've always dreamed of going to Alaska. My family never ventured very far out of Alabama, until we moved here," she said bashfully, visions of traveling the world swirled through her head.

"Well, I've gotta go up there at some point," he said with determination. "To quote the great Robert Service, 'A promise made, is a debt unpaid, and the trail has its own stern code.' "

He could tell she was curious what some freezing guy had to do with going to Alaska.

Tanner followed up with, "I made a promise to my family that I would work in an Alaskan cannery at least one college summer. My dad says it will change my perspective on life and get a true understanding of what 'working long hours' really means."

Feeling uneasy about sharing something personal, Tanner deflected the focus back to Stefanie.

"So, you're from Alabama? You don't have that much of an accent. To tell you the truth, all I know about Alabama is they are borderline insane over football and Bessemer is the hometown of the greatest athletes on the planet, Bo Jackson."

She perked up, "You know my neighbor Bo Jackson? That's kind of weird. Small world I guess."

Astonished, he leaned forward with great intrigue, "What do you mean, 'your neighbor?' " he asked. "Edward Vincent Jackson, commonly known in households around the world as 'Bo,' is one of my idols. Well, maybe not an idol, because that would go against one of the Ten Commandments. The second commandment at that, but you catch my drift."

Throwing her head back in laughter, she said, "My dad told me he was some kind of athlete, but I don't follow many sports besides volleyball."

"Some kind of athlete is a gross understatement, he is superior to any athlete in the world. It doesn't matter the sport, he would dominate Olympic curling or badminton if he wanted to."

She reached over to grab her soda, taking a sip from the straw, she teased, "Sounds like someone has a bit of a man-crush."

Stefanie continued to sip on her soda, with her big eyes coyly smiling at Tanner.

"Anyway, he's a great guy. At least he was anytime he came over for dinner."

Tanner nearly lost his mind. Shaking his head in disbelief, and trying to decode his thoughts, he looked passed his incredulity and made his move.

"So, I was hoping I could take y'all out sometime and introduce you to the town and a little treat we call Pepsi. I reckon yous dunnbe the caddywompus newbie in these parts, fixin' to find a po' boy sammich. I might could swing by in my buggy as a lagniappe. What do you say?" he asked with his best southern accent.

"Puddin', my dad said that I shouldn't date anyone as soon as we moved to town. He told me that the first person I would meet doubtlessly would be a loser. However, I don't think my dad knew that guys like you exist," she said with a flirty grin.

Overjoyed, and surprisingly embarrassed, he simply reciprocated the grin.

"Well, then it's a date, no need to bring your pocketbook. I've got work this week, but how's your Wednesday lookin'?"

"You sure-plum got yourself a deal mister Skilli," she said, playing into her southern drawl.

"Skilli?" he questioned.

"From your jacket, silly. That thing has come in tremendously handy. I actually thought your name was Taylor until I saw 'Tanner' on the front."

"I have certainly been called worse," he chuckled.

With a glance down at his watch, Tanner computed the fuzzy-math his head and gambled that he could make the next day on six hours of sleep, no problem. Any less sleep than that and he would be a hurting unit come morning.

"Hey, I'm glad we finally got a chance to chat, but I've gotta hit the road. I work first thing in the morning," he said with great disappointment.

"No problem at all, I'm used to it. My father gets up stupidly early every morning, or so I'm told. Since we have been in Wellington, I have yet to wake up with him home. Being the new Operations Manager over at the Tall Oak Mill, the lumberyard expansion project has been keeping him busy," she explained.

"What did you say your last name was? Not Stefanie Tucker?" he asked intrinsically.

"Yep, that's the one, but I don't remember ever saying that, Stalker," she replied.

They both sat in silence for a minute before Tanner confessed.

"Your father is my boss. I'm one of his summer grunts working on the lumberyard expansion. When I said I've been called worse than Taylor, most of those adoring pet-names have come from Mr. Tucker. He usually defaults to 'Numb-nuts' or 'Shit-for-brains,' but he will occasionally toss in a 'Sweet-cheeks' when he is feeling froggy."

Slightly shrugging her shoulders she said, "Yep, that sounds like my daddy. At least it won't be too awkward when you pick me up on Wednesday."

8

SCHOLARS DRAW DOLLARS

By the time their senior year rolled around, Tanner and Stefanie had become a power couple. Not only of Wellington but the entire west coast. When the Wellington Lions won their second consecutive regional basketball championship, less than two quarters remained until graduation. Tanner continued to receive dozens of scholarship offers from reputable college programs.

Most of the offers came from PAC-10 schools, but the school that piqued his interest the most was a hidden school called Gonzaga, pronounced Gone-zag-uh. He had heard that the boys up there in Spokane, had something special brewing. They were being led by a basketball wizard named Mark Few. The Bulldogs were soon to be on the national radar. God willing, they would one day be the headline topic of a late night talk show. Then, perhaps, people would stop mispronouncing their school's name like it were Malagasy.

Stefanie was also getting recognition and scholarship offers for her leadership and performance during volleyball season. She enjoyed the praise and attention and was unwilling to admit her jealousy for the extra attention Tanner received.

On a spring evening, Tanner stopped by Stefanie's home to do a routine check-in. He was such a regular at the house, he no longer made the effort to knock. In fact, Stefanie's mother usually prepared him a dinner plate with no certainty of him stopping by, but the odds were in her favor. Tanner and Stefanie appeared as a naturally happy couple. He felt as though he was already part of the family and they had been married for years.

Walking into the kitchen, Tanner pecked Mrs. Tucker on the cheek. He paused for a moment and slowly inhaled the decadent aroma of a home-cooked meal.

"Great to see you, Mrs. Tucker. Looking beautiful as always. Is the other lady of the house around?" he asked with a sparkle in his eye.

Tanner then heard the sound of her gentle footsteps making their way down the staircase.

Stefanie appeared from around the corner wearing the coveted denim overalls, with a white halter-top snuggly securing her curves. She threw her hands in the air and Tanner began to chuckle.

"I know it's your favorite," she said with a grin, pulling him in for a quick hello kiss.

"Yep, that outfit was how you won my heart," Tanner said with his arms wrapped around her shoulders. He had the dinner schedule down to a fine science and had conveniently arrived just in time for the gourmet dish of the night.

"Mrs. Tucker, any chance you need help getting rid of some of the beef stroganoff?" he asked with bashful eyes.

"Well Tanner, you're in luck. I may have doubled the recipe on accident and I don't want to waste good food. Would you be a peach and help us Southern Belles out? We would be delighted to have you join us," she grinned.

It was a scripted conversation, which had been rehearsed for the better part of a year. Both enjoyed the role-play as if it were a special occasion each night. Some nights the theatrics were comically drawn out, depending on their hunger pains. Mrs. Tucker would use Tanner's urgency, or lack thereof, to grade her cooking for the night. She figured, the better the meal, the less willing he would be to play along.

Each dining experience allowed them to learn something new about one another. Sharing stories from their past and views on the world. Mrs. Tucker loved to tell stories about little Stefanie growing up in Alabama and how cute she was as a little girl. Mr. Tucker received a promotion that required him to spend time on the road, attending conferences and meetings with vendors. During his summer at the mill, Tanner proved his worthiness to court young Ms. Tucker. Tanner was happy to fill the role as the man of the house in his absence and gazed upon Stefanie as if she was already his wife.

After dinner, Tanner helped clean up the dishes before heading up to Stefanie's room. When he arrived she was seated in front of her vanity mirror touching up her makeup. She asked if Tanner has figured out which school they are going to enroll at for college. Before he had a chance to say a word, Stefanie told Tanner she couldn't bear to attend a school named after the big hairy guy off of Sesame Street, Snuffleupagus. Tanner was perplexed by her obtuse thinking.

"I don't follow," he paused. "Because of a crazy connection you have in your mind between the school's founder, Saint Aloysius Gonzaga, and a children's character?"

She was busy applying her lip liner when she turned around.

"Yes, they are both named Aloysius," she said before pressing her lips together with sass.

Stefanie was raised as a princess and had routinely gotten her way. Absent the consideration for Tanner's best interest, Stefanie pushed her own agenda.

Regretfully, Gonzaga was removed from the options on the table, leading Tanner to migrate his decision toward the University of Oregon. Home of the Mighty Ducks. Not *the* Mighty Ducks in that awesome hockey movie where they fly in a *V* with Emilio Estevez. Oregon is simply known as "The Ducks."

Stefanie loved the idea of being showered with Nike clothing. In her eyes, the decision made itself. She threw her arms around him and kissed him repeatedly, smearing fresh lip gloss on him.

"I can't believe we're going to college, Babe. It is going to be so wonderful."

National Letter of Intent Day had developed into the most anticipated day of the year for college fans. One could argue that it was more exciting than the NBA draft. Playing ball at the higher level was the equivalent of a full-time job and college ball was the final step in the interview process. The reason the stakes were so much higher for the NLI day was that colleges could not pay players. At least they weren't supposed to, but that doesn't necessarily mean the rules had not been bent at times.

The NBA scouts and agents thought they had it easy. When a

ballplayer reaches the NBA level, players negotiate multi-million dollar deals in exchange for their services. Furthermore, they could establish a player on a team for more than just a few years and take a healthy cut. College recruiters believe the money was in the turnover. More volume at a lesser margin was their business model.

Before there was a Pacific Coast Conference established, playing collegiate sports was a form of survival and self-preservation. The schools did not have a lot of money. A warm meal each day and a guaranteed part-time job on campus were sufficient enough for boys to accept a spot on any collegiate team. Most of the young men were out on their own, simply because their families were too poor to feed another mouth. For them, playing for the school was an honor and gave them purpose in life. The comradery of being a part of something larger than themselves was an award in itself.

Then, money changed things. As the schools progressed into holding higher prestige and became revenue producers, they were able to offer more than just a warm meal and a roof over the athlete's heads. The recruiting efforts to draw the greatest talent in all of the country quickly spiraled to greater heights.

College recruiters in those days leaned heavily on their only bargaining chips. Education, facilities, and school history. The promise of an experience of a lifetime was their bread and butter pitch. The good recruiters had the best job security in the country. Even if they were able to get highly rated players to commit to their school, the likelihood of them staying for more than three years was marginal at best. Fortunately, there would always be new young talent to seek out.

Since Tanner was one of the most sought after players from his district, the local news broadcasted the ceremony for his much-awaited college selection. The morning of the NLI day was bittersweet, due to an oversight by the school guidance counselor. Stefanie requested that her transcripts be sent out to all of her top prospective colleges. At the time, she didn't think there could possibly be an issue. She was an above-average student maintaining a 3.83 GPA. The University of Oregon was the first school to contact her. She was pulled out of the first period, at the request of her guidance counselor.

Walking into the office she saw the principal standing alongside the counselor's desk.

"Stefanie, I just received a call from an assistant coach at Oregon. Upon reviewing your transcript, they stated that your credentials do not qualify to attend their University. They have to rescind their scholarship offer. It looks like we forgot to sign you up for Senior English," the counselor said with deep remorse.

Senior English was only offered in the fall of their senior year. Upon transferring to Wellington High, Stefanie met with the same counselor. It was during their initial meeting that the counselor made a comment about not needing the course because of the way credits were transferred from her school in Alabama. Although the oversight was completely at the fault of the high school administration, she would later receive multiple calls from recruiters who had been pursuing her throughout the year. Each recruiter delivered the same message about academic guidelines they had to abide by.

The timing of the oversight discovery could not have been worse. Stefanie stood frozen in the counselor's office, replaying his words over and over in her head. Being turned down by her top school for something that wasn't even her fault, had her reconsidering every aspect of her life and on the verge of an emotional breakdown. Meanwhile, Tanner was about to walk into a press conference and publicize to the nation which basketball program he was going to commit to playing college hoops.

As badly as he wanted to be a Gonzaga Bulldog, he was deciding to pick a school based on Stefanie's dreams. When he walked into the room, the local media had everything set up. They made it a much bigger deal than he had anticipated. The room was set up like a professional press conference. Any of the people tuning in to watch the coverage would have never known it was being broadcast out of some small room off the school cafeteria.

Tanner sighed heavily before taking his seat. From behind a table decorated with dark green linens, he prepared himself to address the local crowd, coaching staff, his parents, but Stefanie was nowhere in sight.

"Wow, how exciting is this," he said wide-eyed.

"When I first picked up a basketball back in Casper, Wyoming, never would I have imagined that I would be so blessed to get an opportunity such as this. I thank you all for taking time out of your day to share this special moment with me. I am truly blessed," he said with candor.

The kid was a natural. His presence behind the microphone was exceptional. Tanner's delivery was so polished, it was if he had delivered eloquent speeches a million times. Leading up to the big reveal, he spoke a few words of appreciation for his family and the coaching staff.

Taking a short breath, he paused for dramatic effect, "It is with great honor that I am pleased to accept the scholarship offer to play basketball at the great University of Oregon. Go Ducks!"

The room erupted with a cheer. He looked over at his parents and Tripp Skilli was holding up a victorious clenched fist. It was one of the greatest moments in the life of Tanner Skilli. He had made his parents proud.

The Wellington head coach grabbed the microphone and started in on how excited he was that Tanner was going to play for the Ducks. Most of the coach's time was spent on promoting himself and the Wellington program. Once the small crowd realized it was a helpless plug for himself, they quickly lost interest and began to tune him out. Coach wrapped things up with a brief closing statement and called the meeting adjourned. As the room cleared out Tanner noticed a casually dressed man at the back of the room. He looked familiar, but Tanner could not place him. After hugging his parents, Tanner made his way back to the man of mystery.

"Sir, thank you for being present to share in this experience. It's a dream come true," he said.

The gentleman extended his right hand in congratulations, "The name is Phil. I'm an Oregon Duck alumni. We are looking forward to seeing your contributions on the court these next four years. We have a decent football team up in Eugene, but the basketball program lacks luster. The team needs a spark to ignite them to the next level."

Mr. Phil Knight then reached into his pocket and pulled out a very tiny envelope.

"Just a little something to say welcome to the team," he smiled warmly.

They started to chat about Phil's college experience when Stefanie walked into the room. Her eyes were puffy and her hair looked like she had just been mauled by a raccoon. She ran over and threw her arms around Tanner's neck. After a long embrace, Tanner slowly pried her away.

"Stef, this is Phil, he's an Oregon Duck alumnus. He made the trip down from Oregon just to attend my announcement. How amazing is that?"

Stefanie shook Mr. Knight's hand promptly and then turned back and gave Tanner a "We need to talk" look. They thanked Mr. Knight once again and Tanner assured him that he would not be disappointed next fall.

Stefanie pulled Tanner to the side of the room and delivered the upsetting news about her scholarship offers being withdrawn. After belittling the school administration for several minutes, she stepped back from him and stared aimlessly at the ground.

"This means we're not going to go to college together. Unless my father wants to pay for it," she looked at him hopelessly through swollen eyes.

He extended his right arm and nestled his pointer-finger beneath her chin.

Gently lifting her head, "Stefanie Tucker, you are the woman of my dreams. I don't care what life throws at us, we will always have each other. You are my person in life. We will get this figured out." Who knows, maybe we should spend the first year of college apart. We're going to be so busy, it's not like we would have a whole lot of time to hang out. That way we won't feel like we are neglecting one another. Maybe this is a sign. A message from the Universe that the strength of our love is being tested."

Dropping her head once again, she looked down at his left hand.

"What's that?" she asked. "Don't tell me some other girl is passing you a love note now that you are officially college-bound."

Tanner looked down at the envelope he had already forgotten about.

"Phil gave it to me. I haven't had a chance to open it yet," he said with hesitant excitement.

Inside the card was a titanium metallic green Nike gift card. Engraved in the card was "Future No. 1 Draft-Pick."

Stefanie's eyes lit up, "What's on the card?"

He pulled it out of the dark-green envelope and read it aloud.

Tanner Skilli,
Congratulations on making the best decision of your life. Being a Duck is more than just attending a school, it is a way of life. When I first arrived in Eugene I was a wandering soul. The deep history, breathtaking surroundings, and creative energy at Oregon is like nothing you can experience anywhere else in the country. Being a Duck gave me the confidence and passion to pursue my dreams and to take my own path in life. My wish for you is that the University of Oregon allows you to become a man of great honor.

There is an unspoken rule in Eugene, which the town strictly abides by as if it were the 11th commandment. Nike is the only true sports brand in the world, hence it is the only brand you should ever wear. Please put this gift card to good use, so you don't get shunned your first day walking on campus. Initially, we loaded the card with $5, which would barely get you a pair of shoelaces. That's why we put $5 on there for every point you scored your junior season.
Go Ducks!
Phil Knight
Nike - Founder

"Wait, what? That was the founder of Nike?" Stefanie questioned.

Disgusted by her ill-mannered exchange with him, she shook her head in disbelief. Both were overwhelmed with a delayed shock of being star-struck. Stefanie's tune quickly shifted toward making sure she was still a priority.

"You are going to take your No. 1 girlfriend shopping for a new wardrobe, aren't you?" she asked in her sweetest voice. "Regardless of if I end up enrolling at Oregon, I'll at least be a regular visitor. I don't want to get casted with stones, from wearing something with three stripes instead of a Nike Swish."

"It's a swoosh, Babe. They are equally likely to cast stones for calling it a swish," he joked, lightly bumping hips against hers.

Stefanie's dreams of playing college volleyball were not over. She received a call from the Arizona State recruiter. The recruiter began telling her that she had heard the news about the other school withdrawing their offer, but she wanted to reassure Stefanie that the Sun Devils remained interested in having her play in

Tempe, Arizona. The chance for competition on the court made Stefanie's heart at peace. She had no choice but to accept the only standing offer from a PAC-10 school.

At the time, Oregon was mostly known for its football program. The fans at Autzen were not properly classified as fans, they were borderline lunatics when it came to Duck football. Many of the fans feel that football should be played year-round. Unfortunately, for them, it only lasted from August to December. When the team was playing well, they had the benefit of extending their season with a January bowl game. For Duck fans, the football season was always short-lived. In the shadows of the football program hid the basketball team, but that was before *Skilli* was on the roster.

9

TIME TO SHINE

The fall of Tanner's sophomore year, he was amped and ready to turn the school's interest to Duck basketball. After only getting to see a few minutes on the court as a freshman, he was ready to show Duck Nation that he was the real deal. In high school, Tanner was able to chalk up *NBA Jams* stats on opponents six inches shorter than him. The elevated level of play in the PAC-10 was humbling. Tanner Skilli wasn't always the most athletic player on the team, but his hustle and determination during his freshman season won the hearts of the fans and coaching staff.

Over the summer Tanner worked diligently on improving his ball-handling and memorizing the offense and defense. Each day would be concluded with his routine one hundred free throws, followed by countless hours of watching opponent game film. Coaches continued to ask him if he was ready for the upcoming season.

Tanner would always fire back with, "Coach, I'm ready to go."

Something was off though and Tanner couldn't figure it out, both with the coaches and with himself.

Coach Kent continually praised him off the court, but as soon as they stepped into practice it was a different story.

"I just don't get it, man," Tanner said to his center, Zeke Mills, after doing wind-sprints. "Is it just me, or are the coaches riding my ass more than ever. I mean, what the heck did I do to piss them off?"

He stood with hands over his head, gasping for air.

"You got me. All I know is, better you than me, brother," Zeke replied.

Coach blew the whistle and instructed them back on the line. Tanner had turned on autopilot trying to phase them out as he went through the motions. He was too busy trying to sort out the mixed signals he was receiving and questioned if he was really playing that poorly. Tanner couldn't make sense of the situation, causing him to struggle even more through the remainder of practice. The chip on his shoulder grew with mounting frustration each time the whistle blew to point out his flaws. Already on edge, he was unable to interpret the critiques as anything other than a personal attack on his abilities.

At the pinnacle of his disastrous performance, Tanner got a little too fancy. The team was running a half court drill, when Tanner ended up turning a no-look pass into a no-look no-pass, to anyone. He swore he saw a flash on the baseline, but there was not a soul in the vicinity.

"When did the Harlem Globetrotter bus pull into town?" the coach yelled from across the court. "Skilli, pull it together, you just threw the ball to a damn folding chair. Last time I checked, that chair wasn't on scholarship. We might just have one come available if you don't get your act together. You read me, son?"

Following practice, an intended quick shower turned into a prolonged mental strife. Tanner found comfort in the cleansing of his skin to the point his fingers began to prune. Oregon spared no expense, or rather Uncle Phil spared no expense when it came to the athletic facilities. The showerheads cascaded water from the ceiling like a waterfall while Tanner was lost trying to make sense of his place in the world.

After wrapping a highlighter-yellow towel around his waist, Tanner hobbled back to his locker and took a seat on the bench. Caught in the crossfire between anger and confusion, he blankly stared at the floor while his emotions clashed. Tanner could not understand his feelings but knew his body and mind were worn down and in dire need of rest. As Mills was headed out, he acknowledged his friend struggling. At a loss for words, he said the first thing that came to mind.

"Hey Skilli, keep your head up," he said as he pointed to the banner wrapping the perimeter of the room.

Tanner looked up in the direction Mills was pointing, where it read, "Duck! Fight! Go! Fight!" The message was heard loud and clear. Tanner nodded to Mills and then began bundling up for the brisk evening stroll through Eugene.

The walk from the gym to his apartment was a fifteen-minute jaunt, time Tanner usually spent talking to Stefanie. Over the last few weeks, it seemed as though Stefanie was never around when he called. He reached into his pocket and grabbed his flip-phone. With only six numbers programmed, he didn't have to scroll very far to get to "Sexy Mama's" number.

He walked slowly down the path, head hanging low watching the bits of rock and litter pass by his feet. After a few rings she answered and he immediately released his frustrations from the day.

"I had the worst fucking practice today. Coaches were all over me and even threatened to pull my scholie. I wasn't even playing that bad. Sure I had a few missed shots, but they were all clean looks."

"Sorry, Babe," Stefanie simply replied, taken aback by his flood of negativity.

After a short pause, came the next wave of emotions.

"What happened to all that bullshit they were feeding me when I was being recruited," he raged.

Stefanie paused with confusion and sought clarification, "What do you mean? You got kicked off the team?"

Tanner's walking pace picked up as his frustration continued to mount.

"No, I'm still on the team, but they are treating me like they wish I wasn't."

Stefanie took a deep breath, finally letting her frustration of being Tanner's new punching bag show.

"Well I had a fantastic day, thank you for asking."

"What"— he stopped on the trail and pulled the phone away from his ear and looked at it with disgust — "in the world are you talking about?"

"Never mind. It's nothing. Don't worry about it. It sounds like you had a rough day. You should go back to your apartment and relax for the rest of the evening," she said softly.

"I can't, I've got a stupid psych paper to write on why relationships in colder climates are stronger," Tanner snapped back, rubbing his eyes and brow.

"It's probably because they are forced to cuddle with each other to conserve heat at night. Their actions out of necessity provide them with the comfort their hearts crave," Stefanie said with an enlightened chuckle.

Her insight was cast to the side and shot down in the light cross-fire that ensued. Both felt a sense of relief when the conversation came to an end.

Tanner had finally reached his tipping-point and attempted to muster some sincerity to end the call, "I love you, but I'll have to call you tomorrow."

Rounding the final block to his apartment, he felt another gentle vibration in his pockets.

"What is her deal now?" he hastily muttered to himself.

Without looking at the phone, he flipped it open.

"I said I'd call you tomorrow," he barked.

"Tanner, is that you? It's your father. Don't forget we're coming up for the big game next weekend. We wouldn't miss watching our boy play in the Civil War."

Tripp Skilli was driving up to Banff National Park in Alberta, Canada for a week-long trip and bringing his new girlfriend along.

Tanner had yet to meet his father's new love interest. To say he was looking forward to it would have been a joke. Tripp and Judy decided it was in their best interest to get a divorce, due to irreconcilable differences. They tried to hide it from Tanner as long as possible, but they finally mustered up the courage to tell him after a year. He had only seen his father once since receiving the news of the separation. The cut from the breakup was still fresh at the time, so they never discussed what happened back home in Wellington.

"Hey, Pops. Sorry, I was just talking with Stef and she's in *a mood*. I can't wait to see you. I put your name on the guest list. You have to check-in at will call and they will have two tickets with your name on them," Tanner said. "Be sure to bring some heavy artillery. Those Beaver fans have a bit of a chip on their shoulder since Uncle Phil only gives them pittance."

Tripp said his goodbye as Tanner arrived at his front door. Before closing his phone, he looked at the grain picture that

Stefanie had added to his background. Tanner tossed together a small mound of nachos, before settling down at his desk to start in on the paper he had been putting off for weeks. Staring at the blinking black cursor on his screen, he could finally process Stefanie's words. That night he wrote the best paper of his life for the sake of making his heart yearn for companionship and the touch of another body. Thinking about Eskimos bundled up in their igloos made him miss Stefanie.

10

TEN-COUNT TANNER

The week leading up to the big rivalry game was less than civil. Alumni from both teams pulled out the same dirty laundry and used their words as artillery. When Friday finally arrived the team was ready to battle for their rightful claim of their shared state. Tanner and the team stayed at the Corvallis Hilton Garden Inn. The Saturday game was against their orange and black rivals at Oregon State, the barefooted Beavers. Even though it is a quick drive up Interstate 5 from Eugene, the coaches wanted to drive the team up the evening before. Not only did the early precautions eliminate any travel issues, with traffic delays, but it also kept the team from messing up and going out and partying the night before the big game.

Following a team dinner, Tanner headed back to the hotel room with Zeke Mills. He grabbed his phone and saw that he had missed calls and a message. Mills grabbed a coat and suspiciously motioned that he would be back shortly. Tanner flipped open the phone and had to hit the download button to receive the message. After a minute and a half of loading, a distorted video came through of Stefanie making out with a friend at a party.

"Since you're not here, I had to make out with Carmen instead," she said as she tossed her head back and raised a half-empty cocktail in the air.

Tanner called her back several times before going to bed, only to receive a notification that the mailbox he is trying to reach was full.

At 7 a.m. the next morning, the hotel phone thundered a vexatious ring. Tanner blindly reached over to the nightstand, head still resting on the pillow. He pulled the phone over to his exposed ear.

"Hello. Is this an emergency?" he asked with a groggy voice.

"No, Sir. I'm afraid not. Well, I'm not afraid that this isn't an emergency," he paused. "You know what I mean. This is your requested morning wake-up call. Have a brilliant day."

The ill-timed call was a classic Dermot stunt. The two had been engaged in a prank war for the better part of a decade. It seemed like twisted logic, but it was a subtle way the two expressed that they cared for one another. Nothing says I care for a friend, like making him miserable. Tanner lightly snickered to himself and repositioned his head back on the pillow seeking more rest.

Tanner was slow to rise until he picked up his phone and a sudden panic kicked in. He had five missed calls from Stefanie. Rising from the bed, he pressed the voicemail button and took a seat on the couch, bracing for impact as he navigated through the voice automation. The first message was filled with riot-like background noise. He could only translate something about not needing to call her since she was out on the town with the girls. The next three jumbled messages were filled with drunken gibberish that lacked any resemblance to English. Nerves rising, he got up from the couch and grabbed his green Gatorade bottle, the final message began to play.

"Hey Tanner, I made it home. We had a great time tonight. It was a much-needed girl's night out. I tried calling you a few times but you never answered. I'm not sure how to say this, but here it goes. I think we should start seeing other people. We are in college now and supposed to be living the glory years of our lives. I love you so much and I never want to hurt you. I've wanted to be with you for so long, but—" there was a long tone followed by an automated "End of messages."

Staring at his phone, Tanner went into a puzzled trance. So many thoughts were racing through his mind simultaneously, his brain couldn't handle the flood of conflicting thoughts and emotions. Mills rolled over from his coma-like sleep to see Tanner wide-eyed and on the verge of breaking down.

"Skilli, you alright man?" Mills asked with sincere concern.

"Yep, I'm good to go," Tanner numbly replied, autopilot taking over.

"Listen, man, if you need anything you just let me know. I'm no dating doctor, but I know there are plenty of fine fish in the college sea," Mills said softly with a big grin.

Tanner looked up at Mills and was obviously perplexed as to why Mills was whispering so softly.

"In fact, my lure had the right bait on it last night, if you know what I mean," Mills said as he pulled back the sheets and revealed a freshman brunette he smuggled into their room the night before.

She was still sleeping, but not for long.

"You dog, you," Tanner said incredulously.

In an effort to escape the room before their guest woke up, Tanner tossed on his luxurious Nike gear, slipped on a pair of flip-flops and made his way toward the door.

"Bro, if you're going to grab food, I would strongly suggest, and much appreciate it, if you could bring back an extra plate in, oh say, fifteen to twenty-five minutes. Just a minor request for your good friend. You know I would do the same for you," Mills said with an "I'll trust you will do the right thing" tone.

After a morning of watching game film, it was finally time to make their way to the sub-par locker room to dress down. Fighting the urge to call Stefanie, Tanner struggled to find focus. *Was it over? Just like that?* Tanner asked himself. To his credit, he wanted to work up his script before making the dreaded call. He felt that the walls of his world were breaking off like glaciers and sending growlers into the sea of his emotions.

The more he thought about it, the more he realized a phone call to Stefanie would not rekindle their relationship. Ever since the day he announced he was going to be a Duck, they began drifting their own ways. He sensed it was inevitably going to happen, but it didn't help soften the blow. What was once a special bond, was nothing more than a distant memory.

An hour before tip off, Coach walked in to give them a few final words of encouragement and to post the lineup. Tanner wasn't paying much attention to what the coach had to say until he heard the name of the other point guard on the team. The sound drained from the room as he sat there, the world turned from slow-motion to light-speed before catching back up to the current moment. He was going to be riding the pine for the start of the game.

"Okay. So that's how it's going to be," Tanner murmured to himself.

As they ran out of the tunnel for the pregame warmup, Coach stood at the end of the tunnel as Tanner passed him.

"Let's go get 'em Skilli," the coach yelled as Tanner ran by with fire in his eyes.

"I ain't giving them shit if I'm not on the court," he sneered, louder than expected.

Going through their routine, Tanner was surprisingly dialed in. Everything he was throwing up was hitting nothing but the bottom of the net. He was in the zone and ready to start caulking up some stats. As the lights dimmed at Gill Coliseum, the spotlight tracked the starting players, as their names were being announced over the state-of-the-art sound system in perfect clarity.

Each starter shook hands with the opponent and referees. Tanner sat on the bench in the dark, staring at his size thirteen Nike Air Jordan's. Coach Kent thought the demotion would spark the energy Tanner seemed to be lacking in the past few weeks. Six minutes into the game, Coach called Tanner's number and told him to check-in. After a personal foul, the ball was called dead as the referee blew his whistle and walked over to the score table. He reported the perpetrator as if he were a policeman who had just caught a bank robber.

"We got one-two with the reach-in. One-two with the reach-in, at 13:23. One-three-two-three. The ball will be taken out on the west sideline. Following my whistle blow, resume the clock." He locked eyes with Tanner.

"Substitute player, you may enter the game," he said while gesturing Tanner on to the court like a traffic controller.

From the sideline, the Ducks inbounded the ball. Tanner dribbled left and then swung the ball around the perimeter. After a quick jab-step to his left, he cut right and rubbed shoulders with Mills, who was setting a blindside pick. Tanner curled off the pick and received a perfect bounce-pass from the guard in the corner. As he went up for an easy layup his feet were swept out from under him.

From a spectator's point of view, it was an obvious flagrant foul by all regulatory standards. The Beaver guard wasn't even making a play on the ball. The referee blew the whistle before Tanner's body had time to flop on the hardwood. A pushing match ensued immediately. The guilty party was surrounded by his larger teammates as protection. Coaches from both benches ran in and assisted the referees with breaking up the scuffle.

After both teams settled down, the head referee walked over to the score table to report the foul.

"We got zero-zero with the personal foul. Zero-zero with the personal foul, at 9:55. Nine-five-five. Two shots will be taken by number two-two. Resume the clock when the ball hits the rim on the second attempt."

The Duck Nation section erupted with an outraged Tripp Skilli leading the charge from the corner bleachers. The faithful fans started to voice their displeasure for the call in such eloquent ways you would be surprised any of them graduated from junior high. Reaching up to his double-Windsor with this right hand, the coach ripped off his tie and threw it at the assistant coach behind him.

"You have got to be kidding me. That's the easiest flagrant to call in the history of basketball. The midget took out his legs," he screamed inches from the referee's face.

"Coach, I don't want to hear another word out of you about the call or about little people," the referee said with a single figure pointing at the coach's face.

"That's a bullshit call. You know it and I know it. Hell, everyone in this arena knows it. Your mother must have been a Beaver!" the coach said with saliva flinging from his lips.

The referee took a step back and gestured to the coach, both hands up, that everything was fine and there was no need to over-react.

The referee then turned to the score table and said, "Technical Foul, Oregon Coach. The coach is ejected from the game. The home team will shoot two free throws, following the visitor's two free throws, and the home team will have possession of the ball."

Everyone in the crowd, who wasn't already standing, jumped to their feet with an explosion of cheers, curses, and amazement.

Tanner took his place at the line, right toe on the nail mark. He tossed the ball with backspin twice, rotated the ball until he located the embossed Nike logo. After he placed his middle finger in the center of the logo, he bent his knees and felt a shooting pain down his right side. The ball hit the right side of the rim, bounced off the backboard, and fell in the hands of the baseline referee. The referee delivered a hard bounce-pass back to Tanner. He went through his same routine and attempted his second shot. Nothing but net - that is, the bottom of the net.

The crowd chanted in unison, "Air ball, air ball, air ball."

The whistle blew and the referees walked the ball down to the other end of the court to allow the Beavers to take their two shots for the technical foul.

The Duck's assistant coach looked down the bench and signaled for the other point guard to check back in.

The junior guard ran out to relieve Tanner from his duties and asked, "Hey man, we still running Flex-3?"

Tanner shrugged his shoulders and walked over to the bench. He was handed a towel, which he promptly slung over his head, as he took his seat on the end.

"Skilli, keep your head in the game," his teammate said with encouragement and a light elbow-jab to his side.

With three minutes remaining in the first half, the Ducks were down by six.

The assistant coach yelled down, "Skilli, time to go to work."

On the first play down the court, he dribbled the ball off his toe but quickly regained control. He passed the ball to the right guard, who promptly sent it back. Tanner turned to his left and hesitated for a moment. He telegraphed a weak pass as he swung the ball to the left guard. A Beaver defender jumped the pass and stole the ball for a wide-open breakaway. Tanner retreated to the other end of the court and caught up to the player as he was going up for a monster one-handed jam. As he breezed under the player, he tried not to make matters worse and pick-up an unnecessary foul. The senior Beaver, Scott Nall, kicked his feet to the side, initiating some light contact. Nall bellowed out a loud groan as if he had just been mauled by a grizzly bear.

A whistle from half-court was blown by a referee who clearly did not have a good angle of the situation. Tanner ran face-first into the mats surrounding the hoop. After hearing the whistle, he rolled to his right and smashed his shoulder again the mat and flung his head back in frustration. What he didn't account for was a metal *Go Beavs!* sign set in the padding supporting the arm of the hoop. When Tanner bashed his head back in a fit of rage, he expected it to be cushioned by the padding. Instead, he ended up cracking his skull against the solid metal sign. Oregon State is known for its engineering program, but their credibility came into question. Whoever designed the pads were not taking into account the height of the players when choosing the placement of the sign.

"Down goes Skilli," the radio announcer yelled out. "Down goes Skilli."

His body collapsed to his left as if his legs were over-cooked spaghetti noodles.

"What did we just witness?" the other announcer shouted with great astonishment. "Skilli is out cold."

Both teams rushed over to his twitching body. Tripp barreled down the aisle and hopped the three-foot fence at the bottom. He bolted out onto the court before the trainer even had a chance to grab his gear. The coach signaled to the medics to get the stretcher, while a trainer made her way onto the court with a neck brace in hand.

"Give us some room here folks," the trainer instructed the crowd surrounding him. "Give him some room to breathe, please."

Tripp kneeled down next to his son and placed his hand on Tanner's ice-cold arm.

"Sir, I'm going to ask that you take a step back and let us get him stabilized," the trainer instructed.

Coach Kent was informed of the accident and rushed out from the locker room. He walked around the perimeter of the crowd until he was able to reach Tripp. He reached out and placed his hand on Tripp's shoulder.

"Your son is going to be okay, Mr. Skilli. He's a champion, and champions always rise up," he said, giving his shoulder an empathetic squeeze.

Woken up by sirens ringing in his head, Tanner jolted forward, shouting, "Where the hell am I?"

The emergency crew followed protocol to the letter. A mere eighteen minutes had passed from the time his body collapsed to the hardwood until the ambulance doors were shut. Baffled by all the commotion, he suspiciously surveyed the back of the ambulance.

"Hey, this is a moving vehicle. Why don't you have to wear a seatbelt?" Tanner rambled with droopy eyes. "It's just something I have always wondered. That and who the heck is this Don Gloves fellow that they always talk about in medical school."

The EMT informed Tanner of the events that had transpired leading to the fun ride in the back of an ambulance.

"What a knucklehead!" Tanner shouted.

Trying to hit his forehead with the palm of his hand, he grasped the seriousness of the situation. It quickly registered that he was strapped down in restraints like a hostage.

"Don't move Tanner," Tripp Skilli said. "We've got to get you to the hospital to ensure your noggin is still intact."

Looking at the EMT out of the corner of his eye, Tanner said in disbelief, "My Dad is an angel, I can hear him speaking to me."

Tripp was sitting in the seat furthest toward the cab. He leaned over and positioned himself to be in Tanner's line of sight.

"I hate to disappoint you son, but I'm not an angel. I am here though," he said, gently resting his hand on Tanner's shoulder.

The McKenzie Willamette hospital took a series of x-rays and drew blood from Tanner's left arm. Tanner was then carted to a private room in the corner of the hospital. When they reached the room, a troop of nurses made their way in to help with the bed transfer.

"I appreciate the royal service, but I'm perfectly capable of getting into a bed by myself," he said, leaning forward to get up.

A nurse placed her arm across his chest and slowly pushed him back to a lying position.

"We've been instructed to take extra special care of you, Son," the charge nurse said from the corner of the room.

Three nurses lifted him into the new bed and a nurse asked if there was anything he needed to make him more comfortable.

"A Sprite would be wonderful," Tanner grumbled.

She timorously nodded and left the room. The accommodating nurse returned moments later with a can of Sprite and a small white cup filled with ice. Tanner extended his hand to take it from her, but instead, she placed it on the corner table. *Some kind of royal treatment*, he thought to himself.

"Sorry Mr. Skilli, you are on NPO until the doctor evaluates you," she said apologetically.

He began racking his brain trying to figure out what the acronym stood for, but came up with nothing that logically would be applicable.

"It's short for nil per os, if you're curious," the doctor said as he walked into the room with commanding authority. "I'm not entirely sure why the medical field insists on holding on to Latin terms. It just means nothing through the mouth."

After a quick evaluation, the doctor lifted the NPO restrictions. Once the room began to thin out, Tanner cracked open the Sprite and poured it into the paper cup. He cautiously leaned forward to take a sip of the lemon and lime deliciousness for fear that a nurse would swoop in and push him back in restraint. As he lowered the cup, Tripp and his new girlfriend Lorraine entered the room.

"I was planning on meeting you under better circumstances, but I'm Lorraine," she said as she stepped to the end of his bed and rested her hand on his blanket-covered feet.

"Better circumstances, what do you mean? This is the life," he said with a grin.

Tripp started bragging about all the great accomplishments Lorraine has made in her life, reciting her entire resume. She was nice, Tanner would give her that, but she was not his mom. Nor would that be chronologically possible, since she appeared to be about Tanner's same age. For a brief moment, he analyzed her face and tried to figure out if they had a class together last semester. There was an uncontrollable sense of resentment against her, but he did his best to remain cordial.

They sat in the room for a few hours discussing very little. The doctor had instructed them to not ask Tanner too many questions, as they wanted his mind to be at absolute ease. As Tripp and Lorraine talked amongst themselves, Tanner was finding it difficult to understand his father. Tanner questioned how Tripp could tolerate the schoolgirl mentality of his new love interest. When Judy walked through the door, a dreary cloud draped over the room.

"Mom, what are you doing here? I thought Uncle Perry sold his helicopter," he said in an attempt to lighten the mood.

"Of course I'm here. The moment I saw you go down on the television, I caught the next flight out of town," she said.

Tanner was glad to see his mother and did not want her to feel like he did not appreciate her thoughtfulness. He extended his arms as an invitation to come and give him a hug. As she walked over to the foot of the bed, Lorraine quietly pulled her feet out of the way. The two embraced as Judy gave Tanner a light scolding about how bad he had scared his mother, as though he had purposefully intended to knock himself unconscious. When they separated from each other's arms, Judy turned around to address the black-sheep in the room. Judy asked Tripp how much he was being paid.

"Paid, for what," he questioned.

"Oh I'm sorry, I thought you were just babysitting this nice young gal," she said with a devilish leer. "I'm just kidding dear, I'm the obnoxious ex-wife. That's all."

Judy extended her slightly cupped hand.

In the following moments that slowly ticked by, the room grew increasingly tense and awkward. Tanner was never so thankful for a doctor to walk in and divert the conversation.

"Well Mr. Skilli, it looks like your brain carrier took a bit of a hit. For the record, I didn't think you fouled him either," Doctor Mejia said as he pulled up the X-Rays on the monitor. "To complement your concussion, you've developed a tiny bump on your parietal lobe. It's likely no big deal, but we will continue to monitor it. You'll be back on the court in no time."

Following the good news, Doctor Mejia instructed Tanner to stay the night and to just sit back and relax. No television, no music, not even a book. Just to sit in absolute silence. He asked Tripp, Judy, and Lorraine to say their goodbyes for the night and leave Tanner alone with only the company of his thoughts.

Alone in his room, Tanner began self-reflecting. He had lost the love of his life, his parents had separated, and his performance on the court had been less than impressive. Worthless. His life appeared worthless and without meaning. Everything he knew to be real was nothing more than smoke and mirrors. Dreams of marrying his high school sweetheart and becoming an NBA Superstar were tossed out the window. He could never live the fairytale life he had always envisioned. Why carry on if it's only going to lead to struggle and disappointment, he questioned. All was lost and could never be found.

It was a dark and lonely night in the corner hospital room. The nurse performed her midnight rounds and found Tanner propped up in his bed and wide-eyed. She was not sure if he was sad or angry. His eyes were glazed over and bloodshot.

"Are you okay, Mr. Skilli?" she asked.

"Yeah, I'm fine. Just finding it difficult to calm my nerves and to stop thinking. Not having any external stimulus to distract me from reality, isn't helping," he replied.

The nurse left the room and returned with a small Dixie cup

and a glass of water. He looked down into the cup and saw two small pills.

"They will help with your anxiety, so you can relax," she said.

She was not kidding. Whatever was inside those pills was nothing shy of magical. Tanner was sent into a whimsical voyage of blissful happiness.

When he woke the next morning, Tanner saw Tripp sitting in the corner of the room.

"Hey there champ! I mean, Son. Too early for boxing references?" he said with a chuckle.

Tanner closed his eyes and tried to slip back into the euphoric sleep. Tripp informed him that he had been released and they were free to leave whenever he was ready. The pills lingered in his veins and created a hazy and distorted reality. He was slow to rise and had not yet got his sea-legs back. Even though Tripp was parked directly in front of the hospital, the journey to the Bronco was exhausting and seemed to be a Lewis and Clark trek across the entire state of Oregon.

"Did you already throw Lorraine to the curb? Or did her parents run out of money?" Tanner asked as they drove down Highway 126 back towards campus.

"Good one son, nice morning jab at the little filly. No, I dropped her off on campus so she could take a self-guided tour," Tripp replied.

Tanner looked around as they drove down the highway and could not help but think she knew her way around campus pretty well, given that she was likely a student.

"Are we in Eugene already? Dad, you drive like a madman," he said with confusion.

"They insisted on sending you back down to Eugene to prevent any dirty play from that Beaver-infested podunk hospital in Corvallis," Tripp said.

Tanner had been stewing over his parents' break-up all night. He knew that they were in route to pick up Lorraine, and that would be the only time he would get to speak to his father man to man.

"So, Dad, I've gotta ask. What happened between you and Mom? I mean, things weren't that bad, were they?" Tanner asked.

Tripp looked over towards the passenger's seat and started from the beginning, which promptly led to the ending.

"Well son, what happened was you. When your Mother got pregnant, we weren't even dating. I thought marriage was the answer to help shield us from the shame, but we never really loved each other like a husband and wife. We shared a common love for you, and that's what kept us together during all the difficult times. Once you left the house, we had a tough time even making casual conversation. It didn't take long for us to agree that our goal was reached, and it was time to move on with the lives we had originally intended. You were the glue, Son. I will always be grateful to Judy for bringing you into this world. Our love for you is no different, we will just have to express it independently," he said as they made their way through downtown.

"So are you going to marry this Lorraine gal," Tanner asked.

"Son, why would a man who had just escaped from Alcatraz, try to sneak back on the island?" he said with laughter, "I'm just having fun and enjoying the change of scenery. Speaking of, we are headed up the Banff Canada."

Tanner reached under the seat in an attempt to gain some legroom. The seat would barely slide back and forth, apparently hung up on something in the track. With his left hand on the wheel, Tripp reached back with his right arm and started feeling behind the seat. The tips of his fingers brushed across the leather. He arched his back to give him a little extra extension. Finally, he pulled up the object that was hindering the seat.

"Oh shoot, I forgot I had this in here. Those Canadian Mounties probably won't let me bring my trusty Bulldog .44 Special," he said while placing the revolver in his lap. Would you mind hanging on to her for me?"

He picked it up and handed it over to Tanner.

Tanner unzipped the leather case and pulled out the polished revolver. For such a compact gun, it was deceivingly heavy.

"Is it loaded? I don't see any ammo," he asked.

"How many times do I have to tell you? You should treat every gun as if it were loaded, it only takes one remember," Tripp said.

Tanner flipped the cylinder to the side and saw the single round. They pulled into a parking lot to see Lorraine sitting on the bench reading Jon Krakauer's *Into the Wild*. She glanced up and saw her chariot had arrived. Tanner's chivalrous nature compelled him to crawl in the cramped back seat to offer up the roomy front seat to his father's girlfriend.

Tripp drove Tanner and Lorraine down to The Original Pancake House for brunch. Hospitals were rarely known for their exquisite cuisine, but the good folks at McKenzie-Willamette had whipped up a delicious breakfast that morning. When Tanner woke up in a daze he was not all that hungry and it pained him to let the meal go to waste. He had taken a few nibbles, to set his conscience at ease, but only ate enough to make him starving by the time they reached the restaurant. Tanner thought it would be a good opportunity to learn more about the imposter that was traveling around with his father.

A timorous Lorraine tried to lighten the mood with some recent political gossip, but Tanner heard her words as white noise. The thought of immersing himself into their famous club sandwich took precedence. Her political talk stood no chance against the anticipation of the delicious basket of fries smothered in ranch dressing. The hostess sat them in a corner booth. After handing out the menus, she asked if they were waiting for one more.

Tanner began to politely say, "I think we are all set."

Tripp interjected, "I'm afraid we are waiting on one more."

The waitress could sense the awkward miscommunication and gently placed the menu at the empty setting and smiled.

Judy was not about to be sidelined by Tripp and his decoy. When she caught wind of them having breakfast together she insisted on joining. The drink orders were being returned to the table when Judy arrived.

"I took the liberty of ordering you a coffee without sugar or creamer. I know how you prefer it black, like your men," Tripp said with a smirk.

Lorraine looked up from her menu and thought, "Well, this ought to be entertaining."

Right out of the gates Tripp and Judy started taking cheap shots at one another, while Tanner and Lorraine sat quietly watching two parents fighting again. They were reasonably discreet and managed to not make that much of a scene. At times Judy wanted to scream out, she would lean forward and speak in a very aggressive whisper. However, her deeply harbored feelings were difficult to keep at bay.

Eventually, Judy was able to regain her composure. She hastily shifted her conversation to Tanner and gave Tripp and Lorraine the cold-shoulder. The first questions she asked were about

Stefanie, asking how things were going for the lovebirds.

"Mom, I am not sure how to say this, but things are a bit on the rocks between us. In fact, she pulled the plug on our relationship just yesterday. I was kind of expecting it though, but always thought that things would work themselves out. Looking back on it, I pretty much gave up on us a few months back. My heart just was not in it and I stopped making an effort."

Tanner reached for his drink and began taking small sips as he gathered his thoughts.

"Yeah, I'm sad, but part of me is relieved. I was too much of a coward to just man up and call it quits when I knew the spark had faded. Now that I think about it, I thought it would be less heartache for her if she was the one who called it off. I saw where the train was going, and I did not do anything to prevent it from derailing," he said as the waitress delivered their food to the table.

Tanner took a bite of his sandwich and then dipped his fries into the ramekin of ranch, only to find his appetite was lost. He knew his mother was only trying to make casual conversation and did not mean to stir up any hurtful emotions. Judy could see that her son was in pain and encouraged him to eat at least half of his sandwich.

"One more bite from my big boy?" she said with a motherly smile.

When the check arrived, the waitress placed the leather folder to the left of Tripp. Judy promptly lunged over him and grabbed it, she reached into her purse to grab a credit card.

As Judy slid the Visa into the plastic pocket and placed it at over the edge of the table, she looked over at Tripp and said, "Don't worry I've got it. I know babysitting isn't the most lucrative of careers."

He snarled at her and then placed his hand on Lorraine's.

Walking out to the parking lot, Judy announced that she would be taking Tanner back to his apartment. She wanted to drop him off before running to get everything they would need during the recovery process. Judy had made a point to park her rental car on the passenger side of Tripp's Ford Bronco, with her tires well over the white lines, to make entry difficult for the toothpick-sized Lorraine.

Judy said with empty encouragement, "Oh, Honey, I know you are skinny. I'm sure those yoga pants will help you squeeze in between the vehicles."

The thought of ramming the heavy Bronco door into her little Toyota Corolla crossed Lorraine's mind, but she refrained. Being that the car was only a rental made the act of defiance less devilish.

Tanner hugged his father goodbye and wished them safe travels north.

"I almost forgot, thanks for the reminder, son. Would you mind hanging on to the revolver for me, so it doesn't get confiscated at the border crossing?" his father asked. "This gun has been in the family for years and I would hate for them to misplace it at Customs."

He dropped the back gate and reached for the leather case on the seat.

"Hope you feel better soon, Son. No rush, you'll be back on the court before you know it," he said as he handed over the cased gun, "Take good care of her. In the unfortunate event that you need it, there is always one in the chamber."

Although he was released to play two weeks later, Tanner's mind had a looming cloud, creating a dark depression. The doctor had given him a huge bottle of ten milligram hydrocodone pills to help with the headaches. After a few days of popping them like candy, they sent him deeper into misery. On the court, he tried to conceal his mental impairment, but it was obvious that he was not himself. The coaches took note of the difference and launched an aggressive approach to snap him out of it with good ol' fashion tough love. They continued to be on his case throughout the week, micro-analyzing his every move. Nothing he was doing seemed to be right, despite Tanner's best efforts. Coaches made certain to point out every error as if Tanner was unaware of his failure. Due to the received scrutiny from the coaching staff, teammates began to distance themselves from Tanner. No other player wanted to get on the same radar as Skilli.

During water breaks, Tanner would rush to the toilet and throw up copious amounts of orange fluid. His head continued to pound, but he was not willing to risk his position on the team. When the final whistle blew, Tanner had nothing left in the tank. His body showed obvious signs of dehydration as he blindly went through the motions of leaving practice. Not a single player said a word to him as they showered and got dressed in the luxurious locker room.

When Tanner arrived home, he turned on ESPN to catch the scores from around the country. Instead of highlights, they were replying blooper reels from the month. Tanner had always enjoyed the segment. To be a potential feature on the show made the viewing unbearable. Sure enough, they were destined to show his folly. When they aired the clip, Tanner grew furious and outraged. The fact that they looped the knockout in slow motion sent him over the edge.

Tanner raced around his apartment, huffing and puffing with white-knuckle clenched fists. He punched a hole in the wall as he stormed into his bathroom, frantically searching for the pill bottle. He grabbed three white pills and walked briskly to the fridge, in search of an ice-cold Busch Light to wash the medicine down. At the moment, stopping at just one beer did not seem like a *wise* decision. So one after another, he cracked them open and guzzled the magnificent splendor of liquid courage.

Pacing back and forth in the kitchen, the thoughts in his mind continued to darken. All of the buried hurt suppressed deep down inside began to rise to the surface. With his blood boiling, Tanner felt empty for his failure to live up to the expectations of others. Without basketball and Stefanie, what was he? There was no reason to keep wasting space on earth if all he was going to do was disappoint the people he loved most. Tanner chugged the final beer in the fridge and slammed it on the countertop. Gripping the side of the can, his inner Hulk demolished the aluminum with the mighty crush of his hand.

Stumbling down the hallway Tanner continued to mumble, "F' it! F' this place! F' it all!"

When he managed to find his way to his room, he saw the gun case resting on his desk chair.

Removing the revolver from the holster, Tanner felt the weight of the heavy barrel, its power resonating through his hands, up to his arm, and hitting him square in the chest. As if he were appraising the Bulldog Special at a pawn shop, he held the gun in the palm of his right hand, admiring every detail, the snub nose glinting in the faint light of his apartment, the solid chamber turning until it clicked into place. *Let's see if I'm supposed to spend another day on this earth,* he thought.

With his right hand firmly on the grip, Tanner opened the cylinder to confirm what he already knew, there was a single round loaded. He flipped the cylinder closed and secured it into place. Adjusting his grip, palms starting to become clammy, he started thinking of any reason, any thought, that would justify pulling the trigger.

They probably won't even miss me anyway. Really, they'd all be better off without me. A better team, parents free from worry, and Stefanie could move on.

With his left hand, he spun the cylinder and placed the barrel in his mouth. Lightly biting down, the metallic taste hit his tongue, making him grimaced with fear.

Slowly moving his finger off of the guard and back to the trigger, he noticed the beads of sweat dripping down his face, into his eyes, and down his neck. His hands felt a rush of warmth as he slowly withdrew the spring-loaded hammer. Tanner's entire life was resting in his hands. His breathing grew more rapid as he repositioned his finger on the trigger. Taking one brief moment to pause, Tanner moved his finger back to the rest on the trigger guard.

The hydrocodone and beer concoction made it difficult for Tanner to remain focused. His feet began to squirm as terror consumed him.

"Fuck it!" he yelled, pulling the trigger.

The hammer barreled down as Tanner pressed his eyes together and unconsciously shrugged his shoulders bracing for the impact. A blaring white-noise echoed through his head, following the deafening clap of metal on metal. All that remained was silence. The revolver fell from his weak hands onto a mound of dirty clothes. Feeble legs forced his body to follow behind, sending him crashing to the floor.

Rolling over to his back, Tanner slowly, almost unconsciously, started counting limbs, feeling the solidness of the ground under him. Lying in a foreign state of consciousness allowed his yogic breathing to prolong exhalation. The fitful beat of his heart yearned for recognition, becoming more vitalized than ever before.

He breathed in and out, at a decelerating rate, feeling numb to the world. After several minutes, Tanner slowly began to open his eyes. He fluttered his eyelids several times to untangle his intertwined lashes, from being mashed together with unusual force. Staring aimlessly at the ceiling, his mind drifted into oblivion. Questioning his recent act of stupidity, made him immediately hate himself. Tears began streaming down the side of his face as he beat himself up in his mind.

"You are such a piece of shit, Skilli. That was f'ing dumb. That was really f'ing dumb," he berated.

Leaning forward, Tanner began canvassing his room. He refused to believe he was overly sentimental, but childhood mementos took him down memory lane. A cribbage board was sitting on the floor next to his bed, reminding him of the trip he and his parents took up to Wallowa Lake many moons ago. Looking over to his dresser he saw the blue-framed picture of Kurt floating across the water. Dermot had snapped it back in high school to document their first successful double-up. Tanner could not suppress a smile when remembering back on that eventful day.

Tanner had gained the needed clarity that his struggles were minor in comparison to throwing in the surrender towel. He had left it up the universe to give him a sign and the universe answered. The dry fire had killed off a part of him that had been anchoring him down. There was a more adventurous life in store for Tanner Skilli.

"I guess you have a divine plan for my life after all. I apologize for doubting you. Thank you for my life, I will live every day forward as if it were my last," he mumbled as a promise to God.

Tanner closed his eyes and welcomed the narcotics and alcohol to anesthetize his mind and soul.

The next morning arrived in a hurry. Conditioning practice was about to start in less than an hour and he felt as though he had only been asleep for a few minutes. Tanner blankly looked up at his nightstand with puffy eyes. All he could see was a red blur of numbers, but the repeated beeping indicated it was time to get up. Stumbling over to his bed, he tried to catch his fall. As he placed his hand down on the mattress, he felt a shooting pain through his nervous system. Punching the wall had caused a boxing fracture on his right knuckles. Tanner popped another hydro to help ease the pain and chugged a quart of orange-flavored Gatorade.

Conditioning practice was a waste of time. Tanner was better off staying home and curling up with the toilet. For the first time he was thankful they conditioned outside. It only took three wind-sprints before he began spouting orange liquid on the grass.

"Skilli, get your ass over here," Coach Joe yelled out.

Tanner was hunched over and signaled he would be there in

just a second. The coach didn't take lightly the fact that he was now on Skilli time. The gesture violated the chain of command hierarchy. Rarely did players respond to coach by holding up a finger, but he could relate to what Tanner was going through and offered him grace.

After several dry-heaves, Tanner towed his body over to Coach Joe. Coach blew his whistle and told the guys to get hydrated before putting his arm on Tanner's shoulder. Normally it wouldn't be a problem, but Tanner was having difficulty supporting his own weight. Trying to keep his knees from buckling, his legs began to quiver as the coach tried to look him in the eye.

"I know what you're going through Skilli. It's not your fault. Those doctors should have never released you to get back on the court after rocking your head that hard. Does it feel like a haunting storm is circling in your mind all the time and you feel trapped in a nightmare? I've been there too. They probably sent you home with a bottle of pills to take care of the problem, not realizing the collateral damage their actions would foster. I'm not going to say a word to the other coaches, because I could potentially lose my job. Take the rest of the day to get yourself cleaned up and ditch those pills before you do anything else. Those pills might make your body feel good temporarily, but they will destroy your mind. I will tell the coaches that I excused you from practice to nurse a sprained ankle. Maybe hobble a bit when you come into practice tomorrow."

Tanner looked at Coach Joe with swollen eyes and couldn't help but feel like he was disappointing his coach. Since the doctors gave him the green light to play, Tanner knew he was expected to perform as usual.

External pressures were becoming overwhelming, but hearing the words of Coach Joe was refreshing encouragement. A reminder that the head coaches and doctors were only concerned with winning games for the University of Oregon. Coach Joe gave him a reassuring pat on the back and Tanner simply nodded.

As Tanner headed for the locker room, he turned and asked coach, "Which leg?"

Coach Joe smirked, "I've always been told to choose the right."

Arriving back at his apartment, he further regretted his irrational charades from the night before. First, he cleaned up the kitchen. Then, tidied up the living room. Not ready to go back in his room to face the revolver, he showered and tried to eat some Cheerios. Walking around the kitchen in his towel was fine initially. That was until his once warm skin, from the scalding hot water, began to chill him clean through to the bone. It was time to face the gauntlet. Unless he was preparing to join a nudist colony for the rest of his life as an icicle, his options were limited.

As he walked in the room, Tanner refused to make direct eye contact with the revolver. The revolver had adopted its own identity as both a friend and an enemy sitting in his chair. When he got to the dresser, he had to put out his left hand to prevent himself from falling to the floor. Everything went blurry and triggered a distant memory of being spun around, at ridiculous speeds on the county fair Gravitron. His vision narrowed, sending him into a state of panic.

On the verge of hyperventilating, Tanner took a seat on the floor and wrapped his arms around his knees. He continued to lose strength and was forced to lay down with his back against the shag carpet. Tanner finally was able to relax his breathing. He closed his eyes and eventually drifted off to sleep. Three hours later, he awoke to his neighbor slamming the door. Lying in only a towel, his body felt frozen. Unconsciously, at some point, he had draped an old sweatshirt across his chest. That sweatshirt was his only saving grace at retaining any warmth. Dragging his body across the floor, he crawled into his bed, where he remained until the next morning.

Before practice on the following day, Coach pulled Tanner aside. He told him he wanted to make him captain of the team next year, and that's why he continued to hound him.

"I want you to step up and lead this team," Coach Kent said bluntly.

It was difficult to hear those words after feeling completely worthless in the days prior.

"The secret may sound selfish, but I can assure you it is not. Great players do not play for their girlfriend, their parents, or for the fans. Great players play for their team and the men around them. Don't be the star of the show to impress the masses. Be the star of the show because it fuels your soul knowing you are making the men around you great. This, I promise you- internal joy is contagious to everyone around you. Fortunately, for a talented young man like yourself, you have a large stage to perform on all season long. What you don't realize is how many lives are inspired by your determination, competitive spirit, and your loyalty. It has to be authentic and come from within if you truly want to have an impact on the world. True competitors look beyond appeasing the fanatics, they fight to reassure their soul that their gifts are not being wasted."

Following practice, the words from both coaches echoed in Tanner's head during the dark walk home. A surprising gust of crisp air hit his face as he rounded a brick wall. Catching the tailing chill of the breeze, Tanner involuntarily placed his hand in his sweatshirt pocket. The sound of small maracas caught his attention like Ivan Pavlov.

Even though Coach Joe let him off the hook with specific instructions, Tanner thought different. He could not bring himself to dispose of the few remaining pills. Throwing them away wasn't the toughest struggle, he successfully reached that point several times. Overcoming the next steps of taking out the trash, and watching the dump truck haul the pills away, was damn near impossible.

The talk with Coach Kent confused Tanner. Reflecting back on the past three weeks of practice, he tried to comprehend how he had misread the situation so terribly wrong. Tanner's narrow-minded perspective prevented him from seeing the coaches were trying to push him to the next level. The talk with coach occurred at an indeed peculiar time. Tanner briefly nodded his head and smiled, acknowledging the subtle reminder of the promise he made to God.

Passing a tent town, in an abandoned parking lot, Tanner reached into his pocket and then casually tossed the bottle of pills to an old man sitting on a milk crate. He felt like a smooth gangster monitoring his turf. Tossing the bottle through the air like he was kicking a foot soldier his cut of a deal, Tanner pictured himself as the bossman who ran those streets. The bottle hit the man directly in the forehead and fell to the ground.

Most passersby never noticed the chronic homeless man was missing both arms, neither did Tanner until the bottle was already in slow motion flight towards the man's face. Tanner lurked forward, but it was out of reach. All he could do was brace for impact and prepare to defend himself from the PTSD about to erupt from the army veteran.

Much to Tanner's surprise, there was no retaliation for the act of war he had just initiated. Tanner began apologizing extensively, but his words were not heard. After a minute of peace offerings, the old man looked over at Tanner.

"Hey there partner, is it chow time yet?" he said in a battered voice.

"What's your name, friend?" Tanner asked, taking a knee beside him.

"My name? I don't know that anyone has asked me my name in quite some time."

He thought about it for a good long while before reaching a conclusion.

"Leonard. I think my name is Leonard."

Tanner lowered his head, as he had just heard the saddest answer of his life. The pure truth and deep pain in Leonard's words shattered his heart to pieces.

Realizing Leonard's mind was off on a beach soaking up the sun when the bottle of pills hit him, Tanner casually picked it up and shoved it back into his pocket. He knew the price of popping the pills and Leonard couldn't afford to shoulder any more sadness in his life. Leonard's strength and perseverance, helped Tanner realize that it was time to start a new rebuilding chapter in his life. He said a quick farewell to his new friend and on his way out, he catapulted the bottle of pills in an unoccupied burn barrel. A huge burden was lifted, knowing he could not disappoint himself and continue falling in the same dark pit.

11

ALPHA MALE

Word around campus started to spread in the following weeks. Tanner's transformation to get his life back in order was paying dividends and he was almost prepared to get back on the dating market. One of his friends was a writer for the school paper and wanted to accelerate the process by publishing a third-page story about the most eligible bachelor on campus. Women came out of the woodwork, in addition to a few teacher aides, in search of love and potential luxury. They all had the same dream of being the arm-candy of the school's star basketball player who was destined to play at the next level.

Tanner arrived at his first class of the day and felt the eyes of the room fixated on his every move. He conspicuously placed his Nike pack on the floor and began surveying his surroundings. Feeling like a bohemian, he pulled out his notebook, blue pen, and a copy of the school paper he had grabbed from the rack in front of the bookstore.

Sinking low into his chair, he pulled his ball cap down unusually low and flipped the paper over to the back. The crossword puzzle that day was a tester. He had picked off a few of the normal words but for the life of him could not figure out what a male turkey was called. Mills arrived moments before the bell. He slung his backpack over the chair between them.

"Well if it ain't Big Dick Nick on campus!"

Tanner looked at him with confusion.

"What are you talking about man? What am I missing? I feel like everyone is staring at us, and I don't know why."

Flipping to the third page of The Daily Eugene, Mills turned the page around to show Tanner. The vibrant colors filled half of the page with a photo of Tanner shooting a jump-shot. The headline read, "The Most Eligible Bachelor on Campus, Tanner Skilli. He's a Real Knockout." Tanner placed both hands over his face and leaned forward, resting his forehead on the old worn-out chair in front of him.

"Steve has got it coming to him," he mumbled under his breath.

His so-called buddy, Steve Tillman, wrote for the paper and thought he would do a human interest piece on Tanner without asking permission. The article was partially to poke fun at his friend, but it was primarily done with good intentions. Steve wanted his buddy to get back in the game and to enjoy some of the beauties of college life.

Throughout the lecture, Tanner could overhear whispering and felt mild paranoia that fingers were being pointed in his direction. That sort of attention made him extremely uncomfortable, which was strange considering he was routinely performing in sold-out arenas. On the basketball court, praise and recognition from the crowd were his primary motivators. Dropping a clutch three-pointer, then looking up to see people rise from their chairs in applause, gave Tanner special powers.

His need and desire for approval and praise from others stemmed from an early age on and off the court; however, it had gradually morphed into something more powerful and ungovernable. An addiction of being fulfilled by the spotlight and the euphoric feeling through approval of spectators was a constant struggle.

The cheering crowds and hearing his name being chanted gave him the satisfaction that he was in a sense bringing happiness and joy to others. The joy from applause was the only feeling that was able to shake Tanner enough to reassure himself he was enough in life. In those moments, he loved himself.

Off the court was different however. Tanner tried to avoid the limelight as much as possible. He did his best to maintain a low profile, but his cover was blown. The article had exposed personal aspects of his life that he would rather not have publicly displayed.

After class, he pulled his hoodie over his head and quickly slipped out the side door to avoid any rabid jersey-chaser attacks.

Walking along the campus mall, his eyes were fixated on the brick path. He thought he could seek refuge in the gym; he thought wrong. After dressing down, in his Nike-issued apparel, he stepped into the weight room. The football team was just starting to clear out. Knute Abernathy was the starting quarterback that year and enjoyed the perks that came with the title. Abernathy was the guy on campus; the ruler of the kingdom. There is only one starting quarterback on the team and that was him. Knute's life was arguably the most desirable life by any male under forty. When Knute locked eyes with Tanner, he stoically walked up to him and extended his right hand.

"It's an honor to be in your presence, Champ," Knute said.

Tanner reluctantly extended his hand and endured a bone-breaking clench. Knute stepped back and started the most passionate slow-clap in Oregon Duck history. The entire weight room joined in, as the clapping intensified. Tanner shook his head, as Knute reached over and grabbed him by the wrist. Hoisting his arm to the sky like Tanner had just won a boxing title fight. Coach Tony stepped in and told the guys to get their asses out to the practice field for sprints.

Once the football team cleared out, Tanner loaded the bench bar for his warm-up set. After repping out a quick twenty, he racked the weights and laid on the bench. It was at that moment the reality of his situation gained clarity. For the first time in his college career, he was single. Tanner had always pictured spending the rest of his life with Stefanie. Faithfully, he did his best to not admire any of the marvelous talent the student body had to offer. Perhaps it is time that I start pursuing other female companionship, he thought.

After the gym, Tanner headed to biology lab. The class paired everyone up at random at the beginning of the semester. When he got teamed up with the petite brunette, Tanner immediately labeled her as being the brainy-type, simply because she wore glasses. Her name was Annika and was far from being a nerd. She wasn't in the Greek system and couldn't care less about athletics, which made her somewhat of a nomad at the University of Oregon. Beyond the sports' world, the Eugene culture complemented her lifestyle well and she loved being only a few hours away from the ocean.

Walking across campus to lab, Tanner thought, *Here we go again. More people to whisper and point at me.* He arrived minutes before the rest of the class trickled in for the evening. Annika was already at the lab station gathering up all the equipment they would need for their assignment.

Acknowledging his presence, Annika glanced over and smiled.

"Oh, hey there. How's your day going?" she asked.

Tanner was unsure if she was making reference to the spread in the paper, or if she was genuinely asking how he was doing.

Looking up from the ground, he replied, "It's been a bit of an embarrassing roller coaster, but I'm getting through it. I am definitely looking forward to this day being over."

Annika didn't inquire any further.

"There's always tomorrow," she said, continuing to prep the station while softly humming a joyful melody.

"That was rude of me. I apologize, I'm apparently a bit too self-indulgent. How was your day, Ms. Annika?" Tanner cordially asked.

She lightly chuckled.

"Well, to tell you the truth, I'm both excited and nervous about this weekend. My high school boyfriend, Luke, wanted to surprise me by coming up from Colorado to visit, but I already told my girlfriends I would go to the coast with them. I'm not sure how excited Luke is going to be when he is surrounded by a bunch of girls."

She securely fastened her safety goggles before diving into step one of the assignment. Not yet attuned to her form of dialect, Tanner couldn't help but wonder why she was dating a high school boy.

Annika untwisted the cap from the red reagent and began using the specified titration methods in the beaker. After the third pendant drop fell into the solution, she paused, appearing to be in deep thought.

"Hey, any chance you want to join us? It's only for a night," she asked in passing. "He is a great guy, I think you two would get along well."

Taken aback by the breach of their acquaintance barrier and the recent discovery of her strange attraction to younger men, he replied carefully, "I've got to think about it. I get along with just about everyone, but I'm not sure how much enlightenment I'm going to gain from hanging out with an underage kid. Honestly, I feel bad drinking around young people because I suspect it accelerates their desire to do things just to fit in with a group."

Although she quickly identified her poor choice of words that led to the miscommunication, Annika was curious where his rant would end and allowed him to finish.

"No, Sweetie," she smiled and shook her head. "Luke is my boyfriend that I started dating when we were in high school. He's getting his bachelor's degree in criminal justice this year. Don't go thinking I'm some sort cradle robber."

"Oh, snap! That is not at all what I thought. I mean, I'll be honest, it did make consider deducting a few of your awesome-points," Tanner said with a laugh. "We have a Thursday game and coach is giving us the weekend. As long as I get a quick run in while we're there, I'll be fine. So, as a matter-of-fact, you can count me in."

Praying she wasn't up on the current news, he braced himself for some reference to his newly acquired "Ten-count Tanner" nickname. Instead of saying, "I'll just put you down for one, rather than ten," Annika nodded that it was a done deal.

Their interaction outside of the lab had been minimal up to that point. They both attended a few group study sessions and exchanged the occasional greeting when they passed each other in the Knight Library, but that was the extent of it. Albeit, Tanner felt comfortable with Annika for some unclear reason. When together, he could be himself and shed the stigma of being a lazy jock.

Annika put the final lab conclusions at the bottom of the assignment and handed the papers to Tanner for his stamp of approval.

"If you don't mind a running partner in the morning, I'd be happy to join you. Luke isn't much of a runner, and I don't like running by myself when I don't know my surroundings."

She smiled and looked up at Tanner.

"By not much of a runner, I mean he's not a runner on any level," she said through an uncomfortable chuckle. "Unfortunately, Luke isn't athletic, at all, and purposely avoids recreational activities. But I assure you, he's a great guy in need of a weekend wingman."

12

DIG DEEP

Once the weekend hit, everyone piling into the car they headed for the coast, destined for the Surf Rider Inn off of Highway 101. Being the slower time of year, they were able to get a sweetheart deal on two adjoining rooms. Despite the full car-load, the two-hour trip was relatively quiet. Luke drove Annika's Honda Civic with the three girls packed tightly into the back seat. They were kind enough to give Tanner the passenger seat to accommodate his long legs.

The conversation on the trip predominantly surrounded Annika's friend, Danelle. She had been going through a difficult break up with her boyfriend of three years. It was difficult to sympathize with Danelle since she would still sleep with him every time she got drunk and struck out at the bars. She always regretted it the following morning and refused to learn from her mistakes. Had she rebounded once or twice would be one thing, but she was on regret number nine already.

Annika and Kimber were staggeringly supportive of Danelle's struggle. Luke and Tanner sat up front and exchanged eye-rolling glances. Both were anticipating, and hoping, that one of the girls would tell her to stop being a fool and to take a little more pride in her body. Instead, they joined her pity party for the duration of their ride west.

The group stopped to grab sandwiches and beer at the local deli before reaching their destination for the night. They checked into their rooms, changed into some warmer clothes, and made their way down the seventy-five step path to the beach. Tanner and Luke were exhausted by the time they reached the bottom.

Whoever thought it was a great idea to get extra bags of ice, obviously had no intention of carrying the cooler down the steps themselves. The guys tried to catch their breath before starting their driftwood search, but the cooler carry was worse than most practice-ending conditioning sessions. After a few minutes, they slowly hobbled their way into the beachy tundra and scored massive logs that were waiting to be sacrificed to the bonfire. When they returned from their successful hunt, the girls had commandeered the perfect setting. The anonymous artist of the fire pit had put in some serious work because their masterpiece was a structural marvel.

The guys twisted up pages from *The Oregonian* and tried to get the damp wood to take to the flames. Much to their surprise, it ignited with ease and they began heaping on their driftwood treasures for Pele. Everyone got settled in and took their seats around the blaze. The sun was beginning to escape behind the distant backdrop of the horizon and Tanner couldn't take his eyes off his picturesque view displayed before him.

"This is the most beautiful sight I have ever witnessed. Thank you so much for letting me join you this weekend," he said to Annika. "I had no idea what I have been missing my whole life. This is a moment I will forever be grateful for."

His eyes glinted in the lingering sunlight.

Overhearing his comment, Danelle looked over toward him.

"Are you crying? It's like you've never seen the ocean before," she said with a kind-hearted snicker.

"I haven't, this is my first time," Tanner replied with embarrassment.

"But I thought you were a California kid?" Luke chimed in.

"I am a Californian mostly, but we were nowhere near the ocean. It is a common misconception. California only has about eight hundred miles of coastline. People automatically stereotype all Californian's as coastal dwelling surfers. It would be physically impossible for an entire population of twenty-two million, to live on the ocean and surf every day. My hometown had a small river, but that was pretty much the extent of the town's water mass. It was nothing like this, that's for sure," he said, keeping his eyes fixated on the gorgeous sunset.

"Holy, Encyclopedia Britannica. Sorry to judge," Danelle snarked.

Tanner instantly understood why Danelle's ex wanted to keep his distance.

As the night continued, an unexpected connection began to spark between Annika and Tanner around the crackling fire. The topic train was running full steam ahead and the conversation jumped from one random subject to the next. Luke was too distracted playing with his phone that had a rotating camera, while the others carried on. Each time Annika would speak, it was as if she was reading a chapter from the unpublished book titled: *How to Win the Heart of a Skilli*. Her choice of words was fascinating and her approach to life was beautiful. As the sun finally crested over the distant horizon, the temperature dropped quickly. Kimber stood up to grab another drink from the cooler. Instead of returning to her seat, she walked over to Tanner and asked if she could share a blanket with him. He didn't see any harm in being friendly, so he welcomed the proposal.

Kimber sat down in front of Tanner and leaned back between his legs, resting her arms on his knees. It had been a long time since he had felt the warmth of a female body. A strange tingle started in his toes and worked its way up to his head. Annika followed suit and repositioned herself in front of Luke. As she leaned back, she rested her head in the arrow of her left elbow, perched on Luke's leg. She gazed in Tanner's direction, making him unsure as to how he should interpret the look.

Annika's beautiful eyes were saying, "You are the one I should be with."

The tingling stopped in an instant, as Tanner realized that his heart wanted nothing to do with Kimber. The warmth of her body on his exposed legs was comforting, so he made the best of the situation in typical Skilli fashion.

Far-fetched stories swirled around the campfire air, with the sound of the waves crashing behind them. Everyone was having an amazing time until basketball was mentioned.

"Hey Tanner, don't you play basketball for Oregon? Are you any good?" Annika asked.

With great reluctance, he replied, "Yeah, I guess you could say that I play. I used to think I was good, but that's not so much the case these days."

Luke perked up as if he had just made an astonishing revelation, "You're not 10-Count Tanner, are you?"

All eyes made his the center of focus.

"Yep, that's me. The numbskull who knocked himself out. In my defense, that was a huge game, and emotions were at an all-time climax. I also didn't realize that they were brutal enough to cut out a chunk of the protective pad. It was an obvious setup, or poor planning if you ask me," Tanner explained.

Kimber laughed as she said, "At least you made Sports Center. Not everyone can claim that in their lifetime."

Danelle closed the cooler lid and announced that their well had "runneth dry." She had continued to silently drown her sorrows that night and had consumed the lion's share of the alcohol. Tanner glanced down at his watch noticing,

"It's a few ticks after 1 a.m. folks. I don't want to sound like an old man, but it's past my bedtime."

Kimber tilted her head back, looking up at the night sky. Seeing no harm in being kind, Tanner leaned forward and kissed her on the forehead.

"Old man, would you be a doll and carry me up the stairs?" she pleaded with a drunken tone.

"As enticing as that might sound, I think you'll manage just fine. How about I help you up the stairs? And you audaciously call me an old man?" he said with laughter.

Before making their way back up the stairs to turn-in for the night, the guys doused the fire with the liquid their livers had to suffer through processing.

Bright and painfully early, Tanner was woken up by Annika making small circles on his nose with her pointer finger. She had quietly snuck over from her room like a highly-skilled ninja.

"You up for a run on the beach?" she asked quietly.

Tanner rolled to his side and pushed the mound of sheets off his legs. He had used the sheets for a makeshift bed into the corner of the room, to avoid any potential casualties. Kimber had made a few drunken attempts to coerce him to snuggle naked. After passing on the first offer, she countered with "Topless Ten Minutes," which entailed starting topless and then having absolute freedom for the next ten minutes. In which, alcohol had a tendency to accelerate the rate of inappropriate touching. As enticing as it may have been for a college guy to turn down TTM, Tanner courageously declined the offer and curled up next to her bedside.

Tanner had slept on much worse in his life and chose the floor as a more inviting option. Any pain or discomfort from the non-padded carpet would be handsomely rewarded later in his life. The sleeping quarters reminded him of his old bed back in the trailer. Reaching into his backpack he pulled out a pair of size 13 Nike running shoes.

"One of the disadvantages of having big feet is your shoes take up the majority of the space in your backpack," he whispered across the room.

Annika had her back turned away from him and was locked into a trance by the morning beauty of the gently rolling tide.

They crept out of the room and slowly closed the door behind them. It was a perfect escape. Everyone else was either still sleeping or too hungover to move. Before heading down the stairs, they stood at the top and gazed out at the calm ocean. Tanner's eyes lit up.

"Did you see that?" he asked while pointing off the shore.

"I think it was a whale spouting," she said, confirming his theory.

"That's incredible. I've never seen a whale outside of an aquarium. What magnificent creatures they are," Tanner said in awe.

Tanner tried to absorb his surroundings as quickly as possible. A strong sense of energy filled the air. Something incredible was on the horizon. They stood in silence, cherishing each moment that past. Overwhelmed by a backdrop of perfection, he experienced his happiest thought. Out of gratitude for the work, he said a soft prayer to himself as the waves crashed onto the shores below him. *This is a beautiful creation. Well done, my man, well done. I thank you for my life and for the opportunity to experience joy on such a grand level. All praise to you, my Lord.*

Tanner and Annika unintentionally choreographed a deep breath in through their noses and powerfully exhaled. She gestured him to follow her as she took off down the stairs. Blissfully forgetting the doomsday climb from the night before, they hoped it would be a refreshing cool down after their run.

Annika was the first to reach the bottom step and took off in a dash.

"It's a great day for yoga pants, wouldn't you say?" Tanner said from a few meters behind her. "I mean I was going to wear mine too but they are in the wash."

Uncertain as to what compelled him to make such an honestly bold statement, he chuckled to himself and flashed a pearly white smile. Annika glanced over her shoulder at him with a flirty squint and then promptly turned back when she started to feel the blood rushing to her cheeks.

As it turns out, the beach wasn't as long as they expected. Not wanting to depart from the remarkable setting so soon, they continued running back and forth between the north and south ends. They ran as close to the water as possible. Tanner found the perfect shade of sand that would squish beneath his shoes, but not splash like he was stepping in tiny puddles.

Slowly jogging side-by-side, Annika started peppering Tanner with questions about the night before, but not in the way he was hoping. Rather than asking if he felt the unmistakable energy while sitting across the fire, she asked if any sparks were flying between him and Kimber once they got up to the room.

"Nothing happened," he said casually. "We all just went to bed after the endless stair climb. I think I ended up carrying ninety percent of Kimber's body weight up the stairs. It initially was a gentle lean on my shoulder at the bottom steps, but after reaching the top I was wearing her like a tiger skin-cloaked king."

On their seventh lap, Tanner added, "I'm not sure what it is about this morning, but I feel like I could run forever."

For a guy who compulsively looked at his Nike watch, as if it were the shot-clock of life, it was astonishing that more than an hour had passed since he last checked the time.

Listening to the sounds of the ocean, Tanner reflected on how effortless the conversation flowed with Annika and smiled in her direction. Out of the corner of her eye, she could see him smile and began to blush.

A seagull cawed on the beach, disrupting their gaze and bringing them back to reality. Annika's current relationship and Tanner's lack thereof was yet again top of mind. Neither one said a word for the next few minutes. They ran elbow to elbow as if they had been doing this for years, and it was all too perfect. Both accepted the fact that their utopic morning would eventually come to an end and be nothing more than a memory.

They made their way to the south end of the beach, stopping to take in the scenery before making their last turn. As badly as Tanner wanted to tell her how he felt, he knew it wasn't right. It went against the bro code to pursue a woman that is spoken for already.

Instead, he just smiled and admired how the morning sun created soft amber flecks of light in her hair.

"This has been great, Annika. Thank you for allowing me to tag along this weekend. There is no question about it, this has been one of the greatest weekends of my life. Hands down."

She lightly punched him in the arm and jested, "You are an incredible guy, Mr. Skilli. This trip would not have been the same without you."

The tide had reached its lowest point, exposing tide pools throughout the beach. Rather than running back, they took their time and stopped to look at each pool. Some had small fish swimming around, starfish clinging to the rocks, and occasionally an adolescent red rock crab learning how to fish. When they reached the halfway point, Tanner suddenly stopped dead in his tracks. He quickly turned to Annika with a look reminiscent of Ace Ventura and pointed just ahead along the beach.

"I need your help. If that is what I think it is, we are in for a treat. There is no time to explain. Are you with me?" he asked urgently.

She wasn't quite sure how to react, but the determination in his eyes was convincing enough.

"Yes, of course. What are we doing?" she asked.

Tanner beelined thirty yards ahead and dove face-first into the sand, grabbing what is known as a geoduck by the neck. Annika ran over in hot pursuit.

"OH MY GOSH, WHAT ARE YOU DOING?" she blurted out.

"I have always read about these, but started to think they were another folktale. I need you to dig around my hands, and just keep digging. This thing I'm holding onto is the neck of a ginormous clam buried maybe three or four feet deep. They have been known to weigh up to eight pounds," he said enthusiastically, wrestling the long, slimy sand creature.

In the heat of the moment, Annika began digging with

complete disregard for her running attire. She was flinging sand left and right at an incredible rate, but her endless efforts seemed to be of little impact. Each time she got a little deeper, the hole refilled itself like quicksand.

The farther down they went, the soupier the sand became making it more challenging to scoop to the side. They took turns holding the neck, while the other person used various creative techniques to extract the sand. They continued to laugh about how ridiculous the idea was but knew it was a memory that they'd never forget.

A faint noise came from up above the beach cliff. Annika turned around and saw Luke standing at the top of the stairs. He was shouting something. They could hear sounds but were unable to make out even a single word.

Annika stopped digging to try and translate.

"I've got this. I'm a two-state charades champion. I'll see what he is yapping about."

Rising to her feet, she tried brushing the wet dirt off her hands and pants. Looking up at the hillside she motioned for Luke to grab a few pots and pans to use as digging tools. She made a motion of flipping flapjacks on a hot skillet, followed by a gesture to come down to the beach.

Luke looked down from above and attempted to yell out a message over the crashing waves that never made it to their ears, *"Got it. We'll start making some breakfast."*

Mirroring the signals she had just given him, followed by a thumbs-up.

"And that my friend is how it is done," Annika said with a smile, "The cavalry is en route, they should be down here in no time."

Twenty minutes passed without a sign of their reinforcements. The two began their epic dig with even more intensity and determination, but they quickly lost steam. The faster they dug, the quicker the hole would refill itself with sand and water.

A conversation about their childhood surfaced and the speed of their dig transformed into an archaeology discovery. Tanner found himself talking about the small trailer he used to live in before moving to their excessive home in California. Followed by how he realized he was nothing more than a product of a summer camp dare and his parents' marriage was a sham.

"You can find purpose in everything that happens to you in life, Tanner. It may not be fair, but had it not been for their adolescent mistake, I might have never experienced digging up some dinosaur-size clam on the Oregon Coast with you. I'm grateful for their mischievous actions," Annika said sincerely.

Tanner adjusted his grip on the phallic-shaped neck of the clam and stared into the sand. For a moment he was lost in his own mind and forgot where he was or what he was doing. Her words were so simple, yet so enlightening. Annika took a break from digging when Tanner was no longer responsive.

"Get it together, Skilli, my curiosity about what this creature is going to look like is increasing by the second. What are you even doing over there? Make sure you've got a good handle on that thing. A wise man once told me, 'A man's grip on his geoduck, is like a man's grip on his life.' You're about to let this opportunity slip away if you don't adjust your grip," she said with sheer determination.

Tanner had bottled up deep-seated emotions for so long and had refused to ever put down his guard. With Annika, it seemed natural to open up and allow his inner soul to breathe for once. Even though he brought up memories that haunted him, he couldn't help but smile at her. A few deeply scarring moments replayed in his mind. The times he was bullied because his family didn't have money, which led him to remember fights that he and Stefanie had over the most minuscule issues.

As Tanner gripped the geoduck, he suddenly remembered the feeling of his hand wrapped around the handle of the revolver. He glanced up at Annika thoroughly enjoying the experience and realized how foolish he had been. The loss of Stefanie was really for the best and certainly not the end of the world. Tanner hated himself for gambling away so carelessly with his gift of life. His actions placed him right back to his original state, making it difficult to justify the risk.

He paused for a moment and then mumbled an old saying from his grandpa, "You must desire life like water, yet drink death like wine."

However reckless it may have been, being inches from death had revived his spirit and refocused the way in which he viewed the world. Annika was a great listener and said all the right things to help him find peace with his struggles. She was right, if Tripp and

Judy Skilli had given up on life after one mistake, Tanner would have missed out on the opportunity to see the ocean and to enjoy an amazing experience with this incredible woman.

It was pushing a quarter after eight when they changed digging roles for the umpteenth time. As they continued to dig deeper and deeper into the sand, each took shifts holding the neck while the other one dug. Tanner reached blindly into the soft sand and felt something hard. He slowly positioned his hand beneath the shell and loosened the surrounding sand.

"Okay, you are on dig duty again. We are on the verge of hitting the jackpot," he said optimistically.

"What's the plan here?" she asked.

"Annika, I need you to fully commit and to get down in there. Extend those go-go Gadget arms if necessary. You've got this"

"Is that what I think it is?" she exclaimed. "We've finally hit pay-dirt."

She placed her petite hands beneath the shell and began wiggling it out like a Jenga puzzle piece. The clam finally conceded to their unrelenting will. Annika gently lifted the geoduck from the soft sand. It was the strangest, yet most beautiful clam she had ever seen, let alone held. She held the geoduck high above her head like Rafiki introducing Simba to the pride.

"What do we do with it now?" she questioned.

"I think we should run up and get the camera, find out what is taking them so long, and then send him back home," Tanner said with satisfied exhaustion.

From his studies, he knew a geoduck could survive more than a day out of the water, so they decided to haul it up the stairs to show the others. They made the hike up the mountain of stairs with minimal moans or groans.

"There you guys are," Luke said with annoyance. "What the heck took so long? That must have been some sandcastle you were building. Child's play if you ask me."

Annika was walking directly in front of Tanner, shielding their new friend they decided to name, Huey. She was taken aback by Luke's rudeness but dismissed it for the moment. When Danelle and Kimber walked around the corner, Annika stepped to the side. Tanner wanted to showcase Huey like one of the 'Barker-beauties' from The Price Is Right, but his moral-fiber and masculinity would not allow him.

"That thing is huge!" Kimber exclaimed.

Acting bashful, Tanner replied, "So I've been told."

He paused and smirked.

"Oh, the geoduck. Yes, that's right, it's gigantic too."

None of them had ever seen a clam of that magnitude. It looked as though the laser from *Honey, I Blew Up the Kid* zapped a butter-clam. After each person took turns getting pictures, they returned Huey to his home near the sea.

Checkout time come quickly after breakfast. When a sleepy and slightly hungover Danelle heard it was time to get moving, she grabbed her backpack, headed out to the Civic, crawled in the backseat and quickly fell asleep. Last-minute checks for any potential items they might leave behind proved to be a fast job. Having traveled light, final rounds were quick.

They dropped the keys at the front desk, and just like that, they were headed back to Eugene. Tanner had his eyes glued on the ocean, and rolled down his window to get a few more minutes of that ocean breeze. As it turns out, the candle impression is nothing like the real scent. Ocean sightings were quick to fade once they reached Newport. Before turning left onto Highway 20, Tanner asked Luke to pull over into a parking lot. Although surprised by the spontaneous request, he obliged.

"Does anyone have a specific time they have to be back? Can you spare me a few hours? I want to get a tattoo to commemorate this weekend," Tanner asked while looking over at the parlor door.

They all shrugged their shoulders, giving the universal sign for "I don't have anything better to do than to watch a grown man cry from a needle."

Danelle remained in the car while the other four walked in the parlor. The local artist looked like she had one too many the night before, which didn't alleviate any of the first-time tattoo jitters. She introduced herself as "Skittles," which turned out was her breaker-name. Tanner was taken aback by how her name created such a vivid picture in his mind. A name like Skittles was fitting handle for her. The common, yet uniqueness of her, fascinated Tanner the most. The thought that Newport, Oregon allowed break-dance fighting helped calm Tanner's pre-tattoo jitters. He chuckled to himself thinking the ancient art's popularity would run rampant if people knew they got an awesome nickname to use in the workplace.

"Oh, you should get this one Tanner," Kimber said while pointing to a hideous elephant holding a flower in its trunk.

"About that, you see," he paused reluctantly. "My mom said she would disown me if I ever got an elephant tattoo, but I'll fully support you if you want to get it for yourself."

That trip was the first time the two had ever hung out, he wasn't quite sure if she was being serious or sarcastic. Turning the page of the book, predominantly aimed at the male-driven egos, he found the one.

"That's it," he said, pointing at the page.

He asked Skittles to sketch it up with some script below. Skittles then posed a bold question, "Do you trust me?"

At that point, she knew nothing about Tanner, other than his name. One could say they were acquaintances, at best.

"What do you have in mind?" he curiously questioned.

"Two things, actually. How do you feel about an alternate spelling? I also like the look of free-handed letters. Are you ready to do this?" she asked.

Tanner figured that if her confidence was strong enough to ask a complete stranger if they trusted her on that level, then he was willing to let Skittles work her magic.

Positioning himself in the chair, he extended his right arm and pointed to his inner forearm.

"Right here, about this big," he said, giving her a reference with his thumb and pointer finger extended two inches.

"To quote the great Flea," she started.

" 'You pick it. I stick it.' "

Skittles prepped his arm and went to work.

The pain was unlike anything he had expected. It was more of an uncomfortable stinging sensation rather than actual throbbing pain. She was a true artist and had a decent voice as well. They could tell she was in her zone as she sang along with Alicia Keys playing in the background. After twenty minutes, Skittles asked Tanner to take a look at the finished product, as she made her last swipe with the towel to remove any remaining ink or blood. Tanner looked down in amazement of the final result.

The .44 caliber bullet was virtually to scale. "Goiduck" was flawlessly drawn below in a Slab Serif inspired font.

"You are a true artist Skittles," Tanner said while still entranced by its simplistic beauty.

"I've got to ask," she said. "What's the symbolism?"

He looked up and made direct eye contact with Skittles.

"It's a constant reminder to give more than I think I have to offer and to always dig deep. I prefer the alternate spelling, thank you for the recommendation," he said attempting to remain stoic and philosophic.

Placing a bandage over the new ink she prodded, "And the .44 caliber bullet?"

Tanner paused as he chose his words carefully.

"Oh yeah, that—. A single bullet gave me newfound love and appreciation for my life."

Annika was wandering around the tattoo parlor, admiring all the photos of Skittles' work. When she overheard the discussion, she paused and stared at the floor. Annika tried to make sense of Tanner's cryptic response about the ink selection but couldn't make the pieces fit together. He was someone special and the fact that he would commemorate such an incredible memory of their time at the beach warmed her heart.

13
PRE'S ROCK

The following Tuesday Annika and Tanner reunited for bio lab. That week they were learning about genetics and DNA. Both recounted events from the weekend, yet neither let on that there was an extra dash of magic in the ocean breeze.

Tanner glanced her way.

"You are a pretty good running mate. I will be honest; I didn't think you'd be able to keep up with my gazelle strides."

She giggled looking down at the lab counter, not sure how to take the indirect compliment.

"I was a little surprised myself. I didn't think those little chicken legs would keep up with my cheetah-like speed."

Tanner clapped his hands together.

"Oh, that's how it is going to be?" he asked. "It takes a lot of courage to step on the same sand as the 'King of the Beach.' I admire your valor."

Annika snickered at his inflated male ego, trying to deny defeat. The two worked through the lab instructions, taking their time and enjoying the company. Once the lab was complete, each pair of students was free to leave. When they finally completed their lab assignment, they looked around the room. It was only the two of them and the grad-student remaining. Both were so engrossed in the conversation, neither noticed the departure of other students.

The sun was moments from setting behind the hills when they

exited the science building. Tanner being the chivalrous soul that he was, offered to walk Annika to her car parked two blocks away. He had been dealing with a lot of chaos in his life and fighting a continuous internal battle about self-worth and direction since the accident that put him in the hospital. Every distraction and struggle was cast to the side when he was around Annika. Walking a few blocks was well worth the extra effort. She had a way about herself; her confidence was undeniably attractive. Everyone had their issues in life, but she possessed a special quality that made her see the beauty and simplicity in everything.

Tanner knew he needed to get refocused but couldn't figure out how to break out of the mental block. When they reached Annika's Civic, she opened the back door to throw her backpack on the seat.

She turned and looked up at Tanner.

"I don't know if you'd be interested in another morning run, but I have a special place I want to take you," she said.

Tanner perked up.

"As long as your special place isn't where you take your lab partners to kill them."

She laughed as she realized how it could appear a bit creepy.

"No, I want to take you up to Pre's Rock. I've mentioned him in passing a few times, and I could tell you were unfamiliar with the legend. I'm not sure if I should be appalled or jealous that you don't worship him as an Oregon Godsend. He ranks among the most famous Oregon Ducks of all time," she explained.

"The guy running in front of the fountain?" Tanner asked. "I walk by that place all the time and the water is never on."

Annika rested her hands on her hips.

"You've got to be kidding me—. Fountain? His name is Stephen Prefontaine. There's no water fountain there silly. It's his name on the memorial. It's no longer up for debate, I'll skull-drag you up the hill if that's what it takes."

Tanner squeamishly shrugged his shoulders and nodded in approval.

"That makes so much more sense now," he said. "I just figured the water pump was broken and they never got around to fixing it."

Annika smirked at him getting into the car. Pulling away from the curb, she rolled down the window and waved as Tanner watcher her drive away.

They agreed to meet up in front of the memorial the following morning. Annika wore another pair of snuggly-fit yoga pants and a highlighter-yellow sports bra. Tanner was quite impressed with the view but did his best to not let his eyes linger. Her normal attire was very loose-fitting and extremely modest. Back when she was in sixth grade, a few of the popular girls would tease her about being fat. She had never been overweight, but mean girls instilled a body-image issue that lingered with her like a faint shadow. There was nothing to be ashamed about, so he struggled with understanding why she took jealous words to heart.

The run was a novice 1.3 miles up to Pre's Rock. Tanner and Annika made poor use of time as they make their way down East 13th Street, over to Franklin Boulevard, and then up Birch Lane. Both valued their relationship and enjoyed each moment running side by side. Turning right onto Skyline Boulevard, Annika stopped just before the road bent left up the hill.

"Well, here it is. This is Pre's Rock. After runners win a big race, they will make the same trip from campus to deliver their shoes here. As you can see, he continues to make an impact in many runner's lives," she said as she pointed down at the heaps of Nikes piled beside the rock.

Tanner looked around perplexed as to why the rock was in the middle of a normal residential neighborhood. He crouched down in front of the memorial and shook his head in disbelief.

"He was only twenty-four."

"Each time I'm here, it is more difficult to wrap your mind around the tragedy," Annika said softly. "It was a fluke of a situation too. He was out at a football party. After enjoying a couple of drinks, he drove some buddies home in his orange 1973 MGB convertible. They say, he dropped off his friends and then was speeding around corners. One miscalculated bend in the road was all it took. The collision against the rock flipped his car over and trapped him underneath. A neighbor heard the loud crash outside and contacted the authorities before rushing to the scene. The courageous man found Steve alive, but he was unable to free him on his own. Then, by the time the medics arrived, it was too late."

Annika paused for a moment and rested her hand on Tanner's shoulder.

"I come up here from time to time as a reminder of how fragile life can be. He was one of us. A crazy college kid with a bright future ahead of him. Everything, including his life, was taken away in a single night."

She looked down at the slated-black rock.

"His words always resound in my mind, 'To give anything less than your best, is to sacrifice the gift.' "

The last few months raced through Tanner's mind. The internal battle was forced to ceasefire. Despite any self-worth issues he was struggling with, that moment reminded him to be thankful. Steve Prefontaine was an Olympic athlete who sacrificed his career for the betterment of others. He never got to reach the finish line to his life journey. Tanner had yet to achieve the level of success that of Pre, but he still had breath in his lungs and a beat in his heart. Tanner Skilli had time remaining to experience life on Earth.

Before the pools in his eyes became raging rivers, Tanner stood up and wiped his face to mask the tears.

"Sometimes when I stop running, the sweat seems to start pouring down. It's a cross I have to bear," he said while rubbing his eyes with his left sleeve. "I gotta say, Annika, this is truly incredible. I needed this more than you will ever know."

"Well, I'm glad you enjoyed it. I could tell you have had a lot on your mind. I thought a little inspiration from one Duck to another would do the trick," she said, leaning over and resting her head on his arm.

They continued their way along Skyline Boulevard until it looped back into Birch Lane. At the end of the road, they turned right and circled back to campus via Summit Avenue.

14

NAKNEK

On the north shore of Bristol Bay, Alaska sat the summer home for Tanner leading into his junior year. When he gave his coaches notice that he was going to take a puddle-jumper to the small town of Naknek, they asked him to reconsider. Aside from booting him from the team, there was nothing they could say or do to change his mind.

Following the calamitous Civil War game between the Ducks from the South and the Beavers from the North, Tanner was slowly able to work his way back into the starting rotation. By the end of the season, he was consistently scoring in the double digits and grabbing a half-dozen rebounds each game. The coaching staff had no choice but to grant him a summer pass.

Fulfilling his promise to Tripp and Judy was at the top of Tanner's bucket list. He hopped a train from Eugene to Sea-Tac and then caught a flight to Anchorage. Tanner had grandiose visions of plush forests outlining the mammoth glaciers spread across the Alaskan landscape. Unfortunately, the window was commandeered by a teenage boy named Liam, who continually raised and lowered the window-shade to create a strobe light effect. Tanner felt that they had three hours together in the world, so he made the best of the situation. They were seated next to the wing, making it difficult to view the final frontier from the air. From his body language, Tanner could sense Liam's discomfort. It wasn't from fear of Tanner, but rather a lack of exposure talking with adults.

The pilot announced they were flying over Dall Island and had officially entered Alaska airspace. First-timers applauded in victory, while most were plugged into their electronic devices and missed the message completely.

Liam started in on a story about his parents being super strict when a passenger across the aisle in a hot pink shirt captured Tanner's attention. The blinding shirt only amplified the strangeness of the behavior.

Tanner gently extended his arm across Liam like a protector and said, "That guy's mind has him in a different universe right now. Look at him, there is a haunting fear in his eyes. This is a life lesson of why you should never do drugs. The walking-dream he is experiencing right now will forever change the way he thinks for the rest of his life. I'm going to make sure he doesn't do anything might land him in a federal penitentiary."

The drugs took over his body and the young man eventually fell asleep and the drool began to cascade from his mouth like Multnomah Falls. Liam and Tanner continued with their conversation about the unfairness in the world. Hearing Liam speak about the struggles struck a deep nerve with Tanner.

Liam was going through the same issues with his parents and school that Tanner did growing up. In the back of Tanner's mind, he had always believed that his upbringing was uniquely difficult. The baggage he carried with him through life was based on the notion that others had it easy and he was simply dealt a poor hand and unfortunate circumstances. Tanner gathered his thoughts while looking over to check on the crazy guy in the pink shirt, for curious reasons above all else. He turned back and nudged Liam with his shoulder, "It will get better, Champ. Tough times suck, there is no denying that. However, without challenges, you never have the opportunity to succeed. I promise you, it will get better. Just take one day at a time and you'll be alright. There have been several times in my life that I wanted to call it quits because I didn't feel adequate enough. Rather than let others push you down, you need to stand up for yourself because they don't control your destiny."

When Tanner paused to catch his breath, he looked over at a shell-shocked Liam. Tanner realized his emotions sent him on an unguided rant. Liam must have been watching daily talk shows with his mother.

He looked at Tanner and said, "Nah, man, it's alright. Keep

going, get it all out. This is good for you to hear it voiced."

Liam had the talk show script down and was tickled-pink with himself, even though he had heard enough wise words from some college boy going to work in a salmon factory. Tanner thought he was getting through to young Liam, but he could tell Liam's short attention span forced him to lose interest.

As it turned out, the guy in pink, who was tripping on mushrooms, was the human resource manager's nephew, Patrick. He was a third-year veteran, who was fortunately recognized by other returning workers. They assisted Patrick to their connecting flight from Anchorage and told the attendants that he took sleeping pills due to his fear of heights.

When the Boeing 737 touched down at the King Salmon airport, the scenery was underwhelming. The passengers stepped off the plane and saw two ladies with long-braided ponytails holding clipboards. The nice ladies directed the workers to their respective yellow school buses. Handwritten script on the sides of buses read "Robert" and "Ernest" to help distinguish one from the other.

Tanner was thankful to board the same bus as the pink shirt from the plane, as he was dying to know what was going on in his mind during their flight. Patrick was still in a light fog and stumbled his way to the back. Entertaining himself, he began rapping his unique rendition of Outkast's "Rosa Parks" single, "Hush that fuss, Sexy Patrick be movin' to the back of the bus."

Looking out the window as they rode down the bumpy highway, it suddenly became apparent to Tanner why Naknek was a fishing community. No one in their right mind would want to live out there if they didn't have to fish for survival. They say there are two types of people in Naknek. Those who were born there and those who are trying to get away from something they are ashamed to face.

The ride was silent for the most part. Whispers began between friends taking the adventure together, as well as the occasional comments from the veteran workers who wanted it to be very clear that it was not their first rodeo. A few minutes shy from an hour rolled by and the bus finally pulled into the cannery.

One of the veterans, who was later nicknamed "Nancy Boy" shouted out, "Home sweet hell on water!"

The workers piled out of the bus, each lugging around their

over-packed duffle bags. Tanner wanted to experience as much of Alaska as possible. He embraced the role by only bringing his Kelty Coyote camping backpack. As they stood in line to get their room assignments, he noticed a bright yellow hat with a green O embroidered on the front.

"A fellow Duck, I see," Tanner said as he extended his right arm, exposing his tattoo.

Looking down at the ink on his forearm, Gavin squinted and tried to process it all without making it seem like he was staring or confused. Thinking it read "Go duck," he instantly pegged Tanner as a diehard fan with a golden sense of humor. Although he didn't understand the .44 caliber round, it was too early to delve into the deeper meaning behind the piece.

"Heck yeah, Go Ducks! The name is Gavin, Gavin Silva, it's a pleasure to make your acquaintance," he said, delivering a strong manly handshake.

Gavin was a Freshman English major at the University of Oregon. He too was fulfilling a promise he made to his family but was also looking for inspiration for his first novel. The two had an instant bond as both acknowledged their journey in Naknek officially began.

Day one in Alaska started two hours after sunrise, throwing a curveball into his sleep pattern. Tanner frantically rolled off his single-wide mattress thinking he had overslept. It was described as an *extra-long* bed, which must have implied that the mattress makers believe people over six foot three inches to be giants. Tanner brought a small black travel alarm that was perched precariously on top of an old wooden spool displaying 6 a.m. That was the "table" they referenced in their hiring pamphlet, highlighting the *luxurious* accommodations the Alaska General Seafood LLC had to offer.

Already on his feet, Tanner threw on his cannery-issued deep yellow rain slicker and rubber boots. There was no need to shower, so he headed over to the Chow Hall for a *morning delight*. Much to his amazement, the food was surprisingly delicious. They offered a large variety of entrees at every meal, in an effort to show respect and admiration for the prevalent Filipino community.

Over sixty Filipino men and woman made the journey over for the summer to work. They took great pride in the undesired jobs that were considered below the privileged standards of American workers. Keeping this in mind, the kitchen staff concocted a few native delicacies to provide the Filipinos with a comforting taste of home.

During one lunch, Tanner's olfactories were sent into overdrive when he caught a whiff of the soup of the day. He grabbed the ladle and began swirling the soup from the bottom of the pot, taking in the full strength of the enticing aroma as the rising steam enhanced the potency. Tanner lowered his face above the soup as he mouth began to water. The experience was simply spellbinding.

He closed his eyes as he inhaled deeply through his excited nasal passages. When he opened his eyes and peered down at the soup, in preparation to dive in and begin devouring, he was startled by a large fish eyeball bobbing at its surface staring directly back at him. Not only did the soup offer a decadent juicy eyeball, for an end-of-meal treat, but many were also accompanied by the entire head. The cooks didn't mess around when it came to *isda ng ulo sopas*. They were going to give the people what they wanted. Not one, but rather a two fish eyeball bonanza.

Before Tanner left for Naknek, he told Annika he would drop a postcard in the mail upon arrival. It was mentioned in passing on their last day of lab, and neither thought much of it. As the two said their summer good-byes, they exchanged mailing addresses. From an outside perspective, it would have appeared to be innocent. They never pursued, let alone acknowledged, their undeniable attraction for one another.

On the surface, it looked like a couple of friends who went on a few harmless runs. Had Luke not been a part of the equation, they would have been the hottest couple on campus. Internally, Tanner denied his lust was breaching the outer barriers of the bro-code, as he continued to tread through the grey waters. Secretly Tanner was picturing Annika returning home for the summer and figuring out that Luke is a minimum of three rungs below her on the Human Awesomeness Scale.

Midway through the summer, the salmon catch began thinning out in a hurry. All the foremen were huffing and puffing on the docks at the lack of fish. The cannery workers couldn't have cared less at that point. They were getting paid by the hour, but most of them were only working for next semester's beer money anyway. The foremen, including the warehouse foreman known to everyone as Fish, worked purely on a catch-share percentage. Less salmon meant less money. There were only so many long workdays one can endure consecutively, before starting to become delirious.

For the majority of the crew, it was day 33 of burning the midnight oil, and their bodies reflected the sleep deprivation. The highlights of each day were the doughnut breaks every two hours, thanks to the Union, along with the scrumptious late-night meals. Tanner was a warehouse worker, which was the last stage in the entire canning process. Salmon were fed down the slime-line, as they called it, and then smashed into a metal can containing a single cube of salt. The fish bones hung out the sides of the cans, then removed by the sheer-fisted women at the next station. Three women stood on each side of the conveyor belt tasked with the job of making certain there would not be a single bone that would prevent an airtight seal. Those cans fortunate enough to make it through the gauntlet of ruthless Filipino women would receive the honor of having a lid pressed and sealed firmly on top.

That same lid feeding station was where Tommy "Knucks" Davey became "Naknek famous" as they like to call it. If you asked Tommy, the lid feeding station was the pinnacle point of the salmon canning operations. Tommy appeared to be born to man the helm of 'Lid Distribution Central', or LDC as he insisted the station be referenced. He took tremendous pride in his work, perhaps too much for the monotonous task. There was no doubt he was a true artist of his craft. If the line was running at optimal conditions, his line could process 200,000 cans in a single day.

The infamous story is told that Tommy was trying to beat his personal record the day after he shacked up with a native Inuit woman. He didn't have much of a choice in the matter. She was from a dry village and downed a pint of Jim Beam before breaking down his door and forcing herself upon him. Had she simply knocked, he would have graciously invited her in for a little dancing in the sheets.

The morning shift was off to a promising start until Tommy made a rookie mistake. Once blessed with a lid from the LDC, the salmon were intended to glide down the conveyor belt, then over to the enormous cooking chambers. Thermal processing at high volumes required them to be over thirteen yards deep, if they were an inch. Ten crates of salmon cans could be wheeled into a chamber per batch.

Another cannery legend that was often retold, was about a time a worker wasn't seen in the darkness of a chamber and another employee closed the door behind him without realizing. As the story goes, the boiler cooked him to death with the salmon, because no one could hear him banging cans against the walls. Those cheeky bastards sold all the cans that were in there with him anyway. Hopefully, the FDA made them put a disclaimer on the label that "No dolphins, but one human was killed while making this batch." Fishermen say they can hear his ghost early in the morning while the cannery workers are catching some shut-eye. Echoing sounds of the metal on metal haunt the dense fog as the fishermen board their ships for another day at sea.

Personal record day at the cannery had arrived, at least for one master of all things lid related. Tommy had the machine singing the sweet tune of efficiency. When someone thought it would be funny to put extra tape on his next box of lids to test his skills. It took precisely thirty-two seconds from the time that he stacked seventy lids in the column until they were all gone, if everything was running perfect. However, if the lid feeder emptied completely, the backlash would be catastrophic. The mishap would result in salmon being strewn about the entire cannery.

Tommy struggled with opening the heavily taped box for longer than anticipated. It was reaching the point that he had to choose between shutting the line down, crushing his dream about beating his record, or flirting with disaster. He calculated the risks and the gamble paid off, at least for the next ten seconds. Tommy's ego refused to go "'line-down" on such a glorious day and felt compelled to take extraordinary measures.

Emulating He-Man, Tommy summoned The Power of Greyskull and the box finally opened from the side. As he reached in to pull out the next stack of lids, he did the unforgivable and accidentally grabbed a stack with an inverted lid.

The first rule of operating the lid station was simple: If an inverted lid was loaded into the column feeder, it led to an automatic shutdown, no questions asked. Tommy interpreted the established procedures as more or less guidelines for the unskilled workers and clearly not applicable to the Protector of Eternia. He figured all he had to do was wait until the inverted lid got to the bottom of the stack. Then he would simply grab the single perpetrator and refill the column. Easy peasy, or so he thought, better to lose a few cans than shut down the whole operation. As the inverted lid began to shuffle its way down the stack, Tommy readied his hands for the upcoming big move.

Within seconds of reaching down, Tommy noticed blood squirting everywhere and he looked down to see all four fingers had been lopped off, each to the second knuckle. The lid feeding hooks had whizzed below the feeder and sent his fingers off in a can. To make matters even worse, Tommy dropped to the ground and neglected to shut down the equipment. Screaming out in pain, Tommy was showered by bright pink salmon chunks being tossed from his line.

Whether or not it was intentional is still up for debate among the cannery workers, who heard regurgitated versions of the story. Throughout the summer rumors circulated about getting $5,000 per digit, but no one was dumb enough to go through with it willingly. Some thought Knucks was just crazy enough to earn a buck the hard way. The incident cost American General Seafood over $120,000 in lost revenue, legal fees, and paid out damages. Fortunate for Knucks, the finger massacre landed him 40,000 tax-free dollars and a nickname for life. The alternative nickname option, "Thumbs," took home the silver and "Spet" reeled in the bronze.

During normal operations, after the salmon finishes cooking in the giant chambers, the forklifts shuttled the hot crates from the main building over to the warehouse. The warehouse had to wait for the cans to cool off before paletizing and stocking them. On a typical night, workers from the fishhead oil and egg-house operations would be two hours into their sleep cycle before the warehouse crew was dismissed for the night. Fish thought by keeping the guys moving that he was somehow doing the guys a solid. Anytime they hustled to fast and got caught up, they would be instructed to push the broom around the warehouse. It got to the point that Gavin took great pleasure in discovering a tiny pocket of dirt. At times, that floor was so spotless it could have been used for a dinner table.

One July afternoon, rumors of a short day instantaneously boosted morale on the cannery pier. When the Flinstone-style horn blew for lunch, the crew was strutting the pier like they were about to win the lottery. Staying true to his word, Tanner had mailed a postcard to Annika the first week he arrived. Once a week the postal carrier delivered mail and display it on a cafeteria table. The Skilli family wasn't known for their letter-writing discipline, so

Tanner never even bothered to check the mail to see if anything arrived. Gavin, on the other hand, received amazing care packages from his girlfriend Audrey and was a frequent flyer around the mail table. After Gavin received his third bundle of gifts from Audrey, he started to feel bad about his friend's misfortune. In the past, he had been kind enough to share the homemade cookies and fudge. When they walked into the chow hall on that day they saw the large crowd huddled around the mail table.

Each delivery time ignited extreme emotions in the chow hall. Workers who received mail claimed it as if they'd won an Oscar and walk away with an award-winning smile. Others would hover a bit longer at the table to make sure they didn't overlook any letter or package that may have been sent for them. When they realized no one took time out of their day to send a little love, they'd turn away with a sad look of defeat draped across their faces. Gavin returned to the table that splendid afternoon with his weekly care package and what appeared to be an additional letter.

"Hey, Skilli. Looks like you have a secret admirer from the lower 48. I knew there had to be someone out there who was fond of you," he said as he tossed a letter on the table.

As he right-sided the letter, Tanner recognized the familiar handwriting instantly. Annika had beautiful penmanship and always added a fun tail to her *S*'s.

"Well, aren't you going to open it?" Gavin inquired, interested in this new development.

"I think I'm going to hold on to this one until later. This day couldn't get any better, and this will be the icing on the cake. I'll read it once we are freed for the day, and then it's an early bedtime for this guy," Tanner said, pointing his thumbs towards his chest.

He folded the letter in half and placed it in his back left pocket. His right pocket was considered permanently reserved for his Stanley gloves. Without them, it would be death by a thousand cuts when pulling the strapline for the pallets.

Just as anticipated, the day started to wind down early. First, the egg-house workers started strolling along the pier, followed closely by the can-line workers. The roar of a loud engine echoed through the warehouse as a large boat was taxied to the edge of a pier by a Ford F650. Tanner stood in awe as the massive crane hooked up to the boat and lifted it from the trailer. It swung the vessel over the edge and slowly lowered it in the water. He looked over at the forklift driver Mike, who was also captivated by the whole spectacle.

"You don't see that every day," Tanner said.

"Funny you should mention that. Yesterday, Gavin and I cut out of the doughnut break early to escape the crowd. That same truck brought a boat down, and Gavin said those same exact words. So I guess we do see that every day," Mike chuckled.

They both shrugged their shoulders and went back to their repetitive assignments.

Mike delivered the final row of salmon crates to the conveyor belt queue. Spirits were at an all-time high. The crew sang old Garth Brooks' songs as they arm-swept the can of salmon down the conveyor belt. Their foreman, Fish, made his way down from the office, they referred to as "The Hawks Nest," and told the crew to catch up on some much-needed rest and to not cause too much chaos in the bunkhouse for the rest of the night.

Fish barely finished his sentence before the crew vanished from the warehouse. Tanner and Gavin thought it would be a good idea to head to the local store, named Pirate Booty, to get some supplies for the next few weeks. PB, as they liked to call it, was less than a mile down the road. They figured it wouldn't take much time to make a run before getting back to hit the hay. A night with more than six hours of sleep could certainly help with the deprivation dilutions.

The sun still hung high in the sky, providing the comfort of an evening back home. Tanner and Gavin headed up the steps like two kids playing hooky. They wanted to change into normal street clothes before making the journey to town. When Tanner got back to his bunk, he placed his gloves on the spool and then pulled out the letter from Annika. She had been on his mind ever since he left Oregon. As much as he tried to resist thinking about her, he lacked the will to do so. She was currently off-limits and Tanner had no interest in being the guy who got in the middle of ruining a long-term relationship. If things weren't meant to work out the way Tanner imagined, and she was truly meant to be with Luke, he wouldn't be able to live with himself. He could no longer keep his curiosity at bay, the simplest thought of being with Annika was enough to drive him crazy.

Tanner flipped the envelope over and ran his thumb down the top of the sealed flap. She had hand-written him two full pages. As he began reading, his stomach started to tangle into knots. Luke had proposed. Although there was more to the story than Annika wanted to truly share. When she returned home for the summer, things between her and Luke were all but finished. Luke felt the disconnection.

In a desperate attempt to get things back to where they were in high school, he proposed. Although their paths in life had noticeably drifted apart, it was a last-ditch effort to hang on to a love that had slipped through his fingers.

Annika's childhood fantasy of being the most beautiful bride overshadowed the reluctance of being with Luke for the rest of her life. The letter continued about all the wedding plans that had already been set in motion. The venue had been reserved, her dress picked out, and they were looking forward to sampling the wedding cakes next weekend. Line by line Tanner felt his maturity about Annika and Luke's relationship start to wane.

Tanner started to question her motives and their friendship. *Did the past few months matter at all to her? Why would she devote so much time to a relationship she obviously doesn't value? What a slap in the face.* Tanner's old internal monologue started cycling on repeat. Without consideration for Tanner's heart, she was glorifying the fact that Luke was a winner and Tanner was a loser. Crushing his dream of finding true love, Tanner found himself without direction in life. He felt as though she had been dragging his emotions along only to stomp them into the mud.

Three quarters into the first page Tanner ripped up the letter and tossed it to the floor.

"Forget this place, forget her, and screw that undeserving piece of shit. That sorry excuse for a representation of a man that people are subjected to call Luke!" he yelled out as he exited his bunkroom.

Gavin was standing silently outside the door when Tanner opened it. He was going to flip Tanner crap about taking extra-long to primp for their big night on the town, but after seeing the expression on his friend's face he decided to refrain from commenting. The shouting he heard through the door made it clear fate did not favor him at the moment. So as true brothers do, Gavin didn't ask a single question about the topic at hand. Had Tanner wanted to talk about an issue he would have, but if not, Gavin wouldn't pry. He knew that there are some struggles that simply take time to get through. Gavin's philosophy, whether helpful or not, was the sooner people stop talking about and dwelling on life events that cannot be changed, the sooner the pain will start to fade away.

Not a word was spoken about the letter as they made their way down the dirt road to town. Tanner's mind was quickly freed of the weight from losing Annika. A couple hundred feet into the bushes they heard the most violent scream of agony. They weren't sure if they were witnessing a rape, a person being attacked by a bear, or a combination of the two. Each carried their cannery-issued box knife, which they drew in unison like a swat team.

"What are we going to do with these little, tiny razor blades? I mean, a lot of good they'll do against a bear," Tanner said while trying to catch his breath from the startle.

"Hey, there are some other workers headed this way. Strength in numbers, right?" Gavin said like a warrior preparing for battle.

They tactically motioned for the others to join forces. The reinforcements were far from a US Olympic team when it came to running. Their sorry excuse for hustling displayed their lack of understanding for the situation. When they finally huddled around, they pointed toward the bushes.

Gavin yelled out, "Hey, what are you doing over there? We can see you!"

There was no reaction from the bushes, so he decided the next appropriate thing to do in that situation was to roar like a lion. Much to everyone's surprise, the roar did the trick. A tall, skinny, naked man jumped up and started wrestling with the nearby tree. If he was trying to compare stick sizes, the tree would have won by a lengthy margin.

"What the freak man?" someone from the back of the crowd yelled out.

The naked man quickly bolted through the grass like a finely tuned runner, his technique was flawless.

Tanner motioned for the group to follow him. After ten steps he looked back to see the support he thought was following behind, but no one had moved a foot closer. He had to go make sure nothing tragic had just happened to an innocent victim. Trying to mentally prepare himself for what he could potentially discover, he thought, *This is God's will. This is me serving my purpose in the eyes of the Lord. These are the moments that remind humans that they exist for a reason.*

Tanner walked over to the tree and surveyed the area. There was nothing there. He walked over to where they initially saw the man, but still nothing. The others slowly made their way through the brush and started searching the area. The infamous Alaskan saying, "There are strange things done in the midnight sun," had never rang truer.

Five minutes passed and they decided there was nothing to find. The wild exhibitionist was just passing through and tangling with the trees along the way.

The Pirate's Booty general store was open at times accommodating to the fishermen and cannery workers. They stayed open until 3:30 every morning. Tanner entered the store first with Gavin in tow. Gavin wasn't yet of age to buy alcohol, so he pretended to be shopping for some snacks, while Tanner made the purchases.

"A couple forty-ounce bottles of Olde English "800" should do the trick for tonight," he said while placing the bottles on the counter.

"String-bean, don't you think for one second you are fooling this broad," employee Doris said. "There ain't no way scrawny ol' you gonna drink both them forties and still function tomorrow."

Doris caught Gavin's eye from across the way and motioned with her finger to come up to the counter. He pointed to his chest, questioning if he was the chosen one, even though there was little doubt.

She shook her finger and then sharply pointed it at him like a marksman before shouting, "Yes, you. I don't see no one else around you."

In an Eeyore fashion of defeat, Gavin stepped forward with his chin to his chest.

"Son, I'm up here. Look at me. Let me see them eyes of yours. No respectable man is going to have another man buy his booze for him. You owe me four dollars," Doris said with her palm out.

With his heart rapidly beating, Gavin struggled to pull his wallet from his pocket. He was out of practice since monetary currency was rarely exchange at the cannery.

After a test of her patience, she took his five-dollar bill and looked over at Tanner.

"Yours will be three dollars, String-bean," she said with a grin.

"You boys been working your tails' off to help this town stay alive. If you can work, you can have a cold drink now and then. That's what I say."

The exchange with Doris was remarkably refreshing. Her spunk and spirit were admirable. As quirky as she may have been, she made their trip to town a lasting memory. Before returning to the bunkhouse, they stopped at a small cliff that overlooked Bristol Bay. The two removed their 40-ounce bottles of Olde E' from the plastic bag and cheersed to a crazy summer.

Halfway through their malted liquor, a Spice Girls shirt approached them from the distance. Patrick had just met up with workers from the other cannery and was feeling nice and tuned-up. Tanner and Gavin invited him to join, knowing that he was going to regardless. Tanner was staggeringly intrigued by this fashionisto who referred to himself daily as the greatest catch in the ocean. Gavin too had witnessed the bizarre antics on the flight from Seattle but had never been in a place he felt comfortable enough to ask Patrick the back story.

"Patrick, do you remember much of the flight to Anchorage? Do airplanes bother you?" Gavin asked, hoping he would take the bait.

Patrick was an over-sharer and had no qualms about providing every detail. When they arrived at the Sea-Tac airport, Patrick saw they had drug dogs patrolling the security area. Not wanting to get caught with a bag of mushrooms, he headed for the nearest bathroom to flush them.

"There are pivotal moments in life, and that was one of them for me. I couldn't endure the pain and heartache of flushing a perfect bag of 'shrooms away. So I dove in and polished them off myself," Patrick said as Tanner's eyes widened with anticipation.

Things were going okay for Patrick until they boarded the plane. The flight crew had to escort him to his seat since his brain was no longer functional. Reaching into his fanny pack, Patrick pulled out a warm can of Pabst Blue Ribbon and cracked it open.

"Before we even left the runway I was already floating on clouds. The next thing I know I look out on the wing and some random dude is out there smoking a cigarette. It made me furious initially because I didn't think of it and left my smokes in my other bag. That dude was a trailblazer who knew how to work the system. If the FFA won't allow smoking in the cabin, they have to let you smoke somewhere, right?"

Tanner and Gavin continued to pepper Patrick with questions and each response became more ridiculously outlandish. Laughing with the guys helped Tanner find peace and Annika was nothing more than an afterthought. That night on the cliff overlooking Bristol Bay was forever burned into their memories as it gave them a taste of Alaska's true beauty.

15
IT'S GONNA BE AWESOME BABY!

March Madness, the Big Dance, had finally arrived. The University of Oregon basketball team funneled into the film room to watch the Selection Sunday broadcast. The players nestled into the plush seats wrapped in Ferrari leather before Coach Kent made his opening statement:

"Men, we have come a long way. This season has been one that will go down in Duck history as an all-time great run at the national title, but our work is not finished. I question whether or not we need to watch the selections unfold today, as it does not matter who we will face in the tournament. We will outhustle, outplay, and impose our will on any opponent who is foolish enough to think they are worthy of sharing the same court as us. The time has arrived to test our true potential, so we must dig deep. Let's make them regret their decision! Let's take their souls. Silence the haters and display to the world that the Ducks are a force to be reckoned with! I'm proud of each and every one of you. Look around the room, this team has something special. There is no doubt we have the drive and determination to choose our own fate. I don't know about you, but I'm ready to dance. Start fast and finish hard! Go Fight Like a Duck!"

Coach's inspirational speech led to an uproar in the film room. The team's excitement started to amp up the energy in perfect harmony with faithful Oregon boosters. Each booster had a direct affiliation with a major company in one way or another. The success of the athletic program carried a significant financial impact on each of their company's books. The roar of the room subsided as the announcers appeared on the screen. The perfect acoustics delivered their crisp voices as they announced the seeding and revealed the tournament bracket.

A third seed in the Mid-West seemed adequate based on their season record, but the room found it to be egregious.

An outraged booster yelled out, "A three seed? Are they f-ing kidding me?"

It was an unspoken agreement that events, as such, would be respected as a board meeting. Outbursts like his may be accepted in his office, but that was not the case around this audience. They were a silent fraternity, each with intimate knowledge of the others dark secret. As long as everyone played by the rules, they would never expose one other. The perpetrator regained his composure after the nonverbal ridicule and the meeting proceeded.

Once the tantrums of the crowd simmered down, the team was released until practice later that evening. Tanner began making his way to the exit when a booster approached him and extended his hand holding a card.

"Mr. Skilli—. Son, you have done an amazing job leading the team this season. Why don't you surprise your girlfriend with a nice dress and then take her out for a celebratory dinner," he said with a smile.

Questioning the ethical nature of the gesture, Tanner reluctantly took the card and placed it in his back left pocket. It wasn't the first time a situation as this had occurred, but every occurrence filled him with an ounce of guilt.

"Thank you, Sir. All of these guys are like brothers to me. We have had a great season and hope to keep playing well until the very end," he said.

Just then, other boosters made their way over to talk with Tanner. Each gave him grand praise as if he were the only player on the team. Direct attention of this magnitude wasn't something he was accustomed to receiving. Even though he had a rocky midseason, his transformation after a brush with death took his playing to an elevated level.

Events leading up to their first game were overwhelming. One would think they had just returned from a mission to Mars. A series of rallies were held and began to desensitize the excitement for the game. Between the multiple press conferences and banquets, the team started to lose sight of the actual task at hand. There was so much speculation surrounding the first game, it started to feel like they were never going to play.

When the day finally arrived, the team was police-escorted to the arena and ushered into the locker room. Regardless of which road game locker room they walked into, it would never compare to the luxury of the Oregon Duck locker room back in Eugene. Tanner popped in his "Go Time" mixed tape and started his pregame rituals, as AC/DC's "Thunderstruck" blared through his Sony headphones.

Walking out of the tunnel in his deuce-deuce uniform for the pregame shoot-around, Tanner was stunned by the packed house. The Duck fans had always traveled well, but their numbers were diluted on the neutral territory. Most of the crowd was filled with fans who just love to watch basketball and had no loyalty to either opponent. In order to win their hearts, Tanner knew the Ducks would have to put on a spectacular performance. Being on the court and looking up into the stands made him acknowledge the magnitude of the tournament. A feeling of immense external pressure sent his anxiety through the roof. The warm-up was able to calm his nerves, but he was noticeably off-kilter.

They headed to the locker room for a quick speech from the coach and return to the court for the opening ceremony. The introductions were drawn out and might as well have been sponsored by the Bellagio with such an over-the-top production. From the moment of tip off, the game was mercilessly dominated by the Duck offense. As their lead grew, so did their razzle-dazzle on the court. Showboating, Tanner inadvertently began putting on a passing clinic. He was making phenomenal dishes between his legs, behind his back, and tossing alley-oops that resulted in monster jams. The roar from the crowd nearly blew the roof clean off the arena. They were loving every moment of the performance and it clearly had shifted their loyalty to being Ducks. That caliber of flashy basketball is what they came to see. By the conclusion of the game, it felt like the Ducks were at home.

Final score: 94-74.

The Ducks won by an embarrassing margin. Coach Kent walked into the locker room and raised his hand in victory.

"We conquer and we move on. Enjoy this win for the next eight hours men. After that, it's on to the next victim" he said like a military drill sergeant.

The second game was like Deja-vu. The momentum from their first game continued to conquer their next opponent and advanced them to the Sweet-16. Not only did they have two wins under their belt, but also a gaggle of new bandwagon fans in tow. Allowing their confidence to peak a little too high, things took a turn for the worse.

From the moment the Ducks won the tip in game three, the team fell into a groove. Crazy shots were falling, rebounds were practically landing in their laps, and the crowd was absorbing it all in like a drug. Being on a stage of that magnitude and capturing the hearts of all the fans was a powerful rush Tanner found indescribable.

With the roar of the screaming fans behind him, Tanner dribbled down and was met by the defender six feet behind the three-point line. He picked up his dribble prematurely thinking he saw a window for a bounce pass in the paint, but the defending help-side recovered. After a quick pump-fake, Tanner looked the opponent, Benjamin McAllister dead in the eyes. He pulled up for a ridiculous jump shot, which rolled effortlessly off his fingertips.

"From way downtown," the announcer shouted, "Ladies and Gentleman, Tanner Skilli has just dropped a four-pointer from City Hall in the poster-worthy face of McAllister."

It was the greatest moment of his life; the pinnacle of his existence. Pure confidence rushed through his veins as he looked at the crowd jumping and screaming. The Oregon bench nearly got called for an unsportsmanlike foul as they leaped out of their chairs, covering their mouths with clenched fists in disbelief of what they had just witnessed.

When they came out of the locker room for the second half. The now infamous McAllister had a personal vendetta with number 22. Knowing that he was going to be broadcasted all over ESPN for getting a monster three-pointer dropped in his face during the Sweet-16 struck a nerve with him. All his life he had been pampered by his parents and always told that he was the greatest in the world. McAllister grew up in a family of privilege and dealing with adversity was never taught in his household.

Late in the second half, Tanner stole the ball and had a breakaway. The trailing McAllister, whom he had stripped the ball from, took off after him down the court. Tanner received a flying elbow to the side of his head as he went up for what he thought would be an uncontested lay-in. A power-surge in the arena knocked the lights out, or so it seemed to Tanner. His body crashed to the floor as his head bounced off the hardwood. The trainers sprinted off the bench and the Oregon teammates created a secret service style barricade around Tanner. Mills looked over and saw the shrimp of a point guard McAllister.

"You don't deserve to be on the same court as Skilli, little pissant!" he screamed out.

Tanner appeared lifeless on the hardwood until the trainer pulled out the smelling salts and wafted them beneath his nose. His eyes squinted in discomfort and then finally opened. The team helped him to his feet and let the trainer and Mills guide him to the sideline chairs. His surroundings appeared foreign, as he had forgotten they were playing in the tournament. Coach Kent and the trainers gathered around him as they rushed through their concussion protocol. Coach gave the head trainer the nod of understanding and shifted his focus back to the game. Tanner would remain on the bench for the remainder of the game.

Having the interruption in gameplay, to get Tanner alert and off the floor, took the wind out of the Oregon Ducks' sail. The Maryland Terrapins felt the shift of momentum and went on an 18 point run, getting them back into the game with less than five-minutes remaining. Coach continued to look down the bench, to see who they could put in there to close the deal on the game. He awkwardly locked eyes with Tanner.

After being evaluated the trainers never spoke a word. They just stepped aside and carried on about their day like nothing had happened. Although he felt like he was in a daze, he felt the need to get back on that court. Both he and coach knew he was the key to winning that game, but his number never got called. Tanner had to witness his team crumbling to shambles.

"What just happened?" he said as the final buzzer sounded.

The Terrapins were moving on to the Elite-8 and Tanner was the scapegoat. Had Benjamin McAllister not taken him out, the outcome would have been different. The Oregon fans were ready to riot in the streets, while the Maryland fans conveniently forgot their victory came as a result of foul play. Even worse yet, many praised McAllister for such a bold move to help his team win. In their eyes, he was a genius and a savior.

Dreams of playing in the tournament's Elite-8 games was a devastating blow to the team and the vested alumni. Those final minutes against Maryland were excruciatingly painful for Tanner to watch from the bench. *How could the coach just sideline me like that and make me sit through that type of agony?* he wondered.

Sure he was a bit rattled from the Cobra Kai elbow to the face, but he was the missing link. Once he was pulled from the court, the team imploded. During the flight home, the fuselage reminded virtually silent. Questions about how they let a monster lead get stripped away from them haunted the coaches and players.

16

NUGGETS

When they arrived back on campus, Tanner couldn't help but spend the week rewatching the game film repeatedly. Each time he replayed it, the anger and guilt intensified. Since the day he signed his NLI to play at Oregon, he had received numerous calls from sports agencies that wanted to represent him. They all gave off the used car salesman vibe, which was an immediate disqualifier. Unsure of how he was going to confront the team and the fans he had just let down, he flirted with the idea of taking the coward's way out and contacting an agent.

One of the many lessons Tanner learned in high school was to sell when the stock value was high. According to the Oregon papers, and the media, the decision had already been made, unbeknownst to Tanner.

"An individual close to the program," as the reporter fabricated, spoke in a recent press conference about how number 22, Tanner Skilli, would be foregoing his senior year to pursue his NBA dreams. Speculation and tales started exploding like fireworks in northern California. ESPN analysts weighed in on his decision, with the majority backing his business move. Tanner's phone started ringing off the hook from reporters, scouts, and want-to-be agents.

Maybe it was for the best, Tanner thought to himself. He remembered back to the contract he had signed as a minor. There was nothing in there that specified a time frame in which he had to graduate from college. The financial aspect of playing at the next level was not a factor. Uncle Perry had left their family enough money to live three lifetimes. There was an element of fulfillment about having money he earned himself.

While flipping through the newspaper, Tanner flipped to the business section to see how the market was reacting. If he was going to make a move, there was only one man that Tanner knew he could trust. He picked up the phone and dialed an old friend.

"Coach Baugh, Tanner Skilli here. How the heck is life treating you, Sir?" Tanner asked.

Coach Baugh was delighted to hear from him and was honored by the proposal that Tanner began to outline. In most cases, the agents barter for the highest cut possible. The monetary compensation of playing professional basketball was a key motivator for most, but Tanner craved competition. He told Coach Baugh that he understood the risks of having a rookie agent, but he would rather have a rookie than a snake in his corner. With his new agent onboard, number 22 decided to toss his name in the hat for the upcoming NBA Draft.

Without a crystal ball, it was unknown how early in the draft Tanner would have gone had he chose to play his senior year. The ship had set sail leaving college in its wake. Nights leading up to Draft Day were filled with a cluster of stress and mixed emotions. Tanner returned home to Wellington to watch the draft with his family.

Judy acknowledged the dark sadness and struggles he was facing and did everything she could to remain upbeat and positive. She supported whatever decision her son made. However, she felt his motivation to get out of Eugene in a hurry, was taking the easy way out. As she was in the kitchen making sandwiches for lunch, she watched Tanner out the window shooting his 100 contractual free-throws. Every missed shot would fuel the fire to his inner rage. The uncertainty of his future made him question himself, his doubt fueling his angst.

Walking out on the back deck, Judy leaned on the banister perched high above the court.

"Son, I've watched you shoot hoops for the majority of your life. I can tell that your heart isn't in the right place. Play your game. Shoot the ball like Tanner Skilli. Watching you during the games is like watching poetry in motion. You protect the ball and dribble it with delicate finesse. Right now you are throwing it at the hoop like you're upset at the ball. There is a distinct difference between the two. In fact, I can tell if the ball is going to go in just by watching the way you release it. There's a lot going on right now. You've spent too many hours on that court to give up. Dig deep, right?"

Setting differences aside for the day, Judy invited Tripp and a few of Tanner's high school buddies over to watch the draft. Dermot, Kurt, Coach Baugh, and Anders would never pass on free food at the Skilli residence. Judy had a tendency to provide enough food for a small army. The first round trickled by at a snail's pace and Tanner's phone never rang. Each draft pick would rip out a piece of Tanner's confidence, as it meant one less chance of being an NBA player. Trying to refrain from drowning his sorrows, he declined the offer of a Busch Light. Although the decadent refreshment was quite enticing and would help calm his nerves. Tanner didn't want to answer the call so drunk he couldn't accept an offer to play at the next level.

They sat huddled around the phone in anticipation of it ringing. Alas, they called his number.

"With their third pick in the second round, the Denver Nuggets select Tanner Skilli from the University of Oregon," the announcer publicized.

His dream had come true, it was time to play ball with the big boys.

17

BABY I GOTCHA MONEY

L ife in the NBA was bewildering, to say the least. Following the first practice, the head assistant coach told Tanner that it's a tradition to have a quick team meal to kick off the season. Imported engines purred as the team filled the Outback Steakhouse parking lot, which had been roped off for the evening. Part of the arrangement was that the restaurant would provide parking lot security while the team enjoyed their Aussie experience. Not much security was needed for Tanner's 10-year-old standard cab Toyota pickup. He figured the men in yellow shirts were enlisted to watch over the perimeter for the disgusting assortment of Ferraris, Lambos, and Bugattis on display.

They were ushered into the restaurant by a series of servers and hostesses. The welcoming was over-the-top warm and friendly as if a brave player had just completed his walk-about and is now being recognized as a man. It was an authentic Australian celebration. Aside from the big win from last season playing on every television in the place. Each big dunk replay made the room erupt, which gradually increased as the Fred Flintstone-sized mugs of Fosters continued to be delivered to the tables. For supposed "professionals" these guys were still Frat boys at heart. Frat boy's with a lot of money. The evening was comforting to Tanner as it took him back to college. Perhaps the transition to the next level wasn't going to be as difficult as he anticipated. Once the kitchen staff was cooking on high, they whipped up gourmet entrees of surf and turf, accompanied by the healthy "Awesome Blossom." The evening was such a terrific way to celebrate the start of a new season and to mingle with the new teammates.

Lights began to dim as the sound of a loud drum started filling the air. All the televisions in the place went black, as the sacred ceremony was called to order.

The team slowly began chanting, "Suicide, suicide, suicide!"

It was an innocent fraternity-style ritual, but it struck a nerve with Tanner. Since the day he left Lincoln City with a reminder of his selfish mistake. He never revealed his tattoo in public, primarily because he didn't know how to respond to questions inspiring the piece. It was a mixture of shame and sentiment that he chose to keep hidden from the world. He pulled up his right sleeve and glanced down at the .44 caliber bullet embedded in his arm, sending his heart into a panic.

Thoughts of how close Tanner was to ruining the great life he was now able to live, ran through his mind. The team's chant continued, "Suicide, suicide, suicide," as the wait staff began placing the concoctions in front of them.

A shot of tequila, two limes, and a one hundred dollar bill rested beside a small mound of salt. The shot sequence has many names across the world, but they coined it "The Aussie Suicide." Players began to chuff and scream as they prepared themselves for the challenge that lay ahead.

They began to take the long edge of the Benjamin and straightened the salt out into a small line. In unison, they rolled the bill and placed one end in their nostril. Final screams were let out as they began snorting the line of salt, downing the shot, tilting their heads towards the ceiling, and squeezing the lime juice in their eyes. The ritual straddles the line between bravery and stupidity, but it was a creative way to make a group of full-grown men cry uncontrollably. Laughter and high-fives broke out across the tables in victory. The team settled back to their seats to savor the last few bites of lobster.

Promptly after dinner, everyone started to get up and leave. The universal sound of calling it a night was heard as the players took their final chugs of beer and slammed their empty glasses on the wooden table.

The Irish goodbye only works if one is being discreet and the departure goes unnoticed. When it is a mass exodus, the covertness of the mission is lost. As each player headed toward the front exit, they walked by Tanner and welcomed him to the team. Believing he was the guest of honor, a sense of pride filled his warrior soul that pushed him to overcome challenges. They had accepted him as a teammate. His doubts about leaving before his senior year dissolved as he let the honor of the night sink in.

Then the bomb was dropped. The head server, dressed as a native Aboriginal woman, walked around the corner with a receipt that was darn near dragging on the floor.

"Your generosity is admirable," she said as she placed the invoice off the edge of the table.

"I'm sorry Ma'am, could you please clarify what you mean?" he asked.

"You're the new hotshot rookie, aren't you? You can't break tradition," she said with a smile.

It was the most expensive initiation he could imagine. When he opened the black leather book, his eyes were quickly directed to the large total at the bottom. "Grand Total: $4,800.33" appeared in large bold letters. As savory as that meal had been, Tanner's stomach filled with knots as the cold sweats kicked in. Their deceitful ploy wasn't a situation he had planned to encounter during his first week on the team.

Staying true to his contract with Uncle Perry, he deposited half of his signing bonus in a separate savings account. The cost of the dinner took a good chunk of his remaining disposable income thanks to Uncle Sam. That new Toyota 4Runner he had his eye on, would have to wait until the next paycheck.

The initiation did not upset Tanner until he arrived in the locker room for practice the next day. As the team was dressing down, he overheard multiple conversations about players being disgruntled over their current contracts. It really started to grind his gears when the starting point guard mentioned that his contract was bullshit, and could barely make ends meet. The guy was making well over $3,000,000 a year, yet he couldn't buy his own meal at Outback.

Tanner snickered to himself as he started to think about summer sausage, cheese, and crackers. Back when the Skilli's were living in a trailer park, he'd always hear his parents talking about "trying to make ends meet." He thought the phrase was, "To make ends meat," as in the end pieces of summer sausage. It's usually the part of the meat that people cut off and discard. Since it wasn't highly sought after, it was valued as being nearly worthless. Trying hard to make enough money to even be able to attain the undesirable pieces of meat seemed equally as logical.

The dynamic in the NBA locker room was the polar opposite from college ball. The NBA players were completely narcissistic and self-serving. In college, the egos were inflated but the team played for each other and for the betterment of the school's program. NBA players were more worried about their contracts and playing time. They didn't campaign for more time on the court to help their team win, but rather they wanted an opportunity to attract sponsors and a fan base. Once money was involved, it was no longer a sport.

Tanner knew he had to elevate his game, both on and off the court, or his professional career would be short-lived. He had to remember the National Basketball Association was a business first and foremost.

The luxury of having coaches care about players' feelings was a thing of the past. Tanner reminded himself that he could only control his own actions and that nothing positive would come from comparing himself to others. Rather than feeling self-pity over the other player's contracts, he had to applaud their negotiation skills. Accepting the fact that he signed a contract, and agreed to the terms, allowed him to focus on performing well until his contract was up for renegotiation.

During his rookie season, Tanner only got to see time on the court when the team was up by a considerable margin. When he did get time on the court, he played consistent and selflessly. It was a time when the Denver Nugget franchise was going through a rebuilding phase and the window of opportunity to shine was open.

The coaching staff appreciated the fact he was dependable and never got into trouble. He attempted to keep a low profile as to not make waves with the veteran players. Although he wasn't trying to steal the spotlight, his extra hustle during practice quickly caught the attention of others. When the team was doing wind-sprints he received constant ridicule from the other players, telling him to slow down. The Skilli DNA made it impossible for him to go anything less than full throttle. Remembering back to Steve Prefontaine, he didn't want to sacrifice the gift he was given.

It took three seasons before Tanner made the Nugget's starting line-up. Coach Baugh did a terrific job negotiating a new contract, making Tanner Skilli a millionaire for the first time. Coach took a modest cut from the deal and was able to start a career representing other Pac 10 athletes.

Promptly after putting pen to paper and sealing the deal,

Tanner called Judy to spread the great news. They shared in the joy over the phone, as they reminisced about the days back in Wyoming. His mother constantly said how blessed they were and how she couldn't have been more proud of her son. Throughout his life, she expressed how proud she was of him, but her words finally sank in. Perhaps it was the first time that he was truly proud enough of himself to believe her.

Jersey chasers were ruthless in professional sports' circles. The droves of attractive women that an NBA contract attracted was damn near overwhelming. Tanner rented a small condominium a few miles from the UC Health practice facility and was the only player who would pedal-bike to practice. The court entrance was usually scattered with girls in short skirts, fake boobs, and obvious Botox injections. The players had various nicknames for the girls like Baby's Daddy Snipers, Disease Central, or Worms in honor of the great Dennis Rodman.

Dennis Rodman, to this day, is a man who will out work anyone who dare step foot on his court. He went after every rebound within eyesight with little regard for his surroundings. If a shot went up and he was at half court, there was still a good chance he was going to fight his way to get the coveted ball. He played with more passion and desire to please the fans than any ballplayer in basketball.

Rodman received "The Worm" nickname, due to the fact he could always squirm his way to the perfect position to get the ball to fall into his lap. At least that is what many thought. The true origin can be traced back to the days when he was slapping the paddles on the pinball machine and moving like a worm. There was a multifaceted correlation between Rodman and the jersey chasing floozies. The loose use of "worms" seemed fitting, nonetheless.

When Tanner strolled to work on a bicycle, he could walk right past the gaggle of women. They must have figured he was a ball boy for the team. Plus the bike was a great money-saver. Not only did it save on gas, but it also cut down on his potential child support payments he would have to shell out if he was driving a car the price of a house. The two seemed to go hand in hand according to the league statistics. Other players who took that gamble typically regretted it down the road and now have children spread across the country.

18
J & G

August practices kept Tanner in town, but his schedule was left empty for all but three hours a day. Dermot decided to fly into town to see his old buddy. He could easily identify Tanner's mode of transportation outside the practice facility since it was the only one chained to the bike rack outside. Arriving a few hours early, Dermot had some time on his hands and took the liberty of upgrading Tanner's bike with the complete "Barbie" package. He swapped out the tires for bright pink ones mounted on white rims. Frilly tassels were added to the handlebars, accenting a small chiming bell. The final touches were decorative princess spokes to pull it all together.

Dermot had never been to Colorado before. He and Tanner had plans to meet up after practice to kick off the weekend.

When Tanner arrived at the restaurant, the hostess greeted him by saying, "You must be Mister Jack Mehoff. Your parole officer has already arrived. Please follow me."

Before he could take a seat, drinks were delivered to the table. The kind waitress placed the frosty pint of a Breckenridge King's Dish ale in front of Dermot, before delicately placing a full shot-glass topped with whipped cream in front of Tanner.

"Sir, enjoy your Blowjob. Don't forget to swallow," she said as she released the glass and gave him a flirtatious wink.

"Same old Dermot. You son of a bitch, you," Tanner said as he entwined his fingers behind his back and leaned in to wrap his lips around the scrumptious shot.

"You're hired!" Dermot shouted loud enough for the entire restaurant to hear.

Dermot's trip was not only about catching up with an old friend, there was also a hidden business agenda to boot. He waited until after they finished dinner to bring business to the table. Their conversation prior started to make sense. Dermot was talking up this great company he was starting and how it was going to be a game-changer in the software industry.

The pitch began, "Listen, buddy, I want to cut you in on this deal. I know software has always been your guilty pleasure. Remember that old program we worked on back in college? I want to take it to the next level."

Tanner was caught off guard by the sudden shift in topic, but he was also remembering all the nerdy days he would sit at his desk and code for hours. Coding had always been an outlet when he was growing up and throughout college. Coming from anyone else, Tanner likely would have declined the offer. If Dermot was willing to gamble on a decade long friendship, Tanner trusted his friend and agreed to the joint venture.

Going into a business partnership is a true sign of commitment. Some would argue it's a bigger commitment than marriage if factoring in the liability risks. When Dermot made reference to the old program they worked on, he conveniently forgot a few details. Procrastinating on his final MIS project lead Dermot to bribe Tanner with a case of Busch Light to help. Three beers into the coding session, Tanner hit his stride. Dermot sat next to him watching Van Wilder, as the keys were punched in the corner of the room. It took just under three hours for Tanner to develop "The Mouse Tail."

Back at home, he had the luxury of having two monitors. When he would shift his eyes from one screen to the next, he would lose his spot. 'The Mouse Tail" worked independent from the mouse and would cast a solid highlighter across the page. The bar could be scrolled up and down the page, as a placeholder, and helped reduce the strain of having to refocus back on the page.

To celebrate the new business venture, Dermot insisted on scouting the talent at "Jiggles & Giggles." He thought it was the best of both worlds. A few bucks to get big boobs rubbed in his face while listening to mediocre comedians sounded like a match made in heaven.

They walked up to the bouncer, Dermot leaned over and whispered, "This guy right here is the new star of the Denver Nuggets."

The bouncer called in a "Code-Green." Tanner and Dermot were promptly escorted by two gorgeous, topless women. The bouncer removed a rope, allowing them entrance to prime seats on the stage rail. Before they could get comfortable in their seats, the women quickly positioned themselves on the gentleman's laps.

From the corner stage, an amateur comedian opened his act with, "Does anyone know how many flies it takes to screw in a light bulb? Two, but aren't you curious how they got in there?"

"You guys alive? I feel like I'm talking to a bunch of stiffs."

"Sir! Yes, you in the corner. Please don't stand up, those mesh shorts are hiding that pair of sock you smuggled in."

"From the stage, it looks like you've got a pair of ankle socks tucked into your tighty whities."

"But for real, I've never seen so many blank stares."

"You all look like a bunch of deer in headlights."

Patrons in the audience were less interested in hearing the lame jokes, but it gave the comedian a chance to polish his material for a crowd that would be less distracted by exposed skin.

Dermot continued to order shots of tequila and the two began to get increasingly polluted. Throughout the night, Tanner made several trips to the ATM machine. Each time he reached down to grab the dispensed money, his justification to his conscience was that he was making a simple donation to higher education. He didn't realize how many of the working women were trying to make their way through medical school, but the alcohol encouraged him to be their personal financial aid.

The scenery was quite remarkable that evening. There was one gal in particular that Tanner couldn't take his eyes off of as she walked around the smoke-filled room. She was gorgeous and had a striking resemblance to Annika. Tanner caught a whiff of her intoxicating Fruit Loop fragrance, as her silver stilettos punished the old wooden floorboards behind their silk-backed chairs.

"Next up on the main stage ladies and gentlemen is the smoke show they call 'Assley.' You folks down on 'Sniffer's Row' are in for an exquisite treat. She needs help paying for next semester's tuition. Can we support her better than that bra? Let's dig deep into our pockets gentleman and pull out the distinguished bills. Fun fact, her favorite president was Ulysses S. Grant," the DJ announced over the loudspeaker before pressing play on her chosen song.

The legendary Sir Mix-a-lot's "Don't Call Me Da Da" started pumping through the speakers. Tanner had listened to that song a hundred times and knew that he would never be able to listen to it the same way after watching Assley work the pole with poise and grace.

Tanner immediately reached in his pocket for his roll of twenties to construct his patented "Greenhouse" of bills. Two twenties to make the walls, one for the ceiling, and the last twenty creased on top to form an A-framed roof. The greenhouse was an architectural marvel, or so he thought. Dermot tossed a twenty up on the rail and Assley worked her way over and summoned him with her finger to stand up and come to the rail. She ripped down her shirt and smashed his face between her succulent large breasts while looking Tanner directly in the eyes. There was no question Dermot was getting his money's worth with that twenty bucks. She continued to nibble at his neck and rubbed her hands all over his body. Still, she continued to look Tanner directly in the eyes. After spending extra time with Dermot, she placed her palm on his forehead and pushed him back into his chair. Naturally, Tanner thought he was next in line, but she went the other direction to attend to the other lonely club dwellers.

Sir Mix-a-lot said his final artistic words, and Assley began picking up the cash she had tossed in the center of the stage. She walked over to Tanner and demolished the house as she grabbed the bills and crumbled them in a fist.

"Thanks, Sweetie. I owe you," she said as she turned and exited the stage in her birthday suit.

Dermot turned to Tanner, "Dude, she has you wrapped around her pretty little finger."

The night was getting late, but they stuck around in hopes of getting another chance to bust out one of Dermot's infamous pick-up lines on Assley. They watched her walking around the club and then she'd disappear in five-minute intervals. It was time to call off the pursuit and allow Assley to run wild like the sacred unicorn she was.

When they got up, their chairs were a perfect mold of their butts, leaving the impression they had been at Jiggles and Giggles far too long. From out of nowhere, Assley swooped in and asked where they were trying to run off to. She flagged down her friend Patty, short for "Pass around Patty," who came over and wrapped Dermot's arms around her neck. She was only wearing a thong at the time and strategically positioned his hand on her right breast. Her high school graduation gift from daddy was really benefiting her career.

Before Tanner could talk to her any further, he told her that he had a difficult time calling her "Assley" and was wondering if there is an alternate name she would be comfortable with.

"Oh, my real name is Astra. Astra or Ash would be just fine," she said with a smile.

The ladies invited themselves back to Tanner's place and insisted they wouldn't take no for an answer.

For the duration of the cab ride, the girls sat on Tanner's and Dermot's laps. The driver could hear the sound of gentle kissing and heavy-petting, but he kept his eyes on the road. When they walked into his apartment, Tanner could overhear whispers between the girls about how they were expecting more of a penthouse suite. Astra soon realized that she wasn't going to win the lottery, but rather a scratch-off ticket. Patty had put on a skirt before leaving Jiggles & Giggles. It covered most of her body, aside from her butt cheeks hanging out the back. She was undoubtedly a professional and had that skirt striped off the moment the door closed. She aggressively pulled Dermot into the guest bedroom, knowing it was time to go back to work. Dermot should have had to buy a zoo ticket based on the variety of animal noises that soon started piercing the apartment walls.

"That Patty's a wild one," Astra said as she placed Tanner's hand on her butt and started walking toward his bedroom.

"I'm going to rinse some of this baby powder off real quick if you don't mind me using some of your hot water. Care to join me?" she asked coyly as they entered his bedroom.

When he looked at Astra all he could see was Annika's face. The alcohol could have been a contributing factor to his blurry vision, but his eyes saw what he had been dreaming about. He wanted nothing more than to be with Annika. He envisioned exploring the world with her and starting a family, among other things.

"Where did you go?" Astra interrupted, watching his mind travel to his dreamland future. "Are you coming or what?"

Tanner turned on the shower and waited for the cold water to clear the lines. Astra stood there with her flawless naked body, which promptly brought things to attention. Between her fingers, she gently pinched a small white pill.

When he turned around, she said, "I told you I owe you. Take this, it will blow your mind."

They entered the small shower and began to press their bodies against one another. Astra wet down her hair and pulled it back with both hands, pushing out her chest. She grabbed the bottle of body wash and began lathering her front side, before placing her soapy hands on his throbbing member. Her stage skills were paying dividends, Astra's seduction routine was finely crafted and obviously well-rehearsed. Later, Tanner discovered others had fallen victim to her shameless ways. Two of the poor saps were former players in the league, and the other had just extended his contract with the Celtics. Astra received a hefty child support payment each month from all three baby daddies. With any luck, number four would be baking in the money-oven. She had already started picturing herself in her next new Mercedes G-Class rolling on pink rims.

The euphoric shower experience was interrupted by loud tiger chuffs and roars from the other room. White noise from the shower wasn't powerful enough to drown out Patty's inner feline. Astra promptly dropped to her knees and began stroking Tanner's member. Her bright blue eyes looked up at him as she began nibbling down the sides of his shaft. Tanner looked up to the ceiling as his body filled with raging hormones and the little pill started to infiltrate his bloodstream.

Astra wrapped her hand around the tip of his erection and began lightly flicking his stepchildren with her pierced tongue. She worked her way up towards the tip and replaced her hands with her lips. Slowly lowering her head and pushing him deeper into her mouth, she gazed up at him with doe eyes. She began moaning like she was a fat kid at a buffet with a hankering for dessert. There was no intention of stopping at a shower blowjob. Working her hand simultaneously with her mouth, she could feel the increased blood flow pulsing through his veins. He reached down and gently fondled her soapy breasts as she continued to pleasure him like it was her job. When he started to reach climax, she grabbed the base of his manhood with her right hand and started to apply pressure. She used it like a light switch, instantly descending him from reaching climax.

"Not so fast Mr. Skilli, we're not done yet. You built me a house. I have to repay you," she said as she stood up.

First turning off the water with her left hand, she then opened the glass door and stepped out onto the shag carpet covering the bathroom linoleum.

Tanner felt as though he were floating on air. He looked over to see if his reflection could confirm he had taken flight. Fog, amongst other things, had steamed up the mirrors. Astra pushed on his shoulder to gesture to him to lay on his back. Dry mouth quickly set in as he stared blankly at the light fixture.

"I've got to get something to drink. My mouth feels like the Sahara desert," he said as he stumbled his way over to the sink and placed his head under the faucet.

Astra stood before him water still dripping from her hair down her shoulders, breasts, and midriff. She placed her hands on her hips as she grew impatient. *You've got to be kidding me*, she thought, *how many gallons does this camel hold?* He hadn't fully turned off the faucet when Astra pulled him back from the counter and tried to push him to the ground. His body had shifted into autopilot as he reached for a stash of condoms. Astra quickly grabbed him by the wrist and gently guided him to the rug. Lying flat on his back, she covered his body with hers and whispered, "Don't worry about a thing baby, I'm on the pill. I can take a morning-after pill too, just to play it safe."

That night, Astra never clocked out, she was still at work. Tanner was in a daze of bliss, making her work easier. All of his senses were heightened, and the touch of her skin felt incredible. Music began playing in the back of his mind, as she began her well-choreographed routine. Jiggles and Giggles had apparently relocated to his bathroom for a song. Planting a knee next to each ear, she straddled his face. Oblivious to how many other body parts and objects have been there before, he began licking her manicured baby-maker. Although heavily under the influence, he admired the beauty of her waxed lips and perfectly symmetric landing strip. Going back to his college playbook, he began writing letters with his tongue. Not thinking through the inappropriate timing and twisted nature of his next action, the first letters he pleasured her with were A-N-N-I-K-A.

Time seemed to stand still as the heat of passion filled the apartment bathroom. Astra ran her fingers through Tanner's hair and pressed his face deeper between her legs. It was the way he was brought into the world and considered it only fitting to be his exit as well. On the verge of suffocation, she released her clench from the back of his head and allowed him to gasp for air. Long strokes with his tongue encouraged Astra to rub her breasts and press them together. Looking up, it was one heck of a view.

Releasing her twins, they gently bounced and then returned to their perky resting place. Like a gymnast on a pommel horse, she repositioned herself in the other direction to return the favor. Tugging at his member as she massaged the tip with her tongue. Moaning started echoing off the bathroom walls, which was talent in itself. This girl knew how to multitask. Clawing her fingers into the carpet, she slid down his body and began rubbing her clitoris down his erection. Uncontrollably, he flexed and felt the warmth of her inside.

"Tell me how bad you want it," she said looking back at him over her shoulder.

She caressed the end of him with a slight bouncing motion, making him forget all logic.

Rather than saying something sweet like, "You are a beautiful woman, but I don't even know your last name. Maybe this isn't the best idea," he said, "Pretty fucking bad! Your ass is freaking phenomenal and you feel incredible."

Astra lowered herself down his shaft until she reached the base. She had been with multiple players, but the way she felt him inside was like nothing she had ever experienced. Barely able to contain herself, she paused for a brief moment to feel the corrupt connection between their souls collide. Although drugged, Tanner remained cognizant of the artificial love. With her legs on each side of his stomach, she leaned over, forcing her sculpted butt in the air. Like a fly attracted to a lightbulb, he reached down with both hands and squeezed her firm cheeks. It was evident she had spent hours training on the pole, once she began twerking her amazing body. At that point, it was every man and woman for themselves to seek shelter. Many moons had passed since Tanner was last with a woman. When the volcano blew its top, Astra let out a scream like she had just hit the jackpot. The twerking did not stop, it only slowed down, as she continued to ride the aftershocks of his rock-hard member.

Cuddling on the floor of the bathroom after sex is only appealing for married couples who finally got the kids to sleep early. Astra sat up and repositioned her legs and slowly started to withdraw. As she pulled away she reached down with her right hand. From the base of his member, she began squeezing his shaft like a tube of toothpaste, salvaging every last drop.

"Saving up for winter?" she asked. "That was quite the load."

She stood up and licked his remnants off her finger and then massaged it down below.

The overpowering release left Tanner lifeless on the shag rug. His mind wandered into another universe, as the drugs, alcohol, and hormones battled it out. There was a quiet knock on the door as the handle slowly turned. Patty stepped into the room naked, sporting an iconic JBF hairdo, to tell Astra it was time to go.

"We've only got the sitter until 2 a.m. tonight. Let's get going," she said.

Astra gathered her things as Patty stood over Tanner, surveying the situation as if she were a crime scene investigator.

"Hey Ass, do you think he's got any more in him? That thing looks delicious."

Blitzed out of his gourd, Tanner floated off in space and had no cognizance of his body being molested. Patty grabbed his semi-flaccid magic stick and began licking like she was searching for the Tootsie Roll center of a Tootsie Pop. It took the stallion a few brief seconds for him to return to full mast. She climbed on top and inserted him inside of her. Leaning down she smothered her heavily baby powered breasts in his face. With his eyes rolling back in his head, he laid there and smiled.

"I've got a good feeling about this one," Astra said while Patty continued to work him up and down.

Pulling out slowly until only his tip remained and then sensually lowering herself down its full length.

"This guy has a fucking great cock. The sitter can leave the kids home alone for a while for all I care," Patty said as she looked over at Astra.

"His jump shot is even better. A golden ticket," she replied.

Enjoying every inch of him, Patty started again with her safari noises. They seemed annoying when hearing them through the wall, but seeing her in action was an incredible turn on. Astra stepped away from the counter and began making out with Patty as she continued to grind back and forth.

"How did you finish him off?" she asked.

"I went reverse cowgirl and polished him off in less than a minute," Astra replied.

Patty reached over and spanked Astra's butt.

"With an ass like that, I'm sure you did."

After treating Tanner like a sex mannequin, Patty orgasmed several times as Astra licked her nipples to heighten the sensitivity.

"It's time girl. Face down, ass up. Arch your back a bit more to take him all in," Astra whispered.

Like a Rock Star, Tanner was able to deliver an explosive encore performance.

"Holy shit Ass, you weren't kidding," Patty said as she slowly worked him back and forth.

His involuntary flexing sent tingles to her toes as she came to an abrupt halt like his quarter's worth had expired.

The women briskly threw on some skanky clothes and made their way into the living room. Both Dermot and Tanner continued to be lost in their own minds after encountering two of the most erotic gold-diggers in all of the land. When the guys woke the next morning they had little recollection of the night that had transpired. Still on the bathroom floor, Tanner rolled over on his side and began rubbing his eyes. He was unable to gain focus, and everything was a giant blur. He made his way to the toilet and considered emerging his face to drink the water, but his bladder told him differently. As he felt the release on the horizon, a momentary blockage made his urine burst out all over the side of the toilet. Once got a handle on things, he was able to correct his aim and set a world record for the longest pee in history. It was a record he had awarded himself several times in his life. On multiple occasions in college, he filled his body with copious amounts of Busch Light. He would then spend upward of an hour relieving himself, or so it seemed at the time.

Grabbing one of a dozen pairs of sweatpants, he stepped his legs in and pulled them up to his waist. He flipped on the coffee maker and turned on Sports Center. After watching for thirty minutes, and finishing two cups of coffee, Tanner remembered Dermot. He got up from the couch and walked into the guestroom. Curled up in the fetal position, Dermot laid naked on the floor. His arms were wrapped around a pillow, clenching it for comfort. It was a prime opportunity to "Chief" his old friend, but the target would have been too easy. Tanner placed his hand on Dermot's ankle and started to shake his leg. When he came to, he was in a similar daze.

"All I can hear is the sound of zoo animals echoing in my head," Dermot said as he leaned forward and placed a pillow over his privates.

"I'll be sure to wash that pillow before my next guests arrive," Tanner said as he sat down on the corner of the bed.

Trying to piece the night together, neither could remember anything past getting back to the apartment.

"You want to hear something crazy? I could have sworn Annika was here last night. The image of her was so vivid," Tanner said, staring at the ground.

"I don't recall seeing Annika, but I do remember seeing that vixen Assley," Dermot replied. "Was that unicorn a cat in the sack or what? For your sake, I hope you used three condoms. With an ass like that, I guarantee she sells out her goodies like a vending machine."

Tanner placed his head in his hands and instantly regretted the past twelve hours of his life.

"Now that I got that out of my system, I'll never have to repeat a night like that ever again," he said.

"Ahh, man. It's all part of the famous lifestyle. A small little voice tells me that there will be many similar nights to come," Dermot said with a smile.

19

UNCLE PHIL

The season was off to a great start despite the wild run-in with Astra and Patty. Coaches began working Tanner into the rotation more often and his confidence on the court began to improve. Finally, the world felt right again. Sponsors started calling his agent and requesting commercial plugs. Then a call from a dear friend came through.

Tanner answered the phone and heard the voice of Mr. Knight himself.

"I've always prided myself on being an excellent judge of character and talent. It's time that you officially became a member of the Nike family."

Tanner paused, shocked.

"Sir, I appreciate that so much, especially coming from a man in your position," he said. "I can honestly say I'm a bit perplexed. I already thought I was part of the Nike family."

He laughed nervously.

"Well, yes son, I guess you are right. Even though you left before your senior year, the Duck Nation and Nike still have a special place in their hearts for you," Mr. Knight replied.

They finished the conversation with a contractual arrangement. Mr. Knight was having his team draft up the contract and would be sending it over to Tanner momentarily. Wanting to get some great marketing material, Mr. Knight offered to fly him to Beaverton,

Oregon to hammer out the details.

A cab driver named Farouk picked Tanner up the next morning. The Nike office had contacted him to arrange limousine service to the airport, but he politely declined. Hearing the stories of Farouk's life in Kosovo was well worth the cab ride. Farouk was excited to share the news that his family was finally reuniting after a decade of being apart. His successful older daughter had purchased three townhouses for them to all live in the same vicinity. It was clear that family meant the world to Farouk.

Security gave them trouble at the gate, as the guards were not accustomed to seeing regular cabs on that side of the airport. Once they reached the airport apron, Farouk insisted on retrieving the luggage from the backseat. Tanner gave him a hundred dollar handshake and thanked Farouk for sharing tidbits of his struggles and happiness in life.

"I will remember your story and carry it with me. You are a good man, Farouk. The perseverance it took to find your family is legendary," Tanner said as he slung his pack over his shoulder and headed to board the waiting Gulfstream jet.

Being a Nike sponsored athlete is motivation enough to strive to play at the next level. It launches athletes up on pedestals with the Greek Gods. The perks are phenomenal and the paychecks are even better. The sudden amount of wealth made Tanner uneasy when he thought back to the misfortune of Farouk.

While the rest of the NBA players were buying gold chains and exotic cars, Tanner invested his money. Coach Baugh's methodology started to produce incredible dividends. The first lesson he learned from Coach was that the stock market was a measurement of what has already happened. Great investors work their trades like strategic chess moves and never rely on knee-jerk reactions. Traders who have had success in the market, manage to always stay multiple steps ahead of the curve. Those extra hours in the computer lab were becoming well worth every minute.

Not wanting to be flashy, Tanner decided to use some of his money to build a 6,000 square foot home in Boulder. Without the intention of trying to compete with the home Uncle Perry had designed, Tanner spared no expense designing his custom rustic home. The simplicity of the structure was the beauty. The great room had twenty-five-foot ceilings with large beams crisscrossing. In the middle was a magnificent fireplace wrapped with stone and dark bricks. Plush leather chairs surrounded the fireplace to offer an inviting ambiance for conversation.

Watching the logs being placed like Lincoln Logs, was therapeutic to watch. Tanner was on site nearly every day of the construction trying to stay on the general contractors' good side. The general was not rigid like most in his profession and he enjoyed the flexibility Tanner gave him during the process. As things took shape, they made several field adjustments.

The general always said, "Hey man, you've got to live in this thing. Who am I to tell you what is going to be right for your liking?"

Judy and Tripp managed to put differences aside for milestone events. When they heard Tanner was finally getting the certificate to occupy, they made arrangements to fly in for the weekend. Their little boy was finally all grown up and self-reliant. To celebrate the step into manhood, they decided to throw him a surprise housewarming party.

Before their planes had even touched down, the event trucks arrived at Tanner's new residence in the secluded woods. Throughout the building process, he envisioned the first morning waking up to the sunrise with a spectacular view out the master windows facing the tall mountain range. For that reason, his bed was the only thing he had moved in the day he finally got the keys handed over. A loud knock at the door startled him. He figured it was the landscaping crew coming over to add a few polishing touches to the backyard.

Again, a loud knock echoed throughout the great room. Tanner stumbled to his feet and tossed on a pair of Duck sweatpants. When he opened the door his eyes looked past the gentleman standing in front of him and took note of the three large trucks parked in the driveway.

"Mr. Skilli, we are here to set up the party," the event worker said while glancing down at his clipboard and tapping his pen.

"Sorry man, I didn't order anything. I just moved in last night. Oh shit, are you with the moving company? I get it 'The Party.' Since moving sucks, you guys try to church it up a bit to sound more appealing," Tanner sleepily stammered.

"No, Sir. We are not the moving company. We were told to set up for a party of 150 people," the worker said, flipping through the pages of the contract. "Looks like your wife Judy called and made the arrangements. Classic communication breakdown between married folks, am I right?"

Tanner asked the worker to give him a minute to throw on a long sleeve shirt and make a call. He grabbed his flip-phone and selected "Mom," but the call went directly to voicemail. Psycho-dialing had never been his style, so he politely left his mother a message questioning the party that was in progress. Her plane touched down just after 10:30 a.m. As she exited the plane toward baggage-claim, Judy called her son with overwhelming joy.

"Who's excited for their big day?" she said.

"Am I betrothed to a female worthy of being a suitor? I mean, come on. This may be a bit outside the boundaries," Tanner replied.

"No, Silly-Skilli we're showing off your new house to all your old friends. Although, the marriage thing is not a bad idea. I could use the exercise of chasing little grandchildren around the house," she said, hinting so thickly he could feel it jabbing his ribs.

Tanner tried to explain that it was the first full day of being in his house and he didn't have a single glass, plate, chair, soap bar, towel, or refrigerator for that matter.

"Don't be such a worrier. I've got all the arrangements made. All you have to do is shake hands and drink Busch Light," she said.

"My only request is that the beer be chilled to a crisp 41 degrees. Anything warmer would be a slap in the face to those wizards who marvelously crafted such a fine brew," Tanner said with sincerity.

Caterers and the setup crew were putting the final touches on the party as the sun just started sinking into the Colorado Rocky Mountains. Cars began making their way up the dirt road and quickly clustered Tanner's circular driveway. His hands began to get clammier by the second, as people started piling out of the vehicles in droves.

Who the heck are these folks? he asked himself while his mother greeted the guests with open arms. Occasionally, he spotted a familiar face among the crowd, but they were mostly just strangers at his home.

Each welcomed person treated Tanner like they were long-time buddies. For the life of him, he couldn't place a single face or name. Catching a brief pause before the next wave of cavalry arrived, he stepped to the side and questioned if he was falling victim to some sick joke. Wondering if at some point Ashton Kutcher was going to jump out from some secret lab and tell him how foolish he looked. That would have been a more favorable outcome. Instead, Tanner was forced to mingle with a group of money-hungry leeches.

There had been several times in his life that made him battle discomfort in social gatherings, but that night ranked at the top of the list. Not wanting to make a scene, he played along like a good sport. A chilled beverage never sounded so appealing. Tanner located the watering hole and was pleased to see an ice-cold bucket of Busch Light. Three cans quickly disappeared as he guzzled them in search of liquid courage. Over the years, Tanner had come to believe that there are several magical powers that Busch Light had to offer, but one trumps them all. They blend a secret ingredient into every batch that gives shy people the ability to dance. Although, it's a double-edged sword. The dosage must be consumed with meticulous accuracy, as the formula works on a bell curve. Polluting the bloodstream with the precise amount makes the consumer feel like Fred Astaire, but too much makes them better resemble Fred *Twinkle Toes* Flintstone. After the magical powers started to kick in, Tanner began enjoying the evening with a bunch of random acquaintances. He mingled through the crowd and saw a face he had not seen for many years. Judy took the liberty of inviting Stefanie and her partner Carmen.

"If it isn't Fefanie," he said as he approached the table. "I can hardly even recognize you with all that fancy ink."

She got up out of her chair and threw her arms around his shoulders. After a quick embrace, she stepped back and introduced Carmen.

"I've heard many great things about you, Carmen, especially your exquisite kissing ability," he said with a chuckle. "I'm just messing with you. Can I hug you? I'm kind of a hugger. Looking at this house might make you think differently, but believe you me, I get it. Rest assured that I hugged each and every one of these trees before they were set in place. I love them all like they are my children."

Carmen stood up and said, "I get it, I'll give you a hug."

Tanner capitalized on the moment and turned a brief hug into a long-drawn-out romantic embrace, attempting to make the situation more awkward for Carmen than himself. As he swayed from side to side, he questioned his mother's sanity for inviting his high school sweetheart and her partner. Tanner rambled about how long he had waited for the opportunity to be introduced to the infamous, Carmen. He was thrilled he was to finally meet 'The One." Enough time had passed for her to see the humor in his bizarre behavior, so she cleverly maneuvered her way out of his clenches.

Judy was having a delightful time, being surrounded by all her old friends felt like a reunion. Tripp huddled in the corner with his crew and smoked fine cigars, as the dance party was well underway. Tanner returned to the beer trough to refuel, before pulling Stefanie and Carmen onto the dance floor. For a tall skinny kid, Busch Light worked wonders on his dancing skills. The three of them danced in the center of the floor and began attracting others to join. As inappropriate as it was for Judy and Tripp to launch this surprise party mission on the first weekend in his new home, it turned out to be a great event. Tanner stood in the driveway and said his goodbyes to his new, "old" friends as they headed for their vehicles.

Stefanie and Carmen walked up to him and congratulated him on his new home.

As they embraced with a final hug, Stefanie whispered in his ears, "I will always love you Tanner Skilli. I never stopped. You are one of the good guys in this world."

Stefanie's words hit home with him, but he knew that ship had sailed many moons ago. The night set him free of her in a mysterious way and banished his suppressed heartache.

Walking back to his porch, Tanner looked up into the star-filled sky and was thankful that his heart was completely free from Stefanie. The catering crew was busting their humps trying to clean up the party debris. Tanner couldn't help but pitch in and become one of the crew. At first, the workers looked at him as their boss, until they realized he was just trying to do his part. He made them feel like equals and not just a servant to the wealthy. Tanner loved his life and wanted to share in the joy with others. He believed people should always be kind because they never know whose mercy they are going to be under in their greatest time of need.

20

DON'T GET CAUGHT WATCHING THE PAINT DRY

The beeping of the heart monitor continued in a standard rhythmic pattern. His eyelids felt like fifty-pound weights were anchoring them down. A nurse's hand touched him on his left arm as he reentered the world. Water was all he could think about. His mouth was as dry as the Nubian Desert. Without enough saliva to swallow, it felt like he was choking on sand.

"Water. Water," he began to mumble to the stranger.

After three attempts, she could finally translate what he was saying and placed a small ice chip in his mouth. The ice dissolved like a snowflake in the sun.

"Water," he continued to beg. "Please, water."

Again she reached over and grabbed a small ice chip from the cup and placed it in his mouth.

Rather than asking, "What's a guy have to do to get a drink around this place?" his mind was in a fog and couldn't think beyond simply asking for more water. Whether it was protocol or not, she disregarded the severity of his mouth drought and continued to ration the ice chips.

Across the way, he could see what appeared to be the outline of a ghost hovering in a seated position. A thin white sheet was covering his body as well, but that did not discredit the paranormal sighting. The weight of his eyelids made them difficult to open completely for more than a few moments. At that point, it did not even matter much, as he could not focus on a single object. He overheard the nurse make a phone call, followed by a team of help rushing through the doors. Laying on his back, he felt as though he began floating down the hallway. Flashing blurs cruised by his head at an incredible rate, bearing resemblance to laying alongside a NASCAR race.

After being pushed into a dark cave of a room, the blurs began swarming around him.

"One, two, three, lift," the head nurse in charge ordered.

Floating once again, his body jostled back and forth before being placed on a fluffy cloud with metal rails. Nurses pulled back the sheets, exposing his legs, and began strapping him to the bed. Not for security reasons, but rather to secure the massaging pads to his legs to prevent blood clots from forming. In an anesthesia fog, Tanner glanced around the room trying to understand what in the world was happening. The number of questions racing through his head overwhelmed his mind. Nothing made sense to Tanner in the unfamiliar land with faceless beings touching a moving his body.

Nurses exited as quickly as they entered the room and the chaos came to an abrupt halt. Tanner lay on the hospital bed, hooked up to machines, and gazed at the intensive care unit ceiling. His body was wired to multiple contraptions making intermittent beeping and compression noises. A small tube draped over his ears and was inserted into his nasal passages, delivering a pure stream of oxygen. Several moments passed as he lay motionless in his room and listened to the melody of the machines. Tanner began to question if he was on life support and now at the mercy of modern-day technology to keep him alive. Doctor Lance reported to room 333 and informed Tanner he had just gotten out of surgery. Still partially sedated, he tried to comprehend what the doctor was saying. The room continued to slowly shift in a giant haze, as Tanner attempted to maintain eye contact like an active listener.

Crazy flashbacks to elementary and high school were the only memories Tanner could recall at the moment. His concussion made it difficult for him to understand the complexity of the surgery he had undergone. He was still trying to figure out who he was and why he was there in the first place. Dr. Lance informed Tanner that a large tumor had developed near his parietal lobe and they had to perform an emergency craniotomy. Ironically enough, the symptoms of the tumor were the direct path to its discovery after the fall.

The reason for Tanner's arrival at the hospital was due to a mauling that occurred during the third quarter of his basketball game. Tanner received the ball at the top of the arch and looked up to see a point guards' dream unfolding before his very eyes. Similar to Moses parting the Red Sea, a clear path formed down the heart of the key. Anxiously wanting to shake the defender, he utilized his ankle-breaking crossover and breezed around the defender with perfection. Knowing he was moments from blowing the roof off the house with a monster dunk, he barreled toward the hoop like a missile. From out of nowhere, the large 7' 2" center, weighing over 300 pounds and commonly referred to as "The Key," derailed his path and sent Tanner flying through the air. The sneaky-tumor had already begun affecting the mobility on his left side. When he attempted to brace his fall with his left leg, the message telling his body to move was delayed. Tanner's back smashed to the hardwood, followed by his head crashing down. The lead athletic trainer made the right call when he instructed them to ensure his brain was scanned once he arrived at the hospital. Had it not been for that serendipitous accident, the tumor would have killed him in less than three months.

Once he arrived at the hospital they immediately scheduled him for brain surgery to remove the tumor. Under sedation, they shaved his head with a razor and lathered it with rubbing alcohol. Doctor Lance made his primary incision above Tanner's right ear and worked the 10-blade through his scalp across to his left ear. A nurse stepped in to offer an extra set of hands to help peel back his scalp. She placed her glove-donned hand on the outer-edges while the doctor rolled his skin down to his neckline. The doctor then cut a two-inch by three-inch plate out of Tanner's skull. He described the tumor as being "Very well-fed." Dr. Lance was a man of very few words and thought he was being humorous when providing the narrative of the surgery.

The nurse made a circle with her thumb and pointer finger, charading that it was the size of a golf ball. As quirky and laconic as he was, Dr. Lance was a phenomenal surgeon. A craniotomy of such difficulty would normally last four hours from start to finish. It took less than three hours for a flawless execution. Even the precision of the staples they used to reconnect his flesh was exquisite. Doctor Lance and his team were true masters of their craft.

Morphine made life in the hospital more enjoyable, the magical red button allowed Tanner to self-administer his pain medication. It also gave him a chronic dry mouth he couldn't remedy. Each time a nurse would visit the room, he would politely ask for a different flavor of juice. Not wanting to appear high-maintenance, he used an assortment of accents to soft-pedal the requests.

"I'd love a pint of the hospital's finest cranberry juice. I haven't given that one a whirl yet. I like to think that variety is the spice of life. Am I right or am I right? I think my good buddy Benjamin Franklin said that. That's how he got his gorgeous face on the one-hundo," he said like a Scotsman.

While unconscious, the nurses had inserted a catheter into his manhood, making trips to the restroom unnecessary. With an open tab and a full juice bar, he had zero shame asking for the drinks to keep coming.

Tanner's memory slowly began to resurface, but was still handicapped by the heavy drugs working their way through his polluted organs. There were blank spots of time he could not recall, putting him in a mental state of discomfort. He felt as though he had traveled through time and missed out on a significant event of his life. While the nurses weren't big sports fans, they were overly accommodating to his needs regardless. No one had been able to articulate what actually happened to land him in a hospital bed. All the nurses' information about the incident was strictly hearsay. Scarce snippets of information were all they had to go off of. They knew he had fallen during a basketball game and rocked his head on the hardwood floor. A routine CAT scan found a huge brain tumor that got him a fast-pass to the operating room. Beyond knowing he was a player in the NBA, they were more or less guessing and did not know many factual details.

Night one in the hospital was uncomfortable, especially when Tanner was woken up by a needle being jammed in the bend of his right arm to take blood work. Unfortunately, constant chatter from the hallway and the nurses' station did not contribute to encourage deep sleep. Much to his great fortune, Tanner received exquisite care from a phenomenal nurse named Kathy. Her room presence naturally put him at ease making him instantly grateful to see her refreshing smile.

During her morning rounds, Nurse Kathy stopped in to check on his fifty-four staples arching from ear to ear. She pulled back

Tanner's surgery cap and began lightly touching his bald scalp. His Hollywood hair had been shaved away before surgery. Kathy asked Tanner if he would like to see the war wound as she grabbed a small mirror. A strong resemblance to Frankenstein's monster was seen looking back at him with disgust.

Nurse Kathy encouragingly said, "Not trying to downplay it, but I have seen a lot worse. Our bodies are incredible machines that are constantly regenerating and healing. Enjoy your gnarly war-wound while it lasts. Plus, you were blessed with a perfectly shaped head. No reason to keep it from the world the see."

On her way out the door, Kathy turned on the television mounted in the corner of the hospital room. Knowing he was a sports guy, she changed the channel to Sports Center and put the remote back at his bedside. Less than ten seconds later they began replaying the clip of Tanner versus The Key. The video made it very apparent that Tanner's legs were unresponsive when he took flight. The shots were difficult to watch as he began witnessing his career fall to the ground.

Seeing the fear in Tanner's eyes, Kathy wisely said, "Good or bad, hard to say," before exiting the room.

"What the heck is that supposed to mean?" he asked audibly. "How could this possibly be a good thing?"

Everything he had worked for was lost, causing his internal rage to ignite with a desire for competition. No NBA team was going to let a liability like him step on the court again. He pushed the morphine button repeatedly until his body began to numb his hurting soul.

Tanner could overhear a small commotion in the hallway. Shortly after, Judy appeared in his room. She rushed over to him and gave him a bear hug.

"Oh, Sweetie. It will be okay. Momma is here, son. Your Momma is here," she said, "I tried to tell the doctor that I was going to wheel you out of this joint, but they said it was against the law or something like that."

Tanner thought, *That explains the commotion in the hall. Thanks a lot, Mom.*

"Where is your father?" Judy asked looking around the room, knowing well his flight home from Australia had been delayed.

Two nurses came into the room and asked Judy to kindly take a seat. The older nurses provided him with instruction on how to care for the wound and things they should be aware of during rehab. Both nurse Chi and Nurse Babs were seasoned veterans and were vastly informative. Tanner was grateful for them speaking his language. They didn't try to toss in a bunch of medical terminologies that would only confuse him, a tendency many doctors embraced. They were not there to impress him with their knowledge, but rather to educate him properly. Following their demonstrations, they asked if he had any questions before saying goodbye.

"I think I've got it covered ladies. I appreciate all the help. Your entire staff here has been so incredibly accommodating. I cannot thank you enough," he said sincerely.

Nurse Chi said, "Tanner, I know you've been enjoying not having to get up, but we have to take it out. The nurses said you elected to keep it in, but I don't think you understand the risks of keeping it in. Your body is going to get used to it and will forget how to pee voluntarily. In short, you'll have to pee out of a tube for the rest of your life."

She saw the acknowledging looking in his eyes as he nodded in understanding.

The bell to toe the line was ringing, as nurse Chi leaned out in the hallway and called for intern Nicole. Judy began informing Tanner on their plans following his discharge from the hospital. Mid-sentence, Judy stopped and looked at the breathtaking sight in the doorway. Nurse Nicole walked in and stole the show.

Where has this angel been all my life? Tanner asked himself. She was absolutely stunning in every way.

Tanner was always fascinated by the impression one's voice could make and how it could drastically impact a first impression. Nicole's sweet and comforting voice only added to her goddess-like beauty. When she introduced herself, both Tanner and Judy sat in amazement and didn't listen to a single word. Judy was thinking about all of the beautiful grandchildren they could have running around. Tanner was also thinking about all the beautiful grandchildren he would like this woman to bless upon his mother. Nurse Chi asked Judy if she would mind waiting in the hall for a few minutes. Hoping it was a conjugal visit, she swiftly got up from her chair and made her way out the door.

Nurse Chi informed Tanner they were going to be removing his catheter and asked if it was okay that Nurse Nicole gave it a try.

"A try?" he gruffly questioned.

"She's a nursing student and needs some hands-on practice. She's top of her class, and you know I am always looking out for you," nurse Chi replied with a grin.

Tanner was stuck squandering in a mental pickle. Nurse Nicole was the most beautiful woman he had ever encountered face to face and he knew the definitive destruction of any future romance would soon be lost. To the best of his romance novel recollection, there has never been a love story that blossomed from a female pulling out a tube penetrating down into a urethra. Being hopped up on drugs and the lack of showering didn't improve his chances of the more favorable outcome he wishfully desired.

Wanting to give Nicole and Tanner some space, nurse Chi stepped out into the dim-lit hallway to wait with Judy. The odds of a conjugal visit were improving, but those hopes were short-lived. Nurse Nicole positioned herself on the left side of his bed and pulled around the equipment tray. She grabbed an empty syringe before pulling back the white sheet. Tanner was less than pleased with the *big reveal* and accepted he would not be nominated for the "Best in Show" award.

Resisting her sorority impulses, Nicole remained professional. Everything aside from inadvertently brushing her pointer finger across his sad balls when she was getting situated. Tanner took the kind gesture as a way to take his mind off the pain he was about to endure. The slight touch of her delicate finger led to an uncontrollable flexing of his member. His hangdogged manhood distracted the nurse as it resembled a malnourished beached whale foundering. Nurse Nicole quickly regained her refocus.

"I can't take it out if you are aroused. Sorry about that," she said while gazing up with her bright blue eyes.

The mixed emotions swirled through his mind as he struggled to cast aside inappropriate thoughts. *Just don't do anything stupid,* he thought to himself.

Nicole attached the device to the tube and began adjusting the valves.

"At the end of this thing is a little balloon filled with saline solution. Believe it or not, I have heard that some guys who are jacked up on drugs and alcohol try ripping their catheters out. Can you imagine the irreparable damage?" she asked while looking up at Tanner's fearful face.

"Please make sure to get all of the saline out before giving it a yank," he said with a noticeable quiver in his voice.

Extracting the fluid with poise and grace, Nurse Nicole made certain the balloon was fully evacuated. She removed the syringe from the Foley before placing it back on the tray.

"You ready for this?" she asked as she wrapped her left hand around his now flaccid penis.

All Tanner could think about was trying to resist the temptation of breaking into a modified rendition of, "Hey Nicky, you're so fine you're so fine you blow my mind." Using her right hand, she slowly started to retract the tube from the tip of his penis, sending an intense sensation through his veins. Tanner was left speechless and uncertain of whether or not the experience was torture or pleasure. Not knowing how to handle such dominating emotions, he tilted his head back searching for an answer from above.

Had the event been broadcast on national television or radio, the announcers would have shouted, "Duck for cover! Tanner Skilli's new handle is 'Old Faithful.'" As the tube made its final exit, a golden stream anxiously awaited and was ready to follow freely behind. Feeling completely trapped in a position of no control, Tanner shot out a golden burst that brazed the top of Nurse Nicole's forehead. Too focused on the task at hand, she could not turn away in time to dodge the erupting penile geyser.

"Oh my gosh! I am so sorry—, so incredibly sorry," Tanner began to plea.

"That is a perfectly natural reaction," she said as she wiped the dripping urine from her forehead. "Those practice dummies are nothing like the real thing. I should have expected something like that to happen."

It was time to call the time of death on them being a future married couple with gorgeous babies. Despite Tanner's embarrassment over the incident, Nicole was a great sport about the dismal blooper. Although not as heartbroken as Tanner, she too understood their paths' would never intentionally cross again. Luckily for Tanner, the shame of the moment only lasted up until he was wheeled out of the hospital doors a few days later.

For his rehabilitation, Judy hand-picked a medical team to camp out at her home until Tanner recovered. After several days of captivity in the hospital, he was discharged and flown to Wellington, California. The medical team was amazing but they were a little handsy and almost too helpful for Tanner's liking. He didn't require any additional assistance and felt like a child when they insisted on helping him stand up. Anytime he attempted to be even mildly self-reliant, they sprinted to his side as if they were attempting to rescue him from his own self. His annoyance continued to strengthen after the second day as their nervous hovering intensified. At one point he may have inadvertently cursed a few profound words when they were cleaning his open wound with hydrogen peroxide. The burning sensation felt like his head was having lava poured into his flesh. His large bottle of pain pills could only do so much to soothe his agony.

Not a moment had passed without being under some sort of pain-numbing substance, ever since he awoke in the hospital. There was a lingering discomfort in Tanner's neck he couldn't shake. Occasionally, his trapezoids would rapidly begin to twitch before shooting jolts through his spine. Otherwise, the pain in his body was tolerable. Regardless of his aches, Tanner continued to pop pills religiously. He justified to himself he wanted to stay ahead of the pain to prevent any overwhelming agony from potentially settling in. Snapping at the medical staff was very uncharacteristic of his typical behavior, the pills had begun to transform his social conduct.

The rehabilitation sessions with the trainer were Tanner's most frustrating days of the week. Tanner had been an athlete his entire life and put in the effort it takes to play at the professional level. Losing control over his left arm and leg was a challenge he never thought he would have to cope through. To add insult to injury, he began receiving calls from sponsor representatives inquiring about how he was doing. They must have all been reading from the same script. They would ask about his expected recovery, pretending to care, and then promptly mention that they were going to need a doctor's release allowing him back on the court.

Feeling upset already, the purified opium running through his veins only worsened the situation. Tanner began to snap at the medical staff over the smallest issues and grew increasingly impatient with the sponsors. The motivation of playing in the league seemed to be the only thing to help him suffer through the monotony of rehab drills. Tanner felt at times as if his mind was playing tricks on itself. One side refusing to send the proper signals to his legs, while the other side was becoming increasingly unresponsive. Additionally, his cardiovascular levels were still at an elevated status, providing further confirmation that his mind and body were not firing on all cylinders. The only way he knew to calm himself down was to continually have the painkillers within arm's reach.

21

GOOD GUY GREG

After three weeks of being home in Wellington, Tanner took a flight back to Denver to meet with the team's executive staff. He wore a classic top hat and his favorite suit to the meeting. The mood in the room was somber after the initial formal introductions. The chairman of the staff informed Tanner that they would no longer be able to keep him on the Denver Nuggets' payroll. An assistant placed a 15-page legal document on the table in front of him as the chairman continued to explain the reason for making the move. The document contained all the fine print about the grounds for terminating his contract early and the details about the compensation he would receive as a severance package. Tanner removed his top hat and exposed his ear to ear incision. He pleaded to the staff to let him prove that he is ready to get back on the court and win them a national championship. They applauded his enthusiasm, but the decision was final. As the meeting adjourned a member of the staff, Greg Blanchard, pulled Tanner aside.

"I know that look Mr. Skilli. You are battling some serious demons right now and trying to navigate through difficult waters, but you have got to get clean," he said. Tanner turned away in disregard of the unwarranted advice. "I can tell by the glazed over look in your eyes. Judging by the way you don't want to listen to me, you know I'm right, but you refuse to admit it to me or yourself."

Greg placed his hand on Tanner's shoulder, but Tanner shrugged it off and exited the room.

Greg had experienced the same addiction, which cost him a life of happiness with his family. During a few of his episodes, under the influence, he left a deep destructive path. His wife said she was fearful for her life and the safety of their three children, so she packed them up and he never saw or heard from them again. There were two paths he could have taken, and he chose the path to get help for his addiction. When they first moved out he felt a sense of relief. The burden of having to care for others had been lifted. No one would ask anything of him and life in solitude appeared to be a life of great bliss. Week one passed and the feeling of guilt began to set in. He began to psycho-dial his wife, but she knew better than to answer. She had fallen for his manipulative antics too many times to attempt to reason with him. Pain pills no longer gave him the escape from life that he so desperately craved. Jack Daniels became Greg's newfound friend. From sun up to sun down he continued to pollute his body and try to set his soul at ease.

On night three of a binge, Greg was ready to cash in all his chips. Standing on his office chair, with a noose securely tightened around his neck, he said his last goodbye. With his right leg, he pushed the chair out from beneath him. All 195 pounds of him dropped to the floor. His bound-head smashed to the ground, knocking him unconscious. Nearly thirty minutes passed before he began to flutter his eyes. It was a combination of being concussed and passed out simultaneously. When he peeled his head from the drool covered floor, he looked up to see the beam he had secured the end of the rope to. The sturdy beam had been shattered into pieces. Physics could not explain the miracle. There is no logical explanation for a perfectly good piece of solid lumber to shatter under the force of a middleweight man. Greg took it as a sign from God and surrendered his pride to get help. After assessing the strength of the wood, which had been shattered by divine intervention, Greg rededicated his life to the Lord.

After getting clean and getting his life back in order, he thought about offering an olive branch to his wife and kids but knew it was hopeless. He can remember it vividly. During the last episode they had to witness, he saw an unforgiving look in her eyes. She knew she was going to leave and never look back. Greg wrote apology letters to each of his children and fully funded all of their colleges once he worked his way up the corporate ladder. However great his life may have been after being rebuilt, the regret of destroying a happy family was a regret he was forced to live with for all eternity. Greg prayed that Tanner would not follow that same life-altering path and make the mistakes he did with his life.

Tanner's phone began to ring off the hook before he could reach his car at Nugget's headquarters. The sponsors who once wined and dined him were severing ties. When money is involved, there is no vacancy for loyalty. Sadly, the only calls he received for the next week were disparaging. Calls from "friends" came to an abrupt stop once they found out he would no longer receive his hefty salary. Sob stories began to replay in his mind from all the times that so-called friends would reach out. After signing his new contract old buddies were coming out of the woodwork asking for handouts. All saying the same thing about how times were tough and they could barely put food on the table. Out of guilt, Tanner would always send them money. He figured if they were willing to swallow their pride and ask for a handout, times had to be extremely difficult.

Being that he had the financial wherewithal to make sure children were getting fed, he would oblige their distraught requests. Later to see them on MySpace with their new car or boats. They were nothing but leeching posers. He sat staring at a blank wall, and a hurt began to take over. There wasn't a single soul in the world he was associated with through something other than financial ties. As the days continued, the revelation grew clearer. His phone stopped ringing as he spent the days wandering carelessly around his huge house. With no calls coming in, Tanner began thinking no one cared enough to pick up the phone to ask how he was feeling. Physically, he was not *feeling* much of anything, largely in part to the recent dose of pills.

Mentally, however, was a different story. The world was dark. He could no longer find joy in the things he once loved. Watching Sports Center only worsened the situation, but he continually fought the urges to change it to that painstaking channel. Flipping through the other channels seemed worthless. Reruns of Maury Povich were the only shows he found intriguing. The suspense of finding out which one of these three skaters was the father of this outspoken girl's baby was fascinating.

Flashbacks of his most dramatic life experience began casting a dark shadow over his thoughts. Three months following the night on the town with Dermot, Tanner found himself in the middle of a crazy state of affairs. During the game against the Boston Celtics, Tanner continued to receive cheap shots from an egomaniac point guard named Tyson Vernon. It was clear that Tyson had some sort of beef with Tanner, but it was unbeknownst to Tanner as to the reason. As the players made their way into the locker room for halftime, Tyson lunged with his shoulder and knocked Tanner to the ground.

"Don't ever try to get in the way of me and my family. Stay the fuck away from my girl, or I will slit your throat in your sleep. You ain't no fucking man. You're a sackless fraud, Skilli," Tyson threatened standing over him.

Tanner looked up and tried to defuse the situation.

"I honestly have no idea what you are talking about, man. You've got the wrong guy," he said as his teammates came to his rescue and pulled Tyson away.

It took three players and two security guards to contain him and escort him to the locker room to cool off.

Tanner was confused, to say the least. *Classic case of mistaken identity,* he thought to himself. If nothing else, it gave the reporters something to micro-analyze. Sure enough, those bottom-feeding media researchers were able to get the full scoop before the game was over. Promptly after the final buzzer, the assistant coach pulled Tanner into a media room.

He grabbed him by the jersey, and looked him directly in the eyes, "You're going to want to see this."

They shut the door and began playing the breaking news story. As fate would have it, Astra had announced to the world that she was having Tanner's baby.

"That's impossible," he thought. His voice trailed off as he mumbled, "I thought she said she was on birth control and was going to take the morning-after pill as a precaution."

The coach turned his eyes away from the screen and repositioned them towards Tanner.

"You know this woman? Did you know that she has a child with Tyson Vernon and two more children with former players?"

All of the blood rushed from his head and Tanner became pale as a ghost.

"I would barely say I know her, we're acquaintances at best. She invited herself back to my apartment and we had some wild shower sex. That's the extent of what I know, or remember, about her."

The coach shook his head and said, "Shit Skilli, you know how these loose legs can be. They are like money devouring piranhas. I'll get our PR damage control team together, and we'll get this all worked out. Just try to keep it in your pants unless you truly know the broad."

At the time they discovered the brain tumor, Astra was in her third trimester. As Tanner watched the Maury Povich reveals, he questioned to himself, *How am I expected to one day tell my unborn child that they were the product of a night at a comedy strip club?*

He figured it was one step up from being the result of a camp dare. As if he didn't have any other life issues to deal with, aside from losing the job of his dreams, having a shaved head with a huge gash across the middle, fake friends, and being completely alone in a house he will no longer be able to afford.

Tanner began pacing back and forth between the kitchen and the living room. He looked down at his right forearm and honed in on the .44 caliber bullet.

"It only takes one," he said audibly as if the tattoo was going to talk back.

He grabbed the orange bottle of pills and shook a few into his palm. A nice cold Busch Light did the trick to wash them down. After pounding the remainder of the beer, he cranked up the surround sound stereo and began blaring Van Halen. He called upon the Busch Light Gods to come to his rescue when dry mouth from the pills began setting in. Busch Light was the miracle cure. Not only did it cure his dry mouth, but it also helped chase away the nasty taste of Scotch that he was chugging straight from the bottle.

Internal pain weakened his soul with each word of Eddie Van Halen echoing in his ears. He had lived a great life and it was all downhill from that point forward. Haunting memories stirred up past emotions and guilt. He allowed the darkness to take over and force the happiness aside. Reflecting on his life, he could only recount the bad times and struggles. His hyper-focus on the worse times overshadowed any good memories. Sure there had been ups and downs over the years. Compared to the vast majority of the world, his life was nothing shy of amazing. Beyond his childhood, he had lived the life of privilege. Not ever really having to deal with anything catastrophic made him oblivious to his great fortune.

Searching for a permanent solution to a temporary problem, Tanner stumbled down the hallway and grabbed the trusty Bulldog .44 Special revolver. Knowing well that it had the single round in it, he still popped the cylinder to the side to confirm. It was time for him to hang up his towel and put an end to all the hurt, guilt, and internal pain. With his right hand on the grip, he locked the cylinder into place with his left hand and spun it downward. Looking out his large bedroom window, his reflection looked back at him. He shook his head in disappointment and placed the barrel in his mouth and bit down on the steel. His heart was racing and he was on the verge of hyperventilating. Even though he stood with a gun in his mouth, the fear of suffocation made his breathing intensify. Saliva started pouring down the side of his chin as he continued to struggle. A sweaty palm gripped the revolver as he placed his finger on the trigger. He took a calming, deep breath and locked the hammer into position with his right thumb. Upon exhaling, he squeezed the trigger until it clicked.

The room fell silent. Tanner continued to close his eyes and then slowly removed the revolver from his mouth and tossed it on his bed. Staring at his reflection, he was at a loss.

"If it's not my time, then what am I supposed to do with my life?" he asked, challenging the universe for an answer.

Standing motionless, he could no longer bear the weight of his body. Tanner dropped to the floor and laid on his back. It had been a least twelve minutes since his last dose of pain medicine, so he reached down into his pocket and pulled out the bottle. Pushing himself up with his left arm, he sat up to avoid choking. Unscrewing the cap, he tossed a few pills into the back of his mouth, attempting to numb the empty pit where his soul once inhabited.

He laid back down and let the opiates go to work. Before long the easy release from the medication slipped into a dream. That night, as Tanner lay on the floor, he explored the wonders of being a family man. He envisioned a life of pure happiness with the love of his life. The light in his life had slowly been able to pierce through the darkness. It was all too clear what his intended purpose was meant to be. Oddly enough, he saw a life beyond basketball.

22

GET UP

A wakening out of a deep sleep, Tanner gasped for air as he slowly opened his eyes. *There is more in store for me in this life. I just have to dig deep*, he thought to himself. The pill cocktails had put him down for the count. Gingerly separating his body from the wet floor, he became disgusted with himself. The putrid odor confirmed his suspicion that he had used the floor as a lavatory at least once. Although, at the moment, lying in his own urine was the least of his concerns.

Tanner rose to his feet for brief moments before taking a seat on any object that would hold his weight. Sitting down he stared aimlessly at the floor as his mind tried to reboot. Ashamed to return to his bedroom, he headed for the guest room. Realizing his brush with death was more than just a dream, a grave panic stirred in his mind. Even in his fog, his brain instantly resorted back to his memories of his prior attempts. Tanner was ashamed that he lacked the mental strength to break the pattern.

Trying to sort through his emotions, Tanner grabbed his journal from the hallway stand. The fearful adrenaline high made him grip the journal with the strength of Ares. As he flipped through to find an empty page, a small note floated to the floor. Tanner's heart was nearly bursting out of his chest as he rushed anxiously to get his thoughts on paper. He picked the folded note up in haste, thinking it was one more unnecessary distraction.

The folded note was a scratch paper Annika tore from the corner of her notebook the first day they met in science lab. The ink had faded mostly, but Tanner could still make out her phone number. Just the thought of her put him at ease, but he figured that horse had left the barn. She was probably married and had a least four kids by now.

Tanner's hands fell to his side as his blood pressure began to stabilize. Recalling the run on the beach with Annika, made him suddenly thirsty. Fortunately, he had his beer of choice stockpiled in the fridge. Many of the high-brow patrons at U of O frowned upon his preference in malt liquor. Tanner's grandfather always told him, "If you are drinking beer from another man's refrigerator, you can judge him on the temperature of the beer, but never the variety." It was the only wisdom from his grandfather Tanner carried through life.

While holding the note between his thumb and middle finger, Tanner tipped the beer back and let the light-bodied blend of malt and corn cascade down his throat. The uncertainty of Annika's whereabouts mystified him. At that point, there really wasn't much dignity left for him to lose. Curiosity compelled Tanner to grab his flip-phone and slowly dial the number scribbled down on the note. On the second ring, she picked up.

"This is Annika," he heard from the angelic voice on the other end.

Prior to dialing, he was hyper-focused on getting the numbers correct and neglected to formulate a game plan.

He stammered, trying to find his words, "Hey, Annika. It's been a while. Remember your old lab partner in crime?"

The cheerful tone of hear voice freed his nervousness.

"Of course. How could I ever forget my geoduck running buddy? You wouldn't believe how many times I have told stories about that weekend. How are you? Gosh, it's great to hear from you, Tanner."

Not knowing what to say, he started to ask weather related questions. Annika hesitantly intervened, "We are just getting to dinner with some friends. Can I give you a call tomorrow?"

His head dropped forward with disappointment.

Trying to remain positive, he said, "Yeah, you bet. I don't really have much going on tomorrow. Drop me a line if you have a few minutes to spare."

The following morning was a painful one for the shell of a human that resembled Tanner Skilli. He had woken up face down on the master bathroom tile. His light grey shirt had brown stains streaming down the right side. Pants and a single sock were propping his head up as a makeshift pillow. Rolling onto his back, he stared up at the vaulted ceilings and let out a series of agonizing groans. Slow to get to his feet, he braced his arm on the side of the jetted tub and stumbled to one of the sinks. Reaching with his right hand, he turned on the cold water and then cupped his hands beneath the steady stream. He doused his face repeatedly while imagining he was part of an Oil of Olay commercial. Waiting for his body to snap back to normal, he began growing impatient. An angry glare stared back from the mirror. The poisons and trauma his body endured the night before were going to take more than a few splashes of water to recover.

Although his house paled in comparison to that of most professional athletes, it was a vast improvement from the trailer park back in Casper, Wyoming. On that morning, his house felt empty as he wandered into the kitchen. The granite countertops were scattered with various beer cans and tornado aftermath of random garbage and torn paper. As he began chugging the second pint of water, he was reminded of a shirt that said, "How can I be this thirsty, when I drank so much last night?" It was such a damn good question! Six ounces in, Tanner began hearing the copious amounts of fluid slosh back and forth in his stomach.

It was just after 11 a.m. when he managed to choke down a bowl of Honey Nut Cheerios. Even the thought of any other food led him to dry-heave. After plopping down on the couch, he flipped on ESPN to catch up on all the sports drama. For a show that was founded on the premise of highlighting sports, it sure had become more of a soap opera, focused on exploiting the negative side of sports. The news script had been flipped, and the focus of the topic was drastically different. They used to primarily broadcast sports, and then tossed in a few blurbs about dramatic events that were non-sports related. The athlete's personal lives, opinions, and locker room drama had become the frontrunner of the "sports" segments. Actual sports and appreciation for the games had become the byproduct.

The same stories began to recycle and knocked Tanner out of his daze. When he realized he could commentate on the next segment, he knew he had to get up and do something before his brain rotted to absolute mush. As he got up off the couch, he heard faint vibration coming from the kitchen. It was intermittent so he crouched to make the counter at ear level. He traced the mysterious sound to the back of the silverware drawer. Precisely where he kept his bottle opener. The vibrating stopped as he lifted up the phone and flipped it open. It was Annika, but he didn't make it in time. The dark hardwood floors creaked beneath his pacing bare feet. He took a deep breath and pushed the button to call her back.

Annika picked up on the second ring, and with a Charlie's Angels voice said, "Good morning Mr. Skilli."

A sudden weight was lifted from his shoulders at just the sound of her sweet voice.

"Good morning to you as well. Sorry to interrupt your dinner. I was flipping through an old journal and the scratch paper with your number fell out. It's been a minute since we last spoke and I was curious what you were up to these days," he said.

"Well, I'm glad you did. I don't have the luxury of keeping people updated on my life via ESPN," she said with a chuckle.

"I assure you, it's no luxury," Tanner said. "Having people hang on to your every word, and twisting the truth is part of professional sports that they don't prepare you for in college. I wish I could just live up in the mountains in a quiet cabin, away from all the world's drama. Don't get me wrong, there is a certain sense of pride that you feel when the fans are cheering you on, but boy is their loyalty shallow. They praise you in one breath and curse you in the next."

He stared blankly at the floor as the sounds of angry shouting fans echoed through his head.

Realizing his negativity was beginning to tailspin, he shifted gears.

"So how was dinner with Luke last night?" he asked.

"Oh, I was out with some of my girlfriends. We like to meet up every month for dinner at this little Mediterranean restaurant downtown. They have the best vegetarian dishes in Steam Boat. You should definitely put it at the top of your bucket list. Maybe more toward the bottom now that I think about it. The world is filled with many more experiences to be enjoyed first," she said with a smile he could hear through the receiver.

There seemed to be an odd reluctance in her voice as she spoke of the wonders in the world that must be explored. Her dreams had been suppressed by the corporate world and she discovered she had lost sight of who she wanted to be in life.

Hearing Tanner's voice allowed Annika to remember back to her carefree college days when the world was her oyster. She missed talking to Tanner about random topics and laughing with each other over tiny life events. Even though he would forgive her in a heartbeat, Annika felt like she had let Tanner down with the engagement to Luke.

After graduation, Annika took a marketing job with Nike and was relocated to a satellite branch of the company in Steamboat Springs, Colorado. It was shortly after they broke free from the shackles of their old marketing company. They were the ones that came up with the legendary phrase "Just Do It." Nike felt the marketing company stopped being progressive and forced them to take the efforts in-house. Tanner's ears perked up when he heard she was on the marketing team.

Tanner always had, what he believed to be, a great idea for Nike's next campaign. Even though he was sponsored by them, no one was ever willing to listen.

"Annika, I know you don't tell me how to play basketball, but can I give you a suggestion? Take it as you will. It's something that I always thought would be a perfect campaign and product line for Nike. If you don't like it, throw it right back," he said with determination.

"Sure, what do you got? Who am I to stand in the way of a vision?" she appeased him.

Setting the scene, Tanner began, "Picture a commercial with a Title Fight in the twelfth round. The defending champion takes a solid right hand to the jaw, sending him back against the ropes and collapsing to the canvas. It is the boxer's defining moment in his career. He has won every round up to that point and just needs to get to his feet before the final bell. The champion's corner and the entire arena starts chanting, 'Get Up! Get Up,' as he stumbles to his feet in just the nick of time.

The next frame, a mother goes to wake her son up for morning practice. She says, 'It's time to get up!' A series of clips play depicting athletes rising before dawn for military-style training. Each athlete enduring pain and agony, as sweat streams down their bodies, followed by the athletes holding up trophies from their respective sports. The screen goes black and the voiceover says, 'If you want to make something of your life, you must first Get Up.' Then bold white letters fade into the black background, and 'Get Up' appears on the screen, followed by a swish sweeping in from left to right," he paused trying to catch his breath.

After a moment he continued, "You could then have the 'Nike

Get Up 1.0' shoes and then have a 'My Get Ups' website for people to post pictures of everywhere they have traveled in their shoes. Rather than the Nike I.D.'s, they could start customizing the shoes, so they would have a 'My Get Ups' individualized touch. There are so many different avenues it could take," he carried on.

"Wow, you have put some serious thought into this. It's actually quite impressive, Tanner. I'm not just saying that to make you feel better, it's a phenomenal idea with great potential," she said with sincerity. "If you don't mind, I'd like to bring it up with my team at next week's meeting."

She had always known he was more than just an athlete, but the depth and intelligence of Tanner Skilli never ceased to amaze her. She sat there for a moment and the scene of them running on the beach together started playing in her mind.

"That would be awesome, Annika. Worst case scenario, it gets shot down with the artillery of the US Marines. At least it will feel great to have my ideas heard. That way I don't have to keep carrying it around in my mind, wondering if it would have ever taken off," he said with an odd sense of relief.

"So how many ankle-biters are you chasing around these days?" he asked.

"We have five or six now, I think," she said.

"How can you not be sure how many kids you have? That should be the easiest number in the world to remember," he said.

"Oh, kids. That's funny. I thought you were talking about interns," she chuckled, "I don't have any kids. Heck, I'm not even married or dating for that matter. Work keeps me pretty busy. I've been working on getting a promotion for a few months now. It seems like each fiber of my being has been poured into work."

She stopped for a moment, as she reflected on how empty her life had been, other than the monthly dish of awful falafel. Even though it was her favorite dish, she always referred to it as being awful. Mostly because it is catchy, and fun to say. Even when she would be saying it to herself.

Following hearing "Not married," Tanner regaled his posture and his voice grew deeper. Warmth from his legs began creeping upwards to his already flushed face. Vasodilation sent shooting tingles through his body after receiving the momentous news.

"If you don't mind me asking, what happened with Lukie?" he asked, attempting to be playful and not pry too much.

"It just didn't work out. We started dating back in high school, you know. It was kind of the only life I knew. At the time I thought he was a great guy. That was until I got introduced to a new standard of man I wanted to be with for the rest of my life. Luke, just simply wasn't that, so I broke it off," she said without remorse.

Although filled with elation, Tanner sat there and stared at the floor. A flurry of questions swirled in his mind. He was so grateful to hear her voice, but he thirsted for more details about the aborted wedding. Knowing he could no longer carry the burden of curiosity, he had to ask in search of reconciliation. His heart had to unbury the truth.

"Annika, not trying to be too direct, but can I ask why you said yes when Luke proposed?" Tanner asked.

They sat in silence for a few painstaking moments before she replied.

"You know, it's a valid question. In fact, I've asked myself the same thing dozens of times. When I saw Luke getting down on one knee in Walmart, all I could think of was wearing a white wedding dress. The dream of having my makeup and hair done up like a princess, and experiencing a perfect day of my own, clouded the reality of the situation. The soup aisle should have been my first clue."

They both laughed as Tanner filtered the explanation. To understand the dreams of a female is an equation that even the world's top experts are unable to solve. It was a level of depth he didn't anticipate reaching when he initially made the call.

"Annika, it can't be easy talking about such an emotional event. You never cease to amaze me. Most women in your situation wouldn't have the courage to call it off. Once the wheels are in motion they feel like they are locked in the deal. I applaud you for staying true to yourself, even though there would unavoidably be backlash from people who are only self-serving."

Annika looked down at the single-line wave tattoo on her right ankle and thought, *dig deep, right?*

"Hey, I've got a great idea. Have you ever been to the Rocky Mountain National Park," she asked. "Would you be up for an adventure into nature today? You live in Denver don't you?"

Rising to his feet, he took a long stare at himself in the mirror. Sadly, he felt worse than he looked. And he looked like he had been punished by an insane Yeti.

"Oh. Well, I'm actually in Boulder. I think the park is just north of me, I'd totally be down. If you wouldn't mind making up a few sandwiches, I'll get a side dish or two along with some drinks," he said shifting his eyes from side to side.

It was all happening so fast with the conversation flowing much better than he had anticipated. For a moment, he began questioning if it were nothing more than a dream.

"You've got yourself a date," she said with excitement.

The two arranged a time and place to meet at the park.

Tanner was on the clock and had to pull it in gear if he wished to capitalize on the window of opportunity. Clumsily throwing on his running clothes, time appeared to be moving faster than usual. A quick loop, swoop and pull before he was out the door.

Coach Baugh once mentioned long runs allow the body to sweat out bad toxins and Tanner blindly believed those words wholeheartedly. Although fearing the toxicity might melt his skin he knew he must cleanse his body from the drugs and alcohol. It was time to put Coach Baugh's earthly wisdom to the ultimate test. Accepting the challenge, Tanner headed down the road. He made it no farther than the first bend before having to stop and purge. With the clock was ticking, he wiped his face on his sleeve and continued along the road.

"Get up, you sissy," he said under his breath.

As his sweat glands opened, the alcohol began pouring out in kegs. By mile three he had completed the loop and returned back to his front porch in just under twenty-three minutes. No thanks to the intermittent stops, his time made him feel like an old washed-out athlete. Dashing through the empty hallway, he scrambled for a cold Gatorade to extinguish his burning throat from dry-heaving.

Shower body sprayers proved their worth that day, as the hot water began blasting harsh oils from Tanner's skin. Scrubbing continued as he replenished his Martin Loofah King exfoliating glove with Old Spice Denali body wash. Slowly turning the shower handle, he paused before shutting it completely off. A rush of cold cascaded over his face as he looked up to the sky, sending a shock to his system. Never experiencing such a joyous pain, he forgot about being in a hurry and focused on controlling his body. Tanner forced himself to absorb the discomfort of the cold and resisted the urge to turn off the water immediately. Fighting through the struggle allowed him to refocus.

Sliding his left leg into his Columbia hiking pants was the easy part. Ever since the tumor was removed, his leg and arm would sporadically become unresponsive. As a result, his trust in allowing his left leg to bear weight had been lost. Paying it no attention, he stood proudly on a mission as he slipped his right leg in and fastened the button. The cold shower had exalted him and provided the courage to go win back the heart of the one that got away.

Turning the keys to the 4Runner, the mighty six-cylinder engine came to life as the ponies warmed up for their run. Tanner heard a faint phone ringing as the center console started to vibrate and rattle the loose change.

Before answering, he dropped his chin to his chest. Discouraging emotions erased the excitement of reuniting. The call could only mean one thing, Annika was canceling their first date. He reluctantly answered the phone to hear the surprising voice of the Denver Nuggets' Director of Public Relations.

"Mr. Skilli, Joseph here from the Nuggets' office. I've got good news and better news. The good news is that skank Astra popped out another kid. The better news is the little gremlin belongs to some third-round draft pick from the Phoenix Suns, Kyle Malinak," Joseph paused as he realized how uncouth his chosen delivery had come across. "I apologize if you were looking forward to becoming a father. I just wanted you to know that your number has not yet been called."

Tanner thanked him for the call and hung up.

Allowing the news to sink in, Tanner stared straight ahead at nothing. Relief from the burden he had been carrying around for the past months made him feel human again. Yet another bullet had been dodged and it was time for life to resume. Rolling the volume knob to the right, he cranked up the volume to the radio. Placing his Toyota into reverse, he slowly backed out of his driveway with a smile spanning from ear to ear. The words to TLC's "Don't Go Chasing Waterfalls" playing through his sound system had never been so profound. Tanner couldn't help but sing his own rendition in celebration as he headed for Colorado National Park.

23

OH MY!

Tanner arrived first at the Beaver Meadows visitor center in the early afternoon. The birds were chirping and calling back to his rumbling stomach. He had polished off his thirty-two-ounce Nalgene water bottle on the drive, but his body remained weak. Thankfully, there was no line to the men's room as he flung open the door in a hurry.

While washing his hands, he was hesitant to look up at his reflection. The energy from the morning shower had faded along the trip, but his heart reminded him it was time to get up and show Annika his true self. Rubbing his hands together he gave himself a quick pep talk before exiting the room.

In search of electrolytes, Tanner headed for the makeshift convenience store/gift shop. A friendly tap on his shoulder startled him as he reached into the beverage cooler positioned next to the post card stand. Tanner slid the glass door shut and anxiously turned around.

"Fancy meeting a big star like you here," Annika said with a huge smile.

She wrapped her arms around Tanner's neck, welcoming him back into her life as if he had returned from war. It was the most powerful embrace he had ever experienced, bringing some peace into his life.

Neither was embarrassed by the duration of their hug, wishing it never had to end. One of the green-vested volunteers killed the moment, as he shoved his way past them to get a blue Powerade from the cooler. Befuddled by the rude behavior, they looked at the old man, who was marching to the beat of his own drum.

Leading with an antagonizing tone the old man said, "How about you get a room and show some respect? It's uncouth in this part of the country to be handsy in public. You must not be from around heres are y'all?"

Releasing his arm from Annika's shoulder, Tanner collected his thoughts before addressing the man.

"Sir. I apologize for my poor judgment and meant no disrespect. I'm also sorry for the fact that out of all the options on display you chose Powerade, and the blue flavor at that. What are they teaching you kids these days? Personally, I find it difficult to trust a blue drink, or anything blue for that matter."

Before they had to resort to old fashioned fisticuffs, an elderly woman behind the counter came to their rescue and defused the challenge.

Briefly glancing at the cooler, Tanner remembered he had a full two liters of water in his hydration pack and a gold bottle of champagne with a spade on the bottle, figuring that should do the trick. He looked up and saw the green vests grumbling away.

"Have a good day, Sir," Tanner said as politely as possible.

Annika and Tanner looked at each other and smiled. "Old people, you gotta love 'em."

Tanner extended his hand, palm facing upward, and Annika obliged by slowly entwined her fingers with his.

Annika grabbed her food-filled pack and tossed it in the 4Runner. They were headed for one of the trailheads, but found themselves torn. Choosing between Ouzel Falls and Timberline Falls was like comparing beautiful with gorgeous. Both were spectacular, but Tanner campaigned for Ouzel Falls once his innards began doing Triple Pike flips. The hike up to the falls was less than three miles, as opposed to four up to Timberline Falls. He was praying his body could make the full round-trip.

Low visibility made it challenging, but they found the trailhead and backed into an empty parking spot. Tanner and Annika cinched their packs as they breathed in the upslope foggy air.

"It looks like there's going to be dew on the trail. Do you want me to grab an extra pair of gaiters?" Tanner asked before closing the back hatch.

Annika pointed down to her ankles, displaying her green Mountain Hardwear gaiters, the University of Oregon edition.

"A woman after my own heart. I must confess, when it comes to athletic gear, I'm Nike, all in. For outdoor gear, I can't get enough Columbia and Mountain Hardwear. There is no rhyme or reason, but all I know is my closet has a bulk of their inventory," he said while doing his final gear checks.

"We share a guilty pleasure. One of the perks of having awesome friends, is getting a pass to the employee store when I'm back in Portland. It is truly a love-hate relationship. I'm ashamed to say it, but there is a good chance my wardrobe I have acquired over the years could clothe all of the homeless communities in Oregon," she said turning toward the trail.

Once they began their hike only a few words were spoken, yet neither felt awkward with the silence. They both were simply content being in each other's company. Taking in the sounds of the wind brushing off the trees gave them time to sort out their emotions. Being back together was all too surreal. Annika had wondered if it was ludicrous to feel such deep emotions for a guy she hadn't seen in years. Tanner was more focused on keeping his fluids down, not wanting to waste his cherished time with her. Glancing back to see Annika's smiling face was the needed reminded of how thankful he should be for his life.

Pulling her camera out of her pocket, Annika stealthy positioned herself to capture a herd of bighorn sheep. She was in awe of their beauty and drawn to their massive spiral horns. Annika was happy to share the planet with such larger mammals that are equipped to fight for their territory, so long as they didn't attack her.

"Psst, Tanner. Psst," she loudly tried to whisper. "Look over here. Psst, Skilli."

Resorting to ancient communication, she picked up a small stone and threw it at him. Dumbfounded, Tanner looked up from the dirt path and turned back. Directing his eyes with the point of her finger, Tanner looked right, out into the field. Locking eyes with an adult ram was unexpected and terrifying. Tanner shifted his feet, assuming a moto-dachi stance, and instinctively placed his hand over the Kershaw pocket knife clipped into his side. On the side of his pack he carried a large canister of bear spray, but he thought it would be absolute overkill for the situation. Deeming them as harmless, Tanner and Annika were allowed to trespass on the land. The sheep worked the camera like they were auditioning for National Geographic. The still-frames would later be their minds gateway to help them remember the wonderful moments in their life together.

Tragedy struck when they reached the Wild Basin sign. Tanner's straw to his water pack was only producing trickles at a time, leaving him in dire need of some H2O and severe light-headedness. The sun was beating down on his back with greater force than usual, wearing down on the remaining grit left in his body. Without warning, his eyes began to flutter sending flickers of black and white before he collapsed face down on the trail. Annika looked around and began yelling for help at the top of her lungs, triggering the sheep to scatter up the mountainside. She was heard by a young Cub Scout coming down the trail, who convinced his Den Leader there was a woman in distress.

Annika rolled Tanner over to his back and checked to see if he was breathing. She continued to call for help until she heard a man's voice drawing near. Tanner's hot breath blasted her in the face as she leaned forward, providing some comfort that he wasn't dead. Den Leader Dan arrived with a dozen young boys in tow. Annika explained what had happened and Dan instantly reached for his canteen.

Looking up toward the sky, Tanner opened his eyes to see Dan and his hairy beard staring down on him.

"What did you do to Annika? Where is she? I swear, if you did anything that caused her pain, I will own you," Tanner said as he failed to get to his feet.

He fell back down and felt the touch of small hands on his back.

Stepping forward, to be in his line of sight, Annika said, "Tanner, I'm right here, and I am perfectly fine. Dan and his boys came to help after I started screaming."

Feeling dippy, he looked around to see all the young eyes on him, Tanner replied, "Well someone is getting a badge for their courageous actions. I'll buy it for them myself."

The scouts had graciously stripped off his pack and laid it beside him. Tanner reached over and pulled out the entire bladder of water. As he unscrewed the lid, the dryness in his mouth grew sticky, forcing him to chug stoutly once he freed the piece of resistance. Dan took the liberty of using the incident as a learning opportunity.

"Hey pack, who can tell me what caused this?" Dan asked.

A small cub from the back raised his hand and kindly explained.

"The old man got dehydrated as a result of not being prepared."

Tanner paused as the water trickled down the corner of his lips. Pressing his eyebrows together, he violently coughed in disbelief of the ageist remark. Absorbing the full strength of the blow, Tanner looked at the boys and tried to make light of the situation before their words could cut deeper.

During his attempt to rectify the kids' belief of his age, he felt a tug on his sleeve. One of the scouts had been gawking over Annika's beauty and leaned over to whisper in Tanner's ear.

"Hey, Mister. Did you fall just so this pretty lady would kiss you? I might have to steal that trick when I'm old like you."

Tanner smiled at the boy and nodded his head yes.

"Well, I'd say this is as good a place as any to dive into that lunch. Care to join us gang?" Tanner asked while wiping the excess water onto his already soaked shirt.

Dan turned down the offer to share a meal, stating there would be mothers in the parking lot looking to hang him if they were late getting back. Before parting ways, Dan made certain to properly educate Tanner in that they were not a gang, but rather a fierce and loyal pack.

Throwing in the towel of surrender, Annika suggested they forget about the falls all together and hike a little farther to Wild Basin Lake. They found a bluff overlooking the glassy lake and set out a blanket for lunch. The fog had lifted, exposing the distant snow-capped mountain peaks and magnificent landscape around the lake. Annika grabbed her camera and attempted to capture the beautiful scenery.

Tanner apologized for all the commotion and confessed that he had somewhat of a rough night, but played it off like he was partying too hard with friends.

Annika reached into her bag and said, "If anything will cure you, it's my special club sandwich."

Tanner reached into his bag and pulled out a tub of macaroni salad and cheese mashed potatoes. Enjoying the reprieve from hiking, they sat on the blanket and reminisced about old times.

The club sandwich was as delicious as promised. Tanner took his time and ate it over the course of a few hours. They were both too caught up in the conversation to eat, and fortunately his stomach was starting to settle.

"I almost forgot. Could I interest you in a little bubbly deliciousness?" Tanner asked while reaching for his pack.

As he pulled out the golden bottle of Ace of Spades, he noticed Annika had missed her mouth at some point and the remnants of potato resting on her cheek made him uncontrollably snicker.

Noticing Tanner actively trying to conceal his laughter, Annika dropped her hands to her side asking, "And just what's so funny over there? Is there a bug on me or something?"

"No, no, you're fine. Let me help you out," Tanner said, positioning his thumb gracefully next to her cheek.

But before wiping her face clean, he hesitated.

"What is it now?" she with a hint of fright. "There really is a bug isn't there?"

Slowly shaking his head no as if in a daze, Tanner locked eyes with Annika and the mountains around them fell into complete silence.

"I had just forgotten how beautiful you are," he said, finally wiping away the potato from her cheek with his thumb.

Without hesitation, she leaned forward and passionately pressed her lips against his. The connection was intense, and immediate.

As their lips parted, Annika saw an entirely new world open in front of her and she whispered, "I didn't realize how badly I have missed you until just now, Mr. Skilli. I want to know everywhere you have been and everything you have seen."

Before Tanner could find the right words to convey what he was feeling, he caught a glimpse of a small black blur shoot across the ridge. Leaping to his feet, he nobly stepped in front of Annika to protect her. There was a good chance that if the black blur was a small cub, it could only mean one thing.

"Do you have any experience with bears, Annika?" he asked with an unsettled voice.

"I have dreams with brown bears all the time, but I usually just wrestle with them," she said as she placed her hands on his shoulders.

"We need to appear like a large object; bears have poor eyesight. I need you to be as big as you can," Tanner said, reaching into his bag and pulling out his can of bear spray.

Grunts soon followed as the branches snapped no less than thirty yards below. In the midst of chasing after her rambunctious cub, mama black bear sensed an intrusion. Tanner assumed she could smell their food and would want to investigate further. Emerging out from the grass, she made her presence clear. Tanner wasn't willing to wrestle with mama bear who was pushing the scale at probably 300 pounds, especially over a few snacks. Unprompted, Annika moved out from behind him and quickly positioned herself to the right of Tanner.

Knowing how startled she gets every time she opened a bottle of champagne, Annika discreetly began removing the protective covering from around the cork. Their muscles tightened as the mama bear moved in closer, but they tried to cloak their fear.

Trying to quarterback the situation and calm their nerves a bit, Tanner explained, "We're not supposed to run unless we are willing to sacrifice our weakest link. It's a terrible idea, but I'd like to keep it as an option on the table."

His attempt at humor was clearly not working for Annika.

Embracing a more serious tone as the stomping paws grew heavier, "A better option would be holding our ground, even if she charges at us. There is no way we can race her. If she gets any closer, we have to be big and bold. Just a forewarning, I may let out a roar, it's worked wonders in the past."

Annika readied herself as the mama bear started stomping her way up the hill.

Tanner positioned his hand on the bear spray trigger and began yelling as loud as his lungs would permit, "Hey, bear, go home!"

Annika gripped the bottle of champagne and gave it a quick shake. Pressing her thumb forward, she launched the cork straight at the forehead of the girthy black bear. Although her aim was slightly off, the loud pop of the cork alone was enough to make the mama bear resume chasing after her cub.

The sense of relief that filled the air around them was nearly tangible. The sun was fading into the night's sky, signaling them to gather up their belongings and head back to the trailhead. Annika took the lead, on Tanner's request. In case they had any wildlife stalking them from the rear, he wanted to be the first line of defense. In the wild, it was feeding time and both would be a tasty treat for any predator.

Halfway down the trail Tanner began to commending Annika on her quick actions.

He inquired, "What made you think of using the cork as a weapon? That was some Mission Impossible Infinity action right there."

Firmly gripping the golden bottle, Annika took a pull of the champagne.

"I didn't want the champagne to go to waste before giving it a taste test. If that momma bear charged us, I wanted to have a cold beverage in hand while having to watch her maul your body. If the last drink I ever taste is Ace of Spades, that's fine by me. Let's be honest, if I had to step in and save you, we would hear about it for years. 'Remember that one time I was about to make the bear submit to me? I was just about to make her surrender before you jumped in and stole the spotlight,' " she said in her best Tanner voice. "I'm not afraid to let you fight your own battles."

The unexpected remarks from such a sweet gal made it clear she had a side not to be trifled. Tanner smiled at her dark humor and loved how vulnerable she was to show a different layer of herself. It was the second time in a twenty four hour period his life was at risk. Although the run-in with the bear would be the only story he would willingly share with others.

Arriving back at the trailhead, Tanner had never been so happy to see his 4Runner. He was done walking for the day, maybe even the whole week after that close call. Instinctively, he opened his jockey box and began reaching for his pills to ease the pain shooting up his leg from all the hiking they had done. The sensation became more apparent as the adrenaline from the bear encounter started to wear off. Before he could get to his stash though, Annika was already packed up and ready to head back to get her car.

"Are you okay, Tanner?" Annika asked with concern, sensing something was wrong.

It pained Tanner to lie to someone he had feelings for, but he was ashamed of the truth.

"Yeah, I'll be fine. I'm still going through a bit of rehab. It's all part of the process of rebuilding my body. I want to take a pain pill, but can't bring myself to do it. When they are in my system, I don't like the feeling of not being in control of my own body. I also shouldn't take one if I'm going to be driving, especially since I have extremely precious cargo on board."

Hearing his own words helped him come to terms with the truth: He had become an addict.

"I'm sorry you're in pain, Tanner. I've always believed that it's necessary to allow your body to feel pain. If all you are doing is numbing it, how is your body supposed to know where it is supposed to begin healing? The human body is a mystery, but I don't think some factory-made pill is the answer," she said before leaning over and kissing him on the cheek.

Her affection eased his pain in a way that no pill could, maybe Annika was the real medicine Tanner needed to get clean.

Placing his shaky left hand on the steering wheel, Tanner gave Annika a wink and a smile before putting the Toyota in drive. They were headed back on the road with many adventures before them.

24

LIFE AND LAUGHTER

Laughter and joy produced the only drug Tanner needed when Annika was in his life. Logistically their long-distance relationship was difficult, but the two managed to keep the lines of communication open and met up almost every weekend. It gave them something to look forward to and they spent the weekdays making plans for their next adventure.

Due to a limited amount of time, they perfected their planning skills and could venture farther and farther with every trip. Sleeping during the flights allowed them time to fully take in the sights. Annika was the missing piece in his life.

Thinking the novelty and excitement would eventually fade, he was hesitant to fully commit. If anything, it continued to grow with new memories. Annika had always been a very positive person, but even she began to see the world in a different light. Around the office, co-workers mentioned she looked like she was walking on clouds every morning. Being together was a happy and joyful comfort neither of them had ever experienced.

Able to catch the internet stampede, Dermot and Tanner continued to grow their software company, Dweedoole, which Tanner could now devote more time to since being let go from the Nuggets. In early October, Tanner was hiking around Bobolink Trailhead with Annika on a crisp afternoon. When they reached their halfway point they stopped for a cup of warm cocoa to heat their cores. He reached into his backpack and pulled out a small stove. After fumbling around with it in his left hand before attaching the propane and boiling the water.

Being in the higher elevation accelerated the time it took to reach the boiling temperature of 203 degrees Fahrenheit. The two sat back and enjoyed the comfort of each other while they waited.

Halloween was mentioned in conversation and they began discussing what they were going to do for their joint costumes. Neither of them had ever gone to a party with an actual date, so the pressure to create epic costumes was high. While trying to figure out which fun outfits they were going to wear, Tanner got a sudden spark of inspiration.

"I've got it," he said as he lifted his freshly-poured cup of cocoa away from his lips.

"Oh yeah, what are you thinking?" Annika asked following the announced revelation.

Looking his way, she continued waiting for the response but his mind had gone elsewhere.

Annika set her stainless steel cup on a rock, unintentionally freeing Tanner from his reverie. With a shake of his head, he tried to refocus on the conversation and come up with a great costume idea.

"How about this?" he pitched with his hands out like he was trying to sell her a used car. "What if we go as cheese farmers? You know me, I always like to see you in overalls. I'll go buy a pair and paint them orange, so I can be cheddar cheese. You can wear an old faded pair with holes and be Swiss cheese. Done deal?"

Tanner asked with hopes she was going to buy into the silly idea.

Annika smiled as she tried to comprehend what a cheese farmer was, but she couldn't make logical sense of the proposition.

"At least it will make for a great conversation piece, I suppose."

As much as Tanner tried to take it in the gorgeous mountain view on the hike down, he couldn't wait to get back to a computer. Annika could tell something beyond cheese farmer overalls was brewing upstairs in Tanner's mind. Initially, she was content with him not engaging in the conversation, but her curiosity got the best of her.

"Are you going to tell me what it is, or am I going to have to beat it out of you?" she asked lightly nudging him.

"What if there was a way for you to find out where all the hot parties were on Halloween? Wouldn't that be awesome?" he asked.

At first, she was very unimpressed and couldn't visualize the benefits. Peppering him with questions began to spawn new ideas. On the trail back to their car, they brainstormed different ideas, playing off one another like they were one mind solving a problem.

"Treats and Tricks" was the final product of their hike around Bobolink Trailhead framework. After a lot of hard work and development, they were able to launch their brain-child. Treats and Tricks was an integrated software that made Halloween safe and fun. It provided a map of all the safe neighborhoods for kids to trick-or-treat.

Parents could easily locate the registered sex offenders in specific areas and avoid dangerous parts of town. After the initial success of the application, they expanded it to offer more enlightening features. Children could report back to their parents and have them rate the candy that was given out in ritzy suburbs. Young adults and older party animals could use the application to find out where all the parties were going down. It would inform them if there was a cover charge, theme of costume, and which live band was performing. Revenue from the application downloads launched the company to new elevations.

After celebrating their first success together, Tanner knew he couldn't live without Annika and decided it was time to "make an honest woman" of her, so to speak. To celebrate the purchase of a new building, the company threw an after-hours gathering for the entire staff. It was a small group, but they felt like high-rollers with catered food and fancy bottles of champagne. As the night was winding down, Tanner grabbed the microphone.

"Thank you all for sharing in this amazing adventure with us. Without this team, we would not have been able to reach this level. We have a special guest of honor tonight that deserves to be recognized for all her contributions to bringing great ideas to fruition. The incredibly brilliant and naturally beautiful, Ms. Annika."

With a shaky left hand, he raised his glass in a toast.

"I had no doubt that our company would have gotten to this point, but because of this woman, we were able to get here faster than I ever imagined. She is the talent behind Treats and Tricks and also my inspiration to be a better man. I could not love someone more than I love her. To Annika!"

Everyone joined in the toast, as her cheeks began to blush.

Annika made her way to the front of the room and passionately kissed Tanner.

"I love you too Mr. Skilli, I don't know how I could live my life without you," she said, reaching around and grabbing his butt with her right hand.

He tried to embrace her, but both of his hands were full.

After setting down the microphone, he said, "I forgot there are some very special people that I want to introduce you to."

Guiding her out of the room and through the lobby, they reached the door with a glowing "Exit" sign above.

"Where on earth are you taking me?" she asked as he unbolted the deadlock.

When she stepped outside, sparklers lit up the patio. White lights were strung from post to post. Rose petals lined the perimeter with tall white candles glowing in the moonlight. Judy and Tripp were joined by Annika's parents and grandparents.

She placed her hands over her mouth and uttered, "What is going on? What are you all doing here?"

Tanner intentionally tripped and collapsed down to one knee.

"Is it your leg, Babe?" she asked.

Acting as though he was in pain, he slowly turned and looked up at her.

"I'm fine, but I think I need some help getting up. Could you spare me a hand?" he asked.

When she reached down with her left hand, he slowly turned up to see the worried look in her eyes.

"My leg is just fine, but I was hoping I can add a little decoration to this hand of yours."

He repositioned his legs, so he was down on bended knee and gently took her hand in his.

"Annika, you are nothing shy of amazing. Whether it was chance or fate that brought us together, I'm not sure. Regardless of how or why our paths crossed, I am fortunate they did. There are few certainties in life, but I have zero doubts that you are the woman I was destined to spend the rest of my life with. Would you do me the great honor of becoming my wife and making me the happiest man to ever walk on earth? Annika Joanna DeCuman, will you marry me?"

REVOLV3R: The Story of a Beautiful Murder

Without hesitation, she blurted out, "Yes! I want to spend the rest of my life as Mrs. Skilli!"

Celebration broke out as the teary-eyed mothers quickly swooped in to take a look at the sparkling princess-cut stone. Tripp walked over to Tanner and extended his right hand. When Tanner began to shake it, Tripp pulled him in for a hug. Judy came over and wrapped her arms around the two Skilli men. After congratulating Annika, her father walked over and broke up the group hug. Tripp and Judy stepped to the side, while Tanner received the standard death threats of a protective father being whispered in his ear. Grandpa Stephen was soon to follow suit. He was much briefer, but his message was delivered with potency.

"We did good, Judy," Tripp said as he placed his arm around her shoulders. "We did good."

Judy placed her hand on his and said, "We certainly did. He has become quite the man. I'm so proud of him."

Annika reduced her hours with Nike and worked out a deal that allowed her to work from Boulder. They had watched all of their friends start families over the years and they were in a hurry to catch up. Traditionally, the DeCuman family would have strong objections to their children cohabiting before marriage. Since they got such a late start, no one said a word of disapproval. Dweedoole also reaped the benefits of having Annika closer. She would sit in on the occasional project mapping meetings, but fireside chats were the prime setting for her creative genius to flourish.

25

DERMOT'S DOWNFALL

Business was booming. The company was in a solid state of growth with everyone firing on all cylinders. Dweedoole was becoming one of the prominent names in the industry. Their capture of market shares drew the attention of a large investment group, Operculum Operative Corporation. A meeting was scheduled for Tanner and Dermot to fly down to Austin, Texas to see what the group had to offer. As Tanner packed his bags, he explained the details of the trip to Annika. She asked if he needed a guy's weekend. He explained that he loved her dearly, but a little time away might be mutually beneficial.

When Tanner arrived at the Austin airport he caught a shuttle to the Marriott Hotel. Dermot flew down the night before and had already set up shop in his room. The front desk was hesitant to give him Dermot's room number. After he explained he would be paying for both rooms, they quickly changed their tune. Tanner's room was located on the third floor and Dermot's on the fourth. He stopped by his room and dropped off his backpack and computer, before heading up to meet Dermot. Tanner closed his door and headed up the flight of stairs. When he knocked on his partner's door he heard a small commotion in the room.

"Who is it? We have everything we need. We're good, thank you," a voice from the room shouted out.

He then heard the sound of giggling, female giggling.

REVOLV3R: The Story of a Beautiful Murder

Tanner knocked louder, "I just want to fluff your pillows you big stud. After last night I don't know how I could ever be satisfied by another man."

The door flung open and Dermot stood with a towel around his waist, accented by a small tent pitched below his belly button. Tanner heard a commotion around the corner and needed to investigate. He stepped into the room, as he reminded Dermot this was not a camping trip.

"Looks like you are only smuggling a one-person tent underneath there," he said while rounding the corner.

The sight of seeing a nude woman, standing with her back to him, was enough to make him revert his course and backpedal.

"This is Jackie, she made the trip down with me."

So much for the guy's weekend away, Tanner thought.

He was annoyed Dermot didn't have the consideration to consult him before bringing a distraction to such an important meeting. He apologized to Jackie, swiftly brushed past Dermot, and took the stairs down to the third floor.

The Operculum Operative event planner had arranged for the groups to meet at a local cigar and whiskey saloon. Walking in was like stepping back in time. The old wooden floorboards creaked beneath his shoes with the smokey haze hovering in the dim light. Tanner felt like a mobster walking in to discuss waxing a snitch. The men took their seats, in dark leather chairs, and were promptly poured a glass of 18-year-old malted scotch.

Dermot's decision to bring his latest love interest along flabbergasted Tanner. All four members of the Operculum Operative team stared at her as she walked to the bar in her snug red dress. Jackie took a seat across the room and motioned for the barkeep to fetch her a three-finger pour.

"Only one ice cube. Anything more is a whore's drink," she said while sliding a $20 bill to his side of the counter.

Operculum Operative focused their attention and presented an offer enough to catch Tanner and Dermot attention. Following their agenda, they discussed broad high-level issues. Constant interruptions from Jackie's high-pitched laugh began wearing on the group's nerves. They proceeded on and tried to block her out, but it was impossible. The liquor had awoken her wild side and she was ready for the spotlight.

Upon the conclusion of their presentation, Tanner and Dermot were left with a large decision regarding the future of Dweedoole. Operculum Operative's offer was decent but was not substantial enough to be a no-brainer. Tanner wanted to hear more about their plans for the current employees.

A few glasses into their discussion, Tanner excused himself to the restroom. Like a lion hunting down a wildebeest, Jackie followed him around the corner. She grabbed Tanner by the shoulder, spun him to the side, and pushed him up against the wall.

"I know you liked what you saw earlier," she said as she started undoing his belt.

"Nope, this can't happen. This is wrong on so many levels," he said while trying to pry away her death gripped hands.

She lunged forward and began kissing him, with her hands now securely around the back of his head.

Tanner reached back and pulled her hands away from his body.

"Please stop. If I gave you the wrong impression, then I am sorry," he said while crossing his arms in defense.

Jackie punched at his stomach, but only caught a piece of his elbow. She stormed off down the hall and back into the seating area.

Finishing up in the bathroom, Tanner gave himself a quick glance in the mirror. It was his traditional bathroom routine. After drying off his hands he would rub them together, while slightly bouncing, and then put his hands out to the side like he was trying to quiet a room.

Staring at his reflection he asked, "What the hell was that all about?"

A deep breath helped him regain his composure before walking back to his seat.

When Tanner rounded the corner back into the lounge area, he saw all the men had stood up and were looking at him with shame.

"Gentleman. Are we all finished up here?" he asked with his hands out to the side and palms facing upward.

"Looks as though that is the case, no thanks to you old friend," Dermot snarked at him.

The Operculum Operative executives shook their heads and made their way toward the exit.

"Apparently I missed something," Tanner said with a befuddled look.

"Where do you get off trying to force yourself on Jackie? Well, I know where you were trying to get off you sick bastard. She's not like those cheap floozy jersey chasers in the league. You ruined this entire deal. You know what, I don't even care anymore."

Dermot grabbed his jacket off the chair and gave Jackie a head nod toward the exit. Walking over she shot Tanner a bone-chilling look as she grabbed Dermot's arm and headed out the door.

"Dude, this is bullshit. You know that's not who I am," Tanner pleaded as they turned and walked away.

26

DWEEDOOLE DUMB

The number of new struggles that had just been created in his life were at no fault of his own. There was no silver lining for this situation. Recounting the events that led up to his run-in with Jackie, replayed in his mind. There was not a thing he could have done different, aside from sprinting to the restroom and locking the door behind him like he was being chased by a grizzly.

How was Annika going to take the news? He saw no way he could possibly explain it without her losing trust in him. Knowing he was completely innocent did not negate the fact he needed to tell her his account of the ambush.

Tanner's flight back from Texas touched down a few clicks after 8 p.m. Annika was at the gates to welcome him home with a giant "WELCOME BACK FROM SEX REHAB" sign. She was oh so thoughtful. The two shared a quick laugh and hug before bolting to the door. Annika had parked outside in a spot clearly designated for security vehicles. She figured sometimes the rules had to be bent to increase efficiency.

On the drive home, she could sense the trip hadn't gone well. He tried to put on a fake smile, but couldn't muster up the will.

"I take it, it did not go as planned," she assumed, squeezing his leg to comfort him.

"Annika, you know I love you more than anything in the world, right?" he asked taking his eyes off the road in an effort to make eye contact with her.

"Of course. What could have possibly been so traumatic for you to feel compelled to question that?" she asked.

The entire flight home, Tanner rehearsed the best possible delivery of the entrapment situation. He explained that when he arrived at the hotel, Dermot had brought along some gal. She later was at the cigar bar during the meeting and cornered him when he went to use the bathroom. When he denied her sexual proposition, she flipped the script and claimed that she was the victim.

"Nothing happened. I promise from the bottom of my heart," he spoke with natural honesty.

"So you did not kiss, or touch her in any way," Annika asked.

Tanner took a deep breath and tried to compose himself.

"Yes, my lips touched hers. Did I want them to? No. It was like a setup in the movies. I'm not sure if Dermot was in on it, but it seemed staged. I didn't instigate a thing, and I pushed her away as quickly as I could. I won't deny that our lips did touch, but it was passionless," Tanner attempted to explain himself, trying to stay in his lane as he glanced between Annika and the road. "Babe, I cannot begin to tell you how messed up this whole thing is. I've thought about every different scenario and there is no way I could have prevented this. I am truly sorry if this makes you doubt my love for you, but I was an innocent victim. You are the love of my life and there is not another woman in this world that could capture my soul the way you have. Please trust me when I say that I would never jeopardize what we have, I can assure you that."

Annika paused, and looked down at her sparkling ring, "I trust you, Tanner. I love what we have together and I love you for always being forthcoming with me."

The sound of rubber on the road and the faint voice of Jack Johnson. Jack was serenading them with his fantastic "Brushfire Fairytales" on the radio, as they rounded the corners. Annika was trying to be understanding but had a few further interrogation questions about the trip. Concerned more with the fact that some Jackie chick was invited, she felt left out. Texas was on her list of states that she wanted to visit and she loved to fly in the sky.

Mounting tension between them began to dissipate as they made their way through the city. The tires rolled to a complete stop once they reached a red light and both were processing their own thoughts. Dead silence flooded the air as Tanner began to feel like the world was messing with him. Looking left, then right, there were no headlights of any other cars. Trapped in the middle of a Truman Show production, three minutes passed without a single car in sight. Tanner backed up and then moved forward and tried to trigger the light sensor by flashing his high-beams.

"Screw it. This light is jank," he said as he popped the clutch and drove through the red light.

Less than a quarter-mile down the road, their cab was filled with red and blue flashing lights.

"You have got to be kidding me. Where the heck was he hiding? I bet he was controlling those dumb lights and this whole thing is entrapment," he said as he pulled the car to the side of the road.

Remembering back to what his father always told him, he rolled down the window and placed both hands on the steering wheel. Loud footsteps approached his window after the loud slamming of a door echoed off the city-building brick walls.

"What seems to be the problem officer?" he asked automatically.

Looking down at his chest in displeasure of his opening line, he removed his Oregon ball cap and placed it in his lap.

"Holy crap man, that has to be the most gnarly battle wound I have ever seen in person," the officer said as he peered in their vehicle.

When Tanner looked up, the officer took a step back. "Tanner Skilli, for real? I loved watching you play, man. Sorry to hear about the accident. I have watched that replay dozens of times. I didn't know you cracked your skull open."

"Not this guy, I'm afraid. His skull is as thick as they come," Annika said as she leaned over toward the driver window.

She had her top pulled down a bit, hoping the additional distraction might help them out a bit. Normally she was very modest, but she figured it wouldn't hurt their chances of getting by with only a warning. The officer went through his typical protocol and asked for license and registration before returning to his squad car. Ten minutes passed and the two began getting incredibly anxious.

"What could be taking so long?" Tanner asked, looking back at the red and blue flashing lights in the rearview mirror.

He watched as the officer got out of his car. Making his way back to their vehicle, he tapped Tanner's driver's license on the registration.

"Well Mr. Skilli, it seems like we got ourselves a little bit of a situation. You see, I was just going to run your information through the system real quick and let you folks go with a warning. The problem of the matter is there is a bench warrant out for your arrest. I'm supposed to take you down to the station. I made a call and confirmed it was for some dumb parking ticket from months ago. Being that you have done great things for this town, I would not be able to live with myself to take away from your family time over some judicial formality. If I let you go with a warning, can I trust that you will get this old parking ticket taken care of in a reasonable manner of time?"

Tanner finally took a whole breath and promised that he would make it a priority.

Shaking the officer's hand, Tanner thanked him for his service. Like a boyfriend dropping off his girlfriend and waiting until she goes inside to pull out of the driveway, Tanner sat and watched the officer walk back to his squad car.

"I guess I can put the twins away now," Annika joked. "Great work ladies, way to be extra perky."

Tanner laughed and said, "I hate that you know how strong of a mental weapon your boobs are. I mean, it is sort of unfair. I don't have any part of my body that I can just flaunt as I please and get my way."

"Would you rather I didn't have them?" she asked.

He reached over with his right hand and squeezed her left breast gently.

"I love everything there is about you. I'd like to think of your breasts as more of a bonus prize. A phenomenal prize at that. You are perfect, babe, inside and out," he said before reaching over and grabbing the right one as well -- not wanting it to feel forgotten.

After their brief run-in with the fuzz, Tanner wasn't ready to go home yet. Their house was a sacred place that they tried to fill with only positive energy. Any bad moods had to be dealt with ahead of time or left at the door. They took a back road that wound them through a series of switchbacks along the hillside. The 4Runner lights lit up the large rock wall before the left-hand turn. Tanner applied the break until slowing to five miles per hour. Slowly navigating the turn as both he and Annika were fixated on the blasted rock. Once the road straightened out, Annika placed her hand on his leg.

"Skilli, you are the man of my dreams. I remember back to when we made the run up to Pre's Rock. That was the second time I fell in love with you," she said as she squeezed his thigh. "For the record, I think you are dead wrong."

Tanner pressed his eyebrows in and drew his head back. "Wrong about what?" he asked with confusion.

"You've got these little chicken legs to use as your sexual tractor beam. Oh, baby! I can't wait to get home and get you into a pair of Larry Bird shorts. Let the world see those luscious legs," she said while failing to remain serious.

"Very cute, babe. Very cute. It's a good thing you like them because you're stuck with them for a good long time. That is until you wise up and realize that I'm a three at best and you are a solid twenty. If you leave me, you only get one of them. Split it fifty-fifty, right?" he asked with a smirk.

"No, I don't want half. I'll take it all once I bury your body. I've been scouting a few potential drop spots along this road. Ever been skull-dragged?" she asked while holding up her thumb, pointer, and middle finger.

Tanner glanced to the back seat, which had been folded down. He didn't see a shovel, duct tape, or rope and figured he would at least get to live through the night. The odds were in his favor, making him less fearful for the moment.

Annika grabbed his hand and slowly entwined her fingers. She leaned over and rested her head on his shoulder. Tanner tilted his head and rested it on top of hers as they continued down a long country road.

"I trust you with all my heart," Annika said. "I have never wanted to give someone my full love so naturally. If you say that you were an innocent bystander in this deal, then I believe you. When I look in your eyes I see my soul's recognition of the man I want to spend the rest of my days with. I love you, Tanner Skilli. For the record, you are at least a solid eight in my book," she said as she nestled into his shoulder. "You could use a few more inches to get you up to a nine, potentially even a 10."

They sat in silence for a moment before bursting out in laughter.

"Okay, that's not what I meant. I was referring to your height. You know, because you tower over me. That is all. I didn't hear the implication until the words were coming out," she said as she felt her cheeks become rosy red.

27

DAMAGE CONTROL

Operculum Operative was still willing to talk after the Texas mishap, although their offer came in much lower than the initial offer. It wasn't the ideal buyout situation, but it was time to close that chapter of his life. Having his character questioned was the ultimate insult to Tanner and he was unwilling to leave rumors unaddressed. Later that week Dermot's phone rang on his morning drive to the gym.

"D, it's Skilli. Let's get this thing hashed out and behind us," Tanner said bluntly.

Ever since returning home, Tanner had been on edge over the mistrust and poor judgment from his so-called friend. Proposing they sell off the business to Operculum Operative looked slightly suspicious, but he knew that he could no longer put his faith and loyalty behind a partner that didn't trust him. A lesson Tanner's grandfather passed down to him was that perception is oftentimes reality and trust is difficult to rebuild, regardless of the circumstances. Those words confirmed to him that he was making the right decision.

The buyout took less than two months to complete. Both Dermot and Tanner were able to make a sizable return on their investment. They could feel the hands of Uncle Sam reaching into their pockets before the wire transfers were completed. Had they met with a tax advisor ahead of time, they would have opted for an installment payment plan. Instead, they were left with just over half, after the IRS took their cut.

On the day of signing their company over, Dermot and Tanner headed to a local pub to *celebrate* the sale. Grabbing a beer seemed like the right thing to do after selling off a company for millions of dollars, but it was painfully uncomfortable.

Texas was still lingering in the back of Dermot's mind, feeling like he was the victim in the scenario. The two tried to force conversation to no avail. Sitting in the corner booth, they minded their pints and quarts of Irish Lager. It was clear Dermot had been stewing for the past few months and wasn't willing to hear an opposing account of what transpired between Jackie and Tanner.

Liquid courage began to kick in halfway into his beer stein and Dermot let the floodgates open.

"You know how shitty of a situation this is Tanner?" Dermot asked before taking another swig. "We had a great thing going, and you messed it up because you can't keep your ego in check. Not every girl in the world wants you. You know what, man? Stefanie and I hooked up the first summer you left for Oregon. Bet she never told you that little tidbit."

He raised his glass with a toasting gesture. Regardless of the validity behind his claim, it was a shot to the gut and the irony was lost on Dermot.

Tanner stared at the rim of his glass for a few moments and then began to release his inner rage.

"So you're telling me that you hooked up with my high school sweetheart the first chance you had, led me to believe we were friends in college, and then had the audacity to come begging for money? I find it amusing that you conveniently neglected the fact that the computer code that started our company was one hundred percent my work. The only thing you did was turn it into your professor and pawned it off as your own. You're a snake," Tanner said in disgust.

Perhaps the cards were falling right where they needed to fall. Dermot tried to rebuttal, but it fell on deaf ears. Tanner was confident in himself and now knew the truth about his friend's loyalty.

"Maybe that trick Jackie is the best skank to come into my life. Had you never brought her down to one of the most important meetings of our life, without first checking with your *partner*, you would still be forced to live with your lies. I would say guilt, but it's clear you are too arrogant to realize you have been riding my coattails since we were teens. Don't ever try to call me again you leech. We are no longer partners, and certainly not friends," Tanner said as he reached into his wallet and placed a hundred dollar bill on the table before exiting.

28

CLEAR THE AIR

The following week, Tanner headed down to the courthouse and the plague of Dermot lingered. He pulled a number and took a seat on the wooden bench. For a place not known for their promptness, one would think they would provide more comfortable seating accommodations. As he sat waiting in the lobby, he was fascinated by the amazing people-watching the courthouse had to offer. It was difficult to not eavesdrop on conversations, as most patrons occupying the seats had less than polished inside etiquette.

Number 33 appeared on the "Now Serving" screen. Tanner walked up to the window and informed the clerk of the situation. As it turned out, the weekend that Dermot came to town to visit, he had borrowed Tanner's 4Runner one morning to go grab a coffee.

What Dermot neglected to tell Tanner, was that he was a selfish prick and parked in a handicap space while in the coffee shop checking emails. He watched the officer issue a ticket and place it on the windshield, but Dermot aloofly remained clicking away at his computer. To hide the evidence, he tore up the ticket and threw it away in the coffee shop trash. Since it occurred right before Tanner moved, the notice went to his old address and never got forwarded.

Eight hundred fifty dollars later, Tanner walked out of the

courthouse and was no longer a fugitive of the law. On the drive home, his cellphone rang. He took his eyes off the road and glanced down to see that it was Dermot. Although reluctant to answer, he felt compelled.

"Hey, man," Dermot began, "I know that shit got out of control, mostly impart to actions of my own. Shit."

Dermot paused as he began to lose his composure. With a quivering voice he resumed.

"You were right, Jackie is a trick. The other night when I came home from the bar, I found her sandwiched between two garage-band dweebs. Nothing like coming home to a few random dudes running a train on your girlfriend."

Tanner could tell his old friend was in a world of pain, and rightfully so, but had difficulty mustering up any sympathy. Dermot had to deal with the consequences of his actions.

"I'm not sure what to say, to be honest. I think everything must happen for a reason. Although there are difficult times in life, it is all part of a plan that is greater than either one of us. We are just pawns in the grand scheme of things. On the other side of these dark times lies greater adventures and happiness. Thank you for the call Dermot. This too shall pass. Bye for now," he said as he closed his phone.

The dark cloud of Dermot lifted from Tanner's world as he drove down the interstate toward home. With the radio turned off, the sunroof back, and windows down, he breathed easy and enjoyed the peace. Annika promised she believed him, but he couldn't help but imagine there was a hint of doubt. When he arrived home he grabbed a bottle of Sawtooth Syrah and two glasses off the rack.

"What is this?" Annika asked. "Someone's in a good mood."

Tanner inserted the wine key and displayed his sommelier talents.

"You have always been amazing. I am not proud of everything I have done in my life. Being that you are willing to accept me for who I am, flaws and all, makes me love you even more. I spoke with Dermot on the drive home. I refrained from telling him that he owes me an additional $850, but he admitted that the Jackie situation was a severe lapse of judgment.

Jackie had unintentionally confessed to the entire thing or at least allowed for her true colors to be seen. Dermot arrived home and caught her being the bologna in a sandwich of two random married men. Apparently, she has a lengthy history of falsely accusing people in hopes of being paid hush money. I know you said you believed me, but I wanted to let you know. I promise you on this day, and every day there is a beat in my chest, I would never do anything to lose your trust," he said, raising his glass.

She softly smiled and clinked her glass with his. "Thanks, honey. Know that I will always trust you. Because if you ever break that trust, I have scouted several hidden places where no one will ever find your body."

She gave him a devilish smirk before taking a sip of the Syrah.

29

WHAT ARE THEY BITING ON

Since their summer in Alaska, Gavin and Tanner had loosely stayed in contact. Gavin was somewhat of a nomad and spent his time traveling the country and fly fishing. Tanner couldn't recall how Gavin said he made his money, something about Bogging or Blobbing on the internet. It was a foreign concept to Tanner.

"Why anyone would be interested in following the life of another person online, is beyond me," he said perplexed.

It was the perfect fit for Gavin though. He was able to make a career out of the two things he loved the most, writing and fly fishing, just like Paul Maclean. The difference was Gavin didn't work for a news press and was fortunate enough to not have some pompous editor breathing down his neck all the time. Most trips would last a week or two, and he would post the tales of the adventure. At the end of each blog, he would provide a little teaser about where his ventures were taking him next.

People make their living in many fascinating ways. It was difficult to argue that Gavin had a pretty sweet gig. Not only would his traveling expenses be covered by sponsors, but they would also outfit him with all the top new gear. Tanner needed a retreat with a true friend and also had some business to discuss with Gavin. It took a few days to track him down, but Gavin finally returned Tanner's calls.

"Hey buddy, how are things?" Gavin asked.

"That's a difficult question to answer. Not sure where to begin or how much I want you to repeat in your next boggle. Things are great," Tanner replied, half teasing.

Gavin had just returned from a trip up Hells Canyon, where he broke away from his normal routine and went sturgeon fishing. Sturgeon are unlike any other fish, those creatures are Jurassic monsters.

On day two of the expedition, the tip of the rod dove toward the water. They hooked Gavin into a chair, so he wouldn't be pulled overboard during an hour and a half battle with a giant lurking in the waters below. It wasn't until then he could fully understand the pain and agony of the old man in the sea when reeling in the huge sailfish.

The experience was incredible and provided Gavin with enough material to write a short article, later published in the Field and Stream magazine. His storytelling ability was polished. Tanner would sit back and listen as he envisioned himself in each adventure.

"Gavin, you have always been a loyal friend. I am going to marry the woman of my dreams, and I would like to ask you to do me the honor of being my best man at our wedding. What do you say?" Tanner asked.

"The honor is all mine, buddy. Congratulations on finding the one meant for you," Gavin replied.

The early release night in Alaska was a night they'd never forget. A piece of Tanner's soul was ripped out after reading the letter, the front page at least. The memory of their trip to town, getting a lesson from Doris, and then stumbling back to the bunkhouse from the bluff, was burned into his mind.

What he had not realized in his drunken stooper, was that Gavin saw the letter torn up on the floor. He folded it up and placed it in his pocket before both threw up deuces and went back to their rooms. At that moment, Gavin realized the cause of his friend's pain. He was heartbroken.

All summer long Tanner had been talking about this great girl back in the lower 48. It was more than lust, it was true love he felt for her. Knowing how much she meant to Tanner, Gavin read the first page and got a pit in his stomach. Reading the words of the woman his friend cared about was agonizing.

Page two was a different story. Her writing had changed. Rather than further elaborating on the wedding plans, she cryptically expressed her love for Tanner. It was a cry of desperation and an attempt to confess that her gut told her it was wrong. Gavin sat back and tried to wrap his mind around how ludicrous this charades of emotions was unfolding. Her words were sincere and beautiful. Feeling embarrassed and ashamed, she did not have the courage to write a follow-up letter to apologize. The vision of having a Cinderella wedding distracted her from seeing the future until she admitted to herself it was a grave mistake to say yes to Luke.

Reflecting on the few weeks before the proposal, their relationship was awful and painstaking. The signs were clear to both Annika and Luke that their high school love story was coming to an end. When he proposed out of desperation, she reluctantly went along with it instead of staying true to herself. Ashamed and lost, she didn't know what to do. Knowing that she had broken Tanner's heart, with one failing error, crushed her soul. In the days and years that followed, her outlet was to focus on work and self-improvement, closing herself off to the outside world and the dating scene.

Time flew by as Tanner and Gavin talked for nearly half an hour, picking up right where they left off. Their paths in life crossed in Naknek, Alaska of all places, and there was something unexplainable about their loyalty to one another. Looking back on the summer, Tanner recalled several people asking if they were cousins or grew up in the same town. They both had their reasons for working in Alaska, but they were able to find joy experiencing the venture together. Having Gavin accept the offer to be his best man gave Tanner happiness. Shameless to say it, but it made him giddy like a schoolgirl.

A slow beep, signaling a low battery, urged Gavin to end the conversation. They would have carried on for hours otherwise, so it was for the best. A lot of ground was covered and the voice of an old friend was refreshing. Tanner closed his phone and sat back on the couch. He raised his arms above his shoulders and then placed his palms on his cleanly-shaven head.

Sitting in silence, he began dwelling on the dark place he was in after being hopped up on pills and slowly wasting his life away. Negativity filled his every thought and anything truly meaningful was looked over.

"Why didn't I try to reach out to Gavin to let him know that I was struggling?" he questioned.

No doubt about it, had Tanner picked up the phone and called, Gavin would have taken the next flight out of some distant part of the world. Even though it felt like all was lost, there were so many positives in his life. The drugs, pain, and self-pity made him incapable of seeing the truth. Tanner was thankful for his new life and especially thankful for Annika.

30

WHALES AND WONDERS

In the previous years, Tanner attended weddings of his teammates and friends. His standard method of attendance was going stag and sitting as far back in the venue as possible. It allowed him to be within earshot of the wedding-party scattering about in preparation for the big show. Hearing the chaos behind the scenes made Tanner question why women feel compelled to endure the potential stress that accompanies such a theatrical production.

He concluded that wedding planning had to be an unspoken rite of passage. Each bride must be forced to maneuver through the same mentally-taxing gauntlet in order to become a true woman. If that weren't the case, then it would be difficult to explain why an engaged couple would be willing to sign up for such a stressful day of unity.

Sitting in a church pew, or a white folded chair on a lawn, Tanner had a tendency to share his thoughts with the guests around him. Telling them that it must be a sick joke that women convince brides that they have to follow all of the inconvenient traditions or their fairytale wedding will be an endless disappointment. Most of them would just nod and smile while trying to mask their judgment about his cynical and unromantic ideology of weddings.

Given that Annika's previous experience of planning a wedding became more about the event and losing herself. She lost focus of what she truly desired. This time around, her sole focus was on marrying Tanner and celebrating them becoming one. She had learned from her previous mistakes and wasn't willing to repeat them. It didn't matter which entrée they were serving, the cake filling flavor, or any of the other hundred mandatory checklist items a "real" wedding must entail. Instead, she kept the planning simple and booked a block of rooms at the Surf Rider Inn, where the story of he and Annika first started.

August 20th was incredible, an absolutely picture-perfect day. The guest list was short and simply included their parents, grandparents, Annika's brother and sister, Kimber, and Gavin. Everyone arrived on Friday and began preparations for the main event. They were all expecting to check-in at the hotel before retreating to their rooms for the afternoon. Tanner helped carry in the last piece of grandma's luggage and got them situated at their weekend home.

Walking over to the sliding patio door, Tanner saw whales spouting fifty yards offshore. The waves were softly cresting before trying to run up the beach. Looking out at the baby-blue backdrop, only a few scattered clouds floated across the sky. It was a subtle reassurance that he was making the right commitment.

"The time has finally arrived. Let's do this," he said after taking in a deep breath.

Turning away from the door, he faced Annika's grandfather and asked if he would mind doing the ceremony a day early.

"Right now? Well, we best get going. We're burning good daylight," grandpa said while shifting into high-gear.

Changing anything about a wedding is a guaranteed recipe for disaster. Unless the aim is to drive the bride to insanity, then it is the perfect method. Tanner hustled back to their room and found Annika standing on the balcony. She was fixated on the horizon and didn't even realize someone was in the room. He made a gentle bird call, in an attempt to not startle her too badly. Hearing the familiar call made her chuckle.

"Come join me," she said. "This is where I want to be when we are old and wrinkly. This is where it all began, the first time I fell in love with you."

Tanner pulled back the screen door and wrapped his arms around her shoulders.

"It was meant to be," he said as he pulled her in tightly.

"We can't let this day go to waste," Annika said as she watched the whales spouting in the distance. "Too ambitious? I just don't want to spend another day without officially being Mrs. Skilli."

Tanner spun her around with great relief.

"Babe, this is why I love you. Few brides in the world would change the day she is getting married the day before her wedding."

She kissed him softly on the lips, "Well, we better get going, we're burning good daylight. We should probably tell the others."

Tanner chuckled to himself and slowly began grabbing his button-down shirt, shorts, and flip-flops.

"Babe, since when are you a sloth? We have to get the word out to the others that this is going down for real," she hastened, tossing random objects on the bed.

It didn't encourage his sense of urgency, as he found himself trying to analyze what purpose all the strange devices on the bed served. It explained the weight of her luggage when he was hauling it up the stairs. He kissed her on the cheek and asked how long she needed.

"One hour, that's all this bride-to-be needs," she said, applying lip gloss in the mirror.

As Tanner fled the room, Kimber appeared in the doorway.

"You ready for this, sister?" she asked Annika.

"Ready for what?" she said with confusion.

"For the big day. We've got one hour to get that hair and makeup done before trying to squeeze those big boobs into a little white dress," Kimber said while holding up yet another device Tanner had never seen before.

With a tender smirk, Annika glanced in Tanner's direction with delight, "And that is why I love you Mr. Skilli. You know me oh so well. Now get a move on it, mister."

With his thumbs to the sky and his pointer-fingers aimed, he shot her guns and a wink before closing the door behind him.

31

BOBBY J TO BRIGHTEN THE DAY

On the earlier drive-in, they saw an older gentleman on the side of the road jamming away on his guitar. Laying opened in front of him was his guitar case, with a note propped up that said, "Trying to make it to Hollywood." He was the closest person to a "Street Performer" that Depot Bay, Oregon had to offer. They pulled the car to the side of the road and rolled down the windows. Folks called him "Bobby J" and he could wail. Annika glanced over at Tanner and shrugged her shoulders.

"What are you thinking, sugar-plum? Should I see if he is interested in making a few extra bucks?" Tanner asked.

She smiled back and Tanner jumped out of the car.

An offer to play his first real gig brought joy to Bobby J's face. They helped him gather his belongings and loaded them into the back of the 4Runner.

Along the way, Bobby J shared his story and explained what landed him in Depot Bay. He had lived a fascinating life and had experienced tremendous struggle. Music remained as the only constant that allowed him to keep his sanity. When they checked-in at the Surf Rider, Bobby J grabbed his belongings and started making his way toward the thin trees on the side of the Inn.

"Where on earth are you trying to run off to? You have to get stage-ready," Tanner said to his back.

"I was going to head down to the beach and set up camp for the weekend. Spots go for a premium on nice weekends," Bobby J replied.

Annika walked over and grabbed the guitar away from him.

"You, Sir, are the main entertainment for our big day! You're not sleeping on the beach," she said while walking toward the room.

They handed him a set of keys to a room on the third floor. It was the best room the Inn had to offer. Originally it was supposed to be theirs, but they figured Bobby J would appreciate it more.

Tanner arrived at Gavin's room to change with forty-five minutes before the wedding tipoff. He was greeted with a shot of Pendleton whiskey.

"Hold that thought," Tanner said as he walked over to the phone.

He called up Bobby J and asked him to come down to join them for a pregame toast.

"I'd be honored. Make mine a blue dolphin and you've got yourself a deal," he said.

Bobby J hung up the phone and made his way down the flight of stairs. Walking into the room he saw Tanner still holding the phone with a perplexed look.

"What on earth is a blue dolphin, Bobby J?" he asked.

"I've been off the bottle for three years now. That stuff will kill you, you know. A blue dolphin is my mixologist term for water. Tap or bottled, I don't really have a preference. So long as it's cold," he said with a smile.

The hour to get ready felt like only a couple minutes, but everyone took their places on the beach with orchestrated precision. Bobby J began strumming his guitar as Annika arrived at the top step. Looking like a Disney princess, she made her way down the endless staircase. Remembering how daunting it was to walk down the stairs, she planned accordingly. Her perfect dress was accented with an old pair of Nike running shoes, the same ones she wore on their first trip to the beach.

Annika was greeted by her father at the bottom of the stairs. Arm in arm they walked toward a landing of sand, just beyond the tide's reach. Gavin standing at Tanner's side leaned over and gave him a quick hug.

"She makes for one beautiful bride my friend. Congratulations on reeling in a keeper," he said as she approached.

Annika's grandfather began the ceremony by asking who had the honor of giving such a beautiful bride away. Her father proudly announced that he and her mother were blessed to have such a wonderful daughter and a new son. Throughout the ceremony, Gavin was fixated on the stream running through the middle of the beach. The ocean is the final destination for all water. He realized that he was standing at the very place where the most essential element on earth has its journey's end, and his best friend's real journey was about to begin.

For not having any prior experience conducting a ceremony, Stephen performed like he was born for it. Being able to unite his favorite granddaughter with her partner in life, was a lifelong aspiration. He was able to cross off one of the last remaining items on his bucket list. Skydiving, sailing the world, and freeing baby turtles, were of the few life experiences that remained unfulfilled.

Being the selfless man that he was, Stephen and his wife Rose decided to book the newlyweds a honeymoon trip to Costa Rica for a week. Following the ceremony, they surprised the couple and made the announcement. Part of their honeymoon package included a morning excursion to help usher newly hatched turtles along their maiden voyage to the open ocean. All Stephen asked was that spare no detail when reporting back about the trip and that they take a lot of pictures.

He reminded them of the wise words from the Cobra Kai Sensei, "Enemy deserves no mercy. Don't be afraid to shoot down some of them gulls trying to pick off the helpless little guys. Level the playing field and give them a fair shot to explore life under the sea."

It was an incredibly generous gift. Tanner vowed to fulfill Stephen's dream and promised to be the over-watchman for the boys and girls in green.

To celebrate their unity, they got permission to have a bonfire on the beach. Due to the spontaneous timing of the ceremony, they weren't prepared for the festivities that followed. The wedding party headed up to their rooms to put on warmer clothing since the sun was on the brink of setting. Magic was truly in the air, but it was about to be tested. At the base of the stairs, Tanner stopped abruptly. He asked Annika to hold up as she placed her right foot on the bottom stair.

"A proper gentleman is supposed to carry his beautiful bride up the stairs on the night of the wedding. I want you to have the full royal treatment," he said with an ear to ear smile.

Worried about his left arm and leg, and self-preservation, she suggested a compromise. The last thing she wanted on her wedding day was to get dropped and tumble down several flights of stairs. Sleeping in a hotel bed was much more appealing than a hospital bed.

Gavin heard the compromise and bolted up the stairs to fetch his camera from the room. Tanner and Annika walked hand in hand up the stairs and enjoyed the feeling of being married. They were the same couple in love that morning, but the commitment of marriage provided a heightened level of comfort and unity. At the last push to the top of the stairs, they paused and took in the amazing backdrop. Unable to appropriately express themselves, they stood in silence with their arms wrapped around each other.

"Okay, sweet wife of mine," he said as he swept her off her feet and into his arms.

Nervous about his left arm giving out, he focused intently on every step. When they reached the top step, Gavin captured a moment that was the essence of their relationship. It was simply beautiful. Annika's cheeks began to hurt from smiling so much; she was in absolute bliss.

She kissed him on the cheek and said, "When I pictured my perfect life, you were always in the frame. I love you, husband."

Back in the room, Tanner gathered up clothes and supplies for the beach. He looked over at the bottle of Whiskey sitting on the nightstand, and the variety pack of microbrews chilling on the porch.

He announced, "Tonight is a night to celebrate the joy of life and sobriety. I want to look back on this night and remember every facet, and to be present in the moment."

Kimber knocked on the door and asked Annika to come up to her room for a little surprise. Annika grabbed a few things and kissed Tanner goodbye.

"I'll see you down there, hot stuff," she said shutting the door.

Kimber had stopped by the lingerie boutique and had picked out a risqué set of evening attire.

"Girl, wait until he sees you in this. You'll render him speechless. Guaranteed."

"That certainly doesn't leave much to the imagination. Those darn yoga classes better pay off," Annika giggled, holding it up over her wedding dress.

The simple wedding dress had served its purpose. Annika thought about wearing the lucent satin lingerie beneath her beach clothing but decided she would want to rinse off after sitting around a beach fire. She and Kimber headed down to the beach together before the boys. Hustling down the stairs, Tanner saw the large crowd that had surrounded their fire. As he and Gavin made their way toward the beach, they began to hear a guitar accompanied by an incredible voice. When they reached the sand, Annika rushed over and threw her arms around Tanner's neck. She kissed him repeatedly before pulling him over toward the fire. The moment was incredible. Sitting on a blanket in the sand, and listening to Bobby J jamming, Annika leaned over and snuggled into Tanner's arms.

"This is where I belong. Life has a funny way of making things work out better than imagined. I love you," she said and she looked up at him.

He leaned down to kiss her and said, "I couldn't agree more. With you is where I belong. I love you too, Wifey."

Bobby J put on a solo performance that exceeded any, and all, expectations. Beachcombers continued to join the festivities around the fire. They all danced and sang along as Bobby J put his own spin on the timeless classics. Logs continued to be thrown on the already heaping bonfire. It was the first time in history that Oregon hosted "The Burning Man Festival," or so it would appear. Unlike any traditional wedding reception, the night was a perfect way to enjoy their special milestone. They were thankful to have their toes in the sand, over a stuffy prom setting in a town hall.

Out of respect for Bobby J's triumph over addiction, the Skilli Crew decided to remain sober all night. Annika and Tanner loved every minute of the evening as they sipped their *blue dolphins*. Others in the crowd were consuming adult beverages and missed out on the true beauty that surrounded them.

The evening was filled with amazing energy and elated spirits. After three hours, without taking more than a few breaks between songs, Bobby J announced that the next one would be his last. A set of that magnitude started to put a strain on his vocals, or he would have gladly played until the fire was down to coals. He slowly began strumming his acoustic guitar, to cap off the night. As the freestyle intro to Journey's "Faithfully" began, Gavin knew it was finally time to free himself from a burden he carried.

Gavin pulled out a folded up paper he had kept in his back left pocket for many moons. He had saved the letter that crushed Tanner's heart up in Naknek. Unsure how to tell his friend that he was intrusive, and had read Annika's sensitive words, he always looked for an opportunity to tell Tanner what he missed out on.

"Hey buddy, mind if I have a seat," Gavin asked with the pages in his hand.

The newlyweds invited him to join, and he plopped down on the sand next to their blanket.

"I've got something that I think it is finally time for you to see."

Gavin said while handing the note to Tanner. Annika leaned over and saw the familiar writing and felt a sense of guilt take over her.

Before Tanner unfolded the letter, reconstructed long ago with clear tape, he knew exactly what the message contained. Gavin's actions were very unorthodox. Bringing up past memories, which pained him deeply, was the last thing they wanted on their special night.

"Buddy, I was there the day you received this, heck I was the one who pulled it off the mail table. That was the first time I ever saw you in such a vulnerable state of mind. I cannot explain it, but when I saw the letter on the floor my curiosity got the best of me. I couldn't help but start reading them. There is something that tells me you never read the second page," Gavin shared, resting his arm on Tanner's shoulder. "You were always her first pick."

Up to that point, Tanner had been staring blankly at the pages. He remembered every word and knew exactly what it said. Even though he just married the woman who broke his heart, actually reading the words wasn't a memory Tanner wanted to relive.

Tanner tossed the first page on the blanket and began reading the second to himself. The excitement in Annika's writing began to fade, as the acceptance of her true emotions became apparent through her words. It was a cryptic love confession, embedded in a plea for liberation from Luke. Annika leaned over and told them that she called off the wedding the same day she dropped the letter off at the post office.

"That's when I knew. That's when I revealed to myself who the true man of my dreams was all along," she said. "It was always you, Tanner."

Gavin apologized for bringing up the emotionally infused letter but felt compelled to be transparent with his friends.

"I couldn't be happier for the two of you. I love you both like my brother and sister. Annika, I'm sorry for bringing it up on your wedding night, but Tanner needed to know that your heart never stopped loving him."

It was further proof that life has a funny way of working things out. Annika grabbed the pages and stood up. She extended her arm to assist Tanner to his feet. They walked over to the bonfire and listened to the final chorus of "Faithfully" as they tossed the pages into the fire. She wrapped her arms around his shoulders and kissed him.

"It was always you," she said as they began to sway back and forth, with their toes in the sand.

One of the locals gathered up as many Tiki torches as he and his son could carry. They strategically placed the torches along the beach, lighting up the path back to the stairs. The lit beach was a marvelous spectacle to cap off a perfect wedding celebration. Bobby J received a huge round of applause and cheers, before grabbing his gear and trekking up to his room for the night. Ever since they checked in, he had been anticipating sleeping on a king-size bed for the first time.

At 9:30 the next morning, Tanner and Annika were greeted by a nice housekeeper. She walked into the room, with her headphones on, and started down her checklist. The Skillis looked at one another with terror, pulled the sheets up, and remained in bed.

"Hello, Ma'am! You're not alone. Excuse me, Ma'am!" Tanner shouted without a response.

She finally rounded the corner and jumped back against the dresser. Ripping her headphones off, she began apologizing profusely. They assured her it was no big deal and said that they would be out of the room in a half-hour if she wouldn't mind coming back.

A morning run on the beach is what every married couple deserves. On their first morning as newlyweds, Tanner and Annika wanted to relive the steps that led them to fall in love. They made their way down the stairs, as the clouds were glowing a magnificent gold. The air was warmer than the day before and brought with it a light coastal fog of romance. In the blink of an eye, gale-force winds forced the coast guard to evacuate the beaches and cutting their run short. Before reaching the south end of the beach, they were instructed that a large storm was rolling in.

"The tide rips through here like a mother fucker," the coastguard said.

Tanner wasn't fearful, he loved crazy storms. His stoic persona gave Annika comfort that they weren't in harm's way.

Slowly making their way back to the stairs they were pushed around by the heavy wind gusts. Holding on to each other at the waist, they stumbled their way. Annika reached down and pulled off her shoes, so she could feel the warm sand between her toes. Seeing the undeniable joy it was bringing to her, Tanner followed suit and removed his shoes as well.

A huge gust blasted them from the side. Tanner's arms reacted like a martial artist and wrapped around Annika, as he shifted his hips to the side. One might believe he was using her as a shield from the wind, rather than being a valiant gentleman using his body as a safety net. They staggered to the side and then smashed into the sand. Tanner's back hit first and absorbed the impact from the fall. Annika fell on top of him making it all worthwhile. All 120 pounds of her felt like a twig in comparison to what he had anticipated.

"Well aren't you clever," she said. "You just couldn't wait until we got back up to the room."

It was far from his intention, but she was known to have much better ideas than him.

Annika looked down the beach, in both directions, but they were the only ones foolish enough to still be out in the storm. The coast guard had left the premises and the beach was all theirs. She looked up and realized the bluff above them was blocking the view from the hotel.

"I was only partially joking about waiting until the room," she said as she rubbed her hands on the outside of his mesh shorts and quickly excited Tanner junior.

Without warning, warm rain began to fall from the sky. The dark clouds overhead began to rumble with thunder.

"Babe, are you serious. Right here?" he asked.

"I don't know why not, we've got a lot of catching up to do," she said with a grin.

Tanner, caught off guard by her vixen-like invitation, showed brief resistance. Not expecting such directness from his normally timid wife, he became nervous like it was his first time. Not realizing the power of the ring, and the Pandora's Box that he had inadvertently opened, he looked at Annika in a different light. She slowly began to kiss his pillowy lips. After a few moments, Annika turned her head as a hint for Tanner to kiss her neck, which was her favorite. He gently ran his tongue down the length of her neck and softly kissed every inch from her ear to nape.

She nibbled on his ear whispering, "I'm all yours, baby."

Tanner ripped his shirt off, faster than the wind blowing, and nestled into the warm sand. Annika leaned up, and quickly stripped off her shirt, leaving her sports bra on to remain modest. As Tanner seductively kissed Annika down her chest and stomach, he began to slip her yoga pants to her ankles. The salt from the sand and dampness from the rain added to the moment, along with the clouds booming thunder.

Looking down, Annika said, "Don't forget yours, you big hunk."

As she watched and giggled at him as he struggled to get his shorts off in a hurry. She pushed him into the bed of sand and demanded to be loved.

It didn't take long for things to escalate. Being in the wet sand provided an interesting twist. As the wind blew Annika's hair, she took charge of pleasing Tanner. The grinding against small pebbles of rock was distressingly painful. Any discomfort was overshadowed by the feeling of being as close to his wife and feeling her energy. Even though it was short-lived, Annika was more than pleased with Tanner's performance.

Cuddling on the beach allowed them to experience the intensity of the storm passing over, creating an unforgettable memory. The growing sound of the waves crashing drew closer, so they decided to gather their scattered clothes that had started to blow away, and they headed back to their room. Tanner had envisioned making love on the beach to be more comfortable. He had never really put much thought into what he should have expected. One time was enough for him, at least without a blanket to rest on. He hoped a few of the small cuts on his back would leave scars to commemorate their scandalous ways.

32

CHELONIIDAE IN COSTA RICA

Turbulence shook the plane violently triggering the oxygen masks to be deployed from the ceiling. Dying thirty-three miles from Juan Santamaria International Airport (SJO) was not how the newlyweds imagined their honeymoon. The cabin rocked back and forth evoking panicked screams from the passengers.

Annika had commandeered the desired window seat and was mesmerized by the Star Trek show witnessed on the wing. The anti-collision strobe light reflected off the tiny droplets of water racing by at 500 miles per hour. Watching the intermittent white streaks against the darkness of the sky made her feel like she was traveling at warp speed. Tanner had been in much worse conditions flying into King Salmon when he first learned the ways of the crab-walk landing.

The stewardess continued to announce over the intercom, "Please remain calm. The plane is equipped for these conditions. Please remain calm. We are going to land soon."

Tanner began to get increasingly annoyed as he began thinking to himself how airplane passengers are such jerks. The pilots didn't do anything wrong, yet the passengers thought it was perfectly acceptable to scream like they own the place. Perhaps that's why the pilots wear their headphones -- to block out the external distractions allowing them to focus on their technical job.

Deafening screams of panic shrieked out from what they thought to be teenage girls seated behind them. Even the oxygen masks weren't mighty enough to muffle the painful 120 plus decibels. Tanner looked back to express his distaste for the behavior and then began to chuckle. The seats behind them were occupied by two grown men in their forties who were terrified of being in the air.

Tanner pulled the breathing apparatus away from his mouth and prominently shouted, "Babe, if we crash in the ocean you know the sharks are going to eat you first, right? I'm too gamy for the bull sharks down in these parts."

Annika glanced over her shoulder and could tell Tanner was becoming annoyed by the theatrics.

She smiled and chimed in, "At least we won't have to tread water that long before joining the circle of life. We'll probably freeze before the sharks have time to hunt us down. I just hope I'm a tasty meal."

As they descended into the SJO airport, they broke through the turbulence allowing tension in the cabin to begin settling. Passengers felt the landing gear release from the undercarriage in preparation for landing. The hysteria behind Tanner and Annika tapered off as they made their approach to the runway. They touched down at Juan Santamaria International late in the afternoon and boarded a small shuttle for a three-hour road trip to their Costa Rican getaway.

Hearing the recap of their flight from the other eight passengers on the bus was amusing. Had they not experienced it themselves, Tanner and Annika would have believed it to be the most terrifying flight in the history of aviation. The foreshadowing and character development was Oscar-worthy nonetheless and helped pass the time along the way. Stepping off the shuttle, Tanner had to turn his hat around backward. The winds were so strong they were using his bill as a sail. Annika got off behind him and leaned in for a kiss.

"I find you super sexy when you wear your hat like that," she admired.

By the time they checked in and made their way to their bungalow it was pitch black outside. A heavy dark cloud shielded the late first quarter moon, amplifying their senses to hear the crashing waves over the roaring winds. Exhausted from their journey, they opened the bottle of resort-provided champagne and hit the pillow soon thereafter.

The rain continued pummeling the roof of the beach bungalow their first day in paradise. Tanner drew the blinds before he changed into his lounging sweatpants.

"Skilli, there is no need for modesty. We are on a beach 3,000 miles from home and we will never see any of these people ever again. No one knows you in this part of the world. Plus, what are you bashful about? There is no shame in your game," she said with a wink and a smile.

Annika sat up and removed her tank top. She motioned him to crawl back into bed and offered a spirited round of topless ten minutes as she slowly sank into her pillow.

Tanner slipped his hand under the small nook behind her neck. He slowly stroked his finger across her stomach before relocating his touch to greater pastures.

While giving each other Eskimo kisses Tanner whispered, "Mrs. Skilli, your game is off the charts."

She bashfully chuckled and gradually opened her eyes. "Mr. Skilli, I cannot wait to have a church full of beautiful children with you," she replied.

Lying in bed they kissed each other softly and enjoyed the warmth of each other's bodies. A bellowing gust of wind shook their bungalow and triggered a local emergency siren. Tanner leapt out of bed and staggered into the wall.

"One too many last night there Skilli? Maybe you should hydrate a bit," Annika said with a comforting laugh.

When he made his urgent exit, his unfaithful left leg was bearing most of his weight. Diverting the attention away from an impairment he was self-conscious about was much appreciated. They both knew the true reason for the mishap, but they both did their best to disregard the reminder of his unfortunate struggle.

Brochure pictures of the Tortuguero Resort must have been taken when it was first constructed. Tanner feared the ancient walls were going to collapse in on themselves. They looked sturdy in the photographs but were in great need of some TLC.

Tanner decided to lead the charge to seek stronger shelter. Annika didn't share the same fear but humored him about the mission. She opened their front door and felt the 75-degree air brush by her body. Tanner was busy gathering up necessary belongings, while Annika stood in the doorway breathless. Since drunk tourists and undertow stories never have a happy ending, they had closed off the lower part of the beach below the bungalows. Making the water forbidden only increased her desire to plant her toes in the sand and feel the ocean splash on her feet.

Slinging the backpack over his shoulder Tanner also caught a glimpse of the miraculous scenery. Tanner loved angry seas, especially when he was on the shoreline or anchored in a protected cove. He believed the blowing winds and crashing waves were Mother Nature's reminder of her power. Seeing her express emotion in such a subtle but boisterous manner was impactful. Operation Seeking Shelter was scrapped following the sudden desire for adventure.

Annika looked down the shoreline and saw a barefoot old man taking his morning stroll, holding a bottle at his side. He was wearing rolled-up white pants and a navy blue buttoned-down shirt. The top few of his buttons were undone, allowing the wind to expose his grey hairy chest.

"Something tells me that that man kicking sand knows how to party. We should go talk to him," she said with intrigue.

Tanner nodded in agreeance and they exited their safe-haven in search of wisdom. As they approached the man, who they would soon find to be named Finnigan, he gave them a welcoming wave.

Tanner joked, "It looks like you're hitting the sauce early. I admire your stamina. If I drink in the morning, there's nothing more I want to do then go back to bed."

Finn, as he liked to be called, placed the bottle in the sand and wiped his weathered hand on his pants before establishing a physical connection. Tanner instantly became exceptionally fond of their new friend. Annika then extended her arm. Finn positioned his hand beneath hers with the comfort of an old grandfather. Placing his left hand on top of hers and lightly motioning up and down Annika felt the warmth of his dear old soul and was delighted to make his acquaintance.

Finn could tell they were looking down at the bottle with judgment. When Tanner joked about drinking early, he had no idea that Finn had endured several rounds battling an addiction with alcoholism.

In broken English, he said, "No, my friends. I don't dance with that stuff anymore. I thought it was a lucky message in a bottle when I picked it up. They don't make them like they used to, that's for sure. This one is nothing more than a Coors Light bottle with a Carlo Rossi cork. There was a note inside that requested money, but no return address."

Tanner asked Finn what drew him to the beach that morning. He shifted his focus away from the newlyweds and proclaimed how happy he was to see such a mighty wind blowing. Annika could see the delight on his face and a sense of Pura Vita. Her curiosity piqued.

"Can I ask you why you're so happy in this weather? I would guess that most people who live down here don't enjoy it as much as you do."

Not trying to be offensive, Finn explained to them that only those who are selfish are angry by such a storm. They are only thinking of themselves and not the other creatures on this planet. The stronger the wind blows, the more sand gets swept up to the higher ground. He went on to explain that a shifting of the sand makes it easier for the little turtle hatchlings and that they were entitled to every advantage they can get in life.

Tanner and Annika looked at each other with a new understanding and perspective. Finn told them that the storm was by design and not just chance.

"We need to remember that Mother Nature is a mother to all life. Her reach is not limited to just humans, but all creatures of life," the wise man told them.

Like a seasoned meteorologist, Finn predicted, with unwavering certainty, the events that would unfold. His eyes fixated on the ocean as he analyzed the patterns of the rolling waves.

"This evening it will be calm, no more wind. We shall give thanks tonight and then celebrate the hatching in the morning," he said as he casually proceeded with his morning walk.

They thanked him for his words and Finn raised his left hand holding the bottle, while his right hand secured his straw hat from blowing away.

In the flash of an eye Annika blurted out, "I can't take it any longer. I have to feel the ocean. Pura Vida!"

She darted down the beach and hurdled the cheap barriers. Tanner followed suit and took off behind her. He was more focused on the safety aspect of the expedition and wanted to protect her from the riptide current. They felt like they were running in slow motion as the winds continued to resist their efforts. Annika had always been known for her resilience and after several seconds she stopped. With her feet placed close together, she started twisting back and forth like she was squishing a giant bug. She began to slowly sink into the beach as the smashing waves hit against the front of her ankles. Tanner stood ten steps behind his wife and was taken aback by her natural beauty. With her arms open wide to the sides, she tilted her head to the sky and smiled. All she needed was a quick recharge. Before Tanner could even make it over to her, she had already gotten her ocean fix and was ready to head back.

Their afternoon was spent back in the bungalow playing cribbage and talking about their dreams. Elliot Smith played in the background as the Skillis spoke freely and continued to peel back the layers to their souls. They had scratched the surface on broad thoughts of their future, covering all their major bases, but Annika had a much greater detailed picture of what she dreamed for their lives.

Tanner simply knew that he loved his wife unconditionally and had never intentionally given the future much thought. He had always lived his life one moment at a time. Rather than focusing on the finish line, his efforts were only to get over the next hurdle. In his mind, Annika was his person in life. Beyond that, he had never given thought to worry. Following his modus operandi, he was waiting for the next hurdle. With Annika by his side, he experienced new confidence. Tanner was ready for the next obstacle but lacked the vision of how their story was to unfold.

Annika cut the deck and Tanner flipped over the Jack of Spades.

"What do you want, babe? What is it that you want most in this world?" Tanner asked while pegging his two points for nobs.

She looked at her hand and tried to maintain her best poker face.

"In short, I want to make a positive impact on this world and for us to be happy. I don't think that is setting the bar too high."

Leading with the queen of hearts, Annika sat back in silence. For such a positive ambition, Tanner could tell something was troubling her.

"What else is going on in there? I can tell something's weighing on you. There are few guarantees in life, but there is one for certain. Like in the sea of life, we are always going to experience dips and swells. Power is gained from resistance. If we never had to endure times of resistance, we would never grow stronger," Tanner said, digging deep for his inner philosopher.

Looking down at his cards, he contemplated his next move.

"You are gorgeous, there is no question about that, but it is your inner drive and view on the world that attracts me the most. I know that, together, we can overcome any obstacle that gets thrown at us. In the end, our bond will continue to gain strength," Tanner said while playing a five of diamonds.

Taking his two points, he looked Annika in the eye and said, "I love everything about you, Mrs. Skilli. Not to sound selfish, but I love who I am when I am with you."

Annika leaned over to kiss Tanner while trying not to disclose her double-run hand.

"I love you too, Mr. Skilli. I have loved you ever since our first beach experience and surprise surprise, look where we have ended up," she said.

The reassurance of having a partner in life provided them with the confidence to reach for greater heights. Discussing their visions of the future allowed them to draft the outline for their path forward. They had so much in common, but that didn't mean they were without opposing views on various subjects. With a mutual understanding that the light would always overcome the darkness, in that moment, both Tanner and Annika felt at peace.

The remainder of the day was spent curled up in bed and enjoying each other. They faded in and out of sleep until the beat of a loud drum echoed throughout the village three times. Annika got out of bed and made her way to the door. Tanner sat up in bed as he felt the warm ocean air fill their room.

"Finnigan called it," she said as she stepped out of their bungalow wearing only her undergarments.

The drum reverberated off the trees three more times. Annika rounded the corner in an attempt to locate the source of the calling. Colorful lights were displayed above a coved rock formation. Dancing flames from Tiki torches created an inviting perimeter in the sand.

"Thank goodness, I packed the perfect evening dress for such an occasion," she said while rifling through her suitcase.

"Well, the odds were in your favor. The deadweight of your luggage felt like you brought your entire closet," he said with a grin.

"That's just silly nonsense. I tried several times and I couldn't get it zipped up," she replied.

Walking hand in hand they approached the festivities. The volume of the local music grew louder as they made their entrance, providing a warm welcoming. They were promptly greeted by a sweet woman with green cups filled with Miguelito.

She handed a cup to Annika, "For the beautiful lady."

Then she turned to Tanner with excited eyes.

"Their journey is about to begin. Pura Vida," she said with enchantment.

Food started flooding the tables like an orchestrated symphony, as native chants began stirring from the servers. It was a production like they had never observed.

Sitting at a table, feast laid before them, Tanner looked over at Annika in awe, "Babe, this is all for you. Everything you see, hear, smell, and taste was all part of my masterful plan. Happy honeymoon, love."

Annika knew he was full of it, but kind of liked the thought of being a princess for a night.

She looked up at Tanner and sarcastically stated, "You are so thoughtful Mr. Skilli. That must have taken a lot of coordinating to get all these people to pedal their bicycles and coconut carts here tonight."

Tanner looked over and saw the beautiful chaos of a thousand bikes and carts lined up. With pedal bikes being the town's primary mode of transportation, they seemed to be the only ones enamored by the pile of metal and rubber arranged in an organized madness fashion.

The newlyweds enjoyed their night dancing under the full moon and conversing with the fascinating locals. Tanner quickly learned that anytime he said "Imperial," a delicious beer would arrive in his hand. His dance moves had diminished over the years, but he was searching to find them at the bottom of one of those beers. When it got to the point he was trusting his left leg like the old days, they decided to call it a night. They stumbled their way through the sand and back to their bungalow. Annika flopped down on the bed and threw her inviting arms in the air.

"What a night! That was so incredible I don't know how I will ever repay you for going to such great lengths to impress me. Mission accomplished, is all I can say. Mission accomplished. How can I even begin to repay you?" she asked, through a steady stream of Miguelito-infused giggles.

Calling it sleep would have been a stretch, a nap would be more appropriate. The last time Tanner saw on the clock was 3:37 and when he woke it read 5:15 in the morning. Tanner made a promise to Grandpa Stephen and he wasn't about to let sleep deprivation stop him from being true to his word.

Tanner gently kissed Annika on the neck and whispered, "Time to wake up sleepyhead, you've been in bed for almost twelve hours."

After glancing at the clock she closed her eyes.

"Cute, babe. Real cute. I couldn't live with myself if they all made it to the sea before I could grab a few of those adorable little guys to take home."

Nearly every local from the night before was still in attendance on the beach that morning. Tanner and Annika appeared to be the only lightweights in the group. The sun was slowly beginning to rise from behind them, casting rays of light to warm the sand. Finn saw the couple walking hand-in-hand and gave them a native greeting.

"Mother Nature has been kind to us and kind to our friends. Today we will watch them begin their journey in this world. Many will not make it, but that is simply a part of life. Others will benefit from their misfortune but in this case, it does not bring me sadness for they have served their purpose on Earth," Finn said while pointing down to the shifting sand in the nest.

A small charcoal grey neck peeked out of the sand followed by the Olive Ridley turtle's left arm. Annika leaned into Tanner and placed her arm across his chest. Annika bounced up and down like a high school cheerleader overwhelmed with spirit. It took every bit of strength to resist the temptation of dropping to her knees and begin digging them out like she was closing in on a geoduck. The nest came to life in a matter of seconds. One by one the turtles emerged from the only home they had ever known. Immediately allowing their natural instincts to take over, they pointed their noses toward the water and started scooting their tiny bodies across the sand.

Tanner expected to see a couple of dozen turtles hatch from each nest. Eventually, there were upward of 800 little Olive Ridley turtles that emerged from the single nest. Instinctively, the turtles knew where they were going, but that didn't stop the Costa Ricans from unrolling the red carpet for them along the way. Tiki torches outlined their path, light percussions were heard over the clasping waves, while young boys stood guard with slingshots to fend off any predator air raids from the sky.

A strange phenomenon, that Tanner didn't become aware of until later in life, was that he had an instant connection with everything in his surroundings. There wasn't a single turtle in the nest that Tanner had ever seen before yet he still cared deeply for their wellbeing. That uncontrollable desire to hold onto every relationship and connection was both Tanner's best and worst trait. Annika had a similar tendency, but was less impulsive and used a higher level of scrutiny before fully trusting. They balanced each other well and loved every minute of their life as one. Tanner couldn't help but feel his protective instincts kick in and felt as though it was a personal mission to be the over-watch as the turtles fought their way to the sea.

Annika grabbed her camera to capture the spectacle unfolding before them. Surveilling down the beach they began to cheer on the most adorable creatures from the reptilian class. Thousands of turtles pushed themselves through the trenches in search of water, making it look like a miniature version of the swim portion of an Ironman competition. Tanner was inspired by the will and determination each challenger had with them while battling the gauntlet. Spilling waves reached far up the beach to rescue the hatchlings from dry land. Fortunate turtles would get to feel the ocean water surrounding them with a welcoming hug.

Spectators began cheering on the waves as the masses had already crossed the finish line. It was only the stranglers that remained.

Tanner leaned over and kissed Annika on the forehead, "This is always my favorite part of every race. Watching those who aren't supposed to make it, but know they can, always encourages me to do better."

Tanner was a sucker for the underdog in a fight and loved every turtle on that beach like they were a sibling. The later cresting waves extended the reach of the ocean allowing it to embrace those in need of aid. Wrapping its arms around them, the ocean pulled them toward safety. The clapping and singing allowed the locals and the guests to fuse together in unity. Watching the people put down all walls and express themselves outwardly in such a beautiful way was nothing shy of incredible.

Each picture was better than the previous, making it difficult to put down the camera. Annika focused her lens on Finn standing at the water's edge, raising his hands in victory, and wearing a smile from ear to ear. That still-image would later be mounted on canvas and hung in their entryway at home. The shot was the perfect depiction of what they wished their lives to be. The ability to find happiness in the success of others, and showing appreciation for the opportunity to witness the achievement, turned out to be their life credo. Some would say it was their strongest attributes later in life since it brought them so much joy and happiness.

Arm-in-arm, Tanner and Annika watched the remaining turtles surface from the sand. Stragglers looked like Kevin from *Home Alone* as they had been left behind by their families. Annika grew antsy and was trying to put her desires at bay. A local woman named Takuta took notice of Annika's body language. She presented herself with great honor in the village and appeared to have the authority to grant special privileges. Takuta grabbed Annika by the hand and invited her to join her alongside the calm nest. Placing their hands on the outside of the nest they gently wiggled their way towards the bottom.

"Spread your fingers wide," Takuta instructed.

Annika slowly lifted her hand and soon felt the shells of those that had the most difficult path. They were buried so deeply, it was a struggle in itself to even reach fresh air. The sand spilled through Annika's fingers as she introduced the Olive Ridley turtles to Earth's surface. Tears of happiness started streaming into the nest from both Annika and Takuta. Tanner reached over and pulled the camera from her shoulder. The moment was one that will always be cherished, but the visual reminder evoked the same emotions time and time again.

33

KEYS TO THE KINGDOM

With the wedding and honeymoon behind them, Tanner and Annika focused their efforts on their next business venture. Back at home in Boulder, they were enjoying a nice evening, sitting around the fire and drinking Ninkasi microbrews.

Annika rose to her feet and made her way into the kitchen. She saw the pile of mail sitting on the island and started sorting the bills from the fan mail. Tanner had made his weekly routine stop by the post office to check their box. He had yet to sort through the pile, mostly because he viewed it as a stack of work.

Although Tanner was appreciative of his fans taking the time to write to him, it made him unsettled. Each letter would praise him and tell him how much of a hero he had been, followed by a sad story about why they needed money. The letters would tug at his heart-strings, regardless of their validity. They exploited his generous nature, but after a while, he was very selective to whom he would send monetary aid.

Annika started her typical segregation of the mail. Observing from across the way, Tanner asked her to join him in the living room. Over time, fetching the mail had become a chore. Each letter made him feel anxious, as he expected them to be nothing more than another person to disappoint or another bill to pay. Annika grabbed the stack of bills and began thumbing through them.

"This is so dumb," she said. "Why can't all these bills be consolidated into one? I want to write one check, instead of a dozen small checks. Death by a thousand cuts, I tell ya!"

Tanner grabbed another log and stoked the fire. Annika rejoined him. She cuddled up in the corner of the couch and cradled her pint glass between her hands.

"Maybe that's it, babe. That's what our next business should be. We would meet with all the top service providers in the area, starting with the insurance companies. Medical, dental, vision, health, auto, you name it. Then we contact the professional services. We would have legal, tax, investing, bookkeeping, payroll processor, and various others. As the company grows, we would be able to incorporate banks and mortgage companies. It would be the key to having a central hub for life," he said with conviction.

Kingdom Key, as it was later named, would provide a solution to simplifying busy lives. Throughout the year, and more importantly, at year-end, clients would have the ability to review their finances and bills under a single account. All external agencies would feed information into a single point and provided their clients with ease of access. It was genius.

They maintained a high level of standards for their clientele and their pricing structure reflected their target market. At the end of the year, clients didn't have to run around and collect all the necessary documents for their tax return preparation. If their address, phone number, or banking account changed, they only had to update it on their one account and all agencies would be notified.

Annika and Tanner continued to brainstorm around the fire. They opened a couple of new microbrews and carried on the conversation into the night. Along the way, Annika jotted down key details from the discussion. She knew her inebriated brain was always a little fuzzy on details the next day. Luckily for both of them, those notes became the spark that led to a multi-million dollar company.

With the capital they received from the sale of Dweedoole, and the nest-egg Tanner had stored away thanks to Uncle Perry, they rented an office building and began scheduling meetings with all their prospective partners. Tanner worked the deals like a polished businessman. When they were on the fence, he would drop the name of a competitor. Bending the truth a bit, he would lead them to believe that they have already made a deal with the competitor and outlined how it was going to give them a market edge. One after another, they started growing their network and built their management team. Annika and Tanner made an emphasis to hire the right people at the top. They vowed that they would be involved in the company, but they wanted the executive managers to run the day to day operations.

The beauty of Kingdom Key was it took the guesswork out of tax preparation, applying for loans, insurance, and personal finances. After heavily lobbying in Washington D.C., they were able to pass a bill that required the IRS to show their hand in real-time. Rather than treating tax returns like a game of poker, Kingdom Key had the data available to process tax returns without any hidden surprises. Since their company was submitting the lion's share of the information to the IRS, it was only logical they should have access to see if anything else had been reported. Clients would no longer have to track down W-2 statements, 1099's, mortgage statements, or any of the abundant documents that trickle in at a snail's pace at the beginning of the year.

Philanthropy was an essential focus of Kingdom Key, next to taking care of their valued employees. Not only did they provide an excellent compensation package, but Kingdom Key employees were also given opportunities to join outreach programs across the globe to experience other cultures.

A baseline requirement for those who didn't want to travel was one day out of every month, each employee would have to volunteer their time at a local non-profit organization. They would be paid their full salary for the day, but most of them would elect to have it donated to the organization. Although they received great public relations praise, the Skilli's steered the focus toward helping those who were less fortunate in all walks of life. They knew some people were uncomfortable with volunteering and needed that extra push of motivation to get them involved. The program was a great success and won the hearts of the people they were helping as well as the hearts of their staff and business partners.

Four employees had just returned home from a week in Botswana. Tanner strolled into the break room in search of his morning coffee. As he began pouring his starting dosage into his

REVOLV3R: The Story of a Beautiful Murder

Portland Starbucks mug, he overheard the conversation about the trip. When he turned around, the group locked eyes with him and quickly became silent.

"Good morning Mr. Skilli," one of the workers said before staring directly at the ground.

"What are you folks talking about over there, if you don't mind me asking? Work-related I hope," he said with a grin.

"Yes, Sir. We just got back from Africa. We had a unique opportunity to help build a medical center near one of the Seven Wonders of the World. If you have never seen Victoria Falls in person, you are doing yourself a disservice. The local people were so kind and welcoming. We spent one day as tourists and then focused our energy on getting the med center up and running," the employee said.

Tanner sipped his coffee while looking back at the group of workers and started configuring the logistics in his head. He and Annika were overdue for an adventure and he was plotting out how he could make a trip to Africa work.

"You're Joseph, right? Joseph Sattler?" Tanner asked.

Astonished by the fact that the *bossman* knew his name, he was slow to reply.

"That's correct, Mr. Skilli. We thank you for providing such a wonderful culture in your company. The level of integrity and push for individual growth is unlike any other place I have worked."

Hearing those words was music to Tanner's ears. His vision was gaining traction with workers buying into his ultimate goal.

Impressed by a recent project that Joseph had spearheaded, Tanner continued the exchange with him while the others headed for a kaizen meeting. Receiving that sort of recognition from his boss, sent Joseph over the moon. They chatted further about the trip, noting all the must-stop sites, as well as spots to avoid. Both Joe, as he quickly began to call him, and Tanner hit it off. Creative energy began flourishing as they exchanged ideas and stories before heading to lunch.

On days they were both working in the office, Annika and Tanner met up for lunch at their favorite Mexican Restaurant *Sarten Casara*. His metabolism wasn't what it used to be, but he couldn't resist the Sarten Super Nachos with shredded beef, chicken, sour cream, guacamole, jalapeños, beans, and olives. The extremely crucial three-cheese blend was layered throughout and provided the optimum chip-to-fixin' ratio. Tanner nodded to Omar, their regular server, and requested the usual. Annika ordered the tostada, knowing full well she would be assisting in devouring the nachos.

The kitchen crew took a calculated gamble and started building the nacho creation the minute Tanner walked through the front door. Tanner was known for taking the shortest lunch breaks - if he remembered to eat lunch at all. Since he always took care of the staff and tipped well, they made sure to take extra special care of them. What Tanner appreciated the most was how the entire staff showed respect for his time. In the brief moments they had before the food was served, on what seemed like a magma hot place, he pitched the idea of an African Safari to his beautiful wife.

Since extending their family was more difficult than anticipated. The struggle to get pregnant had been looming over their heads for several months like an ominous cloud that only darkened. Constant visits to the doctors and meeting with specialists were becoming emotionally taxing for both of them.

When Tanner initially proposed the trip to Africa, Annika wasn't immediately sold on the idea. She felt like a disappointment to both Tanner and her fellow women. She felt inadequate in not being able to perform the primary function her body was created for.

Tanner began retelling the stories from the break room earlier that morning, as the plates were delivered to the table. They quickly blessed their meal and dove into the masterpiece dishes placed before them. There is a small window of one and a half to three minutes, tops, to grab the optimal chips smothered in nummy cheesy goodness. The two acknowledged the golden window and ceased conversation until it had passed. Once the cheese started to harden, ever so slightly, they resumed discussing the trip.

Reluctant as she may have been, the trip appeared to be one for the memory books and pictures on the wall. Tanner and Annika carved out two weeks of their schedule, which was the longest duration they had been away from the company since it was founded. They were confident that the management team wouldn't run the company into the ground in a fortnight, but subtle doubts still lingered in the back of their minds.

34

GERTRUDE THE GIRAFFE

When the plane touched down on the dirt runway, they knew they were far from home. The locals helped escort them to the shuttle, which took them to their chosen bed and breakfast. Driving up the road they saw the most magnificent giraffes gracefully walking in the open fields. The driver was desensitized to the beauty and dismissed them in a similar manner to how Tanner and Annika viewed cows in a pasture back home.

Their room had a large window on the second floor, providing an elevated panoramic view of the beautiful scenery. People from all across the globe had taken their own journey to experience the unique setting of the Giraffe Manor. Tanner and Annika quickly discovered the obvious reasons why others would travel such great lengths, it was like nothing they had ever seen before.

Gertrude loved being hand-fed by little humans and was notorious for making her morning rounds to meet and greet the guests. The hospitality crew at the manor took the privilege of providing a bucket of freshly peeled carrots and placed them outside Annika and Tanner's door in case she were to made an appearance.

Tanner sprung out of bed and put on his trusty pair of Oregon sweatpants. Slowly opening the door to find out what the clanging sound was, he looked down and saw the bucket of carrots. Rather than being woken up by a traditional rooster crowing, Tanner turned around and saw the head of a mother giraffe peeking through their window.

Upon seeing the giant snout sniffing across the room for her morning breakfast, Annika thought she was still lingering in a blissful dream. As Tanner shut the door, Annika flinched and grabbed the covers over her head.

"Is that who I think it is? The famous Gertrude?" she asked as she slowly lowered the blankets. "Oh my goodness, she is beautiful. She must have already had her cup of coffee and showered, she is stunning."

Annika's eyes widened. Tanner held up the bucket of carrots and asked Annika if she wanted to feed Gerty. With a carrot resting in the palm of her hand, Annika slowly presented it to her. Gerty's long black tongue wrapped around the carrot and pulled it into her mouth. Watching a creature eat had never been so fascinating. It was by far the most unique way they had ever begun their morning.

Once the bucket was empty, Gerty eased her way out their window and headed to meet her other new friends.

Following a delicious breakfast of their own, they were informed by the front desk that their shipment was due to arrive the next day. Tanner and Annika had arranged for a large shipment of school and medical supplies to be shipped to the Lokichogio airport along with a plethora of other necessities. It is one thing to write a check and donate to a cause, but being present for the joy that generosity brings is incomparable.

Before they would have the opportunity to hand out supplies, they had to first face the actual African lions without being eaten. The instructions were clear: do not wear red, do not run, look straight forward, and most importantly, do not let them sense your fear. Aside from that last part, it seemed like an easy feat. Standing outside of the gate, they watched the trainers, dressed in green military-style fatigue and berets, positioned fearlessly inside the fence with the pride. From a distance, the pride looked like cuddly little stuffed animals, all cute and fluffy. When the lions walked along the fence line, their large meat-devouring teeth and giant paws displayed their distinct ability to maul anything that had a pulse.

Tanner was mentally preparing himself when Annika asked if she could go in first.

"Be my guest, sweetheart," he said with relief. "All I ask for is one last kiss."

As soon as the gate opened, he instantly regretted his chivalry. The promise of never putting his wife in harm's way was being broken before his very eyes. Fears of losing Annika before ever having a family together started to dominate his thoughts. The trainer brought over a lioness with a striking resemblance to Sarabi from The Lion King.

Annika stood at attention as the lioness sashayed over and rubbed against Annika's leg with a docile nudge. The trainer instructed Annika to begin walking. With his stomach in knots, Tanner watched his wife walk side by side with the lioness. It was a beautiful moment. His attraction for her grew even stronger in a way he did not think was possible. Her bravery extended deeper than he knew was possible.

Knowing that Tanner would bust down the gate, and wrestle a pride of lions, gave her the confidence to walk fearlessly. Annika smiled proudly as she guided the lioness to turn right. The trainer trailed behind, but only offered a few words of encouragement. He could tell Annika was in her element and further instructions were unnecessary.

Tanner's heart continued to race as he knew it was going to be a tough act to follow. She did it with such poise and grace. Before parting ways, the lioness nuzzled into her side. Annika looked to the trainer for permission and then proceeded to run her hand down the back of the lioness. The two had created an unspoken bond.

The head trainer, Kota, whistled for the other workers to gather Tanner's walking partner.

Kota called out for Samson, before turning to Tanner with a big grin.

"Samson?" Tanner asked nervously.

"Ah yes, he be considered the King of the Jungle round here, that Samson. As strong and mighty as they come. He has killed enough wildebeests to feed large villages," the trainer replied.

Lured off his prized rock by a cut of zebra hindquarters, Samson stomped over toward them. He shook his mane and let out a pitiful roar, more like a morning yawn. Tanner entered the gate after Samson dismantled the zebra meat. With a mouth dripping fresh blood, Samson lethargically strutted over toward

Kota. Vibrations from his large paws shook the ground beneath them with each step. Despite the African heat, a cold shiver ran up Tanner's spine making the hair on the back of his neck stand to attention.

Annika whispered from outside the gate, "You got this, Studmuffin. You are the real king of the jungle, show that little kitty who runs this town."

Tanner appreciated the words of encouragement but questioned the truth behind the statement.

"Pretty sure, he would eat me like catnip," Tanner said with an unsettled tone.

Samson postured up directly beside Tanner.

"Shoulders back. Now walk," Kota instructed from behind them.

Tanner took his first steps while gasping for quick shallow breaths. Annika walked along the fence line with him and could tell he was frightened to death.

To help put him at ease, she said, "You aren't walking him down the aisle there Skilli. Picture it as two kings going for an afternoon jaunt around their native land. Ask yourself, what would Simba do?"

As they began to make their turn back to the gate, Kota tapped Samson on his hind leg. Rather than turning right, Samson had an agenda of his own and wanted to bank left. Tanner tried to give him space to make the turn, but the large beast continued to lean in toward him.

Kota sternly commanded, "Botonda."

Samson lifted his right paw and pushed Tanner to the side. After stumbling backward, he regained his stature. The next few moments flashed by in an instant, like the scene from a horrible car crash.

Tanner couldn't focus his eyes as Samson rose to his hind feet and placed his paws on Tanner's shoulders. The sheer weight felt like he was preparing to squat a full-size truck. Standing stiff as a board, Tanner didn't know how to react. At that point, Samson had not yet thrown the first punch. Retaliation in self-defense could not be used as a verifiable alibi.

Watching it all unfold, Annika stood on the other side of the fence with her hands cupped over her mouth.

She shot a desperate look at Kota, as to say, "Why aren't you stopping this lion from eating my husband?"

Kota smiled back and winked. She shook her head with confusion but then figured out that it was just a bit to mess with the tourists.

"Sweetheart, I love you. We had a good run, but I guess this is where we say our last goodbyes," she said with fake concern.

Kota then commanded, "Zuppa."

Tanner looking left to right in panic, he softly said, "Does that mean stop?"

"Zuppa, zuppa, zuppa!" he began chanting.

It was like he was whispering sweet nothings into Samson's ear as he tried negotiating with the ferocious beast for his life. A large slimy tongue slapped him across his face, leaving remnants of zebra flesh running down Tanner's cheek.

"Simama," Kota instructed.

Samson pushed off of Tanner's chest and went back down on all fours. Wiping his cheek on his sleeve, Tanner looked over to see Annika nearly collapsing to the ground in laughter. He shifted his eyes to the trainers in the corner, whom where all doubled over and slapping their legs in delight. Tanner locked eyes with Kota, who shrugged his shoulders like an innocent bystander to the prank.

"Samson here may be big, but he would not hurt a flea. Most of his teeth had to be pulled when he was rescued. His claws were getting infected, so the animal doctor removed those too. He's a toothless wonder and wouldn't survive a day in the wild," Kota said while patting Samson on the side as if he were merely an oversized house cat.

Being the butt of a joke is never desirable, but Tanner was a great sport about the whole setup. Kota and the crew had the routine down and used it on any man they felt was a little too big for his britches. Being attacked by a lion is a surefire way to reorder a person's perspective of the food-chain.

Annika reentered the cage after Samson had shifted down to his lowest gear. That was the longest walk he intended on taking that day, so probably figured he should revel in the outing.

As badly as she wanted to, Annika was hesitant to wrap her arms around Tanner. His heart was still racing like crazy and was in desperate need of some coddling. At that point, it didn't matter who provided the hug. He would have settled for any one of the trainers, given the recent mental trauma.

Annika feared that the pride had accepted her as their alpha. Hugging Tanner might send the wrong message to the pride, as it could potentially be misinterpreted as a command to attack the timid man. She resorted to throwing up a high-five and told him how proud she was of him for standing his ground with the *mighty* Samson.

"Hey champ, when we're old and gray, we will look back at this moment knowing that we walked with courageous lions," she said while patting Samson on his back.

Tanner looked down and saw Samson staring directly at him with bashful eyes. Slowly reaching with a shaky left hand, he rested his palm on Samson's head. They had accepted one another as gallant equals.

During the afternoon, they sat on the outside patio and watched the herd of giraffes meander about the manor like old folks around a retirement home. Tanner and Annika began discussing how they envied the giraffe's free lifestyle. With no sense of urgency, minimal expectations, constant snacks, and delicious meals served at their leisure.

"Don't take this the wrong way, but I want to explore the world with you. There are so many incredible places to explore and people to befriend. As enticing as a giraffe's life may be, I don't think I could be confined to a few hundred acres," Annika said while taking a sip of her Beaujolais red wine.

Tanner looked at her with a puzzled expression.

"Why would I take that the wrong way?" he asked.

"I just didn't want you to question my appreciation for this experience. Looking around here, I see tremendous beauty. I am loving every minute of our African adventure together, don't get me wrong. Seeing it with my own eyes has provided me with a deep appreciation for the world. When you told me about the trip, I was super excited but couldn't have imagined it would be this superb. I'm trying to stay in the moment, but it all reminds me that we've got no place to go but everywhere," she said with a delighted exhale.

Evenings at the manor were the epitome of elegant. Guests arrived for the cocktail hour dressed in proper formal attire. Annika wore a deep blue skintight dress that quickly stole the spotlight from the other guests in attendance. Tanner could have been wearing his birthday suit and the other guests wouldn't have paid him any attention. Annika and Tanner tried to engage in conversation with every couple and family. Hearing the individual stories and lives full of trials and tribulations that got them to that point, made the evening pass in a flash. Bottles of wine were passed around the tables and the volume of the room became increasingly louder after each pulled cork.

As the night began to wind down, Tanner and Annika found themselves near an open window to take in the African air. It had been an eventful day and the jet lag was starting to catch up with them. They sat down on a cushioned bench, in front of the window.

"Mr. Skilli, not sure I have told you this recently, but I love you," she said with a twinkle in her eye. "This whole experience wouldn't have been the same if I didn't get to experience it with you."

Looking out the window they saw the silhouettes of giraffes cast beneath the vibrant red skyline.

Tanner placed his right arm around her shoulder and pulled her in close to his body.

Gently swaying from side to side, he softly whispered, "I love you too, babe. At this moment, halfway across the globe, my soul is at peace with you by my side."

Slowly closing her eyes, she took a deep breath and nestled into his body. Reaching over with her right hand, she tightened her fingers and clawed his left chest.

"Alright tiger, take this lioness back to the den and have your way with her. Release that internal King of the Jungle spirit from its cage."

Like a butterfly shedding its cocoon, Annika slinked out of her dress the second their bedroom door closed. Tanner leaned against the bed and had only removed his right shoe when he looked across the room. The faded moonlight cast upon the floor. The window frame created a perfect outlining to display her beauty in the soft tint.

"Holy smokes!" he said in astonishment.

His whole body froze in amazement and grew numb at the sight of her. He was continually reminded of how seeing her never grew old, and in fact, felt almost as if he was seeing her for the first time. She was naturally flawless. Tanner's first thought was about how gorgeous this woman was standing in front of him. Then he smiled from ear to ear when he realized he would soon get that amazing body pressed up against his bare skin.

In a state that resembled shell-shock, Tanner was slow to remove his clothing. Rushing as fast as he could to strip down, he fumbled like he was trapped in a straightjacket. Alas, he removed his final sock. Walking his naked body across the room, he began to question the rate of his strides.

"Don't go too fast and appear over-elated like a kid in their first candy store, but also don't go the pace of a decrepit old man," he thought to himself.

Extending her right arm toward him, she summoned him closer with her finger. When he was within reach, she placed her finger on his chest and slowly began tracing a line down his stomach. She wrapped her hand around him and gently stroked back and forth as they kissed each other passionately. Their bodies ignited with each touch, causing each molecule of air around them to hum from their energy. The exotic setting sun and Giraffe silhouettes added a burst of endorphins into their veins. Annika ushered him into the bathroom and turned on the shower.

Regrettable memories of his night with Astra would soon be erased after what unfolded. Although the whole debacle with Astra was a grave mistake, the thought of them entering the shower was the only image that he ever recalled. Still showing respect as guests, Tanner and Annika didn't want to waste water and quickly got down to business.

Kneeling under the rushing water, her talented tongue worked its way around him, sending tingles throughout his body. Annika took great pleasure in the fact her actions were providing her husband with such erotic satisfaction. Selfishly, she turned off the water and motioned him to kick it into second gear like there was no time to spare. She was ready to go and didn't want the moment to diminish.

Towels were tossed on the floor as they exited the bathroom. Annika grabbed his hand and walked him to the window bench. A warm African breeze blew through the open window into the room. She positioned him to take a seat and then slowly began kissing his chest.

After a few enjoyable minutes, she rose to her feet and then placed her legs on each side of his body. The seat cushions padded her knees as she leaned in and smothered Tanner with her still dripping breasts, allowing him to lick her nipples as she brushed them passed his face.

Annika pressed her body against Tanner and released an uncontrollable moan. He felt incredible inside of her. She slowly shifted from side to side, while they embraced one another. Tanner kissed beneath her chin, and down the side of her neck, as she tilted her head back in enjoyment. The remaining details of that night would later be politely omitted when telling the story about the conception of their first child.

Had the trip ended that next morning, Tanner would have been pleased, incredibly pleased to say the least. At breakfast, Tanner and Annika basked in the memories from the day prior. It had every component to make for a complete day: Adventure, laughter, beautiful scenery, wonderful conversation, and intimate romance. Neither one of them could mask the uncontrollable smiles spanning across their faces. Once they had finished their delicious meal, the next chapter of their journey began.

The manor concierge received confirmation that the Skilli's supplies had arrived at the airport and were being prepped for their final destination: Kakuma Refugee Camp. It was time to say their farewells and head to the airport. The manor staff loaded the Skilli's luggage into a white Land Rover and sent them on their way.

Two hours later, Mr. and Mrs. Skill reached the airport, performed a quick inventory count, and boarded their scheduled flight.

"Kakuma, here we come," Annika said as the plane left the ground.

"There is no one else in this world that I would rather spend these precious moments with, Sweetheart." Tanner said as he leaned across the small seat and kissed her on the cheek.

35

LOKICHOGIO LOCALS

Touching down at Lokichogio Airport was a much different welcoming compared to their previous destination. Once on the ground, Tanner appreciated that his travel agent encouraged the additional security for their shipment. A large crowd swarmed outside the gates with their hands. There was desperation in their eyes for any scraps of food available.

The environment was completely gut-wrenching. The only material possessions the people owned were the unwashed and torn clothing on their backs. Lokichogio was operated by the Kenya Airports Authority, but the security made it look more like a military outpost. The locals had become desensitized to the needs of the helpless people, viewing them as nothing more than pesky insects.

Tanner looked at Annika, silently requesting approval to follow his heart. Without a word spoken, she nodded her head, yes, before breaking her silence.

"These people's lives are just as important as the lives in Kakuma. How can we not help them?" she asked, desperation and sadness filling the spaces between her words.

They asked the hired hands to assist in opening one of the crates. Tanner began pulling out bags of food. Rather than having giant sacks of rice and beans, they packaged the food in smaller bags. It helped ration out the available stock, in hopes no one

REVOLV3R: The Story of a Beautiful Murder

would get left out. Seeing the smiles and hearing the cheers of excitement touch their hearts as Tanner, Annika, and the hired hands helped divvy up the food as quickly as they could to keep their schedule on track.

After distributing what they could spare, the rest of the supplies were loaded on a flatbed. When they were receiving instructions before taking off to their next destination, the guide pointed toward the truck. Tanner couldn't decipher his broken English and thought he was telling them to get into the single cab truck, so he errantly did so with obedience. They hopped in and headed down the dirt roads to Kakuma. It created an awkward experience for everyone. The driver had not anticipated having three people crammed into the cab of his truck, nor was he charmed at the fact that Tanner chose to ride in the middle.

Riding in the middle reminded Tanner of being a kid and driving down the roads in Casper, Wyoming. It was a time when his parents were still married. Even though times were difficult, they were still a complete family.

The legroom in the middle seat was not exactly as he remembered it being back home. Like Tripp's old pickup, the flatbed was a manual. Tanner got to enjoy the uncomfortable feeling of having another man jerking a long stick around between his legs. Some childhood memories are difficult to replicate as an adult and Tanner found that memory to be one of them. His comfort-bubble was continuously being breached with little disregard, as they bounced down the road and made their way to their next location.

36

KAKUMA

The other trucks and security trailed closely behind in a much more accommodating van with two vacant seats in plain view. When they arrived at Kakuma, they could not believe the makeshift housing landscape that surrounded them. Tanner looked at Annika, as she was shaking her head with sorrow.

"Tanner, we should have had them send over a thousand times the supplies. Look at how many people are living in these conditions with nothing, absolutely nothing at all," she said.

When they arrived at the camp they weren't swarmed like the welcoming committee at Lokichogio. People started gathering around, as they saw the trucks pulling through the gate. Annika opened the truck door and stepped out. She had been mentally preparing for a paparazzi-style ambush, but it never happened. One by one the villagers approached Annika and Tanner and offered them praise for their presence and generosity. Regardless of the extent of their gifts, the refugees were overjoyed to see new faces of people who cared.

Surveying the deprived setting created a strange mixture of emotions.

"How can people in America surround themselves with every material item their heart desires and still be unhappy, when these poor souls have nothing and love life? I guess material items do nothing for the soul, and these refugees feel rich in spirit," Annika said to Tanner while heading to the offloaded crates.

They assembled three lines. One to the kitchen, one to the schoolhouse, and one to the common area. The organization was marvelous and made the process go quickly. So quickly, they were mindful of how great the need for assistance and donations had become. Their generosity was appreciated. However, the supplies only scratched the surface of their demand, despite the thirty-six crates.

Accepting an offer to join the villagers for their only meal that day troubled Tanner. By the code of rationing, two people in the camp would have to go without food as a result of the additional guests. Not wanting to be offensive, Tanner and Annika proudly accepted the invitation and divided their plates amongst the skinniest children.

A young Sudanese girl joined them at the table. Rather than scavenging for food, Samiyah was in search of good conversation. For being a 14-year-old girl, with limited access to education, she spoke English well.

"I appreciate the way you look at me and the others in this camp," she said.

Annika reached over and placed her hand on Samiyah's.

"Thank you for saying that, but help me understand what you mean. Your words are perfect, but what do you mean by, 'the way we look at you?' "

Samiyah took a deep breath, and then began describing the feeling of being viewed as a real human and not just a refugee.

"I wish for them not to call us refugees, it's a very painful word. We are real people, just like all others in the world. The only difference is we were exiled from our homes and lack freedom," she said with tears in her eyes.

At a loss for words, Annika leaned over and wrapped her arms around Samiyah.

"Precious girl, you are going to do amazing things with your life. There is no doubt in my mind that one day you will have your freedom and a good roof over your head," Annika said with tears streaming down her cheeks.

Tanner watched the two embrace and placed his left hand on Annika's back in comfort. It was a powerful moment and the beginning of a lifelong friendship between the women.

37

SUITABLE FOR SAMIYAH

The following two days were spent helping in the medical tent and the makeshift classrooms. When they had downtime the schoolchildren tried to kick around a deflated soccer ball. Since the ball didn't roll very far they never had a reason to spread out on the playing field. It looked more like bees swarming a nest. Tanner took the calculated risk and interrupted the game, apologizing profusely. The kids began to push him out of anger and started shouting. Although he couldn't understand what they were saying, their inflection made it clear that they were displeased.

"Your ball is flat. Let me help fix it." Tanner said slowly as he walked over to his pack and pulled out an air pump.

After wetting the needle, he began filling the ball with air. The anger quickly subsided. Tanner juggled the ball until his left leg was delayed, causing it to bounce off his shin. The ball rolled back to the smiling kids, as though it was intentional. They spread out and resumed their game.

Smoldering hot days in Kakuma were nearly unbearable. When the sun was highest in the sky, the ground was scorching hot. Tanner had completely soaked through his shirt and was amazed the kids running around didn't even break a sweat. He could feel the heat penetrating from the blistering ground beneath his Nikes while standing on the makeshift field. Annika watched like a mother from the sidelines, amazed over the impact of a single soccer ball.

Samiyah joined Tanner and Annika in the common area on their final night. Rather than trying to speculate, they asked Samiyah what she felt the camp's greatest needs were. The sun was about to set, but the temperature was still in the high 90's. Rather than offering a cup of coffee or tea, Tanner mixed a Gatorade packet with water and stirred it for Samiyah. After tapping the side of the cup with the spoon, he pushed it across the table.

"Would you mind giving this a try, it's the orange flavor," Tanner asked with great anticipation.

The murky tap water made it appear as more of a brown. She cradled the cup with both hands and lifted it to her mouth. Smiling nearly forced a dribble of Gatorade out the side of her mouth.

Beyond the basics of food, water, and clothing there was not much she could think of as a need. In the eyes of an American, they needed everything. Samiyah told them that the women in the camp were severely mistreated. The needs here were much different.

"Girls in the camp know no other life besides being used as a disposable object. The men see us as refugees, rather than people," she said, her eyes a little too knowing for Tanner's comfort.

Tanner took a deep breath as his protective hardwiring sent adrenaline through his veins. Annika rested her right hand on his shaky left hand placed on the table. Samiyah's words pierced through Tanner and Annika's hearts. Being treated as less than a human is a suppression no one should ever be forced to endure. They asked how they could best get in contact with Samiyah, being that they did not have a mail carrier walking their beat around the camp every day. She tried to explain the process. Logistically it was feasible, but not the most efficient way to keep in touch. Communication was certainly an area that could use some improvements.

On the plane ride home to the states, their minds were racing with delusions of saving the world and all of the girls like Samiyah in it. Crafting different ways to put their hearts at ease. Their exposure to giraffes, elephants, hippos, lions, and other exotic animals was wonderful. Seeing one of the Seven Wonders of the World was magnificent. But after all of it, the camp was the only thought weighing on their minds. Tanner looked to Annika, with a glimmer of hope.

"What if we start packaging all the food in clothing? Fill up pants and shirts with rice and beans so they can wear it afterward. We'll start to make the shipping crates out of building materials. We could design a crate that could be broken down and used to build stable structures," he said with a smile.

Annika leaned over and kissed him.

"Husband, you are one incredible man. I am a very lucky woman. You have the presence of a lion."

Annika had proudly accepted the offer to have the coveted window seat. The trip had been mentally exhausting and had taken its toll on her body as well. Before the plane reached cruising altitude, she was down for the count. Tanner flipped open his notebook and started jotting memories of the trip. Hitting the high-level points with the issues that stuck out the most, he tried to develop ideas of how to make a greater impact with his resources. He figured he should start with the basics. Ensure they have a clean source of drinking water. Tanner and Annika were instructed to only drink the water they brought into the camp as the tap water would certainly make them ill. Getting these people clean water was at the top of his list. He proceeded through a plethora of items on the list and made notes next to ones he had afterthoughts about. Looking at it like a business he wanted to grow, he started working through the exhausting details.

38

AFRICA TO BOULDER

Placing his shoe on his front porch step had never felt so victorious. The journey back to Boulder had worn them down mentally and physically. Tanner and Annika walked through the front door and immediately began dropping their bags on the floor. They proceeded directly to their room. Even though they felt sticky from head to toe, their exhaustion overshadowed the fear of dirtying their sacred sleeping quarters.

"We'll wash the sheets in the morning," Annika said while flopping on the bed, "Don't worry about it. I'm running on fumes."

They quickly brushed their teeth, falling short of the dentist's recommended two minute minimum.

Tanner stripped down to his boxers and Annika changed into her pajamas. They sank into their plush memory foam bedding and leaned over for one last kiss before putting their minds to rest. The mattress cradled their bodies. Their pillows gently supported their heads, as to say, "Welcome home." Africa was a journey, which they were not completely mentally prepared to endure. While they were thankful to see another pocket of the world, they were happy to be back in their home once again.

At sunrise, Tanner was awakened by the sound of pine cones dive-bombing the tin roof of the woodshed. Tilting the dark wooden window blinds to confirm his suspicion of the racket, the bright sun infiltrated the room. Judging by the pool of drool on her pillow, Annika did not appear to be phased by the morning light. Tanner walked barefoot down the stairs, craving a real cup of Cabin Coffee's mouthwatering breakfast blend. In an attempt to be as quiet as a church mouse, Tanner opted to brew the lightly roasted beans in their French press.

Not wanting to rush the elegance of the process, Tanner set a timer and took the initiative to get a fire going. It gave him a distraction, while allowing time for the robust brew to steep for four minutes. Quietly opening the fireplace door he began constructing a star fire formation using dry kindling. The newspaper boy had nicely stacked the daily papers on their porch, hidden from the elements and keeping them dry. Tanner grabbed the top few editions from the pyramid and began twisting individual pages.

No matter how many times he did it, he couldn't help but hear Dan Akroyd's voice in his head, "You've got to twist the paper to simulate kindling."

Striking a small flame, vibrant shades of green and purple flames poured off the newspaper as the match went to work. Tanner was fascinated by the comic strip, burning in alluring colors unlike the other sections of the paper. Captivated by the dancing flames, Tanner forgot why the small timer was beeping. The French press was ready. As Tanner pressed the plunger through the soaked coffee grounds, he gave thanks the first person to ever taste test coffee. He wondered how many other beans they first tried in Ethiopia before soaking coffee beans in hot water and giving it a swig. His hat was off to that man or woman, but still holds the first person who tried to eat a chicken egg in the highest of regards.

To watch a little white egg pop out the hind-end of a chicken, and think to themselves "That looks pretty tasty! I say, I think I'll try that for breakfast," takes some serious huevos, as Tanner often liked to say.

Annika walked down the stairs, wearing blue Victoria Secret underwear and a cropped Denver Nuggets shirt. Even first thing in the morning, she was stunning. Tanner slowly began scanning her up and down, making him question what he did right in the world to be so fortunate. Standing there speechless, he was pulled out of his trance when Annika said good morning to him.

"Good morning to you, the love of my life. One whom

coincidentally happens to also be the most beautiful woman in the world. Am I a lucky guy, or what?" he said before reaching for the coffee carafe.

Morning coffee time was typically a coveted ritual in the Skilli home, but Annika politely declined the offer of a freshly brewed cup of Cabin Coffee roast.

"Sorry, Hubmuffin. Nothing against your baristo skills, but coffee doesn't sound good to my tummy," she said while placing her hand on her stomach.

"No offense taken. What can I fetch for you instead?" he asked.

Annika walked over and wrapped her arms around him. With hot coffee in his right hand, Tanner reached his left arm around her and embraced the body he had been lusting over.

"Hot cocoa with extra marshmallows and Nutella sounds amazing," Annika said while squeezing all the air out of him.

Taking their unspoken, but well respected seats on the couch they began recounting their Africa trip. Tanner grabbed his notepad that had little scribbles and arrows pointing in various directions. While Annika was sleeping on the plane, he had drafted a blueprint to help improve their giving potential.

Uncaffeinated and not yet alert, Annika did her best to track the outpour of ideas. She was the first human that Tanner got to tell his idea to and the excitement rushed his words. Annika continued listening as she got up to add hotter water to her cocoa.

Tanner paused at his next bullet point and asked, "Is it too cold for your liking?"

"It was a little too luke-warm for me. The water in the kettle probably still has crab eye bubbles. I'm going to grab a warm-up. Carry on, I can still hear you just fine," she said while turning her eyes to the floor.

The room fell quiet as it was the first time the name Luke was spoken in their home, at least for a very long time.

Holding the warm mug up to her lips, Annika gently blew a small mallow across the top of her cocoa. When she locked eyes with Tanner, she could tell they both heard the same thing.

Annika sat next to Tanner placed her free hand on his leg.

"I'm not sure why, but saying Luke's name makes me feel very uncomfortable. I'm sorry about that. I'd like to propose going forward we call a mildly-warm temperature 'Noah-warm.' I think it could catch on, at least with friends. Noah-warm will be the new standard across the nation. Luke doesn't deserve that type of recognition. Although, it did kind of match his personality," she said with a smile.

The Skillis got back into a rhythm and for an early morning session, it was a brainstorming marvel. Ideas began filling up the page to the point that Tanner had to ask Annika to take over the scribing to relieve his cramping hand. They developed their game plan and couldn't wait to get back to the office and get it implemented.

Annika requested to spearhead the project to allow Tanner to get back to growing other aspects of their business. Kingdom Key sales were at an all-time high. Tanner knew that companies who fail to evolve, through continuous improvements, would ultimately fail. Africa had provided him with a perfect break from office life. Thinking with a clear head, he was able to visualize the next products and services the company could develop. The mission was to help those who were most in need, while also promoting stable growth. Like a dynamic duo, Tanner and Annika's combined efforts provided them with handsome rewards.

At the first boardroom meeting following Africa, they rolled out their plans to the rest of the executive team members. There was slight resistance from a couple of the members, but their minds were eventually persuaded. Bob from accounting was sitting on the sidelines of the meeting taking notes. When Tanner talked about wanting to help the refugee camps in Africa, he noticed Bob unconsciously shaking his head in disapproval. The room fell silent as Tanner stopped mid-sentence and turned to Bob.

"Bob, I'd like to ask you a question. What would you say is the most important aspect of your life?" Tanner asked with his arms crossed. "Right now, what do you cherish the most?"

Bob sat and thought about it for a few seconds and then said, "Probably my Dodge Challenger."

Annika lowered her head in shame. Tanner looked over and asked if she wanted to address Bob. She slowly began nodding her head yes.

"A car? You cherish a material thing the most in your life? I think that somewhat of a twisted mentality," she said while taking a step toward Bob. "How about the love of your family, wife, girlfriend, or whatever you may have? Better yet, that little thing called 'freedom,' Bob. There are men, women, and children living in conditions that you cannot even imagine. We spoke with a young woman named Samiyah. She described to us the horror that unfolded before her very eyes when her village was ransacked by local rebels. Her family had to travel hundreds of miles so they wouldn't get killed. Along the way, she had to help bury the body of her brother who was senselessly stabbed in his crotch. The rebels wanted to rid their genealogy from the pool and discontinue their family tree. This young girl was exiled from her home and lacks freedom. The most basic element of life is to feel human, and they are being deprived of even that."

Bob lowered his head and said, "I wish I could help."

Tanner took Bob's response as being a volunteer. He looked at his administrative assistant and instructed him to find out what projects Bob was working on, get them reassigned, and contact the event coordinators to make the arrangements for Bob's African safari. Tanner looked across the room at the wide-eyed staff.

"What have I always said? Kingdom Key is not a company of good intentions. We are a company of action and resolution. We do not surrender to adversity. Create a plan and execute!"

Tanner's inspirational speech lit a fire under the management team. Company productivity and morale continued to rise as the African outreach efforts began ramping up. They created a separate 501(c)(3) Non-Profit LLC named The Hippo Hopes Foundation. Annika developed a magnificent marketing campaign to roll out, in effort to find well-suited philanthropic partners. They sought out support from Samiyah to help ensure the supplies were being utilized properly. Annika and Tanner made Samiyah the boss of the hired hands that were paid to help at the camp.

Tanner was crystal clear when he said, "If she tells me that anyone treats her in a negative way, none of you will get the remainder of your pay. Samiyah is calling the shots, understood? Treat her with the respect of a princess."

The hierarchy was made clear to everyone on the payroll.

A strange thing occurred after placing a young and brave girl in charge. The empowerment shifted the entire camp culture. Kingdom Key provided a small army of workers to help get Camp Kakuma to have basic accommodations. Their efforts were greatly improved with the receipt of additional capital. The marketing campaign caught fire and donations began pouring in from all corners of the Earth, proving that people across the globe still cared about one another on a human level. Showing concern for another person they have never met, but is in obvious need of help, meant there was still hope for peace someday. It reassured the Skillis that there was still good in the world.

Samiyah was a natural-born leader. It took her a few weeks to get a handle on her new role, but Annika's direct instructions of her responsibilities gave her the courage to take charge. Being the boss of a project is like nothing she had ever dealt with, and it was euphorically invigorating.

Annika's final instructions were that of Peter Parker's wise uncle, "With great power comes great responsibility."

She also wrote about how dealing with power is one of the world's greatest shortcomings. It creates the same feeling of being in the presence of piles of gold. It awakens a strange demon of greed from the depths of a soul, which takes people's minds to a place they should never go.

The tables had turned with the shift in power from male to female. Women in the camp were able to walk with their heads held high and the men also began to act more courteous. Samiyah had an army of muscle behind her to help ensure her safety. It was made clear the abuse of women and girls was to cease immediately. Men and boys caught violating this rule would go without being provided food or water. Naysayers would deem it as barbaric, but the choice was theirs. Be a torturer and starve, or be kind and eat. The decision seemed quite fair.

39

HIPPO HOPES STAMPEDE

Watching the Hippo Hopes Foundation execute the plan they had sketched in their living room, brought great joy to Annika and Tanner. The non-profit company achieved monumental success developing Kakuma to resemble a self-sustaining village. Along the way, Samiyah helped pave the path for future process improvements by providing her intrinsic feedback. The company took those ideas into account when working to develop other struggling villages and camps across the globe.

Marketing was able to significantly reduce their overhead expenses as interest in the Hippo Hopes spread like wildfire. After Kakuma, they began taping each new location they were going to help. They weren't looking for praise. Annika and Tanner simply wanted to show the world a little effort goes a long way. Hearing about the poor conditions or reading about it in the paper didn't adequately serve it justice, primarily because of the difficulty for most to visualize such severe disparity in their minds.

Each project was filmed as its very own documentary. Local television programs back in the United States started picking them up and broadcasting them during premium viewing hours. Following each episode, the floodgates of donations and volunteers poured into the Hippo Hopes Foundation.

Episodes of the recent village developments became a casual

conversation in break rooms around the globe. The marketing efforts became a waste of time and money. Positive word of mouth was enough to create a buzz they had only dreamed of attaining. The emotional connection to helping humans in need put the home and vehicle makeover shows to shame. It was a glorious impact and everyone could take part in playing their role.

Once the infrastructure was in place with Hippo Hopes, and Kingdom Key was firing on all cylinders, Tanner and Annika decided to step down in the company and assumed less time-consuming positions. The time had come to focus more on their family.

After their return home from their Africa trip, Annika began questioning why she had a sudden distaste for coffee. Her motherly instincts were taking over the control tower, unbeknownst to herself. Weeks went by and she had begun feeling different, but she couldn't pinpoint the culprit.

It was a Friday morning when Tanner and Annika were finishing up with an omelet breakfast. Tanner had always taken delight in the flavor profile of the Denver omelet, even before he had moved to Colorado. The coincidence was a subtle sign of fate.

Shortly after they cleaned up the dishes, Annika sprinted to the bathroom and had an involuntary second taste of her meal. Tanner rushed in behind her with a huge grin.

"What on Earth are you smiling about, funny man. Did you poison my food? Not cool Skilli, not cool," she said as she spit into the toilet bowl.

He helped her to her feet and said, "Let me give you a hand there, momma."

Annika was upset she had wasted a perfectly good omelet and only half-listened to his comment. She began washing her hands and then pulled out a spare toothbrush from the drawer. Brushing her teeth she looked at her sad reflection. Tanner stared at her in the mirror with an uncontrollable smile. Annika looked over at him and paused. She spit toothpaste into the sink and leaned down to rinse her mouth out, trying to speak while swishing.

"You really think so?" she shouted with excitement. "That answers a lot of questions now that I think about it."

They rushed up to their room to confirm their suspicion. The test came back positive and they both realized the Skilli family was about to grow.

40

BUN IN THE OVEN

Throughout the pregnancy, Tanner was by Annika's side, making certain she was comfortable and following the doctor's directions. Up until her third trimester, Annika was glowing from head to toe.

At one point Tanner said, "I don't know, Sweets. You would have zero objections from your husband if you want to stay pregnant for a good portion of your life. You are one sexy momma."

He wasn't just saying it to be nice either, Tanner truly meant it. Annika made a stunning pregnant woman. She carried the extra weight like she was taking a stroll through the park and it was just another day in paradise for her.

With her feet kicked up on the ottoman, Annika said, "Twelve more weeks until I can bring this incredible little human into the world."

Right on cue, she felt a wiggle inside of her and called Tanner over.

"Can you feel her moving around in there?" she asked with overwhelming amazement.

Using his patented technique, Tanner slipped his hands up Annika's shirt and placed his hand above her navel. Fluttering kicks continued as the soon-to-be parents looked at each other and shared a short-lived smile. Annika was excited to feel the movement in the womb but quickly became light-headed.

After returning home from a babymoon to Prince Edward Island, Annika began putting on weight at an accelerated rate. While on their trip, they had an opportunity to spend a night on a pristine J/40 sailboat. They were anchored in canoe cove, but the wind still rocked them throughout the night. Annika named seasickness as the culprit until they were back on dry land and her symptoms remained. Her vision began getting intermittently blurry. Regardless of how much water Annika consumed, she continued to get blistering headaches. Tanner noticed the shift in his baby-vessel wife's behavior and tried to remedy the situation any chance he could.

Although he felt helpless most times, he still tried, and the efforts were appreciated. After Annika's excessive vomiting sessions, Tanner would get her cold water to help soothe her throat. She would gargle water and spit it out like a boxer in-between rounds. The acid from her stomach etched away at her teeth. The blood-red was beginning to become absorbed into the pores of her once pearly-white teeth. When the episodes became more frequent, it was crazy to take any further chances. Rather than trying to continue self-diagnosing, they put on their jackets and headed for the hospital.

It didn't take long after arriving at the hospital before doctors gave her a diagnosis of severe preeclampsia. Stammering to get the words out, Annika turned and buried her face in Tanner's chest.

"But it's not time. I'm not ready to be a mother yet," she cried.

Ten more weeks remained until she would carry her baby to full term. Receiving the news was beyond emotional comprehension. Far from excited, or even remotely anxious, she feared for the worst.

41

BED HEAD

D r. Zimmerman reviewed the charts and coldly informed Annika that she would not be going home for a while. Tanner wanted to punch Dr. Zimmerman for the way he delivered the devastating news.

The doctor asked Annika if she liked her job and then quickly followed up with, "It doesn't matter much, you will not be going back anytime soon."

The doctor nonchalantly joking about the life of his wife and little daughter sent Tanner over the edge.

Tanner sternly looked the doctor in the eyes.

"You can go now. My wife and daughter will not be cared for by a heartless individual. How dare you treat them like a disposable commodity?"

At that point, the hospital had contacted Annika's obstetrician, Dr. Archung, and delivered the status of her patient. It was a curveball they had not foreseen. At that point, Annika and Tanner were more baffled than afraid. A few weeks prior, they were traveling up in beautiful Canada and now found themselves isolated in a stuffy little room that cost far more than was justified.

Dr. Archung arrived at the hospital an hour later. Before walking into the room she stopped and took a deep breath, preeclampsia was Dr. Archung's nemesis. It was a lose-lose situation, no matter how they proceeded. Like a tug-o-war between two bodies fighting for a single life, there was no way to win without some form of collateral damage. The longer her baby stayed in Annika's body, the weaker she would become. Innocently, their unborn child was destroying Annika's body for the sake of self-preservation.

They inquired further about the steps that followed. As Dr. Archung went into greater detail about the severity of the diagnosis, Tanner felt a dark cloud form over him. Failing to remain professional and not let her true emotions show, Dr. Archung sorrowfully delivered the message that no parent ever wants to receive.

"The harsh reality is your baby might not make it more than a few days. That it is something we will need to accept as a possibility," she said.

Hearing those words made their hearts sink instantly. They were about to endure the most excruciating waiting game of their lives.

While Annika was relocated to a new room, in a separate wing of the hospital, Tanner ran home to get some clothes. She was escorted from lab to lab and was hooked up to a different fancy machine at every stop. It all happening so quickly and the solitude frightened her. The Skillis were not prepared. They had yet to attend a parenting class and were still three weeks out before their first one. Little good that did for them at the moment. Tanner was about to receive the accelerated fatherhood tutorial.

Before heading back to the hospital, Tanner felt it was necessary to call his mother.

When he told Judy about the conditions, she unconvincingly said, "It's going to be okay, honey."

In Judy's days, preeclampsia was a death sentence for both the mother and the baby. The image was deeply ingrained in Judy's mind. She had lost her younger sister to a similar scenario many years ago. Judy's nephew was delivered, but it was at the cost of her sister's life.

For three days, Judy held her nephew as often as she could before he too passed. Even though the little man's time on Earth was brief, she made sure that her nephew knew he was loved. Judy tried to comfort Tanner but knew there was nothing that could help her son. Both understood how horrible the situation was and neither tried to make light of it. They said their goodbyes and hung up. He sat and stared down at the floor. With a shaky left hand, he grabbed his right forearm.

"Dig Deep," he said faintly.

Tanner tried to reassure himself with the thought that everything happens for a reason. Whether or not he was pleased with the situation, it was beyond his reach and far from his control. His actions were irrelevant. He was forced to be a spectator as he witnessed a much larger plan unfolding before his very eyes. The only thing he could do was comfort his wife through the most torturous moment of their lives. Tanner could not attempt to understand the suffering Annika was combatting.

Annika was instructed to remain on bed rest for the remainder of her pregnancy.

"We cannot afford to have you overexert yourself. Your job for the next few weeks is to do nothing but talk to the little child inside of you. We need her to stay in there as long as she can and to grow as much as possible," Dr. Archung said with an encouraging smile.

Knowing the health of his baby was coming at the expense of his wife was extremely unnerving. All he could do was try and hide his emotions. Being courageous and strong in a situation so complex was another testament to Tanner's character. He stood firmly by her side and tried to keep Annika unperturbed, but bed rest was not improving her condition. Tanner and Annika made jokes about how the bed rest orders felt more like a bad parenting punishment.

Rarely could Annika go for more than an hour without having needles stabbed in her arm or cold gel rubbed on her unbathed body. She felt more like a test subject being used for scientific research and less like a human being in need of compassion and understanding for what she was enduring. The hospital appeared to be more focused on getting data then allowing her to truly get some rest and feel at ease.

Annika's blood pressure continued to elevate and her liver began to slowly deteriorate. After a routine hourly prodding session, Tanner began questioning Annika's mental state. She remained adamant that she could hold on a little while longer and it wasn't yet time. However, it was beginning to appear as though she was preparing to risk her own life for the life of their unborn child.

Without saying a word, Annika rolled to the side of her bed and assumed the little spoon position. Tanner removed his shoes, pulled back the white sheet, and snuggled in behind his wife. Not a single word was spoken as the next hour passed. The nurse making her rounds, slowly opened the door to see the two of them cuddled up in the tiny hospital bed. Tanner leaned his head up and caught the nurse's eyes. She simply nodded and closed the door. It was one of the most impacting moments of their relationship. He was thankful for the life he was given knowing that the two people he cared about, more than anything else in the world, were there in his arms.

Laying in silence, Tanner wanted to show Annika that even through the worst parts of life, he would always be there unconditionally. Pessimistically, Annika had discarded the gestures as being out of love and felt they were performed merely out of obligation. Her negative perception made her blind to see his true motivation. In that moment, she allowed their souls to reconnect. She was reminded of all the reasons she loved him and knew he would do anything for their family. She felt an overdue reassurance of his deep commitment for her.

Later that evening, Dr. Archung arrived in the room with a disconcerting look on her face. Up to that point, everyone had tiptoed around the elephant in the room. Dr. Archung informed Annika she was unwilling to allow her to hold out any longer. Annika tried to reassure her it was a calculated risk she fully accepted.

"Annika, you are my patient. Your life is my number one priority. I understand you want the best for your child, but this little girl —" Dr. Archung paused to gather her composure, "— This little girl is going to need her mother in this world."

Dr. Archung then shifted her eyes to Tanner.

"I'm certain your husband is going to need his wife in this world. The world needs you, Annika."

Tanner tried to hold his wife's hand, but it was like holding a wet noodle. Her energy was completely depleted.

With her last shred of strength, Annika looked up at Tanner and then nodded to the doctor.

"Okay," was all she could bring herself to say.

An emergency cesarean section was ordered. Little Zabriel Skilli was in such a rush to stake her claim in the world, she arrived nine weeks early. Weighing in at a mighty three pounds and three ounces, and measured a hair more than the length of a soda can. Annika had held out as long as she possibly could before giving birth. The brush with death was a state of mind that embedded darkness in her soul. Those final days before the surgery took nearly every ounce of energy from her being.

When little Zabby was cleaned up, Annika didn't have the strength to hold her own precious daughter. Dr. Archung presented their little girl in a swaddled cloth, but Annika passively closed her eyes out of pure exhaustion and tilted her head to the side.

Tanner, on the other hand, jumped at the opportunity to cradle their newest family member. Standing beside the bed, Tanner gently swayed Zabby in his arms alongside Annika's resting body. The new mother's life tank had hit empty. Annika was so worn down, she couldn't even look at her newborn child.

Holding tiny Zabby was incredible, but cut short. After only a few minutes, the doctors informed Tanner they would need to take Zabby to the other room for care. Thankful for the brief moments he got to spend with his daughter, he knew his life had been indelibly altered and their rough journey would continue.

Annika slept for two straight days after the surgery. When she finally awoke, there was a bedside tray with all her favorite snacks and beverages. Tanner was curled up in the corner of the window seat, getting intermittent sleep. It felt like nothing more than a wild and crazy dream to her. Surveilling the room she grew anxious.

"Tanner, sweetie," she said softly.

Tanner nearly fell off the window bench as he jumped to his feet.

"Babe, I was so worried about you," he said while kissing her forehead. "Our family now has a sweet little girl."

Annika smiled, with a glazed-over look on her face. Her world was still foggy, and it would remain that way for several days.

Tanner informed the nurse that Annika was awake. A few minutes later, Dr. Archung entered the room to check in with Annika. She reassured Annika everything was going to be okay, followed by an apology.

"The good news is your daughter is receiving the best care in the world. I know how excited you are to get her home, but Zabby has at least two months. You'll be able to get released soon, but for her it's a 'hurry up and wait' scenario. Her lungs are good, they just need to further develop. When you go home, it will have to be without her, but I promise you I will watch over her personally while you are gone," Dr. Archung said with an assuring smile.

Once Annika began regaining her strength, Tanner and the nurses asked if she wanted to see or hold Zabby, but she continued to decline the offer. Tanner wasn't sure if Annika didn't want their daughter to see her mother in her current condition, or if she was anticipating a magical moment and wanted to be emotionally prepared. Annika's true reason for rejection was one she felt she was unable to share with anyone. She resented Zabby and felt like the worst mother as a result. Part of her had lost hope. She thought it would be too painful to form a relationship with someone who will only live a few days, and who nearly killed her.

Everyone continued to tell her about the special bond formed the instant their baby was born. She didn't share any of those same feelings. If anything, she felt the exact opposite. Annika had prepared her mind for the worst, and it was difficult to recover from such thinking.

The nurse asked Tanner if he would accompany her to the neonatal intensive care unit. Not going to the parenting classes sooner was a huge regret, he had never changed a diaper before. He donned the proper attire and was granted entrance into the NICU "growing lab." Walking in, Tanner could feel the desperation in the room as he caught a glimpse between each set of hanging curtains that separated the babies.

Stepping around the light-blue recliner next to Zabby's incubator, Tanner looked in at his baby girl. Yearning to pass along as much positive energy as possible, he reached in through the padded holes on the side to comfort her. The nurse reached in from the other side and began guiding his hands. His sub-par skill level was obvious, but the nurse could tell that he was trying his best to look like a seasoned veteran.

After battling the first piece of tape, Tanner retreated his alpha dominance and received the non-verbal instructions with an open heart. They made short work of pulling the diaper off, but then came the challenging part. The nurse instructed Tanner to grab Zabby by the legs and to gently lift her a few inches. She was so tiny, making it difficult for Tanner to judge how much strength was required to lift her up. Her legs couldn't have weighed more than a piece of silverware. The nurse assured Tanner he wouldn't hurt her and a fresh diaper would lift her spirits. Once he attached the last piece of tape the mission was complete. It was a small task, but after all they had been through, every little win felt like he had conquered parenting.

Elated by his performance, he returned to the room and gave Annika the full highlight reel. Seeing the blissful happiness on his face, warmed her heart.

"I can't wait to meet her," Annika said with a smile.

"Babe, you have come to the right guy. I have connections and I can make that introduction happen. You just let me know when you are ready. Prepare yourself for when you get a small glimpse of her eyes, it might be staggering. She has her mother's majestic eyes. She will open them for a few brief moments, and then hits the snooze button. It's like looking at a tiny version of you," he said with a charm.

"Your chariot has arrived," the nurse said as she pushed the wheelchair through the door.

"Are you ready for tummy-time? A little 'Kangaroo Care' with your daughter is going to boost both of your spirits and help her regulate her temperature," Tanner said as he assisted Annika out of bed.

Annika scrubbed her hands vigorously before entering the NICU. As she rinsed the soap off, she began mentally preparing herself.

"Okay, I'm ready. Let's do this," Annika said with a sigh.

The nurse assisted them to Zabby's station and addressed Tanner as the parent in charge. She told him that she would give them some time alone, but to holler if they need anything.

A warmth filled her heart as Annika felt the weight of her little girl sleeping on her chest. Tanner rested his right hand on Annika's shoulder and placed his left hand on Zabby's back. The uncontrollable motions from his hand were subtle, as though he were designed to gently rock his baby girl.

For fifteen minutes, Annika cradled her hands around Zabby. She leaned back in the uncomfortable blue chair and closed her eyes to take in the enchantment. Pretending all the tubes and wires hooked up to her girl were non-existent was the only way to find magic in the imperfect set of circumstances.

Their incredible moment took a rapid turn for the worse. Although wrapped up in the moment, Tanner had an impulse to open his eyes. He first looked up to see his wife enjoying an uncharted euphoria, and then looked down to see his daughter turning into Smurfette.

"Nurse!" Tanner began to panic, "Nurse, we got a problem here. Help! Please, help."

Alarms began sounding as a platoon of nurses rushed to their aid. Annika jolted forward, sending her blood pressure off the charts. Tanner began pacing back and forth in a panic. The thought of losing his little girl because he was ill-prepared to be a father, began to rattle him. Nurse Lynn strolled over to Annika's bedside and calmly flicked the bottom of Zabby's tiny foot. She took a few quick breaths and the pigment returned to her skin.

"What on Earth was that all about?" Tanner asked with his hands clenched behind his head.

"Her brain isn't fully programmed to handle the normal involuntary responses when she is sleeping, so she forgets to breathe. All you have to do is flick her foot and it will wake her up," Nurse Lynn said.

The magic in the room vanished after their first parenting crisis, but Tanner wanted to be with his girls as long as he could. Time holding his little girl flashed by in an instant, Zabby had to return to the comforts of her 83-degree incubator to settle. The nurses wheeled over the scale to check her weight before returning her to her incubator.

"Holding strong at a solid 1446 grams," Nurse Lynn announced.

Tanner smiled and thanked the nurses.

"You know, being a NICU nurse is nothing shy of doing the work of an angel. I don't know how you manage the emotions. I fully respect your heart and mental toughness," Tanner said as he watched the nurses swaddle Zabby.

"Sweet dreams, precious child," Annika whispered as Tanner began rolling her away in the wheelchair.

42

WATCHING WATER BOIL

Time stood still for Annika and Tanner after being discharged and returning home. They couldn't focus their energy on anything that would distract them from the situation at hand. Feeling hopeless, Annika began to blame herself. Second-guessing decisions she made during the pregnancy, and faulting herself for being reckless before getting pregnant, made her feel unfit to be a mother.

With each minute that slowly ticked by, her guilt compiled. Tanner tried his best to comfort her, but she was unwilling to open up about her feelings. After several failed attempts to lift her spirits, the weight of the stress and exhaustion from the past few weeks stirred up old demons from within. That same feeling he had after being shoved out of the NBA, being dumped by Stefanie, losing his business partner, all started lingering in the back of his mind. Pulling up his sleeve, he looked down at his tattoo. Tanner felt like a failure once again. The wind was absent from their sails, suspending both Tanner and Annika in lifeless animation.

Trips to the hospital were wonderfully painful. They were allowed three hours each day to hold their daughter, but she had to remain hooked up to equipment. Seeing her in those conditions was excruciating. Zabby continued to be a fighter, developing on schedule and ready to take on any obstacle the world would throw her direction.

The next month passed at a snail's pace. Zabby continued to gain strength in the NICU wing of the hospital. Time was her greatest need. The doctors and nurses loved her spunk and provided her with the best care a preemie could ask for in life. Each week was a new stepping stone. Tubes were slowly removed, as Zabby met her necessary milestones. Although her lungs were developing ahead of schedule, and everything was on track, Annika's daily trip to the hospital grew increasingly challenging. She didn't feel like a mother. It felt like a tease every day and a perceived taunting from the universe took a toll on her emotionally.

Throughout life, Annika always had a positive outlook. In fact, it was one of the first things that Tanner found attractive about her. He was continually fascinated by her ability to see the brighter side of a situation and the beauty in every mess up. From her perspective, mishaps were nothing more than happy little mistakes, a lesson to learn. The newfound sense of emptiness was an unfamiliar place for her. Tanner was worried about Annika, but he was too preoccupied wallowing in his own self-pity.

It was a Monday afternoon when life smacked Tanner across the face. They had returned home from the hospital and began wandering around their seemingly empty home. Nothing was said as they parted ways immediately after walking in the front door. Tanner thought he would make an attempt to display his lasting affection and drew a warm bubble bath for Annika. She was in their bedroom when he arrived to coerce her into the tub for some overdue relaxation. When he walked through the door, he found Annika holding his despised Bulldog revolver.

"Umm babe, whatcha doing with that?" he asked with a hesitant voice.

Slowly taking a step toward her, he calmly told her about the warm bath that awaited her presence.

It was the first time Annika had ever held a gun. She was surprised by the deceivingly heavy weight of the family heirloom, as she cradled the cold, heavy metal in her palms instead of her warm, happy baby. Bouncing the revolver up and down, to judge the weight, it appeared as though she was contemplating something much deeper. The thought of taking her life had not crossed her mind until that point, but Tanner believed she was giving it serious consideration.

"Would you mind if I held the gun, while you inspect it?" he asked with his left hand extended a foot from the revolver.

Without resistance, she complied and placed the gun in his hand. As innocent as her intentions may have been, Tanner knew he had to step up and be strong enough for all three of them. The possibility of his wife having such dark thoughts began to haunt him.

Gavin called the house but was sent to the answering machine with a dozen other missed calls. Tanner and Annika both heard the phone ring but had zero desire to talk to anyone. The speaker was cranked up high and Gavin's voice echoed throughout their house.

"Hey, you crazy kids. I have a very special someone, actually two very special someones, that I want to introduce you to. Well, you already know one of them, but it will be a wonderful surprise. We're headed your way in the morning and would love to grab some lunch or take you out to a nice dinner. I'll give you a call tomorrow, or drop by your house around noon if I don't hear from you."

They dreaded the idea of having guests over to visit but knew Gavin would see right through a fabricated excuse. Annika heard a small knock at the door and reluctantly got up from the couch to welcome them in. To her surprise, her best friend Kimber was holding hands with Gavin, and they had their arms around a little four-year-old girl.

"What? But how," she said in shock.

"Crazy story I would like to tell you," Gavin said. "The Lord works in mysterious ways."

Kimber released Gavin's hand and wrapped her arms around Annika. It was obvious her best friend was not in good spirits. After a much-needed bear-hug, Kimber introduced their new friend. Little Ms. Kyndria was staying with them for a few months after her mother tried to overdose.

Tanner knelt down until he was eye-level with the tiny stranger.

He extended his right hand and said, "Young lady my name is Tanner and this is my beautiful wife, Annika. We are delighted to welcome you to our home."

Kyndria bashfully extended her right arm and shook his hand. She glanced over at Annika and smiled. Tanner had a knack for making people feel welcomed. Throughout his life, he realized the quickest way to earn the trust of a child was to speak to them on their level. The technique worked flawlessly once again and they escorted their friends through the door.

Stepping away from the group, Tanner asked if there was anything he could fetch for them from the kitchen. Expecting beer and wine orders to be tossed his way, Tanner was caught off guard when only water was requested. They circled up in the living room. Gavin and Kimber began telling the story about how on the night of Annika and Tanner's wedding, they fell in love.

"It must have been the romance in the air that evening," Gavin said with a wink.

"We've tried calling countless times to tell you, but we could never get ahold of either one of you," Kimber added.

The mood in the room became unsettling, as the avoidance was blatant. Kyndria could sense that something bad had happened and nestled into Kimber's arms.

"Here sweetie, let's send you off to do some fun kid stuff," Kimber said while rising to her feet.

She reached into her backpack and pulled out some fun puzzles and coloring books. She walked Kyndria up to the loft area and told her that they were going to be talking about boring adult things.

Kimber returned to the room and found Annika on the verge of a meltdown. She asked the boys if they would go watch football or something in the *Man Cave*. Casa de Skilli had a room with a small 35-inch television, making it far from meeting the classification standards of being a man cave. They rarely had any desire to watch television, forcing the great outdoors to be his manly dwelling. Rather than sitting in a decorated room to talk, he opted for fresh air. Gavin was a wizard with the ax. Tanner knew they would fly through a grip of cords in no time, while also catching up on each other's lives.

While the men were outside, and Kyndria in the other room, Annika broke down in tears. She finally was able to open up about her true feelings, knowing that Kimber wouldn't be judgmental. Kimber rubbed Annika's back in comfort, as she described the disappointment that was weighing heavy on her soul.

"I'm supposed to be feeling something that I'm not able to force. I expected it to flood my body and overwhelm me with joy when I saw my daughter for the first time, but I felt nothing. If anything, I resented her in a crazy messed up way. It's so difficult for me to say that, but it's the truth," Annika said with tears streaming down the side of her face.

Kimber smiled as if it were nothing to be ashamed about.

"Sweetie, that is a perfectly natural way to feel. There is nothing wrong with letting life take its course, and not trying to force emotions. You are just getting impatient and it is completely justifiable. All that pain and suffering you went through during pregnancy and delivery may not seem worth it right now, but it will. I promise you that. Once Zabby is released to come home to this beautiful place, with her amazing parents, your pain will become a distant memory. That little girl is going to bring so much joy into your world. I know you will infuse your superb love for adventure in her and raise her to be a strong woman," Kimber said while pulling Annika in from the side.

As the ax blades were flung through the air, Tanner congratulated Gavin on his newfound love.

"Annika and I have joked for a long time about how great of a couple you two would make, but we agreed to never push our agenda. We wanted it to be organic. If we just so happened to host the greatest party in Oregon Coast history, we refuse to take any credit beyond providing the right opportunity."

Gavin appreciated his friend for valuing his journey through life and allowing him to be at the helm to navigate.

"Congratulations goes to you there, Poppa Skilli. You're a father now my friend. We can't wait to meet Zabby the Princess Warrior," Gavin said placing a wedge between two stubborn pieces of wood.

Bottled up emotions could no longer be suppressed. Tanner knew he could tell his friend anything, but it didn't make it any easier.

"I'm struggling, man. There's no way to sugarcoat the issue. My wife was preparing herself for death, and I'm not sure how to deal with that. When Zabby was born, Annika refused to even look at her. I appreciate your kind words, but I honestly don't feel like I'm a father. For the first few months of our daughter's life, she will have been cared for by a medical staff. It's been wearing on Annika worse than me, but I am at my wits' end and just burned-out emotionally," Tanner said while placing freshly cut wood on the stack.

Gavin didn't have a speech prepared, but decided to shoot it to him straight.

"That's a tough one, brother. I, for one, am no expert on the female psychology. They have granted doctorate degrees to those who have studied the subject matter for decades, and they still don't have a clue what triggers female emotion and logic. I do, however, know one thing for certain. If there is a couple that is going to make diamonds out of coal, it is you and Annika. You have had a tremendous amount of struggles in your life. However crappy things seemed at the time, you fought through the pressure. Tanner, believe me when I tell you that you are the most driven and adventure-seeking individual I have ever met. I find it difficult to sympathize with you because I have faith that you will find a way to make everything work out in the end. Zabby will be home in no time and your journey will continue."

The boys came back into the house with canvas totes overflowing with firewood. Tanner took drink refill orders and then convened in the living room. Kyndria was invited down to join them. Tanner placed a small cup of hot cocoa in her little hands after she took her place on the couch. Annika sat next to her and began asking their new friend questions. She acknowledged Annika's swollen eyes and hurt. Annika's vulnerability provided a comfort allowing young Kyndria to open up about her other life. When she spoke about the abuse she went through, before Child Protective Services had to intervene, it was difficult to hear.

"You are a beautiful little girl and you are going to do great things in this world. The world is a better place with you happy. We will help Gavin and Kimber protect you from anything that makes you feel otherwise," Annika said, placing her hand on Kyndria's shoulder.

Following a few runny noses and sniffling, the mood in the room turned for the better.

Annika turned to Kimber, "It's time to come clean. Why have you two been keeping this a secret from us for almost two years? I mean, Tanner and I have talked about how perfect you two would be together."

Kimber began explaining the sudden connection they felt while sitting around the fire and listening to Bobby J sing Otis Redding's "(Sittin' On) The Dock of the Bay." Gavin added that they both wanted to make sure there was a true connection, and not just a wedding infatuation, before declaring they were in an exclusive relationship.

"We love you guys! The last thing we would ever want to do is make things weird with our friendships. When we got together we discussed the potential risk of one day breaking up. In short, we didn't want to put you in a position where you would have to choose sides," Gavin said while looking at Annika and then glancing to Tanner.

Gavin turned his attention to Kyndria and smiled.

"Not going to lie, it has been awesome. Kimber and I have taken several trips, not many into the wilderness, but we have had our fair share of adventures. Then we were blessed to have Kyndria come to stay in our home and life continues to improve for the three of us every day."

They talked about all the wonderful things they had done as a family and where their next adventure would take them. Kyndria perked up when she heard the mention of Disneyland.

Tanner smiled at her, "You'll fit in perfectly with all of the Princesses."

Seeing Gavin and Kimber was a breath of fresh air. The feeling of laughter had been unfamiliar for a long time, although in very high demand. Meeting Kyndria was equally rewarding and helped put their current struggles into perspective. Annika was thankful for the visit, even though she had been adamantly opposed to seeing anyone while they waited to bring their baby home.

43

FIVE POUNDS

Weighing five pounds was the ticket for Zabby to go home and the end of the wait came with a tidal wave of emotions. She would gain a few ounces one day, only to be followed by two days of digression. Eight weeks later, she reached her goal weight. Tanner and Annika had prepared her room with all the necessary accommodations required by the hospital. Zabby still needed to develop and the luxury of the expensive equipment was no longer at her disposal.

The initial days were wonderful. Tanner tried to resist the temptation of bouncing her on his lap. Their neonatologist specifically told them that she needed to first be able to bear the weight of her own body before forcing her legs to engage. Their home felt complete with the three of them sleeping under the same roof for the first time. In the days immediately following her arrival, they sat around the fire. Being snuggled up on the couch with their pint-size angel exceeded their parenting expectations. The room was filled with the sound of a crackling fire and the occasional baby coo. Tanner loved spending time with his two ladies. Each time Zabby would make a noise or smile Annika would look up to Tanner to make sure he had witnessed the adorable performance. His eyes were always fixated on his girl, ensuring he would never miss another moment of her childhood.

As a precautionary measure, Tanner and Annika purchased a pad to monitor Zabby's breathing at night. In the event that little Zabby would forget to breathe, an alarm would sound to wake her. For fear of the other white noises in the room drowning out the alarm, they turned up the volume to the max. At 1 a.m. Tanner was startled by the bloodcurdling scream from the nursery. He rushed in the room, with Annika trailing close behind.

"What is all the commotion about, little lady?" Tanner said while leaning over her crib.

Zabriel was not only terrified, but she was also in excruciating pain. A domino effect of events resulted in her umbilical hernia popping. When she stopped breathing, it triggered the alarms. Since the volume was cranked up, Zabby was startled and let out a harrowing cry for help. It was the loudest sound her little eardrums had been forced to tolerate, sending her body into shock. For being such a compact little thing, her shriek was piercing. Annika could tell it was more than a scream of being afraid. Zabby was experiencing horrific pain. Tanner pulled back her blanket and placed his hand on her tiny stomach. Zabby let out another scream, as he felt her small intestines protruding threw her abdomen.

They quickly loaded up their belongings and headed for the hospital. Annika sat in the passenger seat and buckled the seat belt. Tanner focused intensely as he lowered little Zabby into Annika's lap. Trying to position their daughter into the car seat was not an option. Along the way, Zabby continued to scream at the top of her lungs. Even the slightest shift and bumps in the road sent shooting pain throughout her body. Annika spoke softly and tried to sing her bedtime songs, but it was going to take more than music to remedy her anguish.

The team at the emergency department was spectacular. Rather than making them wait in the lobby, they were given immediate care. When Dr. Emmerson appeared in the room the nurses stepped to the side. He placed his hands on the hernia and in one fluid motion, he shoved the hernia back inside of Zabby's little body. Moments later her breathing began to relax and her cries began to fade. The wailing episode had worn her out and she was finally able to settle down.

Dr. Emmerson placed Zabby in Annika's arms and assured them she was going to be okay.

The doctor turned to Tanner and asked, "Did you see how long that took?"

Tanner nodded, "Yeah, just a few seconds. You made it look easy."

The doctor looked Tanner directly in the eyes.

"I'm going to ask you to go out of your comfort zone and learn the technique I just performed. I know you love this little girl and you want to mitigate the pain and suffering in her life. It took you what, a half-hour to forty-five minutes to drive here? That's unnecessary time for your daughter to be in misery."

"Doc, that's the last thing that I would ever want. What do I have to do?"

"The most important aspect of the technique is to have confidence and to commit. You have to look past your own fears. Once you begin, there is no turning back," the doctor said forcefully.

He shook Tanner's hand and said, "I can see in your eyes that you are one of the good guys. That little girl is lucky to have you as her father."

Before leaving the hospital, they practiced on dolls and received instructions from Nurse Lynn. When she heard the Skillis had returned to the hospital, she requested a break from the NICU to go and check-in with her petite Princess Warrior. They stayed in the hospital an extra hour while Tanner perfected his skills. Keeping his daughter out of pain was his primary focus. He wanted to make certain he wasn't going to harm her if called to action.

In the weeks that followed, there was only one subsequent issue with Zabby's hernia. When she began screaming bloody-murder, Tanner reached into her crib and popped it back in effortlessly. Before he could even rest her on his shoulder, her pain had diminished. From that moment forward, Tanner and Annika took the reins and began experiencing the joy of parenting. They read every parenting book they could get their hands on until they realized it was like golf. There was a lot of insightful information, but there is a drastic difference between reading about it and living it. Had they followed every word of advice, their daughter would never be able to eat or be exposed to anything in nature. Instead, they decided to wing it and hope for the best. Like everything they did together, they excelled at their new roles as mother and father.

Feeding time was always a twisted highlight throughout the day.

In the comfort of their own home, Annika would completely take off her top. Her breasts were engorged with milk and filled to the brim. The restriction from her shirts made her very uncomfortable. Zabby was known to drool all over the place, and it saved them from having to wash another piece of baby soaked clothing. Going topless provided Tanner with an incredible front-row seat.

Tanner sat in a trance while trying to will his eyes in another direction, but was unable to muster the courage or desire.

"Babe, I just had a great idea. If we ever find ourselves in a pickle, I know our way out," Tanner said willing himself to look her in the eyes.

Unimpressed by his teenager like addiction, she humored him.

"Oh yeah, what did you have in mind?" she asked.

Tanner began to outline his strategic plan. If they ever found themselves in a bind, they would have to run *Operation Nipple Balm*. The operation entailed Annika creating a diversion by pretending to have a breastfeeding emergency. The world is blended with those who scrutinize feeding in public and those that view it as a beautiful part of procreation. Drawing attention to such a controversial topic would aid in their ability to carry out the mission. The crowds would be too busy bickering amongst themselves to realize they were being used as decoys. Annika laughed about the foolish plan and switched Zabby from the left to the right feeding source.

44

CASH COW

The executive team at Kingdom Key was polished and business was booming. The Skillis provided the team with an opportunity to take partial ownership in the company before going public. Acknowledging they had poured their hearts into the company as well, it was only acceptable that they too reap the fruit of their labor. Contingencies were set in place regarding the minority shareholder roles, in efforts to ensure the company would not implode in the months following the IPO (Initial Public Offering).

As expected, the IPO was a success. Tanner and Annika were financially set to ensure their great-grandchildren would never have to struggle with monetary difficulties. Despite their riches, the Skillis remained frugal, all things considered, and never lost sight of where they came from. Their mission was to raise a family with strong moral beliefs and an exceptional work ethic. Rather than showering Zabby with material goods, they wanted to provide her with experiences. Annika knew her daughter was going to see the world and wanted her to pack light. She figured it would be easier to carry lasting memories than encumbering material positions.

When Zabby was three years old, they purchased a sailboat and cruised up and down the Pacific coast. They wanted to travel as much as they could before she would have to start school. As a family, they explored each portage and mingled with the locals.

Tanner had promised Annika he would one day take her back to Naknek at some point in their journeys. There wasn't much sightseeing or tourist activities to enjoy in Bristol Bay, but she knew how much of a special place it held in Tanner's heart.

Each time Gavin and Tanner got together they recounted their memories. Annika looked forward to the story about their Red Dog Inn date night and was eager to visit this fine-dining establishment. Tanner hoped a trip back to the cannery with Annika would erase the bad memories that lingered in the back of his mind on certain occasions. It was the place where he thought he had lost his soulmate forever. Tanner found reliving bad events in life, and replacing them with positive memories, provided him with a complete sense of reconciliation. Essentially having a redo of life, but with the wife who he loved, helped soothe his nested pain.

To provide them with a full and authentic re-creation, they started their journey back to Naknek in Anchorage, Alaska. They moored their sailboat at the Anchorage Marina and caught a shuttle to the airport. After passing through security, Tanner instructed his family to head toward the large polar bear for a Christmas card picture. Zabby screamed out, "Kyndee!" Annika looked up and saw Gavin and Kimber had decided to join them on their adventure to provide the true cannery experience. Both Gavin and Tanner wanted to return to the cannery, but neither would have done so alone. It was an unspoken agreement, which both had honored over the years.

The families loaded up in a small twin-engine plane destined for the town of King Salmon. Kyndria loved to fly and asked to sit next to Zabby. Sitting side by side they held hands as the plane left the runway. Tanner had arranged for the local school bus to pick them up at the airport, once they touched down. It was the closest thing to a taxi that King Salmon had to offer. The bus rocked from side to side as it pulled off the main highway and into the Alaska General Seafood cannery row.

"Home sweet hell on water," Gavin said and then quickly apologized to the two young girls for the inappropriate language.

The staff at Alaska General was all fresh faces, but they could appreciate the nostalgic beauty of the visit. Six visitors to Naknek beat the previous record of two, but that was a fluke of a situation. Those two drunks had no idea where they were going and the airport just tossed them on the next plane out to get them out of their terminal.

Walking around the cannery, everything was just as they remembered it. As they headed down the stairs, Kimber started squawking about how the stairs were never-ending. Tanner looked over at Gavin and they shared an internal chuckle. They couldn't begin to recount the number of times they had trekked up and down those stairs throughout their summer. It was clear that Kimber had a deep-seeded hatred for all things stairs related. Tanner was quick to recount the first time they all met. As he recalled, the night ended with Kimber being draped over him for the dreaded hike up the Surf Rider stairs.

They were allowed access to everything, so long as they wore the proper protective and sanitary equipment. The workers on the slime-line thought they were some big-wig bosses who came to see the slave-labor that was making them money. Once Tanner explained that they were old veteran workers, the glares and snide remarks turned to smiles and kind words. Annika carried Zabby as they walked through the cannery, trying to understand the attraction to such a place. Kimber and Kyndria followed behind, while Kimber made comments about how she was so thankful her parents loved her enough to pay for college. Being forced to work in a cannery for a summer, making $5.25 an hour, was not what she would describe as a "Dream Job."

Gavin slugged Tanner on the arm and said, "It is time my friend. Someone promised me they would do something they were too chicken to do years ago."

Tanner had no idea what he was talking about and followed Gavin out of the main canning building. As they headed west, down the pier, Tanner's memory was suddenly jarred.

"Don't try to use that lame brain tumor excuse on me. You remember good and well what is in your future," Gavin said with a smile.

They arrived at the oil house and Gavin made a beeline for the foreman. He explained that they were former workers and a timeless initiation was in order.

Annika saw the fright in Tanner's eyes and grabbed him by the arm.

"Babe, would you mind explaining what is going on here. I feel like they are about to prepare you for sacrifice," she said concerned.

The foreman shouted out, "Bring me the sauce."

Her facial expression made it clear that Annika demanded an explanation.

Nervous about his next beverage, Tanner scrambled for words.

"You see. The sauce is a disgusting shot of fish head oil. Yes, it is exactly as horrible as it sounds. They chop off the fish heads and then smash them down, excreting all of the omega-3 into a pungent concoction," he explained.

"One night we were shooting the breeze, and I may have made a comment about regretting not honoring a Naknek tradition. So yeah, there is that. Gavin took the shot the summer we were here and he has given me crap about it ever since," Tanner said with a quivering voice.

The workers gathered around Tanner as the foreman placed the shot before him.

Kimber was trying to be supportive and said, "Trust me, I've swallowed way worse back in my college days, Skilli."

The comment nearly gave every worker whiplash as their heads snapped around, match a visual to the audio. Kimber owned her past and the dirty confession was enough to put Tanner's mind at ease. He clenched the glass with his right hand and raised it high above his head.

"To Naknek," he said while motioning a cheers.

Annika interrupted and said, "Barkeep, I'll have what he's having."

The workers cheered on her valor as the foreman prepared a second shot of the sauce.

"I figured I would have to taste it on your breath for the rest of the trip anyway, might as well do as the Naknekkians do," she said with a hesitant grin.

Raising her glass in the air, "To Naknek!"

As they walked out of the oil house the crew cheered. They waved good-bye as they began walking on the wooden planks of the dock.

"I want to see where it happened. I need to see where I hurt you," Annika said as she clenched his hand.

They climbed the dreaded staircase back to the bunkhouses. Kimber continued to complain about her quads being on fire and how it has to be the longest stairway in the history of man. Annika looked over at Gavin and apologized for misjudging him. She had always heard about Gavin going on wild adventures into the mountains, but he would always leave Kimber back home. Annika thought he was being selfish and neglecting his wife. Getting a taste of what he would have to deal with, put everything into perspective.

The group approached the entrance to a green building. Gavin put his hand out to the side to stop Kimber and Kyndria from proceeding farther. He looked over at Tanner and gave him a subtle nod. Remembering back to the pain he saw in his friend's eyes, after receiving that letter, was burned into his memory. Gavin knew it was a moment for only the Skilli family. They walked down the hall of the bunkhouse and stopped at the third door on the left.

"This is it," Tanner said after taking a deep breath.

"What's it?" Zabby asked as she looked up into his eyes.

Annika looked at Tanner's puzzled face and could tell he didn't know how to fit the answer into the perspective of a three-year-old. Annika picked Zabby up and told her it was the place her daddy fell in love with mommy.

"Oh," she replied in acceptance of the explanation.

Even though it would have been trespassing, and they had little to gain from his actions, he tried fiddling with the lock on the door. The small combination lock was enough to keep unwanted guests away and served its purpose well. With Zabby in her arms, Annika leaned over and kissed Tanner.

"I love you Tanner Skilli. I'm sorry for ever putting doubt in your mind that would make you feel otherwise. You are my soulmate. You always have been, and you always will be," she said before kissing him again.

Having his family back in the same place that his soul was crushed, lifted the pain he had been harboring for many years. Without a doubt, he was loved. He was thankful for the life he was living and appreciative of the joy his family had brought to him. The return trip to Naknek was turning out to be more fulfilling and redeeming than he had anticipated.

Their last stop, on their unguided tour, was the old Red Dog Inn. They hoofed it down the road, but the old billboard was no longer on the main highway. Gavin jogged down the road ahead of the group and then motioned for them to follow. The Inn had been bought and had undergone a name change. The sign over the door then read *Billy's Barnacle Beef* and the rooms were no longer available to rent by the hour or the night. When they walked in, they received a warm greeting from Billy himself. He introduced himself and then escorted them to the corner table. Tanner made it a point to thank Billy for accommodating their large group without a reservation, but Billy did not see the humor in the joke.

Billy had a familiar face. Tanner leaned over to Gavin, who also took note of the familiarity.

"Do you think that's the same guy from back when we were here?" asked Tanner.

On their last visit to the Red Dog Inn, the host was also their waiter and cook. In the week prior, he had been a fisherman. Then he was "done wrong by the man" and got kicked off the boat.

Leaning across the table Tanner began telling them the back story, "In Billy's version, it was that other deckhand's fault. That jackwagon had it out for him from the start and then tried to knock Billy overboard with a net full of fish. *Naturally,* he decided that he should stab the instigator, which resulted in being kicked off the boat. Every contract in Naknek provided a one-way ticket. In order to get the return trip paid for, the workers had to complete the fishing season. It left knifeman Billy without a flight home."

As it turned out, Billy was still running the show. A few weeks after working at the Inn, his boss Vincent was beaten to death by some enraged cannery worker. Since it was a cash-only business, Billy continued to run the place to make enough money to purchase a ticket home. No one ever came around to ask for rent, or to tell him it was being condemned. After eight weeks, Billy went about business as usual. He was in no rush to get back to the lower 48, and the patrons seemed to enjoy his food, so he figured he would keep it going until someone told him he had to stop. Worst case scenario, he would have to catch a flight home at some point. Money was no longer an issue and he turned the old rooms into his personal dwelling.

Annika looked out the window as they sat on the tarmac awaiting departure from King Salmon. Surveying the landscape, she didn't fully appreciate upon landing, she reached over and grabbed Tanner's hand. That part of Alaska was a small blip on a map, yet it was a setting for many of Tanner's fondest memories. She could now appreciate the nostalgia and beauty of Alaska.

They stopped in at a local grocery store to stock up on supplies before sailing down to Sitka. Gavin and his family joined them since they were going to spend a few days in Anchorage before heading back to the states. As they were leaving the grocery store Annika skimmed over the receipt before placing it in her purse. She noticed that she had been double charged for an item and asked the group to wait up for a minute while she went in to get the oversight corrected. They were chatting outside when Annika flew through the doors and grabbed Tanner by the wrist.

"Babe, you've got that crazy look in your eye. What happened in there," Tanner asked with sheer morbid curiosity.

"It's time," she said as she pulled him towards the entrance.

Annika walked him down the aisle to the peanut butter section.

"Clyde, it's time for 'Operation Nipple Balm.' I'll explain later," she said while looking him directly in the eyes.

They walked around the corner to the toy section and Annika grabbed the only doll she could find. She pulled up her shirt and pressed the red-headed doll into her exposed breast.

"I have to get this baby to a place that I can feed him in privacy," she shouted out while they rushed towards the front door.

"This baby is going to drown from all this milk. My breasts are going to explode if I don't get these mammary tanks emptied soon," she said while trying not to laugh.

The diversion was executed flawlessly. Tanner was able to sneak the peanut butter out the front door without any resistance.

Before leaving the store, Annika tossed the doll into a stranded shopping cart. She threw her hands in the air victoriously, as Tanner began to slowly applaud her performance.

"Okay, you have got to tell us what that was all about," Gavin said with laughter as he tried to keep up with their brisk pace.

"That old hag in there charged me for two things of smooth peanut butter. Had it been the crunchy peanut butter, I may have let it slide, but we're talking about an inferior spread. The kibble is overpriced as is," Annika said with conviction.

"You are telling me that Annika Skilli, one of the most honest and proper women in the world, just stole a jar of peanut butter from a Ma' and Pop store in Alaska?" Gavin asked with disbelief.

Tanner looked at Annika and grinned.

"Bonnie, next time we are going to make a heist, let's reserve that specific operation for a bigger loot. The intrinsic complexity of that operative may have been a bit of an overkill for a jar of peanut butter, even smooth peanut butter," said Tanner.

Ever since plotting the operation, Annika had been anxiously awaiting the window of opportunity to carry out such a silly mission. She acknowledged that it was forced under those circumstances, but was delighted that they got to put it to the test. Fooling two grocery clerks, over seventy years in age, and a single shopper wasn't exactly something to hang her hat on. Regardless, no one cares about the minor details of the flawless execution as it served its designed purpose.

45

FAMILY FIRST

Their life was a perfect blend of silly, serious, caring, and compassion. Above all else, the Skilli family lived for one another. Throughout their half-century of being married, they experienced moments of anger and frustration. The euphoric bliss and happiness woven into their journey helped them cope through difficulties. Regardless of other feelings, they had unconditional love for one another. No matter how challenging something was, they operated as a cohesive unit and navigated through choppy waters. Once they surrendered their individual desires and focused on bringing joy to others in need, they were fulfilled.

Zabby grew up to be a remarkable human being. The day she graduated from Medical School at Washington State University, was at the top of Tanner's proud father moments. Hearing her name called over the loudspeaker and watching her walk across that stage in her cap and gown, was a tribute to their parenting success. She continued to amaze them at each stage in her life. Foolish to think seeing his daughter graduate would be the highlight of her upbringing was soon overshadowed when they found out she was getting married.

Annika and Tanner approved of their future son-in-law, especially since he asked for their blessing before proposing. It was a tradition that Tanner felt should be honored since family was such an important part of their lives. Welcoming an outsider into the coveted circle came with resistance, but they were more accepting of him since he asked to join.

Following the wedding, photos were plastered all over their house. It was a magical day for them all. Annika wore a glow throughout the day and Tanner embraced the honor of walking his little girl down the aisle. They traveled the world as a family and always made a point to spread joy everywhere they went. Tanner and Annika went to great lengths to make sure every one of their friends and family knew they loved them. Some relationships were too difficult to maintain over time, but they still tried to at least send a Christmas card or birthday card out to thousands on their list.

Communication created friction at times, but Annika and Tanner made a commitment to each other that they would always be forthcoming with their struggles. They instilled that same principle with their employees, and most importantly, their daughter. If there was something that needed to be addressed, their approach was to tackle it head-on and without delay. It wasn't always a quick resolution, but they made a promise they would always seek the truth and remain selfless.

46

LOST LOVE

Three weeks after her birthday, with too many candles on the cake to count, Annika became ill. She was able to keep her spirits up while Zabriel brought the grandchildren over to visit, but it took a toll on her body. Before they left the house, Annika made sure to tell Zabriel and the two grandchildren that she loved them. As she squeezed each child, they told her that she was the best grandmother in the world. Their words pierced through to her heart.

"Your grandma loves you both very much. She loves her little girl for being a petite princess warrior. That mother of yours is something special. No matter where you are in life, I will always be with you. I love you kids," Annika said while pulling them in closely.

Zabriel could tell that something was wrong and sensed it wasn't their typical farewell. She wrapped her arms around her mother and squeezed her gently.

"I love you too, Mom. You have been the most amazing person in my life. You and dad have taught me everything I know. A little girl could not ask for better parents. Sometimes I feel embarrassed about the way I was as a child before I could appreciate how blessed I am. You were literally willing to give up your life for me to live. That is a gift that I will never be able to repay. I love you, Mom," she said with tears streaming down her face.

"My precious little girl, you were more than worth it," Annika said with swollen eyes.

Tanner walked in from chopping firewood and saw the four of them huddled in the living room with tissues strewn about. Something was clearly wrong. Annika looked over at him with fear in her eyes, her body was beginning to fail.

Zabriel and the grandchildren said their final farewells.

"I will call you in the morning, Dad. I love you both with all my heart." Zabriel said as she kissed her daddy on the cheek.

They watched the car pull away from their front porch. Following tradition, the little arms stretched out the window and waved until they were out of sight.

"She has her mother's spirit," Tanner said with his arm wrapped around Annika.

He gently hugged his wife and helped her back into the house and up to their room.

"What can I get you to make you feel comfortable?" he asked as he lowered her head into the pillow.

"You. I need you. You are all I have ever needed in this world," she said opening up her hand.

As he intertwined his fingers in hers, it reminded him of the first time they ever held hands. He was amazed at how perfectly they fit together like puzzle pieces finding their only match.

Saying goodbye to his soulmate was the most difficult struggle Tanner had to battle through. He sat at the edge of her bed and softly sang their favorite song. Before he could finish the final verse, Annika motioned him to give her one final kiss.

"You have made all of my dreams come true. I love you," she whispered.

He placed his right hand on her cheek and gently pressed his lips against hers.

"I will see you soon my love," he said as Annika took her last breath.

The person he cared about most in the world was gone. Every cherished memory involved her and each fragment of his shattered soul cried out for her existence. Annika was no longer in pain, but that was the only comfort Tanner could see as a silver-lining. After holding her in his arms for several minutes he stood up. Looking over at the bookshelf he saw the handle of his Bulldog .44 Special protruding out of the case. Tanner staggered over to the shelf and grabbed the case. He slowly pulled out the revolver and admired it from different angles. As he rotated the revolver in his right hand, he began to curse at it in anger.

Flashbacks of wonderful memories and smiles on the faces of his family and friends started replaying in Tanner's mind. Had fate not chosen his side, during the several gambles with committing suicide, he would have missed out on an amazing life. Rather than resenting the revolver, he began to appreciate it for what it helped him realize. Life is worth it; all struggles will eventually pass and hurt will subside with time. No matter how dark the cloud is on one day, does not mean the sun will not shine bright the next. Tanner loved his life and the time he got to spend with his wife and family.

Tears streamed down Tanner's face as he looked over at his wife's lifeless body. He looked at the revolver and considered taking his own life to join her. Ashamed that the thought was still able to cross his mind, he shook his head in disgust of himself. He wasn't going to take the coward's way out. As difficult as it was to come to grips with reality, he was reminded that everything happens for a reason. His day would inescapably arrive, but it wasn't up to him to determine destiny. Tanner pulled open the cylinder and saw the same round that had haunted him his entire life.

"One is all it takes," he said to himself as he clicked the cylinder back into place and spun it downward.

Locked into a trance he was fixated on the trigger. The palms of his hands began to sweat as he contemplated his next move. After several seconds, he decided to bow out of the next roulette round.

As he transferred the revolver to his left hand, he lost control. His sweaty palms and shaky hand were a deadly combination.

Tanner watched in slow motion as the Bulldog .44 Special revolver spiraled its way to the floor. His old age had diminished his once fast reflexes. With both hands flailing, he tried to grab the revolver before it hit the ground. Upon impact the round fired, sending the .44 caliber bullet into his chest. Tanner collapsed to the hardwood as he began to gasp for air. His lungs were filling with blood and his ending was imminent. It took every grain of grit in his body to pull himself over to Annika's bedside, coughing up blood along the way. His final minutes on earth were spent with the woman of his dreams. They had lived a wonderful life together and he could not think of a place he would rather be than by her side. He was a man of his word and honored the promise he made on that beach in Depot Bay: "Until death do us part."

47

TABLOID TALES

The media outlets had a field day with the rumors surrounding the unexpected event. Each article referenced the speculations of others, leaving their citations absent of validity.

The intriguing question that continued to be raised was, "Why would a millionaire kill his wife and then take his own life?"

The fact he had wealth seemed to be the primary focus of each article, leading the readers to believe that money alone ensures happiness. The stories continued to be blasted by news feeds across the country until the autopsy was finally released. When the reports discovered the truth, they refused to accept the facts and looked at the medical report as part of a larger cover-up.

Media outlets hired private investigators to dig up historical dirt on the Skillis, but everything they uncovered painted them in a favorable light. Three months of continual roadblocks made the reporters finally concede. Instead of doing the right thing, or an attempt at rebuilding the family name that they destroyed, the media heads issued an empty apology, they buried a small article in limited papers stating they had incidentally printed false articles based on incorrect information surrounding the Skilli deaths.

Yet another great legacy tarnished by reporters seeking drama over truth. Had their true story been revealed, those who didn't know the Skillis personally would have seen them in a different light. As great as their life appeared from an outside perspective, it was never without pain or struggle. Tanner and Annika exemplified the illusion of a "perfect life," but they still had issues. What distinguished them from other relationships was their desire to explore the mind of their loved one. Being married meant they were living a single life together. Tanner and Annika shared a mutual respect for each other's point of view on the world. No matter how heated an argument got, they always knew their love was unconditional.

48

TANNER'S LAST CAST

Throughout my magnificent life, I overheard people comment about how the world doesn't revolve around me. They were dismissing the fundamental aspect of existence. From the moment I was born, my eyes were the only windows to the world in which I existed. So yes, the world did revolve around me, but I realized that it didn't revolve for only me. The underlying difference in my life compared to others was I learned happiness doesn't fall from the sky like snowflakes on a calm winter morning. I knew I would never wake up and suddenly have a full heart, without putting in the necessary effort.

There were several times I thought my journey was over. Trying to search for a magical cure, to bring a spontaneous burst of joy into my world, only polluted my body and clouded my judgment. During those dark times I could never have envisioned the amazing journey life had in store for me. Taking it to the extreme, I gambled with my life, but fate chose otherwise. I cannot properly articulate how grateful I was for divine intervention during those dark episodes. Rather than facing my struggles, I tried to take the easy way out. I thought my life was worthless and without hope on many occasions. It was difficult living with the shame of knowing I lacked the appreciation for my own life to even consider such drastic measures.

Meeting my amazing wife was undoubtedly the greatest blessing

I ever received. She helped me see the beauty in the world, in ways I was too blind to realize before her. The compassion she showed for others was infectious. As a family, we visited amazing places around the globe and met extraordinary people. Like every married couple, we faced continuous challenges. We had to accept that our marriage was never going to be perfect.

Like a sailboat racer, there was always going to be another obstacle in the way of the finish line. As troublesome as the rough waters got, we were able to navigate through them together. Facing adversity helped us grow closer and strengthened our bond. I cannot begin to tell you how many times I thought to myself, I couldn't possibly love my wife and daughter more than I did in any given instance. But no matter how troublesome the rough waters got, my love for them was always astounding to me because it never stopped evolving. They made me incredibly proud every single day, and I loved them for who they were and who they wanted to become.

Zabby, my adorable little girl, was our only child. We intentionally did not give her a middle name, so she could use Skilli to fill the void once she got married. It made her somewhat of an odd-ball and led to a few strange looks when telling others she was without a middle name. In our minds, it was better than being made fun of for twenty years. Zabby Skilli Skilli sounded more like a cat-call and kids can be harsh. We knew our family name would eventually fade into the tales of time, so we did our best to make a positive impact on as many lives we could with the time we were given. Even though our family tree would end, we hoped our family name would carry on for eternity.

My time on earth was incredible and I would never change a thing. Being able to wake up every morning and look over at my beautiful wife was an excitement and view that never grew dull. Our little girl was eager to enter the world. From the moment she took her very first breath, I knew that I was in trouble. It was nearly impossible to discipline such an adorable little girl, as she always knew how to melt our hearts. Her mother and I counted our blessings every day for the joy and laughter she brought to our world.

From the beginning, our initiative was to instill in our daughter that failure is not a negative outcome, so long as she kept progressing forward. Most importantly, we taught her the value of truly caring for others and that there is no benefit in life to having enemies and no way of reaching your goal if you stop trying.

Our economic status was above the norm, but our business success was not the secret to our happiness. Besides the Bulldog .44, my wife taught me that each day should be treated like your first and your last. With every morning cup of coffee, she left negative memories behind her and settled any looming regrets. Annika enlightened me on how we evolve as people throughout our lives. When I was in my forties, my physical appearance remained similar to when I was twenty-five. My mind and spirit, however, were polar opposites.

The secret to my happiness was dual phased. First, I had to begin each day as a new man. Putting all the troubles behind me allowed me to love myself in my present state. Then I was able to show love for the others in my life. With every rising sun, I remarried Annika in my heart. In each segment of our lives, we had to love each other as the people we had become. The Annika I married, back on that beach in Oregon, was not the same woman I knew later in life. For that, I am thankful. I had no idea that one day I could become as emotionally intertwined with another soul. She always found a way to surprise me and I loved her more with each passing moment.

The true measurement of a person occurs upon death. No one cares about how many material items they surround themselves with, the car they drive, or the size of their home. All that truly matters is the influence they had on others and the positive impact they made in their lives. When I took my last breath I was perfectly at peace. I knew I had lived my life to the fullest and all I ever needed was resting in the palm of my hand.

-     Tanner Skilli

NOTE FROM THE AUTHOR

Even though I grew up thirty-four miles to the south of Pullman it was never a destination for anything other than our yearly school basketball and baseball games. My father loves college football, but he is somewhat of a fair-weather fan. As a result, my childhood weekends were spent inside the comfort of the University of Idaho Kibby Dome. Vandal football was great bonding time with my father, but later I found that the elements of the game that give me life are not found in the climate-controlled domes.

Not appreciating it at the time, my freshman class at Washington State University was incredibly blessed when it came to the Cougar football program. The first game I watched in Martin Stadium was against Stanford, led by Tyrone Willingham. Jason Gesser was lining up behind center for the Cougs and started claiming his mark in the WSU history books. Since that day, I have rarely missed a home game and have a deep love for Washington State, the best in the west. WSU will always be a proud part of my identity and I am proud every day to say that I am a Coug!

On January 17 of 2018, I received a message from my college roommate. We live three hours apart, yet keep in contact better than most neighbors. Each year our families get football season tickets next to each other. It is my favorite tradition to enjoy time together before, during, and after the games. WSU football allows me to spend time with the ones I love the most in the world while being immersed in a beautiful sea of crimson and gray.

When I received the news from my best friend, I simply could not process the words appearing on the screen, *Hilinski took his own life yesterday*. My heart sank and my eyes immediately began to glaze over. Over the last decade, I have attended several funerals. It is not a fear of showing my emotions, but crying is a rare occasion and I can't remember the time prior to that moment. I immediately jumped on Twitter searching for an answer and hoping it was nothing more than a sick and twisted rumor.

Tweets were not providing any clarity, as they were appropriately filled with condolences for the family. At the time, I imagined the impact of 160 limited characters could not begin to fill the emptiness in the hearts of his family. Tyler Hilinski was an amazing human with a skillset and opportunities that the majority

306

of all males dream of having. His impact on people went beyond his performance on the football field. People continue to tell their stories about how he has made an impression on their life and I guess, so do I.

With tears streaming down my face, I tried to make plausible sense why he felt that the world would be a better place without him. I never knew Tyler personally, but the loss of him cut deep like he was a brother. I called my buddy, who had sent me the message. When he answered, I could tell that he was emotional as well. We talk at least twice a week and have since college. That was the first time in our many years of friendship that we both were crying over a shared heartache. Usually, it is just one of us that needs a life pep talk, but that moment was different. We both expressed how it didn't make any logical sense. The thought was so unfathomable, it was difficult to absorb.

In the third overtime of Washington State vs Boise State game, I looked at my son and told him he was witnessing the greatest game of his life. The Cougars had a 0.3% chance of winning the game and Hilinski led the charge to victory. For that incredible memory, I will be forever grateful.

The compulsion to find out Tyler's state of mind in the last moments is something I have questioned every day for the past year. It is an answer that will never be revealed. Tyler's actions inadvertently made me appreciate the gift of life. He had to know that he was loved, but there was something else he was searching for. I pray for his family with the understanding that they are going through struggles on a level I pray I never have to experience.

Movies and television shows tend to follow the same pattern. Things in life get bad, they talk through it in an intelligent and reasonable fashion and then everything is happiness and bliss. The message I want to articulate through my writing is that life is always going to have hurdles. There will never be a moment in our lives when we can just turn off our motors and float downstream, we will always have to paddle. Life is not a race to the finish line, it's a journey of exploring our amazing planet and having deep connections with the humans that we share it with.

The first home game of the 2018 WSU football season is a game I will never forget. Tyler Hilinski's locker remained empty aside from a Hilinski Hope shirt that hung on the back wall. For the opening ceremony against San Jose State, the Hilinski family hoisted the Cougar flag into the air before the coin toss. Tyler's younger brother, Ryan, had his arm around their mother Kym, trying to be strong enough for both of them. With tears streaming from her face, she courageously held up her three fingers in remembrance of her son. My heart sank, as the cameraman zoomed in to capture the moment displayed on the massive jumbotron. Martin Stadium was filled with a strange energy that I will never be able to put into words.

Jordan McNair was an offensive lineman for the University of Maryland who collapsed following a conditioning test on May 29. Jordan tragically passed away on June 13, 2018, at the Maryland Shock Trauma Center. To honor him at the opening game, the team took the field for their opening drive with one man short. An appropriate penalty was called but declined by the University of Texas coach. It was a commendable move by both teams.

When the Cougars took the field for their opening drive against San Jose State, I hoped the Cougs would take the field with ten men and leave the backfield empty. I'm sure psychologists were involved in making the decision not to honor Tyler on the field, being that it could potentially send the wrong message. The angry part of me wanted the Cougar offense take the field without him to show Tyler what he was missing. Not trying to fault him, but my sadness continually wishes that he could see his potential while he was still alive.

Some say the meaning of life is everything while simultaneously being nothing. I believe life is a constant battle within our minds, played out in the actions of our physical beings. Many search for peace on the exterior, when it can truly only be found from within. I will always question why Tyler's path shifted so drastically. He was bound for greatness with faithful support behind him and a team to protect him. Being able to impact fans on so many levels of emotion speaks to the butterfly effect of Tyler Hilinski taking his own life.

A single bullet has created a ripple that carries a message. Mental health issues are running rampant, yet the self-shaming keeps those who suffer silent. I think we live in a world that shies away from the truth if it means being vulnerable or less than perfect. Talking with others about real emotions should not make anyone feel weak, but rather empowered that they are willing to face the music. Regardless of how empty we feel inside, our lives matter to more people on this earth than we realize. I hope Tyler knows that he is loved by people around the globe, including myself. A fan among Cougar Nation, who got to witness Tyler's beauty from the stands.

The Hilinski's Hope Foundation
(www.hilinskishope.org) was formed to help save
lives by eliminating the stigma for student athletes.
It is never too late to get involved to help others.

Made in the USA
Lexington, KY
13 November 2019